Graywolf Press

1992

Other Books

by Robin Hemley

All You Can Eat
The Mouse Town

Graywolf Press

The Last Studebaker

Robin Hemley

Publication of this volume is made possible in part by a grant provided by the Minnesota
State Arts Board, through an appropriation by the Minnesota State Legislature, and by
a grant from the National Endowment for the Arts. Additional support has been provided
by the Jerome Foundation, the Northwest Area Foundation, the Mellon Foundation, the
Lila Wallace/Reader's Digest Fund, and other generous contributions from foundations,
corporations, and individuals. Graywolf Press is a member agency of United Arts, Saint
Paul. To these organizations and individuals who make our work possible, we offer heartfelt
thanks. ·

Published by G R A Y W O L F   P R E S S
2402 University Avenue, Suite 203
Saint Paul, Minnesota 55114
All rights reserved.
Printed in the United States of America.

9   8   7   6   5   4   3   2

First Printing, 1992

Library of Congress Cataloging-in-Publication Data

Hemley, Robin, 1958–
   The last Studebaker / by Robin Hemley.
       p.   cm.
   ISBN 1-55597-167-9 : $20.00
   I. Title.
PS3558.E47915L37   1992
813'.54--Dc20   92-15059

Acknowledgments

"Ballad of Faith," from *William Carlos Williams: Collected Poems, 1939–1962*. Vol. II. Copyright © 1950 by William Carlos Williams. Reprinted by permission of New Directions Publishing Corporation.

"The Banana Boat Song," by Erik Darling, Bob Carey, and Alan Arkin. Copyright © 1956 by Edward B. Marks Music Company. Copyright renewed. Used by permission. All rights reserved.

"True Blue Lou," words and music by Leo Robin, Sam Coslow, and Richard A. Whiting. Copyright © 1929 by Famous Music Corporation. Copyright renewed 1956 and assigned to Famous Music Corporation. Reprinted by permission of Famous Music Corporation.

"Wives and Lovers," by Hal David. Copyright © 1963 by Famous Music Corporation. Reprinted by permission of Famous Music Corporation.

I'd like to thank the North Carolina Arts Council, the University of North Carolina at Charlotte, and the Fine Arts Work Center in Provincetown for their generous support in helping me complete this work. I'm also grateful to Dr. Patrick Furlong of Indiana University at South Bend for his Studebaker expertise, my wife, Beverly, Mark West, and Joe Nordgren, all of whom helped me enormously in completing this work.

For my family,

past and present.

Part I

Garage Sales

Always give the customer more than you promise.

—John M. Studebaker

ONE

You could have paved your driveway with Willy's voice, which was smoother than dirt, but not as even as asphalt. The gravel in it made him sound naturally surly, even when he said hello.

Lois did her best to ignore him. After all, he was her ex-husband. But here they were, rocking like good friends on the porch swing, drinking whiskey out of paper cups, the dogs resting at their feet. Willy drank more than his share while Lois stared into the grayness of the dirt road in front of their yard.

In the field across the road, a ruby light blinked on top of the radio tower, and somewhere overhead she could hear the buzzing of a small plane. Her head felt soggy with liquor. Her thoughts wouldn't focus, but banged away at her forehead like the bugs batting the screen door. She could hardly pay attention to what Willy said.

She and Willy had finally come to an understanding. More like Willy's understanding. He'd told her she had to be out of the house in a week because "my girl wants to move in and there's not room enough for two in the barn." Willy had set up his own bachelor quarters out there.

"That's not true," Lois said. "I know of at least two empty stalls. And there's plenty of hay."

Willy laughed. "Afraid she wouldn't like that," he said. "She's not a horse. The last horse I dated was back in high school. Velma Parkinson."

"Velma," Lois said.

"It shouldn't surprise you," he said.

"It doesn't," she said, but it did. "It's your house. You can do what you like."

"You still have money left, so that shouldn't worry you."

"It doesn't," she said.

What worried her was the coldness in his voice, like she was an employee being terminated, like there was nothing personal, but he just wasn't turning a profit.

"You were the one who wanted this in the first place," he said.

"I know."

Lois surveyed the heap of Studebakers in front of the barn. Willy had been reconditioning the cars for the last seventeen years. Reconditioning in the sense that a wrecked ship eventually becomes indistinguishable from a coral reef. His aims seemed pretty hazy. He didn't actually want to fix or sell them, though that's what he claimed. Sheer accumulation seemed to be the goal. Willy was the king of rusted Studebakers. At least thirty of them sat out there, and none in one piece. Sometimes she thought he wanted to see how much of an eyesore he could create in one lifetime. But in some ways, Lois supposed, the cars served a purpose. They were man-made habitats for all sorts of creatures. Not tropical fish like in shipwrecks, but possums and woodchucks and field mice. The ground was barren beneath their pocked and chipped chassis; weeds twined around their airless tires and mushrooms grew in the cracked upholstery. Unhinged doors made little lean-tos for stray cats. If Marlin Perkins were still around, Lois would have given him the scoop on this wild habitat. She could hear him now. "Even in the harshest desert, life abounds."

"I'm not going to miss *those* at all," Lois told Willy, pointing to the row of cars that looked like a line of hippos along a riverbank. She'd never made a secret of her feelings toward them. She hated not only these particular cars, but all Studebakers. She hated the name. She hated the family.

A couple of Larks sat side by side like the Doublemint twins, their wide grilles sparkling as the light from the porch bounced off the chrome.

"They're just cars," Willy said, his voice harsher than before, and slurred with whiskey. "I can't see why you've always been so stubborn about them. Your old man worked for Stude's. These cars are part of your heritage, your family. They're like your children."

She shivered at that one. How could he compare Gail and Meg to a pack of rusted heaps with deceitful names like Lark and Champion?

"You're a sucker, Willy. Just like everyone else around South Bend." Here she spoke with a mock Southern accent. "They're part of mah heritage, mah family, mah little babies."

Willy took a sip of whiskey. "Yeah, well it's been thirty years." He shook his head and smiled.

"I'm telling you," she warned.

Willy leaned toward her. She nearly suffocated from the fumes he emitted.

She waved her hand in front of her nose. "You sure you haven't been drinking ethanol?" That was supposed to be a dig, but it went right past him. Willy worked at the new ethanol plant in South Bend, and she liked to blame him for the smell of it. South Bend had been a good place to live before the ethanol plant was built. Now a sweet yeasty odor permeated the air from one end of the city to the other. When the plant opened, the ethanol people said they'd get rid of the smell in six months. That was three years ago. What *really* happened was that no one noticed it anymore.

"I've been drinking the same fine Kentucky mash that you've been drinking, my dear," Willy said, and he took a sip to prove it.

"And these cars," he said, waving his hand at the junk heap.

"Keep it down," Lois said. "You're going to wake Gail and Meg."

"These cars," he said louder, "are goddamn classics of design. I wish you could appreciate that. No one designs them like Raymond Loewy anymore. Nothing less than a goddamn genius. There's nothing ugly about them. The girls don't think they're ugly, and Alice doesn't either."

"Then I guess I'm just goddamn wrong," she said. This was the first time he'd mentioned Alice by name. He'd always called her "my girl." Lois hadn't even seen her before. If she ever visited him, he must have smuggled her in late at night or at dawn. Lois didn't see why he acted so secretive about this Alice. As though she cared. But maybe "his girl" embarrassed him. Maybe she was some gawky schoolgirl, some jailbait the same age as Gail. No, he would have been proud of that. After all, Lois had been only sixteen. More likely, Alice feared Lois, feared the Vengeful Wife, the Resentful Daughters, or at least felt awkward about stepping into enemy territory. Maybe she was just the prissy type, and didn't fancy the idea of spending the night with someone in a barn.

Lois felt something in her hair. She reached up and tried to pull out whatever it was. But she couldn't find it. Lois had a nest of red hair that tumbled over her shoulders. A bug, finding its way in there, could be lost for days.

"Here, Willy," she said, showing him her profile. "See what's in my hair."

Willy felt his beard as though something might have found its way in there as well. He took a glance and said, "I don't see anything." That didn't surprise her. He wouldn't have noticed it unless it had been a foot long.

"Look," she said.

Willy took a second glance. "Nope," he said.

Her scalp itched right about her ear. She made pincers of her fingers, then plucked the bug from her hair, and inspected it. Good. It wasn't some foul armored thing with feelers. Just a firefly, pill-shaped, glowing in her palm. The firefly made a graceful circuit of her palm, and its wings lifted. Lois blew to urge it off, but too hard. An updraft carried the bug off her palm, and it dropped onto the pine planks of the porch. The bug's ember flared for a second, died, then sparked again. Slowly, it made a zigzag getaway toward the edge of the porch.

"You know what our problem was?" Willy said after polishing off the last finger of whiskey in his cup.

"Enlighten me," she said.

"We've never enjoyed doing the same things. You're so stubborn. You don't take pleasure in anything I do."

Willy stood up and the dogs rose, too. "It's been real," he said and stretched. "You know, this is the most fun I've had with you in a year."

"I wouldn't call this fun," Lois said.

"No, you wouldn't," he said, holding the chain of the swing. "You don't think it's fun now that I've called your bluff." He used his "facts are facts" voice, not an angry tone, but incontrovertible all the same.

"I haven't been bluffing you," she said. "I've just been waiting for the right moment."

"Waiting," Willy said, and laughed. "You've been holding us hostage."

"Yes, Willy," she said wearily. "You're right."

She waited for Willy to tell her more, to show her where she had failed, but he just looked out into the open field. He balanced his cup in the middle of the swing. "Most fun I've had in a year. I'm just about

out of control with ecstasy right now."

Willy trudged off to the barn. The dogs loped behind him, following their master's whiskied trail.

Lois stared at the empty paper cup on the swing beside her. She kicked off with her feet and swung lightly, and still the cup stayed balanced. Stubborn cup, she thought.

The cup tumbled off the porch swing, and Lois took that as her signal to go inside. She woke Gail, who led Meg to bed, and then she came out again and freed the jar of fireflies Meg had collected in the fields earlier, between favorite television programs. The jar sat on the edge of the porch with three holes poked in the lid for air, the fireflies crawling up the glass and falling to the bottom again, refusing to beam their phosphorescent dots and dashes that Lois had once read were love calls.

She felt too exhausted to sleep, so she drew a bath, kneeling with her hand under the faucet, testing the temperature and letting the water guide her thoughts. Really, she was too tired to think, and as the water spouted down, she couldn't even register if it was too hot or too cold or just right. She couldn't imagine making a decision about it. She just felt like staying in that same position all night with the water splaying her fingers.

She heard Willy's voice behind her. "You cooking a lobster or taking a bath?" he said.

She turned and saw him standing in the doorway, and she wasn't sure what he was talking about or why he was here. They had said good night. She had seen him trudge off to his tiny apartment in the barn, his dogs loping behind him. Now he'd returned, looking like he'd forgotten something. Her clothes lay in a heap beside the door: jeans, the workshirt she'd been wearing, her tapestry vest, her silver locket, her wind-chime earrings.

She looked at her fingers and saw how red they were. Steam puffed out of the tub around her. Pulling back her hand, she drooped her head like a penitent in front of an altar.

"If you put in a little cold, maybe I'll join you," Willy said, his voice a purr of gravel, the sound of a car taking a turn on a back road.

Sometimes she marveled at how slight a gesture or word from Willy could turn her around, could spin her feelings into tenderness again. Maybe that was because he rarely said anything nice to her. When he did, he caught her off guard and her resentment snapped away like a window shade that's been pulled too taut. If Willy were the cunning type, she might have thought he planned it that way. Partial reinforcement, it was called. If you feed a mouse whenever it rings a bell, then it will ring the bell only when it's hungry. But if you withhold food some of the time, then it'll stay at the bell all day long, ringing it in a pathetic mouse frenzy.

Sometimes she rang the bell when she wasn't hungry and sometimes she refused to ring it, preferring to starve. But always, when he offered her some tidbit, she ate it greedily, even now.

Lois gave the cold knob a twist. As the water shot into the tub, she waved her hand back and forth along the surface, waiting for the water to reach the temperature Willy liked best, keenly aware of his touch on the back of her neck.

Willy wanted to be a strong lover. He made love like he was going for a world record in some sporting event, sometimes the javelin throw, other times the marathon, full of tortuous climbs and sweat and pacing, but not much action except for the last five hundred yards. Once she had asked him to tie her up, just to see what Willy's reaction would be. Willy asked her to repeat the question. She refused, but Willy wouldn't let it rest. He rummaged through the dresser drawers for suitable bindings, only turning up a package of shoelaces. He left the room and returned half an hour later with a pair of jumper cables. By this time Lois felt bored and tired. "A jump's not going to do it for me," she told him. "My battery's completely shot. Let's just go to sleep."

Maybe they should have been making love in the bathtub all along, Lois thought now. Suddenly, neither of them was sleepy. Willy leered like a pirate, his heavy beard dripping with water and his eyes bloodshot. "Unhand me, sir," she said in a fainting voice. He responded by dunking his head under water and blowing bubbles into her belly button. She screamed and laughed and Willy grabbed her hips and slid her farther into the water, some of which poured down her throat. She came up gagging and choking. She put her hands on his shoulders and said, "Wait, Willy," between coughs. Willy didn't seem to notice. He thrashed and grabbed her by the rear, kneeling and lifting her halfway out of the tub, one of the old kind with claw feet. Her shoulders rode the porcelain rim, and her arms dangled over.

The water still felt too hot. Willy surged against her and the water made slapping sounds between them. A wave sloshed on the floor. She didn't know if he held her anymore and she became afraid she'd slip and drown. This was too fierce. She thought he might tip her out of the tub. She looked in his eyes and saw that he wanted to make up for things by doing this.

She saw herself sliding down some chute away from him. Bile climbed her throat, but she forced it down. She took him by the shoulders and sunk her nails into his skin. She lifted her chin and Willy brought his mouth to her neck. Now he looked at her again, his whole face wet and shining, but then he gave his head a violent twist, buried his face in her breasts, and pulled her against him.

In that brief look she read a lot. She filled in the blank, said what she thought he might have said, whispered it directly into his ear so there'd be no mistake. Willy took a handful of lukewarm water and dripped it slowly between her breasts, like a boy making a sand castle. She felt all the troubles between them beading off her. When she stepped out of the tub and dried off, the troubles would be gone, soaked into the towel. The next day she'd go out and burn it.

Lois dressed, watching Willy toss in the sheets, the covers bunched over on his side. Sitting down, she pulled the sheet away from him. She remembered how few hairs he'd had on his chest when they were first married, and how she used to annoy him by counting them after they made love. "There's a new sprout," she had said. "I'm putting hairs on your chest." More than anything, Willy had always hated being made fun of, though she hadn't meant it that way. He could make fun of others, but when it came to himself he was humorless. Still, she thought it would be fun to have a contest now for the family. Guess how many hairs Willy has on his chest. The winner gets . . . what? Unconditional love. Forgiveness: now, then, and in the future.

"One, two, three, four," she said.

Willy sat straight up in bed.

"It's all right," she told him. "You just grew another hair. There's a forest down there now."

Willy covered his chest with his hand, and Lois saw he was still dreaming, unsure of what dangerous world he'd come into.

He pressed his hand to his forehead and said, "Is this my head? Who put the elephant head on my body?"

"I think you have Jim Beam to blame for that head," Lois said.

"Son of a bitch. I'll hunt him down. He'll pay." He looked at her unclearly and sagged back down.

"You take it easy," Lois said. "I'll fix breakfast."

"What time is it?" he said, reaching around the bed for his watch. He found it and squinted. "Move," he said, standing up and forcing her off the bed. "I've got to be somewhere." Willy grabbed the bedsheet and wrapped it around him.

"Where do you have to be on Sunday morning?" Lois said. "Have you turned devout all of a sudden?"

"Where are my socks?" Willy said, staring at her as though she should know.

She saw them at the foot of the bed and picked them up. Each sock was in a little ball. She threw them into the hallway.

"Hey," Willy said, reaching for her and stumbling over the bedsheet.

The rest of Willy's clothes were piled on a chair by the door. She grabbed them and walked across the room. "Give them here," he said.

"Not until I see you naked."

"Stop fooling around, Lois. I've got to take a shower. I've got to get rid of this elephant head."

"I'm afraid you were born with it," she said. "As far as the shower goes, we can take one together."

"No we can't," he said.

"We took a bath last night," she said.

"Okay, then you should be satisfied."

"You might as well drop the sheet, Willy. I'm going to see you naked one way or another."

"No you're not," he said. "Now give me my clothes."

Normally Willy could have grabbed the clothes with no problem, but in his weakened state he moved ponderously.

"Give them here," he said wearily, reaching out with one hand while the other held the sheet in place.

"Don't be embarrassed," Lois said. "I'm your ex-wife."

"That's right," he said. "You're my ex."

"All of a sudden you're a prude, Willy? What's up?"

"Nothing's up," he said, taking a step toward her.

She backed away and opened the bedroom window. She threw Willy's clothes outside, trying to arc them past the second-floor eaves. His pants and shirt sailed into the front yard. His underwear caught in the gutter, along with one of his shoes. The other shoe hit the corner of the window and bounced back inside. She picked the lone shoe up and threw it as far as she could, but didn't wait to see where it landed.

"*Now* nothing's up," she said, clasping her hands together and smiling at him like the devoted wife. "Would you like patty or link sausage with your eggs?" she asked.

Willy didn't say a word. He started walking out of the room with the sheet wrapped around him.

Lois followed him and grabbed the sheet and wouldn't let go. "That's my sheet," she said. "Where do you think you're going with it?"

Willy turned around and said, "I'm going to get my clothes."

"Stay here," she said, trying to yank the sheet away.

"I'm going to the barn and get dressed. I was supposed to meet Alice for brunch at Tippecanoe Place and now I'm going to be late because of you."

That stopped her and she let go. "Tippecanoe Place?" Lois said. Lois had never even eaten there. This had been the seat of the Studebaker family wealth, a massive forty-room mansion made of granite, with Romanesque arches, towers, and verandas. Now the building had been renovated and reincarnated into a plush restaurant, full of atmosphere, brimming with South Bend's glorious history. But Lois wouldn't have eaten there even if the ninety-nine-cent special had been pheasant under glass. After all, the Studebakers had broken their promise. They'd promised to give more than they took. They'd promised to treat people decently, like family. As far as she was concerned, the house should have been razed and a plaque erected: Where the Rinky-Dink Studebakers Once Reigned.

"Since when have you started eating at Tippecanoe Place?" Lois said.

Willy started walking slowly down the stairs, dignified as Caesar, his sheet still wrapped around him. Lois followed.

"Brunch is it? When did you learn the world *brunch*, Willy? I thought you only knew the words breakfast, lunch, and dinner. Are we going to eat croissants at brunch? Are we going to drink mimosas?"

"What do you care?" he said.

"I don't. I'm just curious, that's all. I'm just interested in my ex-husband's education. Any time he learns a new word I'm fascinated. Did Alice teach you brunch?"

She stopped at the front door and watched him step onto the front porch. He turned around and faced her. He looked like her husband. He looked like someone she knew better than anyone, even her daughters. He looked like a man whose familiarity made him handsome.

"None of your business," he said.

That was too much for her. "Give me back my sheet," she yelled as loud as she could. She heard the doors to the girls' bedrooms open upstairs.

"I didn't think you'd be upset," he said. "I thought we agreed it was time you and the girls found a new place to live."

"Give me back my sheet," she said as firmly as she could. She wanted this to get through to him, that he couldn't just walk away with her sheet. She'd follow him around all day to get it back if she had to.

"I thought this is what you wanted," he said.

What a ridiculous thing for him to say. A minute ago she'd been counting his chest hairs.

Willy looked away to the road. He seemed to have forgotten Lois stood there. "Damn it, I hope Alice understands."

"Understands what?" Lois said. "*I* don't understand. Tell me."

The previous night was a muddle to her. She remembered too many things. Hardly any of it really happened, she tried to tell herself. "Can I fix breakfast, Willy?" she said, forgetting his brunch date. "Can I do that at least?" She meant a lot more than that, but she couldn't say it. She meant, could she pretend he wasn't telling her these things? Could she get some coffee in him and give him time to wake up? Could they overthrow the old habits and despair just a while longer, at least until she had time to figure out what had really happened last night?

Willy picked at his chest. She just stood there, wondering what he really wanted to do.

He whipped his sheet away and handed it to her. Then he turned around and loped across the yard to the barn, naked as Lois had made him.

TWO

Lois had lived in only two different houses her whole life: her father's and Willy's. She didn't know what it felt like to be without some small utensil or piece of furniture. She was leaving a lot behind with Willy, and had made a list of things to look for at garage sales: dishes, glasses, chairs, window blinds, a coffee table. Also, a glass butter churn. Though she'd never churned butter in her life, she had owned a butter churn before. For fifteen years it sat on the mantle. Then, in the middle of packing up, the churn had slipped and shattered on the floor. Practically speaking, she didn't need a butter churn. Still, it topped her list. She'd discovered that owning something for fifteen years made it pretty close to necessary.

The same could be said of Willy, though she couldn't replace him that easily, and she didn't want to. Still, she added him to the list, down near the bottom. Next to his name, in parentheses, she wrote: "Hah! Good luck." She meant good luck finding him again. She also meant good luck if she *did* find him again. Either way, she wasn't getting a bargain.

Lois searched for garage sales much like a diviner going after water. Instead of scanning the classifieds, she simply aimed her car through neighborhoods, trusted intuition, and watched for signs. In this way, she almost always spotted a garage sale every half hour. Often, there'd be two garage sales on the same block. Giving garage sales tended to be contagious in a neighborhood.

She had discovered the best kinds of sales over the past year, also the ones to avoid. Estate sales consisted of an entire accumulated life dissected on a lawn for people to browse through. Multifamily sales promised bargains, too. Church sales, by comparison, bored Lois. All church sales looked alike, and offered up the same items: heaps of wrinkled clothing, baked goods, Up With People and New Christie Minstrels records, and inspirational books.

Some people held garage sales almost every weekend. Lois didn't appreciate these professional garage-sale givers at all. She considered them charlatans who lured people like herself to sales that had been depleted months before.

Some people didn't know the meaning of garage sales. They seemed to think anything and everything had value, and couldn't differentiate between collectibles and junk. Most of the time, Lois didn't even need to stop at these sales. She could tell the kind of sale just by driving past. The worst ones usually had two racks of faded clothes on the porch or in the yard and a couple of card tables topped by can openers and ancient shavers and waffle irons and jelly-jar glasses. Didn't these people know that only a fool would pay a dollar for a set of five washed-out tin pie plates? Or buy a toaster with a frayed cord? Warped beer coasters with stains? Broken golf clubs? Coverless *People* magazines? Why did these people think they could get away with it? Was this the best show they could put on?

Old garage-sale signs upset Lois the most. A lot of people didn't bother dating their signs, and a lot didn't take them down from telephone poles or the backs of stop signs when the sales were through. Nothing felt emptier than driving past a garage-sale site that had been panned out months ago.

If you wanted to go garage sale-ing with Lois, you had to wake up early. By eleven in the morning, sometimes ten, the best ones had been picked clean. By then, the garage-sale ladies had swarmed over every good garage sale in town. The garage-sale ladies were a bunch of scavengers like Lois, only more organized and deadly. They buzzed from sale to sale like a grasshopper plague, showing up early and devastating the crop, reselling it later to the antique stores around town.

The most thrilling moment at a garage sale for Lois was when she pulled up to the curb in front of a promising one. Her feet magically guided her to the best bargains at the sale, as her eyes scanned each item. Maybe this time she'd come across the find of a lifetime. She didn't know the name of this find, but she thought it waited for her: the one item that would coalesce all her dreams of happiness into one hard relic, one profound bargain.

She parked in front of a brick ranch house. The yard consisted of dirt with patches of weeds and grass surrounding a flagpole without a flag. A lone bush sat beside the cracked concrete walkway. All sorts of debris covered the porch. At first, Lois didn't see anyone there, but then she noticed a man who seemed entombed like a pharaoh in the midst of his possessions. The man wore a porkpie hat decorated with fishing lures, and his face had settled with age into a featureless pudding.

"Real fine day for a sale," the man said when she'd come halfway up the walk.

The fact that the man could speak amazed her. He hardly seemed human. She imagined him shrunken and porcelain-glazed, collecting dust on a junk shop shelf, with his porkpie hat and fishing lures, and a small plaque underneath him: World's Greatest Fisherman.

Lois started ferreting through the piles of knickknacks for bargains. She forgot about her list. It wasn't the real reason she had gone garage sale-ing anyway. Over the last year she'd become a garage-sale junkie. She bought plenty of things she didn't need, plenty of stuff that had nothing to do with her life. Something about garage sales soothed her. Something that made her forget her problems.

She took out her list and scanned the items. Nothing matched. Nothing at this sale seemed even slightly unusual, much less useful to her. While she sorted through the items, the World's Greatest Fisherman smiled and bobbed his head like a dashboard ornament. She tried not to look his way.

A dirt bike set out in front of the porch seemed to be the showpiece of the sale. From there, things got worse. A bowling trophy with a golden man swinging a ball stood in the middle of one of the card tables that had been set up for display. A "Peanuts" lunch box lay on its side next to the trophy, and beside that a set of three "Dukes of Hazzard" TV trays. Also, empty perfume bottles. Giant plastic cups from a convenience store. A plaster statue of a Chinaman with a coolie hat hauling buckets of water. A faucet. A vinyl pocketbook with a broken clasp. A green planter shaped like a frog. A telephone table with its varnish flaking away. Tragedy and tawdriness lingered in these objects. Nothing about them soothed Lois.

"If I could get a bottle and stop up today, I'd make a fortune," the man on the porch told her.

She felt a rush of nonsense knock at her insides, hollering to be let out. She knew it was childish but suffered from some kind of moral or emotional defect that wouldn't let her stop acting like a fool, even when she knew better. Her kids had grown used to it. Willy had, too. But she hadn't. When this headlong foolishness overtook her, she couldn't do anything but surrender. A voice would say, "You don't really mean this," but she always ignored the voice. Until it was too late. Things she didn't mean just burst out of her.

She walked to the porch and grabbed the railing. She put her foot on the top step and leaned forward. The man smiled from his folding chair.

She flipped her hair with her hand. Lois had frizzy and unmanageable red hair that she was forever flipping from one side of her face to the other. She'd sweep her whole arm across her forehead, a dramatic gesture like some vamp in an old movie. Her hair sometimes obstructed her view, but she didn't think of herself as a temptress. Tall and sturdy, she didn't go for much in the way of makeup or current fashions. Her only concessions were the earrings she wore, exotic ones from the Orient that jangled like wind chimes when she walked or swept back her hair. Her favorite earrings were a pair of brass frogs from Malaysia. Most often, she wore jeans and men's workshirts and sometimes an old vest. She also wore a silver locket with the initials SG on it. Inside were turn-of-the-century photographs of a boy about three years old and a girl about six. She didn't know who these children were, but sometimes she'd unhinge the clasp and study their sweet faces, wondering where they were now, if they were still alive, if their lives had been happy. She'd found the locket at a garage sale like this one.

She picked up a dish from the table on the porch. "My lawd, will you look at this?" she said. "It's a genuine JFK plate. My man is Kennedy crazy. Just loco. He must have three dozen of them plates by now. Won't eat off nothin' else. I set out some 'I Like Ike' china the other day, but Mac wouldn't hear nothin' of the sort. He starts hollerin', 'I want my JFK and I want it now.' Lawd, sometimes he's just like a little baby with all his carryin' on."

"You can't find that JFK ware these days," the man said, pointing. "That's a bargain."

"Sure is," Lois said. "I ain't never seen it so low."

She held up the plate to the sunlight and tapped it with her knuckles. She liked the idea of serving a meal on a JFK dinner plate. If you covered it with the right kind of food, say, mashed potatoes and gravy, you'd have a real surprise when you scraped bottom. There'd be Kennedy in full color, resurrected under gravy, leaning across his desk, come back to tell you something momentous.

She didn't think she was doing any harm putting this man on, slipping into his life, wearing him like a forgotten sweater with moth holes. He reminded her of her mother's brother, Uncle Chick. Lois's father had always made fun of Chick, saying, "When God handed out brains, Chick thought he'd said 'Rain,' so he ducked for cover." True, he was slow, but he was Lois's favorite uncle when she was young. She didn't care about his brains. He'd talk about any subject under the sun, whether he knew anything about it or not. And no matter how young the person speaking, or how foolish the words being said, he'd listen patiently to whatever anyone told him.

"Where you visiting from?" the man said to Lois.

"Visiting?" Lois said. "How do you know I'm visiting?"

"Just don't sound like you're from around here."

"West Texas," she said. "Lubbock, to be exact. You ever been there? Best beef in the world."

"No ma'am," the man said. "Never made it that far. Amy and me sightsaw the Tennessee Smokies, but that's the furthest south we got. I sure would have liked to have sightseen Texas, but I guess I ain't gonna make it now." He looked at Lois and smiled. "What you doing up this way?"

The nonsense kicked at her insides again. She bit the JFK plate, rapped it with her knuckles, then put it close to her ear.

"I come up for the garage sale-ing," she said.

"No!" said the old man. "All that way?"

The man stared at her. For an awful moment she felt as though she'd gone inside him, that she'd entered through his open mouth and become trapped there. She flipped her hair back the other way.

She didn't know what to say. She'd carried this too far. She wanted to calm down now and sink back into her normal self. She hoped the man wouldn't say anything else to get her going again.

She started ferreting among the objects on one of the tables: an

Avon bottle in the shape of a rearing stallion, a plastic outhouse with a little boy inside who turned around and peed when you opened the door. She ogled each object as though it was precious and one of a kind, holding each one up against the sun.

Then she noticed a doll that looked like a cross between FDR and Maurice Chevalier, with gray hair and a chiseled jaw. A geriatric Ken doll. The doll had absolutely no dignity, maybe because it had no clothes except for a pair of white plastic gloves that were inseparable from its hands. The doll had a smirk, the seedy grin of an exhibitionist, and seemed completely delighted with its spindly legs and enormous pot belly.

Lois had never seen a doll so odd. She started bending the doll's limbs in all directions. First, she stretched out one leg *en pointe* like a ballet dancer. She made the other leg do a high kick. Then she bent the wrist of the left hand as though extended for a kiss. The other arm dunked an invisible basketball. Meanwhile, the doll, which had a smooth rump and no genitalia, smiled divinely like the belle of the ball.

She looked back at the man on his porch and grinned, imagining what she must look like, a woman in her late thirties fascinated with an elderly Ken doll. The man smiled back and nodded. He seemed to think her behavior perfectly natural.

"I never been down to Texas," the man said, his voice slow with wonder and wistfulness over that fact. "Amy and me sightsaw the Tennessee Smokies, but that's the furthest south we got."

Lois wanted to use her normal voice again, but knew she couldn't without hurting his feelings. She'd committed to this cornball identity. To make up for it, she told him she wanted the Old Ken doll for her daughters.

He flipped the doll over in his hands, studying it like a jeweler examining a diamond. "I'll take a quarter," he said finally.

"How about a nickel?" Lois said, her bargain-hunting instincts too ingrained to ignore.

"I have to get a quarter. How about I throw it in with the JFK ware? I'll give you the lot for five. The little naked feller and the presidential china."

Lois had forgotten about the JFK dinner plates. She didn't want them, but felt obliged after all her foolishness. She gave the man five dollars and gathered up her junk. The man didn't do anything with her money, but just held it in his hand. "You have a pleasant stay in South Bend," he told her.

Lois did not feel good about her purchases. Here she'd gone out to find a place to live and had been sidetracked into a garage sale. Instead of bargains, she'd wound up riding around South Bend with a stack of plastic commemorative plates and a nude doll perched on top of the heap. Just thinking about this made her nearly suicidal.

If Lois had gone directly home, the trip would have taken her fifteen minutes, but at her pace she circled South Bend for half the day. Old Ken joggled and the plates clacked together in the back seat.

Somehow she made her way to the old Studebaker buildings, where her father had worked so many years, though she hadn't planned on ending up there. In one of the old Studebaker plant parking lots, Lois sat in the car with her hands on the steering wheel, staring at a sign above the first floor of one of the buildings: "Avanti." She didn't think about it as the name of a car, but as a philosophy. An arrow shot across the skinny letters on the sign. The letters slanted from left to right as though swept along in the arrow's draft. Lois thought Avanti meant something like "Let's go fast and break our necks" in Italian.

A hundred windows, half of them boarded, lined the brick factory with the Avanti sign. Lois still remembered her father complaining about the Fiberglas hulls of the Avantis, how difficult they were to shape. "This Fiberglas is stubborn," he'd griped to her mom one day. "It doesn't know how to behave. You can't bang it into a sensible shape like metal." This stood out in Lois's memory because her dad didn't usually gripe and didn't like that kind of behavior in others. He believed that griping made people weaker than they already were. "We must know what we're doing or we wouldn't do it," he'd added to make up for his complaint. That's how her dad had always spoken of Studebaker. Not the royal "we" but the familial kind, like management cut him in on every decision it made. Studebaker had encouraged that kind of feeling. The company slogan was "Always give the customer more than you promise," and Lois's dad believed it.

Lois remembered a day when he came home glum and silent for lunch, not griping, but not talkative either. Lois had stayed home from school that day with a slight fever. She didn't say anything when her father mentioned the rumor, and neither did Lois's mother, who set out a bologna sandwich and a bowl of soup in front of him, then snapped on the radio. Lois's father raised his spoon to his mouth, his hand just staying there for three or four full minutes before he pushed his food aside and rested his head on his arms. Lois couldn't remember the words of the radio announcement now, only the somber tone. The plant closed three weeks after Oswald assassinated Kennedy, and, to Lois, the tone of the announcement seemed the same. Just as sudden, just as unbelievable.

"I'm sure we wouldn't have done it if we didn't have to," was all her father said.

"What's this 'we'?" Lois's mom said.

"There's got to be a good explanation," he said.

"A lot of good that'll do." She took a chair and sat down and looked at him directly. "What about your retirement fund?"

"I don't know," he said. "I'll find out." Then he shook his head and said, "They've got to give us an explanation. You don't just drop out without explaining yourself."

Hypocrite, Lois thought now. Well, Avanti to you, Daddy.

A couple of the old buildings at the plant were still in use, but only a store selling old parts had any relation to the old Studebaker. A painting of a Commander adorned the side of the building, and above that the words PARTS FOR STUDEBAKERS. LARK. HAWK, AVANTI. TRUCKS. A chubby man wearing a white shirt and yellow shorts stood beneath the sign, looking in her direction. He wiped his forehead with a handkerchief, and waved to Lois as though she always showed up in the parking lot about this time of day. Lois put the car in reverse and spun gravel.

No matter what, today wasn't going to be a complete waste. She headed for Martin's to buy some necessities for her family.

Lois fought her way through the front door past Willy's dogs. She carried her groceries into the living room and through the den, where Gail sat with her knees up in Willy's leather recliner, her eyes on the tube, her hands picking away at a Fruit Roll-Up. She looked at Lois and said, "Who are you?"

"I'm your mother, I guess," Lois said.

"You guess?" Gail stared at Lois suspiciously and said, "The kitchen's over there."

"Where's Meg?" Lois said.

"You mean the pug-nosed wonder?" Gail said.

"I mean, Meg."

Lois hated the word *pug* and tried to discourage Gail from using it, which made her use it all the more. Pug reminded Lois of Pekinese. True, Meg had a small nose, and in Lois's heart of hearts, she supposed the nose could fairly be called "pug."

Gail stuck her arm out straight, her finger pointed toward the kitchen, her eyes still on the set.

Lois walked into the kitchen, where Meg sat at the table, reading a book. Meg dog-eared a page and set the book down. "My nose isn't pug, is it?" she said.

"Of course not," Lois said, dumping the groceries on the counter.

Gail and Meg didn't look at all alike. Gail, with her short hair and bony figure, looked like some slight teenage boy who one day would shoot into the clouds, to basketball height and beyond. Already she was taller than most girls her age and many boys. In that way, she'd taken after Lois.

Meg, the runt of the family, was shorter than most ten-year-olds. In a family of giants, Willy and Lois had always wondered where Meg might have come from. Her face was round and her hair, which sometimes seemed light red and sometimes blonde, fell long and straight in front of her shoulders. She liked to wear white T-shirts and blue-jean overalls. Gail had a uniform, too, one that Lois thought of as "Dress to Depress." Her normal outfit consisted of a black T-shirt with the lightning-jagged logo of her current favorite band. Today, she wore "Anthrax" across her chest. While Gail preferred black for her torso, she encased her legs in blue, though just barely. She liked to wear jeans with rips and holes, from which frayed threads dangled. Also, bandanas enthralled her. She wore one around her forehead, and one on each leg. She looked like one of the leads in a heavy metal version of *Les Miserables*, her clothes tattered, her wounds tended with tourniquets. Not that Lois minded her daughter's appearance. Gail simply went about in costume for a high-school play on a stage without boundaries.

Lois washed her hands at the kitchen sink and told Meg to help her
with the groceries.

"What about Gail?" Meg said.

"Gail, come in here and help with dinner," Lois yelled.

A few moments later, Gail tromped into the kitchen with a weary
expression and a stiff-jointed monster walk, her arms in front of her.
Lois prepared dinner while Meg and Gail did the dishes from the night
before. Lois asked Gail where Willy was, and Gail got a stern look on
her face and said, "Dad said he wouldn't be home for dinner."

Just like him. They had come to an agreement, and now he'd broken it. For their last week living in the same house, they'd decided to
at least eat dinner together, all four of them. So Gail and Meg wouldn't
think there was any rancor between Lois and Willy.

"Did he say where he'd be?" Lois said.

"God, how would I know. Am I Dad's major confidant? Am I the
FBI?"

Meg, who dried the dishes faster than Gail washed them, stood at
her sister's side and looked in the air as though waiting for a bus to ar-
rive. "Well, I'm standing here," she said.

"You're not supposed to just wipe them off," Gail said. "You're
supposed to put them away, too."

"They're not dry yet."

"So dry them, you twit," Gail said.

Meg looked over at Lois and moaned.

"Okay girls, that's enough."

Gail looked slyly at Lois and said, "By the way, you're in trouble
with Dad. Guess who forgot to take him to work this afternoon?"

Lois picked up a carrot and started to peel. "Was he angry?" she
said.

"Fuming," said Gail.

"Jesus," said Lois, tossing the carrot into the sink. Willy had his
car in the shop and none of his old Studebakers worked.

"We're not even married anymore," she told her daughters, re-
hearsing what she'd tell Willy. "Besides, I was looking for a new place
for us to live."

Neither of the girls said anything to that. Gail picked out the carrot
from the soapsuds and handed it to Meg, who wiped it off with her
towel and set it beside the drying dishes.

To Gail and Meg's horror, Lois served dinner on the JFK plates. She also brought out Old Ken. She straddled the doll on the faucet so that it shot between his legs. His hands clutched the sides of the spigot, and as always, he seemed joyous at his nudity and even more perverse-looking than before.

Gail looked exasperated and said, "Honestly, Mom."

Meg, on the other hand, acted as though she'd never seen anything funnier. She shrieked, covered her mouth with her hand, stabbed her fork in the direction of Old Ken, and gasped, "He looks like he's on a bucking bronco."

"That's not supposed to be a horse between his legs," Gail said.

"I know that," said Meg, putting her fork down and giving her sister a hooded look. "I think it's funny no matter what he's doing. Isn't that right?"

"That's right, honey," Lois said with an enormous grin. "No matter what he's doing," and she tilted back her head and started laughing. Gail joined in, despite her attempt at sullenness. Even Meg, who tried to bite her lip into an angry look, started giggling.

Gail stopped laughing and said, "I suppose you didn't find anywhere for us to live."

"Don't worry, I will," said Lois.

"Dad said if you don't find a place by Wednesday, he's kicking you out in the cold. We can stay."

"How kind of him," Lois said. "But if he wants to kick me out in the cold, he'll have to wait awhile. It's only May."

"Be serious, Mom," Gail said. "Why don't you show some responsibility for once?"

That sounded like Willy talking. Obviously, Gail saw her mom as the villain.

Lois stood up. "Okay then," she said. "Let's find a place to live."

"What do you mean?" Gail said.

"Just what I said."

"Now?" Meg said.

Lois told them to wait in the kitchen. She returned a few minutes later with a globe and a copy of the classified section of the paper. "In case we don't find anything in the classifieds, we'll find some other town, some other country."

"Great," said Meg.

"How about some other planet?" Gail said.

Lois flipped open the classifieds and said, "Nope. Too small." She flipped another page. "Too large." She flipped another page and said, "Too expensive."

The girls exchanged looks and Lois said, "I guess we'll have to go to France or somewhere." She tossed the paper over her head.

"Mom!" said Gail, laughing. "You're crazy."

"So?"

Lois turned her attention to the globe and gazed at it like a crystal ball. Then she passed it to Gail. "Go on, close your eyes," she said.

"What for?"

"We're going to pick our destination. Like this." She gave the globe a spin and stopped it with her finger. "Czechoslovakia," she said. "Here. You have a try."

Gail looked unsure, but then she drew her fingers across the stubble of the Rockies.

"You've flipped out completely," Gail said, but she closed her eyes. Lois felt she'd won a small victory then against the rational step-by-step world Willy lived in. From now on, she'd have to spend more time with her daughters, unteaching them everything they'd learned from Willy.

Gail spun the globe. After a few seconds, she stabbed the air and her finger skidded along the surface of the planet for a thousand miles before stopping in the middle of the Atlantic Ocean. She smiled, but when she opened her eyes she looked disappointed.

"Oh, you know what that means?" Lois said. "You were a citizen of Atlantis in a past life, and your soul wants to return."

"Maybe it just means the planet is two thirds water," Gail said.

"Look, if you want to travel the globe with me, you're going to have to broaden your vision. I don't tell everyone this, but I used to be Gertrude Stein in a past life. That's why I'm so attached to France."

"Who's that?" Meg said. "Did she live in Atlantis, too?"

"That's a good question," Lois said. "She probably did. Go ahead and give it a whirl."

Meg turned the globe. "Here," she said, stopping it with her finger.

"Detroit, Michigan," Lois said. "You can do better than that, can't you?"

"She used to be Henry Ford," Gail said.

"Come on, one more try," Lois said. "No matter what, this next place is where we're headed."

Meg spun the globe while Lois clapped and yelled, "Free spin, free spin!"

"Much better," she said. "Peru."

"Peru," Gail said, groaning.

"Come on," Lois said, standing up.

"I don't want to go to Peru tonight," Gail said. "I'm too tired."

"Where's your sense of adventure?" she said.

Lois grabbed Old Ken and led her daughters to the car. Of course, Gail and Meg fought over who would sit in front, but it was Meg's turn, so Lois promised Gail she could sit in the front on the trip back from Peru, as soon as they started crossing the Andes. Gail said she didn't want to sit in front anyway, and demanded to know where they were really headed at ten in the evening.

Lois put the car in neutral. She hadn't decided yet where to go, though she didn't tell Gail that. Instead, she danced the doll in front of Gail, across the top of the backseat. "We're going to the land of the Incas. Are we there yet? I'm hungry. I've got to go to the sandbox."

She pushed the insanely-smiling doll in her daughter's face.

"Stop that, Mom," Gail shouted, grabbing for the doll. "Stop acting like a child."

Lois was too quick for Gail. Still, she obeyed her daughter and straightened up at the wheel. "Very well," she said in a chauffeur-voice. "Instead of Peru, would daughter prefer Bonnie Doon?"

She saw a pair of headlights pull up the drive in back of them. She couldn't make out the car, but she knew who it was. The car came to a stop and the passenger's door opened. Willy walked around the car out of the glare and bent down by Lois's window, giving her a look.

"Just out for a drive, officer," she said.

"We're going to Peru," Meg said.

Willy nodded like he hadn't heard. He stood up and put a hand on the roof of the car. "You were supposed to take me to work," he said.

"You were supposed to be here for dinner," she said.

"When are you going to grow up?" he said.

Lois shrugged. From the backseat, Gail added, "That's what I keep wondering, Dad."

Willy gave the car a tap and leaned in again. "Anyway, I'm glad you girls are still up. I want you to meet Alice. She's waiting in the car back there. I was thinking we could drive over to Bonnie Doon or Dairy Queen."

Gail stepped out of the car in a flash. "I'll have a Reese's Blizzard," she said.

Meg gave Lois an unsure look. "Go ahead," Lois said. She kissed Meg and told Willy not to keep them out too late. She hoped Meg would ask her about Peru. She wanted to tell her daughter that they'd go some other night, but Meg didn't say a thing. Lois realized that even her youngest daughter didn't believe her.

Lois watched the three of them in her rearview mirror. Both Gail and Meg went into the backseat. Lois tried to make out the features of the woman at the wheel of the car, but the headlights made it impossible.

The car pulled away and Lois just sat there for a while with her car still in neutral. She put the car in gear. Maybe she'd go to Peru on her own, she thought. As she turned around in the drive, she caught something in her headlights, and braked. One of Willy's dogs, a three-legged mutt, blocked her car. Willy had named all his dogs after drivers on the NASCAR circuit. His other dogs were named Rusty Wallace and Bill Elliot. Dale Earnhardt, the three-legged one, tottered and growled softly. Lois toyed with the idea of running Dale down, but instead she tossed Old Ken out the window and watched the mean little dog hobble after it.

THREE

If Henry Martin were a pirate as his landlord claimed, then he held his position in life reluctantly, if not unconsciously. He didn't mean to take things that belonged to others. He didn't mean to break things all the time. He didn't mean to be so forgetful. But if he'd learned one thing over the last two years, it was this: accidents happen. Mysteries abound. Civilizations collapse and disappear. Great dynasties wither away. Fortunes turn to dust. People vanish, explode, self-immolate, are run through, drowned, crushed, minced, diced, or swallowed whole.

A lot of accidents could kill you, and then your only luck was that, generally, only one accident killed you at a time. If you died in a heap of metal and glass on some back road, for instance, that exempted you from being bitten by the deadly coral snake.

Sid Junkins, on the other hand, was a determinist, a logical, decent man with a plan, master of his destiny, who fervently believed a fellow could rise buoyantly from the seventh ring of hell if he found a hobby or girlfriend or, in Sid's case, ran a vitamin franchise.

Henry listened to the Sid Junkins Doctrine respectfully, with the same patient smile he used on Jehovah's Witnesses and Electrolux salesmen.

Sid, silver-haired and bearded, sat cross-legged on the scratchy indoor/outdoor carpet he'd installed in Henry's attic room about 5,000 years ago. Sid's house, a sprawling turn-of-the-century thing on Notre Dame Avenue, had seven bedrooms, four chimneys, and massive limestone pillars. How Junkins afforded the place, Henry could never figure out. One thing was sure: he hadn't made the money with vitamin sales.

As he talked, Sid rolled a joint. "What are you doing here, Henry?" he said. "What are your plans? For the future, I mean."

"For the future?" Henry said, considering. "I think I'm going to Macri's to get some coffee."

"For a hundred dollars I could set you up with your own distributor-ship," Sid said. "You could be a vitamin mogul like me. Think about it."

"I don't want to sell vitamins," Henry said.

Henry looked like a starving POW with his scraggly beard and hollow face. Carla had once told him he had the eyes of a fanatic. Now he seemed more like a frostbite victim whose extremities had chilled pound by pound, leaving only his eyes still glowing.

The rest of him seemed to be shrinking to nothing. In six months, he had lost twenty-five pounds, his hair had thinned, his build had turned wispy, and his ribs had begun to show.

"Here, you want some?" Sid said, handing the joint up to Henry, who sat nearly nude on his bed. He wore only a pair of B.V.D.'s with a striped elastic band that had lost most of its spring over the years. The underwear had a couple of holes in the rear and a faint pee stain in front.

At least he could walk and talk. Eighteen months ago, he'd been comatose, and when he awoke, delirious. For two weeks he'd believed a guy nicknamed Hollywood lived beneath his pillow. He'd known someone named Hollywood ten years earlier, as a freshman in college. Hollywood hadn't even been important to him. The guy had stayed up most nights playing five-card stud and smoking grass until he flunked out. So why, when Henry awoke from a coma in the hospital, did he imagine Hollywood skulking beneath his pillow, yelling out, "Read 'em and weep," and "I cut my baby teeth on this game"? Why didn't he fixate on his mother or, more appropriately, Carla and Matthew? Delirium has its own rules. It had perhaps sent him Hollywood, the most shallow individual Henry had ever known, as punishment, to while away the creeping hospital hours.

Now, more than a year later, he'd been almost completely physically rehabilitated. Tiny scars from broken glass made a patchwork on his forehead and his right hand hung limp, without feeling. Not bad though. Considering.

"What am I doing?" Sid said, snatching the joint away. "You don't need any of that. Your mind's altered enough as is." Sid took a drag and held his breath. His eyes grew small and he smiled faintly. Henry had always thought it strange that a man who sold vitamins for a living also sold pot on the side. Sid claimed this as his only indulgence, besides reggae music. Sid claimed indulgences the way most people take deductions on tax forms.

"I'd give you the boot if I had any sense," said Sid. "But I don't. I'm too understanding. I can't even turn away Bible salesmen. If someone comes to me hungry, I feed them. That's the way I was raised, but there's a limit, even with me. You've got to stop filching other people's food."

Henry understood. He didn't mean to take advantage of his housemates. He'd just forget to eat for a couple of days, then would go downstairs to raid the refrigerator. He thought the food he was taking was his own. He wouldn't have taken it otherwise.

Taking food wasn't the only problem between him and the others. One day, returning home on his bike around dusk he'd pedaled lazily through his neighborhood. The humidity of the day still clung in the air, but Henry enjoyed himself anyway, pedaling forward and backward, just trying to keep his balance and not making headway in any direction.

Henry aimed his bike for the path of a lawn sprinkler making a wide bell of water over the sidewalk. As he launched himself down the street, he heard a distant scream. He stopped and waited. Nothing. The air rasped with insects and the whirring of sprinklers. Still, he waited and heard it again, but this time closer.

A women dressed in a T-shirt and running shorts came sprinting around the corner of a large gray house, through the lawn and the path of the sprinkler. She looked like an evening jogger, only she shrieked as she ran. The woman looked familiar. She wore her hair in a poodle perm and had a wide face and squat body. She barreled right past him with a determined look, as though trying to run a personal best.

"Rhonda?" Henry said.

She stopped, jogging in place, turned around, and shrieked at him. Then she set off again.

Henry dropped his bike and took off after her, yelling, "Wait, what's wrong?"

Rhonda looked over her shoulder and kept screaming. She veered into the street and crossed to the other side. Henry followed.

She changed direction again, ran past Henry and up the front steps of the boarding house. Henry took the steps two at a time, but arrived too late. She slammed the door in his face and locked it. She continued to scream from behind the door, but then her screams turned into wails like an ambulance. The wails retreated down the hall and he heard another door slam. The basement. That's where her apartment was.

He went around the side of the house and knelt by the window of the apartment he thought was hers. He put his face close to the glass and hooded his eyes with his hands while he peered in. Rhonda's face popped up like a balloon in front of him, their two faces separated only by a thin windowpane. Her mouth hung open and her hands shredded the air.

Someone tackled him. He felt he had tumbled into hell, that Rhonda had transformed herself into a demon whose screams would always echo in his head. His arms were pinned to the ground and he heard a voice say, "Hold him. Don't let him go."

Two frat boys, who introduced themselves as Tod and Jimmy, held Henry until the police arrived. One of them sat on his chest, while the other paced the lawn yelling, "It's all right everyone, we got him. Everything's under control." Of course, that made people curious, and they came out of their homes in droves, making a circle around Henry, who remained calm, though he could barely breathe.

While they waited, Tod, the guy who sat on Henry, picked handfuls of grass and talked softly to him. Under different conditions, Henry might have enjoyed their talk. Tod chatted as though sitting on a porch swing rather than Henry, and discussed things that people around there spoke about on calm nights: the dry weather, Notre Dame's prospects for the fall, the race for the pennant in the National League East.

When the police arrived they handcuffed Henry and left him in their patrol car while they went inside to talk to Rhonda. The neighbors hung around and Tod and Jimmy continued to chat with Henry through the patrol car window. When the police returned, they gave him his first clue of what had happened. Someone had tried to force Rhonda into a car while she was out jogging. Henry didn't fit the description of the man and didn't have a car, but the police still refused to let him go. The two of them, a middle-aged man and a young woman, kept asking him variations on the same question. "Why did you chase her?" the man said.

"I didn't know what was wrong."

"Why didn't you stop when she screamed at you?" the woman said.

"I didn't know she was screaming at me. I just thought she was screaming."

"In general?" the man said. "You thought she was screaming just to scream?"

The interrogation lasted half an hour. They didn't arrest him, but they didn't congratulate him either. Henry felt terrible, and tried to apologize: to the police, to Rhonda, to Tod and Jimmy, even to the milling neighbors, but the police could only deal with concrete guilt, not guilt in the abstract. They wanted someone to claim responsibility, not guilt, which was all Henry could offer. Tod just said, "Don't sweat it," and he and Jimmy left with the neighbors. Pam, another of Sid's tenants, looked down from her window. Rhonda stood beside her in the nearly dark room, the flash of the patrol car's blue light streaking across her face and Pam's. Henry wanted to tell Rhonda he was glad she was all right. He hadn't meant to harm her. Other people he hadn't meant to harm weren't so lucky.

Sid waved his hand in front of his face, breaking up a cloud of smoke. "What do you think?" he said. "Do you think I should give you the boot? No, don't answer that. You're the accused. You only have one right in this court, and that's to listen."

Sid seemed to get a charge out of reprimanding Henry, giving him fatherly advice and warnings. Sometimes Henry almost thought Sid *was* his father, but his real father lived in Pasadena, California, not South Bend, Indiana. The only similarity between the two men was that Henry's real father would have made him pay rent for staying at his house, too.

"Wild World" played on Henry's stereo, one of the few possessions he still owned. He traveled light these days. He'd tossed almost all his personal belongings in the Dumpster. A lot of things he hadn't been sure he could part with: Carla's guitar, Matthew's toys, all the things that had defined their life together. For a while, he thought about them, wondered if he'd made a mistake. He missed Carla's guitar most of all. His room in Sid Junkins's boarding house was completely bare except for his bed, his stereo, and his ten-speed. Besides that, he had a hot plate, a mug, and an electric coil to heat water. He only ate food he could stab with his Swiss Army knife.

He owned a house, too, but that wouldn't fit in the Dumpster and he couldn't sell it. He was proud he hadn't sold any of his belongings. He'd left them in plain view for the taking. Maybe he'd do the same with his house.

"If I were you, you know what I'd do?" Sid said. "I'd get out, have some fun, listen to Jah music. I'd buy some clothes. *That* would set you on your feet again. Then you'd be happy and you wouldn't take things that don't belong to you. As they say, clothes make the man. Look at you, sitting there in your underwear. What do you own — two shirts and a pair of jeans?"

Sid, the sharpest dresser Henry knew, looked so confident and easygoing in his present costume, what an Argentine rancher might wear: huaraches, brown shorts, and a military-green knit shirt. Henry wished he could look like that, wished he could even dress himself. Out on a walk the other day, he'd noticed something wrong with his legs. One of them suddenly seemed shorter than the other. By about two inches. He worried until he looked down and saw he had on two different shoes.

Sid also wore a multicolored African belt he'd picked up at a Wailers concert the weekend before, a concert to which he'd tried to drag Henry. He always attempted friendly gestures like that, trying to get Henry interested in life. Henry just wasn't interested.

"I *am* happy," Henry said. "Honestly," and he smiled, but he had morning mouth. His chapped upper lip stuck on one of his eyeeteeth and he snarled rather than smiled.

Sid shook his head and said, "Don't kid a kidder. What about your old job? Maybe you could get it back."

Henry had quit only a year and a half before. He'd worked for his uncle Dan, his mother's brother, who owned an advertising agency in South Bend.

Sid took another hit and said, "You know, we had a meeting last night."

"We?"

"Me and the rest of the house: Tony, Rhonda, Pam, Charlie, and Pete."

"You met without me?" Henry said.

"The meeting was about you."

Sid's other tenants were Notre Dame students. He took an interest in all their lives, keeping track of their grades, their romances, their personal problems. Sid, who was unmarried, even fixed them lavish holiday feasts when they couldn't make it home. Of course, the flip side was that Sid never left anyone alone. He constantly snooped and inquired.

"Do you think 'Wild World' is a true song?" Henry said.

"What do you mean, 'true'?" Sid said.

"I mean, do you think Cat Stevens wrote it about anyone in particular, or about people in general?"

Sid looked blankly at Henry.

"I think you caught the A-train," Sid said, wetting his index finger with his tongue and snubbing out the joint. He dropped the roach in the plastic bag, rolled it up, and stuck it in the pocket of his shorts.

"I bet it's true," Henry said.

He stood and went over to the stereo.

"I'm not through talking to you, Henry, so don't try to divert my attention, you rapscallion."

"The record's stuck," Henry said. "Sorry Cat," he said and took the record from the turntable, but didn't bother to put it back into its dustcover.

He sat down again and said, "You're going to kick me out, aren't you?"

"You've got to start paying attention more," Sid said. "You need to get on with your life."

"Okay," said Henry. "How?"

That kind of advice was easy when you were Sid Junkins. When you had control of your life, out-of-control people frustrated you. Henry could even sympathize with his decent, well-meaning landlord, and he would have accommodated him if he could have. He could see Sid Junkins squeezing his eyes shut in well-meaning frustration, could even hear his well-meaning thoughts: You see, to get hold of yourself, you just grab yourself right here, then you pick yourself up, slap yourself a couple of times, hold steady and don't flinch.

Henry remembered a man at the advertising firm named Malcolm Mooney, who'd been a steady and trusted employee for fifteen years.

One day he'd started baby-talking in the office for no apparent reason. Not only to this colleagues, but to clients as well. The clients began complaining. No one in the office could figure out why gray-haired and straight-backed Malcolm Mooney had all of a sudden started speaking with a lisp in a tiny doll-like register: "Whath the mather? You dough likee my propothal?" he'd ask in the middle of a strategy session. The man mortified everyone, including Henry. Henry's uncle finally took Malcolm aside and told him to quit talking that way or quit the company. Malcolm acted baffled. "Talking what way, you meanie?" he said.

Henry was relieved when his uncle fired Mooney, but now he thought he understood. He wished he could find the man and apologize.

Sid brought a hand to the bridge of his nose. "I think it's going to rain," he said. "My sinuses are killing me."

"South Bend's not a very good climate if you have sinus trouble," Henry said. "The humid summers, the lake-effect snow."

Sid took his hand away and stared at Henry. Then he let out a sharp laugh like a karate yell. He stood and wandered around Henry's bare room, ending up by the open closet. He stretched his arms and touched either side of the door frame, then lifted his head. To Henry, he looked like Samson about to make the temple come crashing down.

"Henry," he said softly, "Come here." Sid stepped aside from the doorway and pointed. "I want to show you something."

"Sure thing," Henry said, and joined his landlord at the closet door.

"What's this?" Sid said.

"Clothes."

"I mean under the clothes."

"A frying pan."

"What's in the frying pan?" Sid said. "That's what I want to know."

Henry extracted the frying pan from the closet. Inside, some gray lumps sat on a bed of hardened noodles. A fine green fuzz made a canopy over the top. Henry sniffed and drew back. "Beef Stroganoff, I think."

Sid took the frying pan from Henry and lifted his index finger. "This is exactly what our meeting was about," he said. "Buy your own refrigerator, tape your mouth shut, feed yourself intravenously. I don't care what it takes."

Henry had never seen Sid so angry. He wondered if he was the cause. Henry thought Sid might have a heart seizure. "Don't worry," Henry said.

"I will."

"I'm sorry."

"You sure are," said Sid.

"I won't do it again," Henry promised.

"Yes you will. I'm afraid you will." Sid shook his finger at Henry and left the room. Henry knew what that shaking finger meant. He had one more chance. He could feel that shaking finger lingering in the air, chasing him wrathfully around the room like some disembodied cartoon finger. One more chance. Henry Martin, you pirate, you scoundrel, you rogue. One more chance to prove you're a normal human being.

Henry ran his bike down three flights of stairs, tires bouncing. Getting the bike out the front door could be a cumbersome process with only one working hand, but Henry had perfected it over the past few months. First, he balanced the bike against his body, let go of the handlebars, then flung the front door open. He whipped out the door and around the front of the bike, grabbing the handlebar at the same time. He braced the door open with his shoulders, flung it back again, and dragged the bike through the door. Outside, he bolted across the porch and scrambled down the front steps.

All this for a cup of coffee. He just wanted a chance to wake up before getting hold of himself, before changing his life, taking responsibility. He didn't want to keep disappointing Sid.

Instead of going directly to Macri's, he went in the opposite direction. He wasn't sure why. He just felt like it. Chance events, disconnected synapses, random neurons firing. These things ruled him.

Henry rode his ten-speed up Notre Dame Avenue to Howard Street. A Mustang passed and honked three times. He turned in its wake and rode in a straight shot down Howard, his bike in tenth gear. He felt his muscles burning as he pumped the pedals. He stood in his seat and took his left hand off the handle. He thrust his chin forward, as if he was bracing against a stiff wind, but the day was muggy and dead calm. The only motion in the air came from the cottonwood spores drifting like snow past him.

He rode past Niles Avenue and down the hill to the bottom, where Leeper Bridge crossed the St. Joseph River. He turned around and started climbing the hill, weaving slowly back and forth so he could make it up without stopping. Hard enough with two hands, the climb seemed nearly impossible with only his left. His veins bulged, but he didn't give up. Another car honked as it passed and someone whistled. They probably thought of him as a hazard, weaving that way. At least if he crashed or hit someone he'd only hurt himself.

He wished he could go faster. He enjoyed going fast on his bike. Of course, braking could be a problem. The left-hand brake stopped only the front wheel, so he had to pump the brake slowly to stop or else he'd tumble over the handlebars. That had happened several times, but he just couldn't stop himself from going fast. When he went slowly, he started remembering too much. He saw himself in the car, arguing with Carla. He remembered the interminable trip, the incredible heat. He remembered following some kind of antique car for miles, and what someone had written in dust on the back of its hood: Clean Me!

By the time he'd reached Niles Avenue, he was weaving from one side of the road to the other to maintain his balance. If a car had been coming over the hill, he wouldn't have been able to see it. He glistened in the heat and his hand kept slipping on the handle. He sang to himself like soldiers do when they're marching, loud bursts to match the rhythm of his bicycling. "Carla and Matthew," he sang, a tuneless song. "Carla and Matthew."

He turned down Niles Avenue and coasted down the hill. Now he could forget again. Life seemed easier and clearer, and he had that old feeling of limitless space in front of him. Every direction he traveled seemed West, every mile a new frontier. He knew he could go faster in a car, but right now, coasting down the hill felt fast enough. He didn't trust himself to go any faster.

As soon as Henry entered Macri's Bakery, he knew something was terribly wrong. The two gray-haired women behind the counter, usually so friendly, just stared at him. He looked down and saw he wore only his stretched-out B.V.D.'s with the pee stain in front and the rips in the rear. Henry and the women faced each other off without saying a word. The women looked like they were about to start dueling, one holding a loaf of Italian bread, the other a sausage.

"Excuse me," he said. "I left something at home." He walked sideways out the door so they wouldn't see the pee stain or the rips in his underwear.

On the bike ride back, he avoided the curious gazes of drivers as they passed, the hoots and whistles. He kept his eyes straight ahead and his jaw set, but he didn't feel too upset. This incident didn't concern him. He'd simply slipped up, made another minor error. Another oversight. Not a big deal. An accident.

FOUR

Despite the gaudiness of the ad, Lois imagined the people on Prospect Avenue bringing over peach preserves, babysitting for each other, popping in for coffee and donuts to eat on their sunlit verandas. She'd always wanted a veranda, though she'd never seen one advertised before in the *South Bend Tribune*. She'd seen porches and patios and sun decks. Sun decks galore filled the rental section of the classifieds. Mostly in complexes with names that could be interchanged with any cemetery or theme park: Enchanted Forest, Lost Hollow, Gitchy Goomy Shores. The paper brimmed with plenty of patios, too. But patios struck her as something for the shuffleboard set. A veranda struck a different chord. Spanish moss dangling in view. The notion entertained her, even though she didn't know for sure what Spanish moss looked like. The ad in the paper stated, "FOR RENT – C/A, W/D conn., Lots O' Room. Veranda!" That's what impressed her, the fact that "veranda" sat off by itself with an exclamation mark, like someone shouting to the entire block, Look here, the genu-wine item!

Lois didn't mind the drive, despite the intense heat of the day and the distance. She and Gail and Meg just rolled down the windows all the way and drank air as it rushed by. The wind rustled Lois's hair and tangled it more than ever, and her earrings jangled furiously in the breeze. Lois had chosen a house as far away from the old one as possible. For twenty years she'd lived in the same farmhouse off Portage Road, within walking distance of the Michigan state line. Now, to get where she wanted, she had to cut a swath through South Bend to Mishawaka. Basically, South Bend and Mishawaka were the same city, so sometimes people put a hyphen between the names and called it that, like a married couple who went by both names. Officially, the area where Lois lived was called Roseland, and even Notre Dame was its own town. All that was too confusing, so people had made up a name for the entire area. Since South Bend was only a few miles from the Michigan border, people called the region Michiana.

Lois drove down Portage past Highland Cemetery, in the middle of which stood the Council Oak, where in 1681 the explorer La Salle held council with 5,000 Miami Indians. Back then, the oak stood in front of the tent of the Miami chief. The 5,000 Miami Indians had since been replaced by 5,000 gravestones, not of Indians, but of Jankowskis and Davenports, McManuses and Gibbonses, their headstones lasting monuments to instability, migration, and betrayal. Lois was living proof of the same instability. Hungarian and Polish on her mother's side, she had Scotch-Irish blood and a pinch of Cherokee on her father's.

She couldn't see the oak from the road. She could see only graves and monuments and mausoleums, and she didn't have time to sightsee. Time only to drive and wish she had more time. Still, she remembered the old tree's serpentine branches running out like weeds along the ground. She wouldn't have minded standing in one place so long, though she'd heard the tree had been struck by lightning the year before. That's what you got for rooting to the same spot for 600 years, she supposed. Anyway, Willy wanted her out in a week. She'd show him. She'd clear out in a day, an hour, a minute. She'd drive in reverse through time and roll away the days and years like miles. She'd make it so he never happened. She'd cut his head out of every family picture and paste in the head of the explorer La Salle.

Gail had taken possession of the paper and busied herself with the travel section, her favorite, and the classifieds. Lately, Gail seemed to think she needed a job. She claimed that would make her more independent. Lois thought if her daughter gained any more independence, she could start issuing her own currency, and lobbying for observer status at the UN. Lois could never sway Gail one way or the other. Gail had just turned sixteen and wouldn't be taking driver's ed. until the fall. A job for Gail meant she'd rely on Lois as her personal chauffeur.

A mile past Highland, Meg, who sat in back, said, "La Pays Mexican Cousin." She had a habit of announcing road signs as the car passed them.

"La Paz," Gail corrected. "And that's cuisine, not cousin."

"It says cousin," Meg insisted.

Lois could see the storm clouds on the dashboard, could feel the static bouncing between Meg and Gail. She turned to Gail and said,

"She's right. That's the Mexican Cousin restaurant. It's a chain. There's also a Dutch Uncle Coffee Shop and a French Aunt Bakery."

"See!" said Meg triumphantly.

"Don't be so gullible," said Gail, turning back to her travel section.

"It's true," Lois said. "You bring your Mexican cousin and you get in free."

Gail laughed unpleasantly. "Come on, Mom," she said. "Even Meg's not that stupid."

Gail smiled, but Lois didn't like her attitude. You used to be so sweet. What happened? she wanted to ask, but didn't dare risk the question. She would rather have thrown a lit cigarette into a field of parched brush.

Gail never showed any mercy, and seemed compelled to dredge up every private shame and weakness in the family. She constantly teased Meg, her sparring partner, about her looks. Because of Gail's jabs, Meg refused to wear glasses anymore, though she could hardly see without them.

Gail seemed to notice the way Lois looked at her. She smiled and said, "What would you think of Cozumel, Mommy dearest? This article says it's the off-season, and we can get a special family package."

"Fine with me," said Lois. "First we need a special family, and then, if you have that kind of dough, daughter dearest, I'm game."

"Meg can be our Mexican cousin, and one of us will get in free. It says so right here." She turned to Meg and said, "Do you want to be my Mexican cousin?"

"Are you making fun of me?" Meg said.

"Hah!" said Gail, rattling the travel section.

Lois gave Gail a look, a preemptive strike aimed at neutralizing the fight before it began. Lois's look was famous in her household.

"The killer look," Gail said, shielding her eyes. "Duck, Meg."

"Watch it," Lois warned.

Gail sat up straight and plastered on a smile. Lois looked in the rearview and saw Meg copying her sister. Pathetic. Meg, the constant object of Gail's scorn, still followed her sister's lead without question.

Lois tried her look on Gail again, but she was empty. She'd run out of laser power. She had to fall back on the tone of her voice. She opened her mouth, but Gail finished her sentence for her.

"I mean it now!" Gail yelled.

"Jerk," Lois said, hating herself for being so predictable.

Lois turned down Angela, driving past Notre Dame. Today the Golden Dome looked like the top of a teapot to her. She imagined the dome rattling, hot water sloshing underneath.

"Here's a job for me," Gail announced. "Full- or part-time help at Flipped Out Records. Will you drive me there later on?"

"We'll see," Lois said. Already, it had started.

"But they'll hire someone else. A million kids would die for this job."

"Then they'd be record martyrs," Lois said, "and they'd go directly to heaven."

"Say you'll drive me," Gail said.

Eventually Lois would cave in, so she saved herself the wasted effort and agreed. Delighted, Gail smiled and regarded Lois with something approaching appreciation.

"Mom, what does reconstituted mean?" Meg said.

"Where did you see it?"

"On a truck."

"Did it have anything else written on it?" Lois said. "Something like lemon juice?"

"It just said reconstituted."

"It just said reconstituted," Gail mimicked.

"You didn't see it," Meg shouted.

"I don't have to. Trucks don't talk. So it couldn't have said anything."

"Reconstituted means something that's been put together again."

"Use it in a sentence," Meg ordered.

"To our surprise, the lemon reconstituted itself." That was the first thing that popped into Lois's head.

"Give me a better one."

She thought some more. "When the founders of this country couldn't agree the first time on a government document, they got back together and reconstituted."

Gail put her paper on her lap and leaned her head all the way back against the seat. "Mother," she said in a tone of supreme annoyance. "Why are you encouraging her?"

"What can I say? I've got an active imagination. Must we take reconstitution so seriously?"

Lois had been about Meg's age when Studebaker shut down in 1963. There'd been talk around South Bend of suicides, break-downs, and divorces. But Lois's dad acted like he'd been promoted to foreman instead of being laid off. He acted like he'd won the Irish Sweepstakes instead of losing all his pension money. Like Studebaker was just another fly-by-night car, another Packard or Pierce-Arrow. He took the shutdown in stride, like it didn't affect him personally, like he hadn't really believed in Studebaker for the past twenty years.

First, he bought a new car, a Ford Fairlane, the only non-Studebaker he ever owned. Then he piled the family in, and they took off for the world's fair. The entire ride east Lois's mother worried about money, detouring them miles out of their way every night just so they could stay in motels with names like the Modernistic Motor Court, where kids slept free. They traveled leisurely and by the time they reached New York, Lois's mother had filled an extra suitcase with Modernistic Motor Court towels and ashtrays and water glasses. Her pocketbook brimmed with dozens of sugar packets with fun facts about the states they traveled through, and paper placemats with riddles. "So we'll have something to occupy ourselves with on the trip," she explained as though talking about a trip through the outback.

Lois's dad never said a word about being out of a job. He never said much of anything else either. Instead, he sang. All the way to Flushing Meadows and the steel gleam of the giant globe at the entrance to the fair. He wouldn't stop singing and he wouldn't let anyone else stop either. When they ran out of songs, he made up new ones and repeated the old ones. About the only song he *didn't* sing was the Studebaker company song, "Rolling Along for One Hundred Years":

> Rolling along for one hundred years,
> Sing of the Studebakers,
> Wagons and buggies and automobiles,
> Sing of the Studebakers.
> Born in the year eighteen-fifty-two,
> Theme of a dream and it all came true,
> Smart as a whip for any old trip,
> Sing of the Studebakers.
> Over America's hills and plains,

Wheels for a mighty nation,
Thundering hoofs and wagon trains,
Spirit of transportation,
Rolling along for a hundred years,
Pride of the grand old makers,
Rolling along for one hundred years,
Sing of the Studebakers.

In 1852 Clem Studebaker and his brothers had started in the wagon business, and for over a hundred years Studebaker had remained a family business, though not the *same* family, but dozens of different ones who worked side by side, generation after generation. There were the eight Wilk Brothers: Stanley, Julius, Joseph, Frank, Charlie, Benny, Ted, and Gus. And the giant Bokon clan: Pop Bokon and all his sons and daughters. There were so many Bokons around, Lois's dad thought Studebaker should make a car called the Bokon. This atmosphere was what he had loved most about his job, even though *he* wasn't descended from generations of wagon and car builders. He'd come to South Bend from Toledo after the War, and never spoke about his parents and brothers or sisters, if he had any. Maybe that lack of feeling for what he'd abandoned had made him all the more fanatical about his two families in South Bend: his wife and kids, and the Studebaker Company.

The first thing Lois saw at the world's fair, the giant steel globe called the Unisphere, didn't impress her at all. To her, it looked like a skeleton, like all the life had fallen off the planet, leaving only the bones of the continents behind. Most other things she enjoyed, especially the twenty-foot cigar that puffed smoke rings.

Lois's family stood in line for an hour before they could enter an immense hall called the March of Progress. During the wait, her father sang songs and her mother kept vanishing and reappearing with free refreshments from the Hall of Beverages. After her fourth Coke, Lois couldn't hold anymore, but her mother kept pushing it at her.

"Drink it. It's free."

The March of Progress contained a museum filled with machines and gadgets. Lois spoke on a video phone to a boy in California. He looked a little older than her, maybe eleven or twelve, and she could see a bunch of other kids crowding behind him. "Hello?" she said.

"Hello?" he responded, and then a man yanked the phone away from her and brandished it at the next kid in line. "Hello?" the boy in California said forlornly, never allowed to get a proper answer from anyone.

Lois and her family walked on until they came to an auditorium without chairs, only a giant circular floor with a railing, and a screen that surrounded them. People jammed the room, which seemed to be lit with hundreds of night-lights. Lois stood in between her parents, her mother still sipping a Coke, her father humming softly, her younger brothers, Jackie and Tim, standing behind her, their heads craned.

On the screen that surrounded them hundreds of pictures flashed by, like a fast-paced dream. Fireworks and galaxies and spaceships zoomed between giant platforms. Stars exploded soundlessly, and then a meteor hurtled through space. Gigantic clouds parted and dispersed, and America grew closer and closer until Lois couldn't see the borders anymore. Still hurtling down into the middle of the country, to Indiana. Things slowed down and a town appeared and then a neighborhood, green lawns and water sprinklers, people waving pleasantly as they jetpacked through a perfect sky. A man with a briefcase hailed a monorail, which stopped for him, and then in one swift moment, hushed by.

Everyone in the room stayed silent, except for her father, who sang softly, "Buffalo Gals, won't you come out tonight?"

A row of metal cubes that all looked alike glowed on the screen. Seamless doors opened and closed silently as people walked in and out of the cubes. Children played in front, pointing up as iron-shaped rockets scorched the sky. Robots walked dogs and raked leaves.

Lois's father bent down and whispered, "That's something, huh?"

"Ssssshhh!" someone said behind him. Lois's father kept on talking. "That's the world of your children," he said. "Every possible convenience at their fingertips."

Lois believed her father, reassured that a peaceful green world with jetpacks and monorails and rockets would come to pass. But no cars, and she knew why. Studebaker, the best car company in the world, had gone out of business. The other companies must have just given up, she figured. With Studebaker gone, there wasn't anything left for them to aim for, and they knew it.

On Prospect Avenue no one jetpacked and there wasn't a monorail in sight. The houses looked as though they had been slapped together in one swoop: brick ranches with two cars parked in each driveway. Here the winning combination seemed to be a pickup truck and a Camaro or Trans Am.

"I absolutely refuse to live here," Gail said.

"Just wait and see, honey," Lois said. "Maybe our house will be different."

"Our house. I knew it," said Gail.

As far as Lois was concerned, she *had* to rent this house, no matter what it looked like. She'd scoured the classifieds, and this was the only house in Mishawaka or South Bend with enough room and the right price. She'd feel too cramped in an apartment, and she certainly couldn't afford to buy a house. She couldn't go up to Willy either and say, I looked for a place, but the prospects weren't good on Prospect Avenue. She would have preferred taking the day off, going garage sale-ing, and not worrying about finding a new home. She wished she could just buy a garage at a garage sale, and live surrounded by hundreds of knickknacks that she'd sell. That way, things would always be new for her and she'd never grow attached to anything again. If something got in her way, she'd sell it. Couches, lamps, cars, husbands, and complaining children.

No reason to get bitter, she thought. No need to lose my patience. Gail will get used to it. Life will settle down as soon as we're reconstituted.

Unfortunately, the house looked like all the others on the block, minus the Camaro and pickup. A Ford Taurus sat in the driveway.

"Oh no, it's a larva," said Gail. That was the family's nickname for Tauruses. Lois was the one who first observed that Tauruses look like bugs in their pupal stage with wheels. Gail remembered it differently. She claimed the idea as hers. Not that Lois cared, but the only way Gail could approve of Lois's words or actions was by co-opting them.

"I like this house," Lois said when they pulled into the driveway behind the Taurus. "It's got lots o' character."

"You live here then," said Gail. "Not me."

True, the house didn't look like much, but Lois held out hope for the veranda.

A man in a navy blue suit and a red bow tie loped over with his arms hanging apelike at his sides. The man had a long sloping face with thick sideburns, but almost no hair on top.

"I'm Gary Ydell, the Real Estate Guy," he said like a testifying regular at AA. A thin brown cigarette burned in one hand. "Do you get cable TV?"

"Yes, I do," Lois said. On closer inspection she saw that he *did* have hair on top, the ghostliest hair she'd ever seen. It stood straight up, but you could see right through to the scalp.

The man exhaled smoke. "Have you seen me before?" he said and tilted his head. He looped his hand in front of his face like someone finishing a soft-shoe routine.

"That's very nice," Lois said, stepping out of the car uncertainly.

The girls waited inside, looking at the man suspiciously. Until then, he had seemed unaware of Gail and Meg, but now he took a step closer. "What have we here?" he said, his eyes wide and blind like Little Orphan Annie's.

The girls shrank back in their seats.

"My daughters," Lois said. "Gail and Meg. Gail's sixteen and Meg turned eleven last month." As soon as she said this, Lois wondered why she'd mentioned their ages. This wasn't a game show.

Trying not to seem obvious, she sneaked another look at the man's hair, which seemed more like arm hair than head hair, like grass sprouts on the lawn of a new house.

"Come on, girls," she said, and the two of them reluctantly stepped out of the car.

"What's my name?" the man said to Meg, who looked down at his feet as though she wanted to stomp on them.

"Don't be embarrassed. No one remembers the first time they're introduced. That's why I use mnemonics. My name is Gary Ydell. *G* as in the *greatest* real estate. *Y* as in *your* money. With mnemonics I don't even need a business card. If you still can't remember, you can call me the Real Estate Guy. Of course, I wasn't born the Real Estate Guy, but that's who I am now. I'm a lot like Spiderman, except I wasn't bitten by a radioactive spider, but by the real-estate bug."

The man bent down to Meg and pointed his brown cigarette at her. "My name also rhymes with Bobby Rydell, but you're too young to remember him."

"Why is your hair so fuzzy?" Meg said.

The man placed his hand on his head as though playing Simon Says. He looked at Lois and said, "By the way, you wouldn't be interested in buying rather than renting would you?"

"I can't afford a house right now," Lois said.

"Condo?" he said.

"I don't think so."

The man looked disappointed, but smiled at Meg and then at Lois. "She's got the cutest pug nose."

Meg looked about to burst into tears. He seemed to notice this. "Let's see. What did Bobby Rydell sing?" He snapped his fingers at Lois and said, "Come on!"

"'Blue Velvet'?"

"Bobby Rydell," the man said. "Not Bobby Vinton." With a gleam in his eyes the man spread his arms and sang.

> For wives should always be lovers, too.
> Run to his arms the moment he comes home to you.
> I'm warning you.

The girls shot killer looks of their own at the man, who plugged his mouth with his brown cigarette and walked stiffly up to the front door.

"I think it's a hair transplant," Lois whispered to Meg.

"What's a hair transplant?" Meg shouted back.

"It's a spacious home, just right for four people," the man said at the door.

"There are only three of us," Lois said.

The man slapped himself. "That's the first law of real estate. Never assume. Unless, of course, you're assuming someone's loan." He started to laugh, but swallowed and gave Lois a pathetic look. "Your wedding band threw me off," he said, pointing to her ring.

Even though she and Willy had been divorced over a year, she still hadn't slipped it off. She didn't know why she still wore it. Willy had removed his ring ages ago. Maybe she wore it for Gail and Meg, so they'd have some hope of reconciliation.

"Our dad kicked us out," Gail offered with a twisted smile. She seemed to relish the idea of being kicked out.

"Then you'll have even more room, won't you?" the man said, unlocking the door and ushering Lois and her kids into the house. As she passed him, the man put his hand on the edge of her shoulder and guided her in as though she was blind. "How gutsy of you," he whispered.

With an expansive gesture, he presented the living room to them. Lois could almost hear the man say *Voila!* He didn't say it, but an air of *Voila!* definitely permeated the space around the Real Estate Guy. He swung through the room with an arm raised, as though spraying a can of air freshener in his path.

The front room felt cavernous because of the lack of furniture. The ceiling looked like it had been spackled with vanilla icing. Birthday candles would have fit in nicely. A chandelier with electric candles dangled from a flimsy chain in the middle of the room, and a burgundy shag rug covered the floor.

"Plush, isn't it?" the Real Estate Guy said to Lois, who stared at the carpet in horror.

Lois turned and saw her daughters transfixed at the living room's large picture window, which lacked curtains and rods. Outside, two boys stared at the girls from the driveway. The boys seemed a year or two older than Gail, seventeen or eighteen, and both wore jams and brightly-colored shirts. One boy's shirt showed blue parrots perched in tropical trees, while the other boy's shirt was tie-dyed in a pattern that looked like the parings of a green apple. The boy with the parrots cradled a skateboard, and the other one rode a small bike with fat tires and a racing number. This boy, dark, pimply, and wearing glasses, made tight circles on his bike while staring at Gail and Meg. At the end of each circle, he jerked his front wheel up in the air and whipped his head around to clear the hair out of his eyes.

Gail turned to Lois and said, "I'm going outside."

"Don't you want to see the rest of the house?" Lois said, slightly disappointed in her daughter's taste in boys.

"I can see it later," she said.

"Can I come, too?" Meg said.

"Yes," Lois said in a voice loud enough to drown out Gail's no. "You can be Gail's chaperone." When she saw Meg's blank look, she added, "It means the same thing as reconstitute. A chaperone keeps things together." Meg still didn't seem to understand. "A chaperone is a snitch."

Gail looked up at the spackled ceiling as though she wished the icing would glop down and smother Lois. But she allowed Meg to follow her outside, though only at a distance. Lois watched Gail stride up to the boys. Immediately, the three of them started talking and laughing.

The Real Estate Guy sprang up beside Lois and announced, "Neighborhood boys."

"Is that supposed to put my mind at ease?" Lois said.

The shriek of a low-flying jet shook the house. The kids in the driveway covered their ears. All except for Meg, who looked up as though seeing the face of God, and waved.

"An occasional jet on its way to the airport," the Real Estate Guy said. "Shall we view the den? The walls are knotty pine."

S ing and drive. Daddy refused to do anything *but* on the way home from the world's fair. Lois knew he was out of a job, but if he didn't care, why should she? He was only acting natural. The way she'd act if she got kicked out of school. Mama seemed to be the only one who cared. From the backseat, Lois heard her windblown worries. Daddy played Soupy Sales to Mama's Chet Huntley. Daddy's silliness reminded Lois of pies in the face and cartoons. Mama used words like *bankrupt* and *layoff*. She made all the motor lodge arrangements, and took over the everyday necessities like food, while he just meandered them west toward Indiana, conducting a never-ending "Sing Along with Mitch." But Lois could never follow the bouncing ball. Like them, the ball bounced erratically, jostled and thrown across the seat by Daddy's funny driving. He kept time on the gas pedal, and when they sang a slow song like "Shenandoah," the car moved like it was in a funeral procession. Traffic swerved around them, horns mooing, but Daddy and the kids just lifted their voices in lilting answer: "Aaaa-way, you rolling river." When the tempo picked up, so did the car, surging forward, Daddy's shoulders wriggling in rhythm, the car shaking, rattling, and rolling between lanes. Lois thought it was the car's fault, that it wasn't a Ford Fairlane, but a Fourlane because that's how many lanes it took up.

When Daddy sang upbeat songs, he pushed his hat up on his head like Maurice Chevalier, and leaned forward, one arm out the window, raised against the wind, his singing voice on full throttle.

> In the Southeast corner of the pigpen
> on the tail of a lonesome hog
> Sat a cross-eyed flea with a dimple on his knee
> picking his teeth with a two-by-three . . .

In this way they passed time, singing like the Von Trapp family, fleeing across the Poconos at night.

Lois loved Daddy's singing voice. He sang better than Burl Ives, better than Mitch Miller. They sang truer and deeper, but always the same way. Daddy changed the way he sang all the time. Sometimes he sang harmony, sometimes he made up new words. His voice jumped, bent, scratched, and shimmied over the asphalt, scouting ahead of the car in three-four time.

Once in a while, he got carried away and closed his eyes while he sang, which made Mama angry. "Keep your eyes on the road, for God's sake," she'd yell.

In back, Lois and her brothers made fun of their mother's voice. Not by actually talking. Mama would have slammed their heads together. No, they made fun of her with signs. They'd point at each other, then turn an invisible steering wheel, back up their index fingers against their chests, spin their fingers around their ears, and screw up their eyes.

Sometimes Daddy's voice scratched in his throat like a worn needle on a record, so he turned on the radio and hummed along. Cruising at night, Daddy's humming blended with the sound of the tires, and sent Lois to sleep. Her head slumped back and forth between her brothers' shoulders until the air around her exploded with the chorus from a song:

> Irene, good night
> Irene, good night
> Good night, Irene
> Good night, Irene
> I'll see you in my dreams

And then he'd return to humming. Fifteen minutes later he'd holler.

Day o, Day o,
Day de light and I wanna go home.

After that, the space between songs grew shorter and shorter, like birth contractions, and soon the car rocketed with sound again. Lois didn't mind the noise. What scared her was the silence when Daddy stopped singing and just looked at Mama with helpless eyes, or shrugged his shoulders as if to say, I forgot the words. At night he never slept. Lois knew this because the family always slept together when they stopped at a motor lodge. The rooms had only one bed in them, always reserved for Mama, who sometimes fell asleep crosswise with all her clothes on. What exhausted her, Lois couldn't figure out. Daddy did all the driving.

As soon as the lights went out, Daddy stood up from the floor in his boxer shorts and socks. Sometimes he put his hat back on, and then tiptoed across the field of children to disappear into the bathroom.

One night, Lois followed him and stood in her nightgown outside the bathroom door, staring at the crack of light underneath. All she could hear from inside was the faint rustling of paper.

She knocked softly. "Daddy?"

He didn't answer, but the rustling grew louder and she heard something being folded.

He opened the door and looked down at her. He held a map, all worn and torn at the creases. Daddy looked torn at the creases, too. For the first time in days she saw his face straight on. So used to seeing only the back of his head, she'd nearly forgotten what the front looked like. Now she saw what her mother had to see all day. Now she understood why her mother seemed so exhausted every night. Daddy was not there at all. He did not live in that face anymore. He'd gone somewhere else, maybe down the road a couple of days. Maybe they'd catch up with him, but Lois feared they wouldn't. Lois feared that somewhere along the way they'd left him behind.

"What are you doing?" she finally said. She meant more than this. She meant, Who are you now? Where are you taking us this time? What happened and when? I missed it staring at the back of your head and singing.

"I'm plotting a course," he said.

"Where are we going? We're almost home, aren't we?"

Daddy knelt down and took her by the shoulders. She wanted to run from him. He looked at her like he had something he didn't want to say, something he wouldn't say unless forced to by circumstances. Maybe someone had died, and sooner or later she'd find out.

"We don't have a home," he said.

Then he started singing to her, his hands still on her shoulders.

> Away, we're bound away
> across the wide Missouri.

In this way, they passed an hour, Daddy quietly singing to her. His voice was a secret between them, something that her brothers still had no knowledge of, and that her mother hadn't penetrated. Lois knew, and she didn't fear him anymore.

The next day Daddy took them off in the wrong direction. Instead of continuing across the top of Ohio, he swung south around Youngstown, heading toward West Virginia.

"As long as we're in the neighborhood," was his only explanation, which bled immediately into "It's a Long Way to Tipperary."

Lois's brothers pointed their index fingers at the back of his head, then turned an imaginary steering wheel.

At a Stuckey's near Parkersburg, Daddy finally stopped. By this time, they were cranky, having made only two rest-room stops, and not eating for a day. Daddy said, "How about a praline? That should do us for a while."

"That's fine, Rudy. You go inside and find us a praline," Mama said.

He smiled and pushed his hat forward like he planned on singing an up-tempo song. Then he scooted out the door and came around to Lois's side. She wouldn't look at him. She felt hungry and homesick and didn't want to trade silly faces with him.

"Hey, honeycomb," he said, rapping his knuckles on the window. "Look at me," but she refused.

"I'm going to get you something special inside. What do you want?"

She wanted one of those games with the golf tees that you move from hole to hole in a triangular block of wood. She knew he'd get it for her if she asked, but she preferred to punish him by ignoring the offer.

"Nothing," she said.

"I'll get you something anyway," he said and gave the door a slap. Only then did Lois turn and see him stepping lightly toward the oasis, belting out "Sixteen Tons."

And that's how they left him. Without a word, Mama slid over to the driver's side and patted the seat next to her. Lois understood and slipped into the dent Mama left in the vinyl seat. The scent of lime from Daddy's after-shave hung around the dashboard.

"Wait," her brother Jackie yelled, looking up from the comic book he'd been reading for the last hundred miles.

Mama didn't wait and she didn't explain.

At first, Lois was glad they'd left Daddy behind, and she felt strong and rueful sitting in Mama's indentation.

Mama looked strange behind the wheel. She leaned forward like Daddy did when singing an upbeat number, but she did it because the seat wasn't adjusted right and her feet barely hit the pedals. She kept her eyes wide open on the road, as though some horrible monster loomed in front of them. She wore an ice-cube of a hat, and altogether she looked like some taxi driver out of *The Mummy's Curse*.

"We can sell the car as soon as we get back," Lois told Mama after a hundred miles of silence. "That should tide us over."

Mama didn't answer. Lois couldn't stand Jackie's crying and Tim's constant questions from the backseat, so she turned on the radio. Mama didn't even let it warm up. She stabbed it off and said, "No more songs."

Mama trembled and Lois wanted to comfort her, but she also wanted to be comforted back. "It'll be all right, I promise," she said.

Mama laughed grimly and said, "A lot of good your promise does me."

"I'm just saying it's going to be all right," Lois said.

"I'm saying back that it won't," Mama said. "We can't live on pralines, and we can't live on songs neither."

And that's when Lois really understood. This was more than a temporary change in plans, a rerouting, a brief detour due to construction. This was fundamental. Monumental. The steady march of progress. The heartbeat change from the wagon to the automobile, the jetpack, the monorail, and the spaceship. A completely new outlook, a new means of transportation, a new future. Mama wouldn't *ever* turn around and pick Daddy up.

Knotty pine just didn't trip her trigger. The Real Estate Guy tugged at one of the den's windows, which had been painted shut, while Lois stayed by the doorway. The stale air almost gave her the dry heaves.

While the Real Estate Guy struggled against the window, Lois daydreamed. She pictured Willy eating his favorite meal: pork chops with gravy and new potatoes. She didn't know why this picture came into her mind at that moment, or why it seemed so important, but it seemed *extremely* important, as though some mystery in that image was still unsolved. He smiled broadly, enjoying every bite, cutting the chops and swirling the meat in the gravy. She guessed she'd probably seen that picture of Willy a hundred times in real life. She'd fixed pork chops and new potatoes for him at least that many times since they were married. She knew the man inside out. She knew what made him happy.

The Real Estate Guy gave up trying to open the window and said, "Of course, you could panel in knotty pine in the basement and you'd have yourself a matching family room."

Lois couldn't believe the man was telling her she should panel a rental house. How would paneling someone else's room improve *her* life?

"What about the veranda?" Lois said.

The man fiddled with his bow tie. "The veranda? In knotty pine?"

"I meant I'd like to see it," Lois said. Really, the man was a pill. Lois wanted to take him by the shoulders, shake him, and say, What is it with you and knotty pine? Is it some kind of code word? Are you trying to tell me something real?

The Real Estate Guy surveyed the study one last time, and then sucked in his breath. He seemed completely enamored with the room. As he whisked by her into the hallway, he snapped his fingers and sang, "'Hey, little girl, comb your hair, fix your makeup,'... I don't remember the rest. Do you?"

Lois shook her head. The tune was "Wives and Lovers," the song by Bobby Rydell he'd mentioned before, and unfortunately, yes, she did remember. She hated the song, but knew it would always be threading somewhere through her mind, along with "Ring around the Collar" (Those dirty rings!) and the theme song from "Mr. Ed." That was the problem with songs. They just kept on singing to her. She'd heard of people mysteriously picking up radio broadcasts from the thirties and forties, but who knew where they came from? She'd heard of other people picking up radio shows with the fillings in their teeth, unwanted tunes jamming their bones. She imagined the voices of people orbiting the earth like junk satellites. You just needed equipment sensitive enough to pick up the sounds. That's how she felt, receiving memories by mistake with no way to turn them off, except to start drilling, or by pulling out all her teeth.

Lois stepped onto a deck of sorts, though not really a deck, because she associated a deck with something made of redwood with a hot tub at one end. This room was enclosed like a porch. Giant screens surrounded the room, and the parts of the walls that weren't screened consisted of wood painted white. The room didn't feel like a porch either, because a porch is something in front of a house, with a swing to sit on and watch traffic go by. This room was attached to the back of the house like a patio, but it definitely didn't have a patio feel. It didn't have lawn chairs or birdbaths. It didn't have any furniture, no Adirondack chairs or white wicker couches and tables, no ferns hanging beside the windows. Through the screens an immense backyard sloped beneath the room and down a long hill. The yard seemed half as long as a football field, and was bordered by some woods. Lois could imagine surviving the rest of the summer in this room, drinking lemon Cokes as she watched the children play boccie ball or aim mallets at distant wickets. Lois had never tasted a lemon Coke, wasn't quite sure how boccie ball was played, and hated croquet. But never mind. She had entered a new dimension.

"Now *this* is a veranda," Lois said.

The Real Estate Guy beamed at her. "You could almost call it a piazza," he said.

"How much did you say the rent is?" Lois said.

Far below, someone yelled. She glanced out the windows and saw Meg running from the woods and up the hill toward the house.

"Mom! Mom!" Meg yelled.

"What honey, what's wrong?" Lois said, but Meg didn't seem to hear her.

Gail tore out of the woods in hot pursuit. Gail, a much faster runner, started gaining on Meg.

"Mom!" Meg shrieked.

"What?" Lois shouted, cupping her hands around her mouth.

Meg stopped and looked around.

"Up here," Lois yelled. Meg shielded her eyes. "I wanted to chaperone on Gail," she yelled, "but she wouldn't let me."

At that moment, Gail caught up and swung Meg around by the arm like a dance partner. Meg lost her balance mid-swing and fell backwards into the grass. Gail took Meg by the arm again and pulled her to her feet.

"Liar!" Gail screamed. She gave Meg a strong shove in the chest, and Meg fell down again.

Someone else emerged from the woods, the boy with the bright jams and green tie-dyed shirt. The boy with the blue parrot shirt stepped alongside him. The two of them looked up the hill at Gail, who now straddled Meg. The boys exchanged looks and nearly collapsed with laughter. One boy raised his hand and the other one dusted it with his palm.

"Gail, stop that," Lois yelled, but it didn't do any good. Gail continued to beat up on her sister.

Lois took a breath and dashed out of the room past the Real Estate Guy. Through the house, out the door, and down the hill.

"Liar!" Gail still shouted as Lois grabbed her by the arm, yanking her off Meg.

Lois had never believed in smacking her children, and still didn't. Her hand came down across Gail's cheek. Gail's head snapped back. One of her five earrings flew off. The black bandana around her forehead was pushed up and tilted.

Lois waited for Gail to say something, but she didn't. Gail acted as though they were playing a game of freeze tag, and no one had unfrozen her yet. Even Meg, who'd been whimpering on the grass, lay silent and still, as though waiting for Lois's anger to come down on her as well.

Lois flipped her hair and said, "Get in the car."

"Good, because I'm not living here."

"Yes you are," Lois said. "You're going to live here because I'm going to live here, and I don't care one bit whether you like it or not."

"Good, because I don't."

"Good," Lois said.

"You're not my mother," Gail said.

Lois shared that feeling. She didn't feel like this girl's mother.

"I wish someone had let me in on that secret sooner," Lois said. "I could have skipped childbirth."

The two boys from the woods stared at her. She took a step toward them. They backed off and vanished among the trees without a word.

"Get in the car," she told Gail.

She almost added an extra look and an "I mean it now!" but she saw it wasn't necessary. Gail turned around and walked silently up the hill.

As Lois and Meg followed, Lois studied the way Gail walked, the sullen dip of her shoulders, her fists clenched. She knew her chances with Gail were not good, that Gail would always blame her for leaving, just as Lois had blamed her mother. For years, Lois had wished her mother had abandoned her, too, at that roadside oasis. A year after they left her father there, she heard "King of the Road" on the radio and convinced herself the song was about her father. She even wrote to Roger Miller to find out if he knew where her father was. After several months, she received a reply saying he hadn't had anyone special in mind when he wrote the song, but he hoped she would catch up with her daddy someday.

After that, she tried to put her father out of her mind, and over time succeeded. By the time Lois married, her father had died a dozen different ways. As a teenager, she daydreamed about it. Whenever she had a fight with her mother, she locked herself in her bedroom and counted the ways he might have died, like one of the devout saying rosaries. She saw him run over by a truck. She saw him starving and stumbling through some snow-crusted forest, being stabbed by a hobo, putting a gun to his head. Thinking of his death made her feel sorry for herself, not him. And, over time, she became certain he had died. She didn't necessarily need proof. After all, she couldn't visit her father's death to make sure it existed, like some kind of monument. She couldn't place a grave marker over it, and she couldn't save up her money and sightsee it someday like a foreign country. She couldn't buy his death like some old piece of furniture picked up at a garage sale. No, he had died too far away for that. He had become too small for the human eye, like a subatomic particle or a quark. She believed in ghosts, too. Always had, and didn't need proof. One night, at age fifteen (she swore she remembered it clearly), he pulled up the sheet around her shoulders and kissed her hair as she was going to bed. She had no doubt he was there, and even thanked him silently and held a soft unspoken conversation in which they shared confidences. She asked him where he lived and he answered with a breeze. She asked him what she should do with her life and he threw colored spots in front of her eyes, which meant she should become an artist or a dancer, depending on whether she followed the movement of the spots or their composition. A plane flew overhead, a sign she should leave or a sign he was leaving. And then silence and the gray dark.

Y ou're not leaving, are you?" she heard a faint voice say from far above.

She turned and looked toward the veranda. She couldn't see anyone, even though she shielded her eyes. She tried to see Willy there, but couldn't. She imagined him asking the same question, but he hadn't. Then she tried to see her father there. She saw him standing in a Stuckey's parking lot near Parkersburg, West Virginia, humming the question to himself.

Part II

Driving Music

Music is continuous; only listening is intermittent.

—HENRY DAVID THOREAU

FIVE

Wreckage pinned Henry beneath the car. He tried to rise, but couldn't. Something pressed against his windpipe and kept him down. Part of the chassis? The wheelbase. In the dark, he recognized the outline of a wheel to his right. He turned and saw another wheel to his left. The tires had apparently burst off the wheels, leaving only metal. The rod connecting the two wheels stretched barely above his neck. He couldn't see any other debris around him. He figured he must have been thrown clear. He lay flat on his back on a scratchy surface, too uniform in length to be weeds. Had he landed on someone's lawn? He didn't remember a yard nearby, only hills and fields for miles around. The last thing he remembered was Carla rubbing his leg, giving him a look, saying, "Are you crazy?"

Why didn't she take this thing off him? Why didn't she check to see if he was all right? What did she want to prove?

With his left hand, he lifted the rod attached to the wheels. He let the rod roll in behind him and he stood up slowly. His eyes started adjusting now. He stumbled to the door and flicked on the light.

In the middle of the room lay a set of barbells Sid had lent him. Sid's latest theory was that Henry was borderline anemic, and that's why Henry acted the way he did. So Sid lent Henry a set of barbells and sold him $300 worth of vitamins at discount. Henry had tried to explain to Sid that no amount of vitamins would unsever the ulnar nerve in his right hand. "Nonsense," Sid replied. "I've given you extra doses of Vitamin E." Henry knew he couldn't tell Sid the truth. His ulnar nerve wasn't severed, though that's what the doctors had thought at first. The doctors hadn't been able to find anything wrong with his hand, but if Sid knew that, then he'd start force-feeding Henry megadoses of vitamins.

Even megadoses couldn't make him lift barbells with one hand. But he wanted to accommodate Sid, so he spent half an hour grunting underneath the weights, making no progress. He succeeded only in exhausting himself, and had finally fallen asleep.

Henry's impromptu nap hadn't refreshed him at all. He felt groggy and disoriented. His mouth was gummy and dry. He decided to ride his bike over to Macri's for coffee. This time, he made sure he dressed. Six months earlier, he'd shown up at Macri's in his underwear. Even now, he hadn't chosen the right clothes for the season. He wore metallic-green shorts, running shoes, and a short-sleeved shirt. He couldn't stand long-sleeved shirts and regular pants anymore, unless he wore gigantic pants that made him look like Tweedledum, the pant waist nearly reaching his chest. Anything tighter made him feel too constricted. He could stand chills and goose bumps. He couldn't stand feeling constricted.

He ran his bike downstairs and banged the front door open. It sprang back and clicked behind him.

He stopped. Sid locked the front door at seven every night. Henry felt his pockets but knew he hadn't brought his keys.

He stood in front of the door as though it might forgive him and open again. It was an oak door with a beveled glass window. The dim bulb that lit the front hall gave way to a brighter light in the kitchen. Through the open kitchen door he could see Rhonda smoking a cigarette and sitting on one of the kitchen chairs, her knees bent to her chin. One of her arms rested on her knees and the other held the cigarette and gestured to someone Henry couldn't see. Probably Pam. Of all Sid's tenants, Rhonda and Pam hated Henry the most. They forgave Henry nothing, regarding every mistake he made as a personal attack.

Henry leaned his bike against the side of the house and sat down by one of the limestone pillars of the porch. This kind of night reminded him of the better times with Carla and Matthew: one night in particular when the three of them had lain on their backs in the yard. They'd stared up at the mix of fireflies and stars, and shouted "Look! Look!" as though the stars were the lights of a distant city and the dipping and weaving bugs were cars buzzing recklessly through its streets. Of course, that night had been in a completely different season. All the fireflies had disappeared by mid-November.

Even so, the essence of this night felt similar to that other night, back in his old life. Maybe the stillness of the air had something to do with this feeling. Of course, this neighborhood and his old one had nothing in common either. He and Carla had lived in a subdivision, not like this old neighborhood with its hedges dividing the lawns. In this place, trees arched over every yard: oaks, maples, poplars, cottonwoods, and a shaggy pine here and there.

Henry knocked on the door again and peered inside, certain Rhonda could see him because the porch light was on. He knocked again, tapping loud enough to be heard but soft enough that he wouldn't offend her too much. This time she looked at him and blew her smoke into the hall. The smoke drifted and swirled around the bare light bulb.

Henry smiled and waved. He pointed down with his index finger, then rattled a make-believe doorknob. He put on his most pathetic face.

She went back to her conversation. Henry knocked a little louder. She looked again. Now she stood up and said something to the invisible person she was talking with. Henry smiled gratefully. He knew she'd yell at him for forgetting his keys again, but if yelling made her happy, so be it. He'd stand there and take it, which would undoubtedly enrage her even more.

Rhonda gave Henry a little wave and kicked the doorstop aside. The door swung back and forth between the intense light of the kitchen and the dim bulb in the hall. And then it closed.

He wished he was still asleep. He wished Sid had never lent him those barbells. He could still feel them pressing against his neck. He still felt that panic of being pinned down, of disorientation, of not knowing if Carla and Matthew were alive or dead. If he hadn't awakened like that, he wouldn't have remembered, and if he hadn't remembered, he wouldn't have rushed out of the room without his keys.

That was one way of seeing things. The other way, to view each event as separate, each outcome as random and accidental, was the safest route; to forget about blame and responsibility, to lead a no-fault life without consequence or conviction. He wished he could impress all the people who wanted to change him with this outlook. On second thought, he didn't wish anything. Wishing was antithetical to Henry's new life. Henry didn't want to want anything.

Unfortunately, he'd come to this conviction much too late in life. He'd been full of so many wants and expectations before that now they'd left a residue of desire behind. He still wanted something very badly, though he couldn't name it. This desired thing haunted him. It tripped him up and made him a bumbler. He broke things in its name. He fed it with food that didn't belong to him. He suffered the constant abuse and lecturing of others who spoke to it through him. It locked him out and caused him to wander naked in the streets of South Bend.

If Carla hadn't died, she could have shown him how to conquer these leftover desires. She had been a master of wanting nothing, though the effort had made her a nervous wreck who avoided people's eyes and laughed in staccato clips. She seemed resigned about most things: the baby she had had in high school, the lousy jobs she'd held, the series of men she'd dated who seemed linked in a loose confederation dedicated to her everlasting abuse. She had a take-what-you're-given attitude that Henry had always tried to battle. She never thought she had the right to refuse, not the high-school boys who had appeared like genies in her arms, not her bosses who overworked her, not her mother who commanded Carla to deliver her a grandson.

But Carla never minded. "Bad luck's in my background, my genes," she used to explain. "I'm half Gypsy, half Indian, you know." Actually, her genes had nothing to do with it. Half German, half Republican, she was the daughter of a GOP judge in the southern Indiana town of Floyd's Knobs, named not after the testicles of the mayor as Henry claimed, but after a couple of notable hills.

She didn't speak much about her old boyfriends, and when she referred to them at all, she lumped them together as "those shitheads," leaving it at that. Luckily, Henry didn't fit into that group, though Carla's son, Matthew, always mistrusted him. Right after Henry and Carla started living together, Matthew, no more than eleven at the time, warned him, "Don't ever hit my mother or I'll kill you."

To Carla, Henry qualified as the opposite of a shithead, whatever that was. One night in bed he and Carla tried to figure it out between caresses and kisses. A rosehead? Yes, something fresh-smelling. A cedarhead? Henry liked that. He savored his role as avenging cedarhead, stepping into the midst of Carla's life and cleaning things up. Only two years out of college, and he could already claim an instant family and a job he'd stepped into as a birthright. With no real effort at all, he'd landed a full and meaningful life.

Eventually, the things that at first attracted him to Carla started grating on him, began to seem like more serious flaws. Her gentleness he saw as submissiveness. The way she always made fun of herself seemed just a sign of spinelessness. He started feeling she'd taken advantage of him. After all, she had six years on him. He wasn't ready to live with a woman who already had a half-grown son.

One of Carla's hobbies was apologizing. "I'm sorry" were her favorite words. If he couldn't find anything to watch on TV, she'd say, "I'm sorry," as though she controlled America's viewing choices. If traffic held Henry up and he arrived home late for dinner, she'd say, "I'm sorry," as though she should have found him a shortcut. If a sunny day turned suddenly cloudy, she'd say, "I'm so sorry."

After a while, he started believing that everything *was* her fault. He started moping around the house thinking, She's the reason I'm so unhappy. Today's the day I'm going to leave her.

Sometimes he looked at her in the middle of a fight and she looked, and they both stopped, breathing hard and waiting. Her face was upturned. She backed up against the door and she waited for him to hit her. They both waited. He almost did it. He wanted to, but he wouldn't. He knew she'd have it over him then. He knew that being hit was her secret weapon. Then she'd be able to keep her bruises and scars in reserve forever, just in case all her prickly apologies didn't sting him to death first with guilt. Then he'd join the rank and file of marching shitheads. Meanwhile, Matthew waited behind the door with a butter knife. Henry never saw the boy during a fight, but he always sensed that he was lurking in the wings, his mother's little avenger if things got out of hand.

On random nights Henry would go driving in his old Buick Skylark with its V-8 engine. The *i* had fallen off the Buick nameplate on the back of the Skylark, so that's what we called his car: Buck. He was reckless. He acted like a jerk. At two or three in the morning, he'd take off for parts unknown, headlights off, rocketing at 90, 100. One December night, he pushed Buck up to 126 with the windows down. He hardly knew his teeth were chattering, that his hands turned blue on the steering wheel.

He tried not to repeat himself on these trips. He did something new on every expedition. Once, he sped on I-465 around Nap Town ten times without being pulled over. Indianapolis bored him. More often, he headed even farther south, to the edges of the state, racing through dozens of small towns: Oolitic in the hills of the limestone belt south of Bloomington, New Albany across the Ohio River from Louisville, Tell City, French Lick, Nashville, Sellersburg, Azalea, Nebraska, Little York, and Pinhook. The towns had their differences: the galleries and antique stores of Nashville, the oddball architecture of Columbus. The county seats like Brownstown and New Bedford and Bloomington, where he'd gone to college, had nearly identical squares with a court-house in the middle and kindred street names from one town to the next: Wabash, Main, Lincolnway, Sycamore. When he arrived in one of these towns he'd circle the square slowly a couple of times, paying his respects, and then scoot off again.

Occasionally, he went west from South Bend to the Region, past the mills of Gary and into South Chicago by the old Falstaff Brewery with its giant concrete cans of beer, the paint chipped and faded from time and pollution. Then he'd turn around and buzz past the concave tower of the power plant that loomed over the orderly houses of Michigan City. When he grew tired he'd pull over in a motel parking lot and stretch across the seat, even if he had only a few more miles before South Bend. The next day he'd head home. He didn't have any real purpose to this roaming. At that time, the state slogan on the license plate was Wander Indiana, and that's exactly what he did: his sole aim being to cover territory with patches of rubber like some crazy dog pee-ing on every no-name bush and shrub to mark as his own. He simply wandered Indiana in a high-speed daze.

He never went farther than Louisville, and then he'd sling back like he was attached to Carla with elastic. No sooner had he walked in the door than he picked a fight, reminding her of the faults he'd forgotten about while he was away. Without even knowing what she'd done, she'd apologize over and over.

The more Carla tried to please him, the guiltier he felt. She always baked him his favorite desserts, bought him trinkets, deferred to him, never disagreed. Instead of appreciating her more, he grew bored with her, ignored her, insulted her. In retaliation, she became a virtual saint. She read his mind and did things for him before he asked. He didn't dare show the slightest sign of displeasure. If he did, she'd just redouble her desperate kindnesses, leaving him choking on the impossibility of appreciating her enough.

One day she suggested they all get away. "Get away?" he said. "From what?"

"You know," she said. "Take a breather, spend some time together?"

"Oh," he said.

"You don't think it's a good idea?" she said.

He hated the idea.

"Where to?" he said.

"Lake Michigan. Warren Dunes."

An even worse idea. He didn't like beaches. He preferred pools, where he could keep track of his laps. And he didn't appreciate sitting around on a blanket doing nothing. Still, he agreed. If he said he didn't want to go to the lake, she'd suggest the ocean, the mountains, Europe, a trip around the world. He'd never make it home again.

The trip took only an hour and a half: a straight shot up Highway 31 to the shoreline. Henry tried to act like this getaway was something he might enjoy, but he couldn't possibly match Carla's enthusiasm on the road. She brought along all kinds of little games with her, including three books of Mad Libs, which Henry hadn't realized existed anymore. When Carla grew tired of Mad Libs, she tried out insults on Henry and Matthew, who sat in back spitting out the window. Not real insults. Gag insults she'd tried to memorize from a book for this trip.

"Listen, Matthew, this one's a hoot. Let's play horse. You be the back end, I'll just be myself."

"You've got it backwards, Mom."

"Oh, right. You be the front end, I'll just be myself."

"You just insulted yourself," Henry said.

"Okay, I'll be the front end, you just be yourself." When neither of them laughed, she ducked her head and said, "You guys! That's funny."

Then Carla did something disgusting. She made sandwiches out of white bread and cold baked beans. At first, Henry thought this was another gag, but she explained that eating cold bean sandwiches was a travel tradition from her childhood. First, she piled thick slabs of butter all over the bread, then poured the beans over the butter.

"How can you eat all that butter?" he said.

"My mom's from Wisconsin," she said. "You don't expect me to eat oleo, do you? I don't see how anyone stands margarine. Come on, let me make you a sandwich."

Henry took his hands off the steering wheel and made a cross with his index fingers, like she was a vampire.

"Suit yourself," she said. "But you're going to be hungry. Matthew and I always eat these on trips. Don't we honey?"

Matthew didn't answer. He'd stuffed the bean sandwich almost whole into his mouth. If he'd tried to say anything at that moment, Henry would have had to stop the car to perform the Heimlich maneuver.

There used to be a commercial showing a happy vacationing family in a station wagon, singing songs and laughing. Suddenly everyone stopped singing as their car entered a blackened and still-smoldering forest. That's almost how Henry felt when they arrived at Warren Dunes. Instead of hundreds of charred trees, Henry and Carla and Matthew confronted thousands of dead fish, a kind called alewives, a little bigger than sardines. They usually lived in saltwater, but they had swum by the millions through the St. Lawrence Seaway into the fresh water of Lake Michigan, where they'd gone belly-up. Now they lined the beach for miles, and a sheet of them floated offshore.

Carla tried to play the glad game. "At least it's a gorgeous day," she said, unfurling the beach blanket over a relatively clean stretch of sand.

"Wasn't there someone you could have called about this?" Henry said. "You could have checked."

Carla started to apologize, but Matthew broke her off. "I'm going over by the dunes. See if anyone's hang gliding."

"Okay," she said. "Be careful."

Henry decided to go for a walk, too. "Can I come?" Carla said, hopping up from the blanket.

"No, stay here," Henry said, "Watch our things." He walked off. Matthew headed in one direction while Henry went the other. Henry looked back and saw Carla combing out her hair on her blanket, and the tiny dot of Matthew receding into the dunes.

When he returned, Carla lay on her back on the blanket. Her eyes fluttered open as though sensing him standing over her. She smiled, shaded her eyes, and said, "Did you have fun?"

He didn't answer her question. Instead, he answered another question she hadn't actually asked, but one that always hung in the air between them.

She looked at him for a long moment. She searched his face with her hand still shielding her forehead. He had expected this look of hers, but it lasted much longer than he had imagined it would. Even so, he hardened himself, feeling like a bastard, but he didn't know any other way. On the other hand, he supposed he could have chosen a better moment. Carla brushed the blanket with her hand, the same motion she used when she brushed her hair. "What have I done?" she said.

Someone had once told him never to answer that question. Nothing could be deadlier than rattling off a soon-to-be-ex-companion's faults. Nothing could be gained. He couldn't have answered anyway. His mouth felt dry and glued shut. This had turned out even worse than he thought it would, seeing her face so open and on the verge of collapse.

Henry looked away and scanned the beach. Some parts of the shore seemed better than others. A few brave swimmers had found pockets of alewife-free water. One large woman in a purple one-piece bathing suit stood still in the lake, and Henry could see she was slowly being encircled by a school of dead fish. Even so, the woman barely moved. With all those fish floating around her, she looked like an ingredient in a giant stockpot. Every once in a while she'd do a half-hearted breast stroke, probably to keep the little fish back.

"Henry, I'm sorry," Carla was telling him. "Are you listening? What more do you want me to say?"

Henry went to the door and tried again. Miraculously, it opened this time. Maybe it hadn't been locked at all. Maybe he'd just imagined it was. He could feel the acid burning his stomach. The last time he could remember eating was – what? A year ago? Impossible, but the last meal he actually remembered eating was at Thanksgiving.

He made his way to the kitchen. Rhonda and Pam had disappeared, though Rhonda's smoke still lingered in the air, and they'd left their dishes and things out. On the table lay a half-eaten sauer-kraut-and-pineapple pizza, which seemed to be the natural food of Rhonda and Pam. Just as koalas eat only eucalyptus leaves, Rhonda and Pam seemed to survive on pineapple-and-sauerkraut pizzas. Pam was from Iowa, where they ate such things. Henry couldn't say for certain that pineapple-and-sauerkraut pizzas tasted disgusting, since he'd never eaten one. Tonight, he felt hungry enough to find out, but the food didn't belong to him, so he closed the box and put it on the bottom shelf of the refrigerator.

Looking inside, he tried to remember which food he could rightfully eat. Almost everything had someone's name on it. Plastic containers in the freezer had Magic Marker labels, cartons of milk had masking-tape labels, even vegetables and fruits had their owner's name scribbled or scratched on. Henry found only two things that didn't obviously belong to someone else: a pat of butter and a carton of extra-large eggs.

Henry stared for a long time at the eggs with the door to the fridge open. He couldn't remember buying them, but he couldn't remember not buying them either. The carton was blue and made of foamy plastic. He remembered seeing such cartons before. He even remembered picking them up at the store and opening them to see if any of the eggs inside were cracked.

He took the box out of the refrigerator and set it on the table. He sat down and stared at the carton some more. He still hadn't opened it, but he guessed there were only five eggs inside. He opened the lid and peeked inside. Five on the button. That proved it. He knew how many were inside, plus he had at one time bought eggs before. Maybe these.

Still, he didn't act. Nonchalantly, he gathered Rhonda's and Pam's dirty plates, holding them with his good hand while balancing them on his right arm. He brought them over to the sink, washed them, and set them to dry beside a frying pan on the dish rack. He picked up the frying pan and turned it over, studying it.

"Something seems to be missing," he said, putting it on the stove.

He turned on the front burner and gas whispered out. He struck a match and held it to the burner. He blew out the match, set it on the stove, then fetched the unclaimed pat of butter and dropped it in the pan.

Still, he hadn't committed himself to the act yet. He looked at the eggs on the table and felt vaguely guilty. They *were* his eggs. Sure now, he clearly remembered how he'd felt after Sid's last talk with him, how he'd gone out then and there and brought home two sacks of groceries. He couldn't remember exactly what he'd purchased, but he must have bought eggs. After all, everyone buys eggs.

That decided it. He lifted an egg out of the carton and cracked it against the rim of the frying pan. Then he plunked the egg into the sizzling butter. He took one more from the carton and repeated the process. The blue flames curved up around the bottom of the pan. Maybe he had it on too high, but the eggs seemed to be cooking fine. Already, the whites bubbled and the yolks started hardening. Smoke rose from the center of the pan, and the smell of food overtook the stale cigarette odor.

H enry and Carla and her son, Matthew, sat in silence on their way back from Warren Dunes. Henry stared straight ahead at the oil slicks that made water mirages in the road, while Carla occupied herself by brushing out her hair, flipping radio stations, and glancing at him uncertainly. Her hair was black and dull but plentiful, and she always brushed it when she was nervous.

Matthew, who sat in back, had inherited his mother's fondness for combs. He had a buzz cut, but kept a comb in his back pocket as though his hair needed constant attention. Matthew still wore his swimming trunks, as dry now as when he'd arrived at the lake. His trunks didn't have a back pocket, so he'd stuck his comb between the elastic of the swimsuit and his rear end, and he'd wandered the beach all day like that. Now he looked sullenly out his rolled-down window. Every ten seconds or so he'd spit. Henry considered neither his sullenness nor his spitting unusual. The boy hardly ever spoke and had developed a habit of spitting all the time. He spit so often he never had more than a penny's worth of moisture in his mouth. Henry and Carla didn't know where the habit came from, though they thought it might have been from watching the Cubs on WGN all the time, where the players spit on cue whenever the camera turned their way.

Carla had the radio tuned to a country station, which kept fuzzing in and out while they drove. Henry hated Carla's taste in music, but he

could tell she was on the verge of tears, so he didn't want to make an issue of it. The radio station played a particularly gushy song by Ronnie
Milsap called "Don't Your Memory Ever Sleep at Night?" As the car
moved along, the reception became more and more distorted. Static
acted as Ronnie's backup singer, making a steady "fup fup fup fup
fup," like the sound of a tire losing its tread.

The music started driving Henry crazy. He clutched the steering
wheel, trying not to let it get to him. That's why Carla had left it on that
station. To get to him. Sonic revenge.

The road, a two-laner, had been twisting and bending for a while,
but now turned into a straightaway, and he could see some kind of old
car in front of him. He quickly gained on it, and forgetting the mood,
wanted to point it out.

"Look, Matthew," he said. "What kind of car do you think that is?
It looks like something out of an old 'Looney Tunes' cartoon."

In the rearview, Henry saw Matthew swivel his head from the window and over Henry's shoulder.

"Don't know," the boy said, turning back to the window to resume
his spitting.

"What kind of car do you think that is?" Henry said to Carla. He
smiled at her and she stopped brushing her hair. She placed the brush
on the seat beside her and gave him an uncomprehending look, like
he'd just asked her if she thought the Salem witches had been guilty or
not.

"You know," she started, but he cut her off by switching the radio
station.

"There's nothing on here," he said. "Just static."

"You know," she said, grabbing the handle of her brush and beating lightly on top of the car seat. "You know I've always wanted to
please you."

Henry didn't want to hear it. He tried to find her station again, but it
had vanished. He wanted to see the antique car, even if no one else
cared. He punched the gas and almost bumped into the car, huge and
brown and snail-like, with a tiny window in back and a roof that made
a hump. It must have been traveling twenty miles an hour, max. It had
been built so low that Henry could barely see its tires. The car, the ug-
liest he'd ever seen, could have been some giant vacuum cleaner
skimming across the countryside.

He tried to read the make, but couldn't see a nameplate. He swung out to pass it just as another car roared at him from the other direction, blasting its horn. Carla clutched his leg and said, "Watch out."

Henry made it back just in time. Carla released his leg and let out her breath. He looked in the rearview and saw the car receding, the sound of its horn speeding away. He caught Matthew's eyes in the mirror. That sullen look had disappeared. Matthew seemed fearful and excited now, and he sat up straight, peering ahead. "Wow," he said, almost in admiration.

As Henry sped up again, so did the car in front, matching Henry's speed, making it impossible to pass. Henry glanced over to see the driver of the other car, a guy in his twenties with a ponytail, grinning maliciously.

Carla picked up her brush again, and started going through her right side, leaning her head over so that she glanced sideways at Henry.

Henry noticed the radio reception had eroded completely to static now. He switched off the knob.

Carla reached out and turned it back on, so loudly that static completely filled the car. "Why do you have to change things now?" she yelled over the noise. For a second, he thought she meant changing stations, turning it off.

Henry didn't answer and she pursed her lips and frowned. Then she smacked him on his bare arm with her hairbrush.

She hit him hard and the bristles made him wince. His foot hit the gas and he nearly collided with the car in front.

"Why now, all of a sudden?"

"It's not all of a sudden," he said.

"Then why didn't you say something before?" she said. "Are you afraid of me or something?"

He didn't say anything, but just looked at her. She wouldn't have been able to change, even if he'd said something earlier, and anyway, this had to do more with him than her. He'd been restless for a while, but hadn't had the guts to do anything.

She looked at him harder, expecting an answer. He shrugged.

She raised her hairbrush to start beating on him again. He grabbed her hand and bent it against her wrist. She dropped the brush on the floor and cried out. She shrunk into her seat. She scooted against the

door and didn't take her eyes off him. He looked back and saw that
Matthew glared at him, too.

"You *are* afraid, aren't you?" she said.

"Of what?" he said, but he didn't let her answer. "If you want to
know the truth," he yelled, "you embarrass me."

He didn't mean that, though he felt embarrassed at this very moment. He hated arguing in front of the boy. He could see what had happened embarrassed Matthew, too. The boy just stared out his window,
not doing anything, not spitting, not combing his hair.

"Why can't you wait?" she said.

"Why can't *you* wait?" he said. "Let's talk about this at home."

Henry had missed his chance to pass the car in front. The straightaway had disappeared, and now the road rolled and curved, and they
crept along.

He tried to be patient. He tried not to make any sudden moves. He
didn't want to say anything else. Carla huddled in the corner of the
seat and curled into herself. She started apologizing over and over, almost chanting, "I'm sorry."

Henry flicked the radio on, then switched it off sharply.

They climbed a hill slowly. Henry tried at least to appreciate the
scenery. A barbed wire fence ran along either side of the road. The
embankment consisted of only bare dirt and rocks and sparse weeds.
Over the sides of the hill, farm fields swelled with crops for miles. In
the distance stood a ramshackle barn with an advertisement for Mail
Pouch chewing tobacco painted on it.

Henry closed his eyes for a moment, just to calm himself, to retreat,
to place himself in a different situation. He opened his eyes again, and
laid on his horn. The car in front seemed almost at a standstill.

He turned on the radio, and amazingly a station came in. Another
country station, but he didn't mind. Anything to muffle Carla's apologies.

Carla's weeping climbed as steadily as the car, her apologies became more hysterical, and she made less and less sense. One moment
she begged him to change his mind. The next moment she threatened
him. Then she moved her head back and forth like some animal shaking off rainwater. She told him now how much she hated herself.

"Just stop, okay?" Henry said.

He felt something warm and wet on the back of his neck. Henry slapped his hand back there, and just as quickly realized what had hit him.

He and the boy exchanged looks in the rearview, the boy daring him to do something.

Oh, he wanted to be home. He wanted this miserable day to be over. He wished he hadn't agreed to go on this trip in the first place. He honked his horn at the car in front. He laid into it, but the car wouldn't pull over. Instead, it seemed to slow down to fifteen. He still didn't know the make. The only thing he could read was something someone had written in the dust on the back: "Clean me!"

Henry swung again into the other lane and slammed on the gas just as a truck crested the hill and bore down on him. Henry started to slow, to get back into his lane, but the boy in the other lane slowed, too. Then the man pointed to his crotch and mouthed words Henry couldn't make out.

Carla reached over and touched his leg again. He read it as tenderness. Almost as tender as the love the singer on the radio was mourning. But her words didn't sound tender. "Are you crazy?" she said, and for the first time that day, Henry wondered if he could possibly have made a mistake.

Henry put the rest of the carton back in the refrigerator, then searched one of the drawers for a spatula. Out of the corner of his eye, he saw something. He looked down the hallway and saw Rhonda and Pam returning.

Henry grabbed a towel from the sink and ran to the stove. He picked the frying pan off the burner and looked for somewhere to put the eggs. He stopped in the middle of the kitchen, frozen to the spot, unsure of what to do. He remembered buying these eggs. They came in a blue container. Only three remained.

Why did he feel so guilty?

He put the frying pan on the floor. He opened the refrigerator, quickly retrieved the frying pan, and shoved it inside. He ran to the stove and turned off the flame. Then he closed the door and sat down at the table just as Rhonda and Pam entered.

They stopped and stared at him. "Oh God, it's Henry," said Pam. "Break out the nuclear weapons."

Rhonda started sniffing.

"I cleaned your dishes," Henry said.

"We're not finished eating," Rhonda told him. She and Pam fanned out across the kitchen, scanning the shelves.

"I didn't eat any of your pizza," Henry said.

"So what *are* you cooking?" Pam said.

Henry sat down at the kitchen table and watched Pam and Rhonda conduct their search. They seemed to have run out of places to look, so he helped them. He pointed to the refrigerator and said, "They're in there."

Rhonda ran to the door of the refrigerator and opened it. A cloud of steam poured from inside, out and around her face.

"My eggs," she shouted.

"Are those really your eggs?" Pam said. "Sid said we had to be sure."

"I'm positive," Rhonda said. For a moment, the two of them stared at the steaming skillet as though identifying a body in a morgue.

"I'm sorry," Henry told Rhonda and Pam. And he was. Sorry for everything in their lives. Sorry for scaring Rhonda when he chased her by mistake. Sorry for taking their food. Even sorry for things he wasn't responsible for. The drought last summer in the Midwest. Inflation. High interest rates. Flash floods in Bangladesh. Riots in Uzbekistan. The moon, the sun, the starry firmament. No one had ever been sorrier than Henry.

H enry didn't know what happened next. Maybe he curled up in his dark room and slept for a couple of days. Maybe he polished off a bottle of Gilbey's.

In any case, by the time he recognized himself again, by the time his head cleared, by the time he could keep track of time, his room had been completely cleaned out. No barbells. Sid had probably revoked them since Henry hadn't lived up to his expectations. No bike or stereo. Pam or Rhonda probably took them as revenge. No hot plate or Swiss Army knife. Even his clothes had vanished, all except for what he had on. He'd been pillaged. The other tenants had swept through his room like the Mongol hordes. Or maybe it was all his own doing. Maybe he'd paced around the room and thrown his belongings out the window. Over the last six months he'd been doing that. Sometimes, he left a pile of things out in the hall for someone to take. Other times he just tossed things out the window: records, books, clothes.

Obviously, he was going mad, though the word *going* implies a steadiness of course, a graphlike climb toward some final and perfect state of mind. Actually, he'd been going mad, off and on, for the last two years, with short intervals of clarity and contentment.

Finally, he turned, gave his key to Sid, and walked off the front porch into the street. "What are you going to do now?" Sid said as he was leaving.

The answer seemed simple to Henry. The open road seemed so full of possibilities. Or at least, flattened animals. Oily patches. Bridges that freeze before the road. Falling rocks. The only problem was that he didn't drive anymore. He hadn't driven, in fact, since the accident. Not because he couldn't afford another car. With the insurance, he could have bought a fleet of them. But simply because. Simply for the same reason he hadn't slept in his house since he'd been discharged from the hospital. For the same reason he'd been living at Sid Junkins's boarding house and had put his house up for sale, and then, when he changed his mind, for rent.

Henry turned north. Toward Michigan, five miles distant. Toward Canada. Maybe he'd run away. Run against the traffic. Start a new underground railway. Life was full of possibilities, and if it wasn't, then at least he could unequivocally state that it was full of one or two.

Maybe he'd return home after all.

SIX

Gail put on her bathrobe and went out in search of semi-intelligent life, namely her mother. Only an hour remained before she had to open the store, so she needed to get her butt in gear. Actually, she already had *her* butt in gear. The butt to worry about was her mother's, which stalled out every time Gail had reason to depend on it.

Gail hadn't gone farther than the kitchen when she saw a note taped to the refrigerator door. She ripped it off, knowing what it said before she read it. She'd *told* her mother she needed a ride this morning, but you just couldn't give that woman any responsibility. The note read:

> Gail –
> Have gone garage sale-ing. Be back sometime. Don't
> leave your sister alone. Do get along.

Gail crumpled the note and tossed it in the trash. It didn't matter. Nathan would understand. Or maybe he wouldn't, but she didn't care. Nothing could be done now. Only a few months before, they'd been a two-car family. Actually, they'd been a thirty-car family, what with all of her dad's rusted Studebakers. But no one besides her dad had ever really considered them cars. Cars worked. That seemed to be the minimum requirement at least.

Her dad had always promised her he'd fix up one of the Studebakers, and give it to her when she finished driver's ed. She'd bet anyone a million dollars he'd forget. So far, driver's ed. was a bore. In the first month of school, she'd been shown half a dozen films of dummies flying through windshields. Almost everyone in class cheered whenever a dummy bought it. Mr. Sims, the driver's ed. teacher, gave her A's on all her papers, proving he had incredibly low standards. Last week he'd assigned them to find the worst intersection in the South Bend/Mishawaka area, and to tell why. She'd chosen the intersection of South Bend, Corby, and Eddy. Under the heading *Why*, she scribbled: "It's patently obvious." He'd given her an A– and had written, "Good choice! For that, I commend you. Your truncated answer, however, leaves too much to the imagination. Next time, try harder." You betcha, Mr. Sims.

Gail headed for the living room. "Here I come," she yelled before entering.

Whenever Lois left Gail alone with Meg, the two girls, by unwritten agreement, divided up the house into two unequal territories. In their old house, Gail had taken the upstairs, and Meg had taken the downstairs. In the new house, their territories had been divided by rooms. Gail had Mom's room, the den, the veranda, the backyard, the kitchen, and her own room. Meg laid claim to all the rest: her room, the front living room with the ice cream ceiling, the hallway, the basement, the garage, and the driveway. The bathroom was no-man's-land. Since Gail was in charge, she could sometimes make forays into Meg's territory, but she had to give warning. If she went into the living room, for instance, she'd yell out, "Here I come." Not for any particular reason. Just as a courtesy. On the other hand, if Meg wanted to go into Gail's territory, she had to ask permission. If she wanted to get a snack, for instance, she'd stand in the middle of the hallway and yell out, "I'm hungry, Gail." Gail would then decide whether or not to hear her sister. If she chose not to hear Meg, then Meg might try a couple of more times to be heard, but after that, she'd have to give up and retreat back to her own land. However, if Gail chose to hear Meg, she'd tell Meg what she could snack on and how long she could remain in the kitchen. The rules between the two sisters were elaborate and had been developed, through trial and error and laboratory testing, over several years together. They'd proven useful in maintaining harmony while Lois was absent. Of course, as soon as their mother returned, all boundaries dropped away. Lois knew nothing of their arrangement.

Gail found Meg on the floor of the living room doing three things at once. Meg was watching a cartoon on TV. She had a book cracked open. And she was busying herself with some kind of shoe-box diorama.

Morning flat nose, Gail wanted to say, but she didn't. Instead, she smiled and said, "Looks like you're having fun."

Meg barely acknowledged her. She just looked up from her reading.

Boxes from the move lay scattered and piled up everywhere. Things still needed to be unpacked even though they'd been living here since June. Gail still hadn't found some of her belongings, and probably never would. Small wonder. She wished her mom and dad could have been a little more organized about the move. After all, they'd put it off for more than a year, and then, when the time finally came, they all ran around like no one had even *mentioned* the move before. Her mom acted especially crazy, stuffing things into plastic garbage bags and packing boxes without labeling them.

Now, no one seemed to have the energy to finish the move. Gail definitely didn't. These days, she just dragged herself around the house, avoiding everyone else. Her mom thought she was angry for some reason. Actually, Gail simply didn't want anyone to see her. She thought they all must know, though *she* wasn't even sure. She'd bought a pregnancy test kit a week before, but so far, it had sat in the bottom of her laundry bag in a corner of her closet. She'd read the directions five times, but that was as far as she got. Still, if Mr. Sims tested her on the pregnancy kit manual instead of driver's ed., she'd probably ace it.

If she knew for certain, she wouldn't feel afraid anymore, but she was afraid of knowing for certain. Still, just knowing would make her feel amazingly calm. Or maybe she wouldn't feel much of anything.

For the time being, she tried to practice compassion and understanding. She even forgave Meg for trying to snitch on her that day they first looked at the house. She'd been getting high in the woods with Drew Dribek and Ricky Greer, a couple of wusses she'd hung around with, then left in the dust, after her first two weeks in the neighborhood. Not that she cared what her parents thought, but she wanted to avoid, if she could help it, a big scene between them.

She picked up the shoe box Meg was working on and looked inside. Sand, sticks, and pebbles filled the box. Meg had made a blue Magic Markered background on the wall. The background had been done in a hurry, so the sky didn't look anything like sky, just a bunch of blue streaks and blotches. A gray plastic boar lay on its side, and cattycorner from it sat a small dish containing sand. A plastic woman with a stick in her hand stood across from the boar. On the front of the box read the caption: "Karana almost kills the leader of the wild dogs, but she doesn't."

"Are you making this for school?" Gail said.

"What do you think?" Meg said, looking up at her suspiciously.

Gail smiled benevolently at her sister and said, "I don't know what to think, but it's good."

"Put it down," Meg said. "You're going to break it."

"Okay, okay," Gail said, setting the diorama down gently on the rug to let her sister know she meant no harm. "Why doesn't she kill the leader?" Gail said.

Meg squinted and said, "Huh? Why do you want to know? Are you trying to make fun of me?"

"I'm just interested, that's all."

Meg shrugged. "You'll have to read the book."

Gail decided to give up. "I'm going in my room now," Gail said, pointing down the hall.

Meg looked at her like she'd just said something incredibly obvious. How would Meg react if Gail turned out to be pregnant? She imagined Meg standing over a crib, turning a mobile, looking in awe. That's the way it should be, Gail thought. Then she and Meg would have to mend their differences and stop constantly fighting. Same with Mom and Dad. This baby would work miracles. It would have a hard lot in life, being the peacemaker, the family saint, but it would have to get used to that role. Gail wouldn't have it any other way. She wouldn't deliver this baby for nothing. She'd expect everyone to get along. In return, Gail would be the kind of older sister she wanted to be to Meg, as well as the perfect daughter.

Gail took the portable phone into her room to call Nathan. Instead of calling right away, she placed the phone on her bed and looked around her room. She shrugged off her bathrobe and started to dress. Today felt like a five-bandana day. She went over to her dresser and sorted through her bandana collection, but some of her best ones were still AWOL from the move. Finally, she settled on a red one and tied it around her forehead. Then she stopped and returned to the bed.

She noticed her driver's ed. manual by the nightstand. Sims expected everyone to take the written test within a month, but so far Gail had barely touched the book. Opening it at random, she read:

Emotions and Distractions

Emotions affect our driving, whether the emotions are good or bad. If we are excited about something like a promotion at work or winning a big prize, we may find our driving is affected. If we are upset about something, we may find that our thoughts are not on our driving and are less likely to see a dangerous situation until it is too late. People whose marriage is breaking up are more likely to have accidents. People who have had a loved one die or who are having other upsetting things happen may be unable to drive safely. At some time almost everyone goes through such conditions. . . .

She started dialing Nathan's home phone. In the middle of the number, she stubbed on the play button of her cassette deck with her toe.

The lights on her tape deck jumped and skidded across the panel. Guitars burned her room, scaling the walls, then crawled along the floorboards with the drum, tense and steady, shaking the plaster ceiling.

Gail could barely hear the phone ringing. She imagined Nathan lying on his bare mattress with a T-shirt and underwear on. That's how he always slept, and when he awoke, he'd just slip on some jeans and he was ready to go. His morning preparations consisted of splashing his face with cold water, running some deodorant under his arms, then wetting a comb and gliding it without resistance through his thinning hair. So he'd told her at least. "In case of nuclear attack, I'm out of South Bend before you can paste on your false eyelashes," he'd said, and she'd replied that she didn't wear false eyelashes. "Doesn't matter. There's got to be something false you put on in the morning. All women do." She'd never actually witnessed his routine because she hadn't yet spent a whole night at his apartment above the store. Her parents didn't even know about Nathan.

On the tenth ring, Nathan picked up the phone. Gail started reading to him from the driver's ed. manual: "If you begin to feel a bumpy ride when there is no obvious reason, stop and check your tires. In this way you may be able to avoid a blowout. Sometimes a tire will blow out without any warning."

Nathan groaned and hung up the phone.

Quickly, Gail redialed. This time Nathan answered on the first ring. "Yeah?"

"Nathan, that was me."

"Yeah?"

"You're going to have to cover for me," she said. "I can't come to work today. My mom fucked up again and I can't get a ride."

When Nathan didn't answer, she said, "Are you there?"

Nathan sighed and said, "Take a cab."

"I can't leave my little sister alone."

Nathan didn't say anything to that.

"Are you there?"

"You know, it's a rare and remarkable person who hasn't been fired from at least one job."

"You're not going to fire me," she said.

"What's that you're playing?" Nathan said. "There's nothing finer than being roused from a sound sleep by heavy metal. Haven't I taught you anything about music?"

The sound of Nathan disappeared, replaced by a loud clacking sound, followed by two thumps. Nathan groaned in the background. She heard a closer grunt and then he said, "I dropped the phone. You still there?"

"Yeah."

"Good. Get to work. Now. And stop fucking with me."

"Get over it," she said.

"Where are my cigarettes?" Nathan said. "God, I hate life. Nothing's where I want it." Nathan's voice lowered to the point where Gail could barely hear it above the music. "How old's your sister anyway? You can leave her alone, can't you? Or bring her into the store."

"Yeah, you'd like that," Gail said. "She's only eleven, Nathan."

"Don't taunt me, darling. I'm your boss."

Nathan's voice sounded pouty. She knew he'd sulk about her not showing up for work, but she also knew he'd get over it. Not that he was all that easy to figure out. A lot of things mystified her, like why he owned a record store when he hated music, and not just metal. All music. Or why he'd chosen to live in South Bend when he could have lived anywhere in the country. He'd done some pretty amazing things in life before going into the record business. He'd been a ballet dancer in New York, a cab driver in San Francisco, had hitchhiked over forty-five thousand miles (a fact, he said, that only Vietnam veterans seemed to appreciate), had sailed the Great Lakes in the merchant marine, slept on a park bench in Chicago for six months, and run contraband pet monkeys into the United States from the Yucatán. He claimed he came to South Bend for the peace and quiet, but he acted like he'd rather be anywhere else in the world. Knowing him, he was most likely hiding out from some loan shark.

Though Nathan was more than twice her age, something about him seemed younger. Even when he acted mean and angry or ordered people around, he didn't seem completely serious. Something about his face, when enraged, said, I'm just having fun. If you take me seriously, you're a fool. Gail often couldn't stop laughing when he yelled at her.

His features were almost feminine, full lips and a petite nose. He wore his dark hair in a ponytail, which added to the aura of girlishness about him. Sometimes, his soft voice masked the cruelty and bitterness of the things he said. The contradictions in him fascinated her. The life he'd led delighted her.

"How's your tattoo?" she said. "Mine still feels kind of tender."

"What do you expect?" he said. "I've never heard of such a stupid place for a tattoo. What's the point? No one can see it."

"It's not stupid," she said. "I just didn't want my dad to see it. I don't care what my mom thinks."

"Gee, how brave," he said. "You shouldn't care what your dad thinks either. I left home when I was your age, and I've never given a single thought to what either of my folks wanted me to do."

"I've got to go," she said. "Go ahead and fire me if you want."

"Who said anything about firing?" he said. "I'm just disappointed in you."

"You're disappointed in everyone," she said.

He paused and said, "That's very astute. You're a bright girl."

"I'm not a girl," she said. Apparently, he'd found his cigarettes. She could hear a rush of air on the other end, and he sounded less harried now.

"You don't expect me to call you a woman, do you?" he said. "Girl suits you better. A woman, by my definition, wouldn't leave her boss in the lurch. A woman wouldn't listen to Guns n' Roses. She wouldn't have to stay home with her little sister. A woman – " he said.

"Ciao, Nathan," Gail said, placing the receiver back on its cradle. She just stared at the wall in front of her. So far, it hadn't been decorated. She hated its blankness.

She inspected her foot as though a splinter had stuck in it. With her index finger she traced the image of a .357 Magnum the size of a penny on her instep, still moist from the bacitracin. Tiny scabs, almost too small to see, had formed where the needle had pricked her skin. She remembered the pain without having to see the scabs. The whole process had felt like a steady burning and pinching.

She and Nathan had this in common. They'd both had tattoos done on the same night, though hers was only a positive/negative image while he'd gone for a full color. Still, this was something permanent between them, even if it didn't feel that way yet.

The gun took less than an hour to put down. Nathan's had taken over four. His tattoo showed a smirking skull in a top hat smoking a cigar. Underneath, a caption read: As I am, you will someday be. She didn't know why Nathan wanted a tattoo now, all of a sudden. He'd been complaining about getting soft lately. He'd pat his small pot belly and say, "I'm turning into a wuss." Gail figured the skull tattoo probably made him feel better about himself. That night, he also wore a T-shirt that read: I'm not in the shit business. I don't give it. I don't take it.

Gail had just come along for kicks; she hadn't planned on getting a tattoo. The guy who did them both had long blond hair and a tattoo on his arm that read: MOTORHEAD. As he put down Nathan's tattoo, Mr. Motorhead and Gail talked metal while Nathan winced, as much from the subject as the pain.

She and Mr. Motorhead hit it off, and he gave her a tattoo even though she was underage, but he made her swear she wouldn't tell anyone who gave it to her. Nathan said she was too young. She told him to fuck off. Sometimes he tried to act like her father. He also thought her instep was a stupid place because no one would ever see it. That was the point.

The fact that she wanted a tattoo on her instep didn't surprise Mr. Motorhead. As he worked, he chatted about some of his customers and the places he'd put tattoos on them. She could hardly pay attention to what he said, it hurt so much. The pain nauseated her. He said he had put tattoos on every imaginable part of people's bodies and showed her some color photos of a man who'd dyed his balls robin's-egg blue. Above them, an eagle flew with its talons out, as though making ready to rob the eggs from their nest.

Nathan snickered and said, "I wouldn't have that done if my life depended on it. I wouldn't have that done for a million dollars. That's the dumbest thing I ever seen. It probably made the guy sterile."

The tattoo artist pointed his machine at Nathan like he planned on tattooing his face. "Man, I didn't tell you this, but those are mine. If anything, I'm more potent now than ever. These are two of the most bodacious balls you'll ever run across."

"I don't want to run across them," Nathan said.

"I tell you, I could have fifteen children if I wanted," Mr. Motorhead said. "I already got two. So don't give me that sterile shit."

Nathan puffed himself up and put his chin right up to Mr. Motorhead's chin. "I got you beat, my man," he said. "I got five kids. That I heard about. Where do you come off showing your bogus gonads to my daughter, anyway?"

Mr. Motorhead fell silent and gave Gail a reverent look. He mumbled an apology and backed off. She could tell Nathan got a charge out of this, but she just felt embarrassed and ashamed. Nathan claimed most people were gullible enough to believe anything if you said it loudly enough and with authority. Maybe that was true, but he still didn't have the right to tell this guy she was his daughter.

Then she did something she hated herself for. She started crying right in front of Nathan and Mr. Motorhead. Nathan looked at her, unsure why she was upset, but accepting it as part of their father-daughter act.

In the car, Nathan started kissing her, but she pulled away and told him to drive her home. She almost directed him to her old house, and nearly forgot how to get to the new one.

Nathan didn't understand how or why she could be so mad at him, and she didn't want to tell him either. Halfway home, she forgave him, but then he started pouting and wouldn't talk to her. "Come on," she said, rubbing the bald spot in the middle of his head. "Stop acting like a little boy. I have enough babies to deal with at home." She almost added, Maybe I have another one to worry about, but she didn't dare.

"Hey," he said, swatting her hand away from his head. He refused to talk, and now she felt guilty. He just stayed glum the whole way home and didn't even say good night.

Wearing only her red bandana, Gail got up and did a kind of snake dance, arms outstretched, a wild smile on her lips. Her head was thrown back, and she danced with ease. Her arms were slender, her legs smooth and strong, spread without self-consciousness. She slowly drew one of her hands across her belly, which she thought showed the beginnings of the fullness of pregnancy.

She imagined herself in a video, not a pretty one. Gail wanted to shock the viewer, to show the young, helpless girl locked in her room. Down on her knees. Begging. Up again, defiant as ever, raging at some unknown attacker, who sang to her:

> You're my ace in the hole, bitch
> Maybe I'm not playin' with a full deck
> but I've got you beat.

Who listens to the words anyway? She sneered and kicked him in the nuts.

Finally, she settled into a split, ending her dance, not one of joy, but of abandon. She bounced up again, throwing her small body onto the bed. She tossed her sweaty bandana to the faceless multitudes, who reached their arms out to catch it, as though it were a rope thrown down from heaven to hell. Then Gail laughed at some private joke, and with a gentle smile lay down on her back, a hand curling gracefully in the air with a beckoning motion.

The door opened and Meg stood there.

Gail jumped up from her bed and grabbed her bathrobe. She couldn't believe Meg had entered the inner sanctum unannounced. She forgot all her resolutions to be a more forgiving, more compassionate human being, and wriggled into her bathrobe, ready to pound Meg into oblivion. "Who told you to come in? What are you doing in my room?"

Meg didn't move, which surprised Gail even more than the fact that

her sister had just barged in. Usually, a little sword-rattling sent Meg
running. Gail had expected Meg to close the door and scurry back to
the living room. Then Gail would have gone back to her music and
waited until later, perhaps while they watched TV that night, to lodge a
formal protest in the form of a punch in the arm. Instead of running,
Meg just stepped farther into the room, and shut the door behind her.

"What is it?" Gail said.

"There's a man here," Meg said. She said this calmly, as though
announcing that the toilet wouldn't stop running.

Gail didn't understand her sister, and didn't want to listen to her
exact words anyway. Still stunned by her presence, she said, "You're
in deep shit. Up to your neck."

"I just thought I should tell you," Meg said. "He's in the kitchen
eating our food."

Gail looked at Meg, but didn't say anything. Usually, she had a lot
to say to Meg, but for now she stayed quiet.

"What man?" she finally asked.

"I don't know," Meg said.

Gail pushed past her sister and locked the bedroom door. Then she
pulled Meg to the bed and made her sit down beside her.

"Now what's going on?" she said in a whisper.

"There's a man in the kitchen," Meg said.

"A stranger," Gail said.

"Yes."

"Are you sure it isn't Dad?"

Meg rolled her eyes. "Yes, I'm sure," she said, raising her voice.

"Okay," Gail said. "Don't get excited."

"You're the one who's excited," said Meg.

"How did he get in?" Gail asked.

"Through the door. I let him in. He said he lived here."

Gail couldn't believe it. Hadn't their mom and dad taught Meg *anything?*

"Well, how was I to know?" Meg whined. "He said he lived here."

"He said he lived here," Gail mimicked. Gail took both of Meg's
hands and said, "Now Meg, I know you're retarded, but I want you to
tell me something? Okay?"

"Not if you call me that," Meg said, yanking away her hands.

"Why did you let a stranger into the house?"

"Because he said he lived here. I already told you."

"You're in deep shit," Gail said. "Getting deeper every minute. If you're lying, you're in about seven feet of shit. If you're not lying, you're in about twenty feet."

"I'm not lying," Meg said, backing away to a corner of the bed, rubbing her nose, and sniffing. She seemed more concerned about having her integrity questioned than her intelligence.

Gail grabbed the phone and dialed her father's number.

"Who are you calling?" Meg said.

Gail ignored Meg. The phone rang five times before she realized she'd called his old number in the barn. He'd moved into the big house when the rest of them had moved to this one. So, she dialed *her* old number and this time a woman's voice answered with a cheery "Kulwicki's Palace of Pleasure."

That stupefied Gail. At first, she didn't know who had answered. For a second, she figured it had to be her mom, but it didn't sound like her mom's voice. Then she recognized the voice as her dad's girlfriend, Alice. What a dumb way to answer.

"Alice?" Gail said.

"Oh my God, Gail?" Alice said. "I thought you were your dad calling."

"Well, I'm not," Gail said.

"Is that Alice?" Meg said. Gail shooed her away with her free hand.

"Your dad's not home," Alice said, "though I wish he was. I miss him. I've just been sitting here, drinking coffee, which I shouldn't. It's giving me such a buzz. You know, he's a great guy. Did you know what a great guy he is? He doesn't like to eat breakfast though. That's my favorite meal of the day. And he doesn't drink coffee. Has he always been like that?"

"Like what?" Gail said. "A great guy or a non—coffee drinker?"

"Mmmmmm," Alice said. "Both, I guess. I mean, I'm sure he's always been a great guy—"

"Maybe we could talk about this some other time, Alice." Gail said.

"Oh sure."

"Is Dad there?" Meg wanted to know. "Are you going to tell him? Don't say I let him in."

"Just be quiet," Gail said, covering the mouthpiece.

Meg straightened up like she'd been deeply offended. She stood up and went by the door. "I'm going out," she announced.

"Good," Gail said. "Now leave me alone." Then she turned back to the phone and said, "This is kind of an emergency. You know where I can reach him?"

"Oh no," Alice said. "I hope nothing's wrong."

No, Gail wanted to say. It's the kind of emergency where nothing's wrong. It's a happy emergency. Gail stopped herself. She didn't want to go through the typical-daughter-from-a-broken-home routine. She didn't hate Alice or even resent her. Gail could definitely sympathize with her dad for jettisoning her mom. But she couldn't quite explain why he'd throw aside one dip for another. Gail had met Alice only once, the night in June they all went out to DQ for ice cream, and that had been enough to see that her dad was making a big mistake. Still, she resolved not to interfere, even though she knew the woman would drive her dad nuts within a few weeks. Alice was a tiny woman, just a little taller than Meg. She acted like a regular on "Hee Haw," some fool with a shit-ass grin in the middle of a cornfield telling dumb jokes. After every other sentence, she yelled out, "I'm *loving* this, Willy. I *love* family. I was made for family." Gail almost felt like creating a tragedy, pushing Meg out onto the gravel road, or having a miscarriage in the backseat. Anything to somber this woman up, to obliterate her slap-happiness.

"I'm going out now," Meg said, putting her hand on the knob. "He's probably still out there."

Gail turned away a bit more. She wanted to know what Alice would do in this situation. She knew she should probably call the police, but the thought embarrassed her. What if she wound up making a fool out of herself? What if Meg had just made the whole thing up? Or maybe the man had some reason to be in the house? A repairman or the land-lord even. She didn't want to start squawking and calling attention to herself before she knew for sure. Just about anything seemed prefer-able to making a fool out of herself.

Gail noticed then that the door stood open. Meg had left. She hit her fist on the bed and yelled, "Meg! Get back here you little twerp."

Now it didn't matter. She'd yelled loud enough so all the psycho-paths in the world could hear.

"Look, Alice," she said, "don't worry. Everything's fine now. Don't even tell my dad I called."

"Are you sure you're all right?"

"Yeah, really. Please don't tell him I called."

"Why not?" Alice said. "He'll want to know."

A tough question. Why didn't she want her father involved all of a sudden? She couldn't be sure, except that it had something to do with the fact that he hadn't been home for her in the first place. He hadn't anticipated an emergency. He didn't even seem to really want to be involved in her or Meg's life anymore. She felt embarrassed that she'd even intruded.

"Just don't," she said. "I'll call him later."

After she hung up, Gail kicked the off button of her stereo. As she dressed, she listened for any sounds outside her room. She didn't hear a thing.

She found Meg at the end of the hallway, by the kitchen, staring in. Gail stopped at the threshold, too. A little man sat at their kitchen table, surrounded by food from the refrigerator and pantry. He just stared ahead in the direction of the kitchen phone on the wall by the mudroom. She couldn't guess his age, though he had to be at least ten years older than her, but definitely younger than her mom and dad.

If someone had asked Gail for a one-word description of the man, she would have answered "pip-squeak." He was a compact man, almost elfin, with a scraggly beard and curly dark hair. Obviously, the man didn't care anything about his appearance. He wore a white shirt with a kangaroo on the pocket, metallic-green shorts, and a pair of red running shoes.

He looked like a long-distance runner stocking up on carbohydrates before a race. He had two jars of pickles around him and a jar of peanut butter. A saltine lay on the table. He tried to spread peanut butter on the cracker with only one of his hands.

His tongue poked out the corner of his mouth as though he'd never attempted a more difficult task in his life. As he slid the knife across the cracker, it broke in half. A look of disappointment flashed across his face. He put the knife down, and then, with the same hand, reached for another cracker from the open package.

"He's hungry," Meg whispered.

The man looked like he belonged. He seemed comfortable in these surroundings, like he'd sat many mornings at this table eating peanut butter, crackers, and pickles. Gail felt as though she'd intruded. She could tell Meg felt the same way. Both of them had stopped at the kitchen door, at first out of fear, but now, almost out of propriety.

"Excuse me," Gail called out, ready to dash for the front door if he made the slightest move.

The man looked up. His new cracker broke in half. "Oh, I'm sorry," he said, but Gail wasn't sure if he'd just apologized to her or the cracker.

Gail had about five seconds to decide what to do: run with Meg in tow or confront the man. In a way, Gail was like someone nearing a hitchhiker. She'd have to make a snap judgment about his character before speeding by. In about two seconds, she sized him up. He definitely looked peculiar, but something about him seemed harmless: maybe his eyes, or his wispy build, or the childlike way he tried to spread peanut butter on a cracker.

The man squeezed the bridge of his nose with his thumb and forefinger. "Do you know Gary Ydell?"

Gail shook her head slowly, and then remembered that it rhymed with Bobby Rydell. "The Real Estate Guy?" she said.

The man nodded.

"What did he tell you?" he said slowly. "I mean, did he tell you anything? Did he act like it was okay?"

Gail didn't know how to answer that. "What do you mean?"

The man looked at the jar of peanut butter and didn't say anything. He seemed kind of spaced-out to Gail. He acted like he was under ten feet of water, like he'd removed himself from the normal dry world, and had somehow learned to live in a place where people needed gills.

"You've moved in?" the man said. "These are your things?" He made a circuit of the room with his eyes. "I'm wondering because this is my house."

"That's my peanut butter," Meg said, pointing.

The man looked down at one of the broken crackers. "Oh," he said.

"That's all right," Meg said. "Help yourself."

The man nodded a thank-you.

Meg, the good little hostess, just wanted people to like her. Even complete strangers.

"I want to know who you are," Gail said. "I've already called the police."

Meg looked at her in shock, as though she'd committed the ultimate act in rude behavior.

The man looked down at the cracker, then back at Gail. "Well, there's definitely a mistake," he said. "Did Gary Ydell tell you to live here?"

"He didn't *tell* us to live here," Gail said. "We paid him. We didn't just barge in like you."

"Gail," said Meg in a disappointed tone. "I told you. I let him in."

The man didn't answer. Instead, he nodded and said, "I'm going to have to call him."

"You say you own this house?" Gail said.

The man looked around, as if to make sure. "Yes. Four-twenty-four Prospect Avenue. Are the Ramseys still around?"

Gail and Meg exchanged looks, wondering how he knew the Ramseys. The man seemed to misunderstand. He raised his hand about three feet from the floor. "An old couple," he said. "They never left their house and kept their shades drawn."

"Mr. Ramsey died right after we moved in," Meg said.

"I didn't know," the man said.

"Mrs. Ramsey's real nice though," said Meg. "Did you know she has a dog named Loverboy?"

"I remember her dog," the man said. "But I don't remember his name."

"Isn't it a peculiar name?" Meg said, and then added, "*I* certainly think so."

"The house on the right's a duplex now," the man said. "That's something new."

Meg nodded solemnly.

"Some college students live there," she said.

"How would you know?" Gail said. "You don't know what college students look like."

"Yes I do." Meg said. "In one of the sides there are two guys who sell rats to laboratories. That's how they're putting themselves through school. Isn't that awful?" she said to the man.

The man didn't reply. He dipped his knife in peanut butter.

"How do you know that?" Gail said.

"I know *everyone* in this neighborhood," Meg said. "I'm very social. It's in my nature."

The man seemed to consider this. He looked down at his right hand, the one he hadn't used, and said, "Not mine."

"Oh," said Meg, looking a little disappointed.

Gail didn't know if he could just do this, if he had the right to walk in and take over. She also knew that people often did what they pleased, regardless of their rights. Not that the man seemed at all hostile. He hadn't even actually said he was kicking them out. Still, she felt flustered, partly because she knew she had to make some kind of snap decision now. That struck her as funny. She realized she'd never had to make a real decision in her life. Yet, she considered herself a decisive person. Even sleeping with Nathan didn't really seem like a decision, but more like something she just fell into. The only decision she could recall making was getting a tattoo of a gun on her instep, something she couldn't even show anybody.

Still, she should have been making her own decisions long before now. This was a good example of where her mother's decisions led. And now, maybe being pregnant, Gail really had to be careful. An awful thought entered her mind. What would happen if her mother took charge of her baby's future? She imagined giving birth on the sidewalk outside of the civic auditorium, no place to live because her mother didn't know how to plan, didn't understand responsibility and consequences the way normal mothers did.

"We're going to have to move again, aren't we?" Meg said, turning to Gail, her eyes wide. For once, Gail didn't have an answer. If the man really did own this house (even if he wasn't certain, he still acted like he belonged here), then they'd have to move again. Kicked out of two houses in a row. Now *that* seemed embarrassing.

"Are you absolutely certain you live here?" Gail said to the man, realizing what a dumb question that was a second after she asked it.

The man didn't seem to think so. He seemed to consider every question with equal seriousness. She could have asked him, Are you a giraffe? and he would have felt his neck before answering. "One time I was assigned the same seat as someone else," he said. Then he paused and said, "Oh, I'm talking about a plane. I think I was on my way to Boston. No, New York. No, it must have been Boston, because it was

Christmas. Wait a minute," he said and looked down at his lap. His lips moved and he seemed to be counting. Then he looked up at Gail and Meg as though they might know. The man acted like this was the most crucial information in his life, and for a second, Gail wanted to help him out, and even believed she could, believed she could help him find out whether he'd been on a flight to Boston or New York.

"New York," he said. "You know, I'm not sure. I used to be sure all the time. Now I'm never sure."

The man looked off toward the mudroom. She felt that he had just let her and Meg in on a great secret. She could even sympathize a little with that feeling of being unsure, of not knowing how to act. She still wondered if she should call the cops, but most likely she'd end up embarrassed. Either way, the situation seemed pretty embarrassing.

"I've been away for a while," he said, as though that explained everything. "I'll call Gary Ydell."

The man walked to the wall phone. He cradled the receiver between his neck and shoulder blade, and started dialing with the same hand he'd used for everything else. Midway, he stopped. Zero-nine or nine-zero?" he said, turning to them. They both looked at him blankly.

"I'm sorry," he told them. He didn't say it the way people do when they're saying, I'm sorry for the inconvenience, I'm sorry that you'll have to move out now. He said it the way people do when you tell them that a close relative has died, as though blaming themselves. Maybe he'd said it for Mr. Ramsey. Maybe he'd had some kind of delayed reaction to the news. Maybe he'd known Mr. Ramsey really well, she thought.

SEVEN

The girls always seemed to find broken and dying things. Sometimes Lois thought that animals came from all over the Midwest to die in her household. The word seemed to be out in the animal kingdom. There's this lady in South Bend who runs an animal hospice.

Gail and Meg always promised to take care of the animals, but the animals never lived. You could see that from the moment they were brought home. You could see the weakness and fear in their eyes, even a kind of sadness. Lois thought whoever said that animals don't understand death never held a dying animal or lived on a farm. Every animal she'd ever seen knew it was going to die, but only after the dying process had started. Only after it started struggling to live. The fallen bird that couldn't lift its neck. The cat trying to stand, though its back had been broken by a dog. People, too, didn't really know they were going to die until things started going wrong.

Lois thought maybe she'd escaped, moving from the country to the city. But no, she hadn't. Now, instead of a bird, they'd brought home a man, grievously wounded, who kept staring at the woods as though he'd fallen from one of the trees.

She tried to find something in his appearance that would give her a clue to his identity. He wore green running shorts and a sports shirt, and didn't seem to have any guns or knives. He looked anything but menacing. He looked like an emaciated man with sad eyes, a scraggly beard, and curly dark hair.

He sat in one of Lois's chairs, gazing out at the back lawn. Even though she'd made a grand entrance, the man didn't budge. His hands lay on the armrests, and a soft drink had spilled by his feet. As soon as Lois had entered the room, she'd felt something go out of her. There was a natural hush in here, and she sensed something wrong. Maybe this man would never move again. All she could hear was the wind through the tops of the trees in the woods at the edge of her yard. The breeze must have been somewhere higher than her house because no air was moving through the screens. There wasn't any air moving in the room at all. Lois felt an impulse to whisper, but she summoned up her anger and yelled at the man. "Hey, what do you think you're doing?" Just a general kind of question. She wasn't sure what kind of answer she expected.

The man didn't answer at all, and didn't move. Lois went around and looked him full in the face. His eyes were open and he was staring, but not blankly like a dead man's stare or someone in a catatonic state. He stared into the woods as though he saw something in them, as though he didn't want to watch, but couldn't help it. He squinted and his eyes blinked in the sunlight. Other than that, he didn't move or speak a word.

The Real Estate Guy, who had been there when Lois came in, walked to the other side of the man. He looked thoughtful for a moment and took a drag on his long cigarette. He exhaled and said, "Actually, something like this happened once when I first started out. There was this ancient couple, the Littles, who used to put their house on the market just so people would visit them. God, I'd almost forgotten about the Littles," and he gave a squeaky little laugh.

Then he seemed to shake himself out of it and he gave the man in the chair a small shove. "Hey, Henry, get up or the lady's going to call the cops."

Henry didn't move.

"You've frightened the lady and her children. That's worse than the Littles even." The Real Estate Guy turned to Lois and said, "Henry lived here with his girlfriend and her son. After they were killed, he asked me to sell the house. I found a buyer in four months who made a very reasonable offer." Here he pushed Henry's shoulder again.

The Real Estate Guy waved his cigarette at her. "He decided not to sell the house after all. He asked me to rent it for a year before I sold it. 'What's a year, more or less?' I asked him. But he wouldn't budge. Now I see he'll probably never let this place go."

Lois wasn't sure why he was so upset. After all, *her* house had been invaded, not his, and the man in the chair had lost his family.

"How did they die?" Lois said, whispering.

The Guy clapped his hands together, but didn't say anything. What did that mean? They'd been squished? He saw how she was looking at him, so he put his hand to her ear and whispered, "Car crash. Head-on."

"Come on, Mr. Martin," the Real Estate Guy said. He tapped the man on the shoulder and spoke in a tone that one would use on a child too young to understand the consequences of his actions. "You've taken up plenty of our time today."

Henry didn't move, so the Real Estate Guy tried to get around him and lift him under the arms. The Real Estate Guy grunted and heaved, but he couldn't move the man even though Henry looked frail compared to the pudgy Real Estate Guy.

"I can't do this alone, Henry. You're going to have to help me. Come on, on the count of three." The Real Estate Guy counted to three and then yelled "Upsy-daisy!" like it was some magical incantation that always worked. Not this time.

Henry seemed a statue or a ghost who had died in the collision along with his girlfriend and her son, haunting his own house, too frightened to move on.

For a while, they talked about him as though he wasn't present. "Something's wrong with his right hand," Meg whispered. "He never uses it."

The Real Estate Guy gave Lois a pathetic look and said, "I can't deal with this. If I worked in a mental hospital, I could deal with this. Or if I was a cop. But I'm the Real Estate Guy. I deal with people's houses, not their lives."

"Should I call the police?" Gail said from the doorway.

Henry lifted a hand slightly off one of the armrests and put it down again.

"Look," Lois said, brushing a hand through her hair. "I don't mean you any harm, but I just wish you'd leave. Please?"

The Real Estate Guy tapped Henry on the shoulder. "She'll call the police and I won't stop her. The house will be yours again in a year. Then you can sit out here all you want. Not now. The lady has a lease, but she's nice and maybe she'll give you visitation rights. Under the provisions of the lease you're allowed to inspect the property with twenty-four hours' notice. You could come and inspect it every week. What do you think of that?"

Apropos of nothing, Henry turned slightly and said, "I just can't remember anymore."

Lois drew back slightly. He seemed to understand so little. It didn't seem right to force him out just yet. Not that she *wanted* him there. She wished he'd never shown up. She wished he was just some small wounded animal that one of her girls had found in the backyard. She felt like she should turn to someone and say, Okay, you can keep him, though only until he's well enough to fly away. He's a wild thing, you know.

"Should I call the cops now?" Gail said.

"No, we can take care of it," Lois said. "Why don't you go get Mommy's Uzi?"

"Really, Mom," Gail said. "What are you going to do?"

"Have a heart, Gail," Lois said. "He's not hurting anyone."

"He doesn't belong here," Gail insisted.

"Maybe I can kick him out better on a full stomach," Lois said.

"You can't say that," Gail said, almost shrieking. "He can't stay. You've got to do something now." More and more, Gail was starting to sound like Willy, full of demands and questions, and always ready to tell her the latest way in which she'd failed to live up to his standards.

"What are you going to do?" Gail said, blocking the doorway.

"Start dinner," Lois said and walked off toward the kitchen.

Her daughters trailed after her into the kitchen, and the Real Estate Guy exited cheerily and told her he might be able to work out some kind of rent reduction for the inconvenience. He seemed to have been made ebullient by Lois's accepting attitude, and the fact that she wasn't blaming him. Maybe this was a mistake, she thought after he'd left, but what was one more mistake to her, the Queen of Mistakes?

Meg was the only one who talked at dinner. She rattled off the most meager events of her day as she did at every meal. This seemed to be Meg's way of keeping order in her life, a sort of running diary that was forgotten as soon as she entered it into the record of family conversation. Usually, Lois listened attentively, and encouraged Meg to continue, but tonight she just stared at the empty fourth plate and nodded her head occasionally. This wasn't good enough for Meg.

"Mom, Mom."

"I'm listening, Meg."

"Look at me."

"I can listen without looking at you."

"No you can't."

So Lois looked into her daughter's eyes, and didn't blink. Gail sat at the end of the table, taking mechanical bites of her food.

"Gail?"

"What!"

"Nothing, just eat your food,"

"I am."

"You know Tad Grover?" Meg said.

"No," Lois said.

"Yes you do. Think back. Tad Grover."

Lois tried to think back, but she couldn't remember Tad Grover. She turned back to the empty plate and stared. She couldn't even remember the last time she'd set a table for four. Maybe Gail was right. Maybe she'd made a mistake. How would she ever get Henry out now? She'd gone only a few months without Willy, and now here was some new man camped out on her veranda.

"He was at my birthday party last year," Meg said.

"Who?"

"Mom, look at me."

"I'm looking. Who?"

"Tad Grover. He called me today. He and Randy McSwain. They said they wrote a love letter for me, but I hung up before they could read it."

Gail stood up from the table and brought her plate to the sink. She scraped her food into the garbage, rinsed the dish, and set it aside. "May I be excused?" she said, which was something she never asked. This, Lois knew, was Gail's subtlest form of antagonism. Act excessively polite so your mother knows you don't love her anymore.

"You may," Lois replied in her sweetest voice.

Now it was dark and Lois knew Henry couldn't see outside anymore. She joined him on the veranda, sat beside him, but on the floor. He turned and peered at her. He looked at her face as though trying to memorize it. She held a plate in her hands and offered it to him.

"Leftovers," she said. "At home, I feed them to Willy's dogs. That's my husband." She paused. "I mean, that used to be my home and he used to be my husband, and they used to be my dogs."

Henry kept looking at her. Then he turned away.

"Not that I mean to insult you," she said. "Those dogs were fed pretty good. As good as we were fed anyway." She lifted the fork, twirled it on the plate, and put it back down. She set it down by his feet. "I wish you'd say something, Henry," she said. "I'd feel a lot more comfortable then. I know you've been through a lot, but you know you can't stay here." Lois laughed and said, "Anyway, Willy's going to find out sooner or later. Probably Gail's calling him right now. I'd just love to see Willy's reaction to all this."

"Who's Willy?" Henry said in a whisper.

His talking startled her, and she sat back. "My ex," she said.

"X?" Henry said.

"Yeah, X, as in marks the spot." He had no visible reaction.

"You can take your time," she said a little more sternly, "but you're going to have to go home soon."

Henry turned to her and looked as though he had something he didn't want to say, something he wouldn't say if he wasn't forced to by circumstances.

"I don't have one," he said.

Lois started hearing sounds she hadn't ever noticed before, maybe the sounds Henry had been listening to all along. She heard the refrigerator start up in the kitchen. She heard the high whine of the overhead lights in the hall, the sniffle of the water pipes, a bird outside, a sudden breeze. Her earrings jangled in response. Then the air started to rumble with the sound of a jet approaching the airport. As it neared, the whole veranda vibrated, but Henry didn't move. She saw he'd fallen asleep, and she didn't move to disturb him. She had the thought that maybe he was an angel of God, and his appearance a test to see how she'd react.

She remembered a time she'd gone to church when she was sixteen. It was Easter Sunday. Her mother had urged her to go to confession and unburden herself, since she hadn't been in years. She went into the confessional, but started telling the priest that she didn't believe in God. The two of them argued about God's existence for half an hour. Finally, the priest told Lois to ask for a sign from God.

"How do you do that?" she asked the priest.

"Just ask him."

So she asked for a sign, and immediately a woman started banging on the outside of the confessional.

"Hurry up in there," the woman yelled. "You're not supposed to take so long. This is Easter Sunday. We're all waiting."

Flustered, the priest told Lois they'd better hurry along. He gave her a few Hail Marys and she left. After that, her mother was too embarrassed to sit with her because she'd been in there so long, supposedly confessing all those sins.

Now she sat in silence with her vagabond landlord. She didn't take her eyes off him. She just listened and waited for a sign. Even though they'd hardly exchanged a word, she thought she could understand Henry a little. Maybe a few months earlier, when she still lived with Willy, she wouldn't have felt so sympathetic, but now she knew how it felt to be kicked out of your own home.

EIGHT

On the other side of Lake Michigan, the sky seems clearer in the winter. That's because the weather fronts pass over the lake, gathering precipitation. Lake-effect snow, it's called. This snow comes more frequently than the regular kind, rising off Lake Michigan and blasting South Bend. Snow plows push it to the side, creating walls that make the roads look like toboggan runs. And the roads discolor with salt. Each splash of a slush puddle leaves its imprint on your car, a salt line like the markings of a seismograph or an EKG.

No one in South Bend can ignore winter for long. South Bend is cloudy most of the winter, and snow and ice storms come as late as the end of spring. Once, ten inches fell in May. By April everyone is sick of the weather. People honk their car horns at the slightest provocation, shove each other in line, mumble under their cloudy breaths.

Economists sometimes call this part of the country the Rust Belt or the Rust Bowl. The weather and economy make it the Rust Belt. Sprinkling salt on the road has its benefits, but it comes back to haunt you. Harsh choices and necessity make this area the Rust Belt. Studebaker had its rust problems, too. Customers often complained that the cars rusted away too easily. Maybe shoddy workmanship wasn't to blame. Maybe it was a conscious decision on management's part, a proud reminder that these cars were constructed in the heart of America's region of rust.

On cold mornings, Lois sat at her dinette table with its Formica swirls and specks like fool's gold, her fingers wrapped around a mug of Early Grey tea, her chair positioned above the heat register. The kitchen had a fifties feel to it: a high ceiling and one old light fixture dangling like an upside-down coolie hat above the dinette table. She liked to sit here in her bathrobe, the hot air swimming up her legs. This is where she did her serious thinking. Or no thinking at all, luxuriating in the time to herself after Gail and Meg had gone off to school.

No one else liked to sit at this table. The legs were spindly and unadorned. Gail had recently taken to eating alone in her room, and Meg usually deposited herself in front of the TV at dinnertime. Gail complained that their old oak dining table was perfectly fine. Lois thought it didn't fit a fifties kitchen at all. She'd picked up the dinette table at a sale, and decided to sell the old one. She didn't have room to store the oak table, so she'd called up Willy one night at 2:00 A. M. to see if he'd keep it temporarily in his barn. She knew she shouldn't call so late, but the problem had been eating at her. Sometimes when business popped into her head, she had to settle it right away or else be tormented all night.

And maybe the late hour was part of the reason she wanted to phone him. She wouldn't have hesitated when they were together. She punched out the first six digits of her old number, and listened to the random music her finger made on the push-button phone. Tonight, those numbers sounded curiously like the opening of the theme song to "My Three Sons." She remembered, for a moment, the cartoon feet that accompanied the theme.

She punched the last number, and right away made the connection. All the way across town, her ex-husband's hand stretched over his girlfriend's body and fumbled for the phone. When he answered, he didn't sound angry. He just listened patiently to what she wanted, and said, "Sure, now go to sleep, Lo."

"What's that?" Lois said.

"I said go to sleep."

"I can't hear you very well," Lois said. "Can you speak a little louder?"

"Lois, I don't have anything to say."

"Wait a second," she said. "I think I know what it is."

She unscrewed the receiver and took out a piece of cotton that she'd smashed inside the week before. Then she screwed the earpiece back on.

"Say something now," she told Willy.

"What do you want me to say?" Willy said.

"That's much better," Lois said.

"What was wrong?" Willy asked.

"I can't tell you," she said. "I'll sound like a complete flake."

"What? Were you speaking into the wrong end?"

"No, but it's almost as bad. Remember last week when we had that fight? You hung up on me, and I was so angry I slammed the phone down. I slammed it so hard that the receiver fell apart. As I was putting it back together I found a piece of cotton and I thought, 'Oh that's nice, the phone company puts little pieces of cotton in the receiver.' I figured that otherwise the sound would be too loud. It took me forever to smash the cotton into the receiver, but I thought it had to be there for a good reason, so I finally got it in."

"You're right, Lois," Willy said. "That sounds pretty flaky. Where did the cotton come from?"

"I don't know. It must have been lying around."

"Go to sleep," he said wearily and he hung up on her again. She stood in the kitchen. He'd hung up on her. She slammed down the phone, and the receiver flew off. The next half hour she spent squashing the cotton ball inside again. Then she stood there in the kitchen, wide awake, astounded by the fact that he always sounded so reasonable, that he never seemed even slightly upset. Maybe he hadn't been awake. Maybe he'd spliced time and distance together, and had mistaken the sleeping body beside him for Lois. Maybe he thought they still lived together, and that she'd simply turned and talked to him rather than phoning. On the other hand, this was Willy's way, this unswerving reasonableness that had bored and irritated her for twenty years.

Lois went into the living room and turned on the TV. She felt exhausted, yet couldn't sleep. Larry King was interviewing Shari Lewis about her puppet, Lamb Chop. In a serious voice, King asked her if she was bothered by the fact that deejay Howard Stern had referred to Lamb Chop's private parts in a radio broadcast.

"Oh no," Shari said. "That doesn't bother me because Lamb Chop *does* have private parts."

"I see," said King.

"Lamb Chop does a Las Vegas act," she went on. "He's not only for kids. He's got an adult side of him, too. When he's in Las Vegas, he has private parts."

With that, Lois turned off the TV and went back to bed, thinking she'd have nightmares if she listened to one word more.

Another thing Lois liked about her kitchen was her black refrigerator. She'd nicknamed it the Wurlitzer because of its rounded jukebox top and chrome highlights. She liked this refrigerator even though it barely worked and constantly needed defrosting. Every week, a layer of ice built up so thick she couldn't close the freezer door. Nevertheless, she didn't want to get rid of it because it was an antique, though not officially. It wasn't fifty years old, but it still had more character than the ones out on the market these days: huge boxy things coated with grainy white plastic. Lois knew the market because she'd priced new fridges one day. The only other colors besides white were avocado and tan. If you wanted black, you had to pay a hundred dollars extra for a translucent black panel that snapped onto the front. And if you didn't want something with sharp corners, forget it. Nothing looked even half as elegant as her Wurlitzer. To her, her temperamental refrigerator had made itself part of the family, and she'd let it stay around as long as it kept things mildly cold.

And finally, what she liked best about her kitchen was the fact that it was hers, and she could eat whatever she wanted. Smoked oysters, for instance. She'd always enjoyed them, but had never been able to eat oysters around Willy. Whenever she opened a can, he'd complain about the smell and make her eat them on the porch. Just the thought of smoked oysters sickened him, and when she bought them, she had to hide the can in the deepest recesses of the pantry. When she finished eating them, she'd wash oyster oil from the can, and bury the can in the garbage. Then she'd brush her teeth. And still, hours later, Willy would sense an oyster presence. He'd sniff around the kitchen like some police drug dog and say, "You been hoovering them mollusks again?"

"I'll never eat them again," she said once.

"Go ahead and eat them all you want," he'd said. "You know I'm just joking."

No, she hadn't known that, but she took him at his word. The next time she wanted smoked oysters, she decided to ignore his remarks, and ate them in front of him.

"You like that fishy taste?" he'd said.

"Yeah," she said, which was simpler than saying they didn't taste fishy to her.

He watched her bring an oyster to her mouth and then he'd said, "Do you think they're still alive when they put them in the can?"

"I don't know," she said, which was simpler than saying, Will you please let me eat my oysters in peace?

"It's kind of remarkable," he'd said, "how they get them to fit so tight like that in them little cans. What makes them look so shriveled and brown?"

"Willy!"

"What? I'm just trying to figure out why you like them," he said.

"Because I'm weird," she'd said. "Because I'm a horrible human being."

Willy thought a second and said, "I guess that about sums it up."

Today, this horrible human being waited for Willy (that picture of perfection) to help her haul the table to his barn. They'd made the date, rain or shine, a week before. No matter what. That's how Willy was. No matter if he still felt like it or not. And it *was* raining, a half-frozen drizzle. And Lois *didn't* feel like hauling away an oak table today. For one thing, a stranger was asleep on her veranda. He'd been asleep all night and had slept through the morning. Lois had held a kind of vigil beside him half the night, then retreated into the kitchen. Twice she'd checked up on him to make sure he wasn't dead or anything: once when Meg and Gail woke up. Meg had trotted into the kitchen like it was Christmas, and asked brightly, "What's he doing?" Together they'd peeked into the veranda, and saw him sitting in one of the chairs, a blanket over his knees, his head lolling to the side. He'd looked like some old man who'd fallen asleep on the deck of a ship.

The next time was right after Willy called to say he'd be over in an hour. After she hung up, she dashed onto the veranda, wondering what she was going to do if Willy found this strange man there. Then she stopped herself. What did she care? She'd stood for a full five minutes in front of Henry, watching him breathe, hoping not to disturb him.

An hour later, on the dot, Willy appeared at her door in a glistening green poncho, his beard sopping. He smiled and barreled past her, stopped in the hall and said, "Okay, let's get this show on the road."

He pulled a pair of work gloves from a back pocket and started to slip his hands into them, like a surgeon making ready. He ran a gloved hand over his beard and said, "It's colder than a witch's tit. You sure picked a fine day to move furniture."

"I'd just as soon wait," Lois said. "To tell you the truth, things have been kind of crazy around here." She didn't like the idea of leaving the house before Henry woke up. Maybe she should go wake him, but then she'd have to bring Willy into this, and he'd just complicate things.

Willy nodded like he hadn't heard a word. He pursed his lips and glanced around the hall and living room. She noticed him looking at some boxes from the move shoved in the corner of the living room.

"Gail and Meg at school?" he said.

"Sure," she said. "Of course."

"Yeah, right," he said. "Of course." He smiled again and said, "Let's get this show on the road."

"Don't be in such a hurry," she said, pulling him by a corner of his poncho. "Come on, have a cup of coffee." She didn't want to go out just yet. She wanted his concern for a little while. She wanted to sit down with him and say, There's a man on my veranda. Now what are you going to do? She wanted to blame him, If you'd been paying attention, you would have watched out for me. You wouldn't have let me make so many mistakes.

Willy glanced back, like someone was waiting for him.

"What do you have, regular coffee?" he said, following her down the hall. "You have any decaf?"

"Decaf?" she shouted. "Are you crazy? When did you start drinking that?"

Willy followed her into the kitchen and pulled off his gloves. He tossed them on one of the seats like he lived there, then pulled his poncho off. The poncho, beaded with water, should have been left out in the hall, but Willy laid it across the chair over the gloves. A little puddle of water started to form on the floor, and Lois looked at it, strangely pleased.

Willy sat down heavily in another one of the chairs around the Formica table. He faced away from the table, toward the center of the kitchen, and he slumped down low, his legs stretched out, his feet balanced on their heels. He smiled wide at her. Willy had the most evil, self-satisfied, pitiless smile. He had big yellow teeth, his skin crinkled and his eyes turned into little glinting shields. Lois adored that smile.

"What is it?" she said, folding her arms and smiling at him. She wanted to be in on the joke.

Willy shook his head. "Decaf," he said. "My God. Decaf. I'm turning into a goddamn decaf drinker." He seemed stunned by the admission. He kept shaking his head and smiling. "What do you make of that, Lo?"

Lois went to the stove and poured him a cup from her metal percolator. She'd left the automatic drip with him, and had found this one at a sale. What surprised her was that it flat out made better coffee than the automatic one. No doubt about it. And it didn't take that much longer. The only real difference was that you had to take it off the stove yourself, and it didn't have a clock.

"Here," she said, handing him a mug of strong, singed coffee. "Drink this. The effects of decaffeinated aren't irreversible."

Lois wondered if it could be this easy, if she could hand Willy this mug of coffee, and feel only a small tug of affection lift and settle back down again. Not quite settle. She had to force it a little. Although glad that it still survived somewhere in her, small and healthy, she knew she had to hold it back all the same.

Willy brought the mug to his lips, and then stopped. His eyes changed and Lois followed them. From the other side of the room, the door to the veranda opened. Her ersatz landlord, curly-haired and anorectic, padded silently in his metallic-green running shorts to the refrigerator. Henry opened the door, looked inside, and took out a small tub of potato salad she had picked up at the deli counter at Martin's.

He gazed at the salad in his hands as though it was the Holy Grail, and he proceeded, head bent, toward the table where Lois and Willy sat. He seemed to sense something. His head jerked up. He looked at Lois and Willy as though someone had shot a bolt of electricity through him. Then it passed and he joined them at the table.

"Hi," he said.

Willy still sat in the same position, slumped down, his legs thrust in front of him. Only he wasn't smiling. He looked confused. He set down his cup of coffee and folded his arms. "Hi," he said.

Lois watched Willy carefully. He looked at her and she wanted to tell him something, but what was there to tell? What horrible timing Henry had. She'd been sharing a cup of coffee with her ex-husband. For the first time in months they'd been alone together, and something had been developing. Not that she wanted it to develop, but she enjoyed forcing it back. To know it was alive had been enough.

"Is this yours?" Henry said to Willy, holding the tub of potato salad out to him.

Willy shook his head.

"You want some?" Henry said, and Willy seemed to freeze.

"No?" Henry stood up. "I guess I need a fork."

He headed for the sink and Willy shook his head and looked at Lois. He said her name softly, hoarsely, in disbelief, as though he'd just caught her eating smoked oysters.

"Willy," she whispered to him. "Henry's not my lover. He's my landlord, sort of."

"Uh-huh," he said, and he smiled that big evil smile of his again, only he didn't look so charming anymore. He just kept smiling and shaking his head, glancing up and down at the man.

"Nice legs," he said to her. "He looks like Gandhi."

She wanted to hit him. "Don't be such a pig," she said. "I felt sorry for him. He needed a place to stay last night and I let him."

Willy didn't say anything to that. She hated how he thought he'd figured everything out. She hit his arm.

"What?" he said. He seemed genuinely surprised, convinced of his innocence, but there wasn't anything innocent about Willy.

"Henry," Lois said. "This is my ex-husband, Willy."

Willy waved and nodded. "Big fan of yours," Willy said. "Saw the movie three times."

Henry looked up at the ceiling, as though trying to sort out this role from among his many. "Thank you," he said. Then he took the plastic lid off the tub and started placidly eating the potato salad by the sink.

She could forgive Henry his rudeness, but not Willy. Let him think what he wanted. She stood up and threw Willy's wet poncho at him. "Come on, let's get this show on the road," she said.

Willy stood up slowly, stretching and moving his shoulders around, obviously some stupid territorial display for poor Henry's sake. Even though Henry was oblivious. But so was Willy.

On the way out she said to Henry, loud enough for Willy to hear, "Seeing as how it's so miserable out, you can stay another day. When I get back, I'll set you up in the garage."

By that time Henry's mouth was full. He nodded at her and went to the kitchen table. Her last sight of him was Henry sitting alone, bent to the task of polishing off the salad. Then she noticed Willy's gloves beside him. She was about to mention it to Willy, but she didn't. Let him freeze his fat fingers, she thought. Let him leave something with me that I'll never return. But out in the garage, where she'd temporarily stored the oak table, he remembered, and he went back inside to fetch the gloves. That was just like him, not to ever leave any loose pieces of himself lying around. She wanted to follow to see what he said to Henry, but she didn't. And when Willy returned, she didn't ask him either. He looked at her, and she knew he'd said something. She didn't want to know what it was. She could live her whole life without ever knowing what stupid thing Willy had told Henry. She could see that Willy was dying to tell her, too, but he didn't. He was famous for his self-control.

NINE

From outside his small room, Henry heard laughter and then a solitary voice booming. Another voice answered in the same loud way. Props lay scattered around, but none of them quite fit: a fireman's helmet, a section of hose, and a large rubber boot. He stared at the large rubber boot and tried to remember his lines, which he'd known only a moment ago. In fact, he had been so sure of them he hadn't even had opening-night jitters. He had never faced this problem before. Usually, he didn't falter one bit with his lines, and people knew him around the company as dependable, if not talented.

Henry opened his eyes, and the props changed, but not the small room. He sat in his shorts and T-shirt on a canvas cot that smelled of mildew, three blankets wrapped tightly around him. Instead of fire gear, he stared at the orange coils of a space heater, its cord suspended from the single overhead light in the garage. Did the space heater frighten him? Was that why he'd transformed it in his dream into fireman's gear? After all, so many fires started from portable heaters. Obviously, he still cared a little about his life, or he wouldn't have bundled himself in three blankets. Or maybe only his body cared, the body shivering under the blankets, more sensible than his mind. His mind wanted nothing, and so his body had taken command, constantly feeding itself, or piling blankets on to correct his mind's mistakes.

Henry heard the laughter again, and the voices, only different now. Not the deep voice of the stage manager or the people on stage, but the voices of young girls. Again, he tried to remember his lines, his place, what people expected of him. Rhonda? Pam? Was Sid Junkins out there? A door was on one side of the room and a window on the other, covered with frost. The voices came from the other side of the door, and then it opened. Henry huddled farther into his blankets.

Three young girls burst in, then stopped and stared. He recognized only one of them. She looked about ten. She had a small nose and black hair and eyes that seemed quick and alert. He remembered her as the younger daughter of the woman who lived in the house. Her two companions looked like sisters. They were both Indian, had dark skin and braided black hair. The older seemed about twelve, and her sister maybe a couple of years younger.

The three girls stood in a line facing him, and scrutinized him openly, as though they were visitors to a zoo. The girl who lived there smiled proudly at him. She turned to her friends and said, "See?"

The older of the Indian girls held a bouquet of plastic flowers, and Henry wondered if they were meant for him. The three girls seemed to be waiting for him to say something.

He raised a hand out of the blanket and said, "Hi."

"Hi," the three girls replied together.

Then the three of them burst into action, as though his word had un-frozen them from a spell. They didn't move toward him. They went away from him, to the other side of the garage. There, they gathered around a black trunk and opened it.

Henry craned his neck. The trunk held clothes, and the girls sorted through them, paying no attention to him at all. "Look at my new dress," the girl who lived at the house shouted.

"Isn't it lovely?" the older Indian girl said.

The girls picked through the wrinkled clothes and sorted them into piles. Henry watched. He hadn't seen kids for so long. He wanted to know what they were doing, and that surprised him. He couldn't re-member the last time he'd been curious.

He wanted to ask them something, but didn't want to startle them by yelling across the garage. So he waited until they were done and started filing past him holding bundles of clothing.

"You carry the flowers," the older Indian girl said to her sister. "It's *your* wedding."

Henry saw this remark as his opening. "Whose wedding is it?" he said.

The three girls stopped and stared at him. "It's hers," the older girl said, as though she'd been caught doing something wrong.

The younger girl laughed at this and hid behind her sister.

"She's getting married?" Henry said. That didn't seem very reason-able to him. Still, he knew that in India people married young.

The girl who lived at the house seemed to sense his confusion and said, "It's only pretend."

For the first time in a long while, Henry felt his face color. "Of course," he said. "I knew that. Who's she marrying?"

"She's not really marrying anyone," the same girl said. "It's just pretend."

"Who's she pretending to marry?" Henry said. He shifted his weight on the cot and rearranged the blankets. Maybe the heater was kicking in.

"She's marrying her cousin," the older Indian girl said, and at that they all laughed, even Henry.

"How old is the boy she's marrying?" he said.

"He's five," the older Indian girl said.

"No, he's six," said the bride-to-be, the first words she'd uttered since Henry began to talk with them.

"She's marrying a younger man," her sister added. Then she strode up to the cot and showed him her hands, palms out. Henry just stared at her hands, wondering what was expected of him. "Here, take it," she said, cupping her hands together as though she held something in them, something small and alive. Henry looked closer, but still couldn't see anything.

"What is it?" Henry said.

"Take it," the girl said.

Henry reached out and grabbed air from the girl's hands. This seemed to satisfy the girl in part. She brushed her hands together as though they'd collected dust, then folded her arms, and regarded him. He still didn't know what this was about, and he wished now that the girls would just leave him, and allow him to go back to sleep.

"Okay, now go ahead and perform the marriage ceremony," said the girl.

Henry just looked from her to his palms.

"It begins: 'Dearly beloved,'" the girl prompted.

The other girls seemed as surprised as Henry. "Who's getting married?" the girl who lived at the house said.

"You and Pia, of course."

The two girls looked at each other in surprise. "I can't marry her," the girl who lived at the house said. "We're both girls."

"And I'm not ready," said the young Indian girl, clutching her flowers. "And what about Naseem. I was going to marry him."

"It doesn't matter what you say," the older girl insisted. "I've arranged this marriage. Anyway, you can get divorced right afterwards. Then you can marry Naseem. This will just be practice."

This explanation seemed to satisfy the other two girls, who linked arms and faced Henry. The older girl nodded at Henry and said in a whisper, "Dearly beloved."

Henry looked down at his palms and pretended to read: "Dearly beloved, we are gathered here to join −"

He looked up at the two young girls. The girl who lived at the house said, "Meg," and the other girl said, "Pia."

"Meg and Pia," he said. In the distance, Henry could hear a jet approaching.

Henry read on, and after barely a minute pronounced them man and wife, though he didn't clarify which was which. Meg and Pia then turned to each other, puckered their lips, and made smooching noises in the air between them. Pia tossed the flowers to her sister, and the three of them broke into giggles.

Henry put the make-believe book aside and said, "Where are you going to spend your honeymoon?"

The girls looked at each other, considering.

The sound of the jet grew closer until it filled the garage and drowned out their voices. The jet seemed close enough for Meg and Pia to reach up and be swept off to their honeymoon right away. Henry remembered how frequently jets flew over on their way to the airport, how he'd always thought of this as the major drawback of his house. Carla, on the other hand, had taken it in stride. She'd made the jets her hobby, memorizing their schedules, their takeoffs and landings. She never seemed particularly interested in flying anywhere herself; she just wanted to know where things were headed.

The three girls still stared at him.

"You're nice," Meg said.

This bold statement shocked him. "No I'm not," he said. "How do you know?"

"I can tell just from talking to you," she said with certainty.

After they left, Henry slowly untangled himself from his blankets.

Then, one by one, he folded the blankets neatly and placed them on the foot of his bed. A thought occurred to him: he was a guest in this house. No, not even that. He didn't belong here at all. A woman and her two children lived here, not Carla and Matthew. Yet, he had nowhere else to go. Soon, he'd have to find a new place to live, but not just yet. He wasn't ready. Something about these people, this place made him want to stay a while longer. He felt confused, but his confusion made him happy. For months, he hadn't even known enough to know he was confused, and now he did. For months, the world had seemed flat, like some painted cardboard set. This was the house he had lived in with Carla and Matthew, but other people lived here now. Two separate sets of people. The girls tramping through the garage had stepped on the same ground he and Carla and Matthew had walked. It was almost like walking through some battleground a hundred years after the battle.

He looked down at his green running shorts. He pinched the fabric of his T-shirt. He wondered what he was doing dressed like this in December. What he wanted now, most of all, were some new clothes.

Slowly, he opened the door to the house and peeked inside. He heard sounds from the kitchen. He crossed the living room and started heading down the hall. Facing him was the older daughter of the woman who lived at the house. The girl, dressed in a blue terrycloth robe, and holding a towel around her hair, stopped and stared at him. Without a word, she turned and ran down the hall. A door slammed. Henry kept walking.

In the kitchen, he found the girls' mother alone, listening to a radio and stirring something in a mixing bowl. This woman with her frizzy hair, broad shoulders, and strong chin seemed the complete opposite of Carla. She seemed like some pioneer woman, determination etched in every bone and feature. Carla, on the other hand, had always looked so weak and small, from her rounded shoulders to her nervous smile and darting eyes.

For a moment, he just watched her from the doorway. He didn't want to upset her the way he seemed to upset her daughter. Right now, she looked imperturbable, her head bent to her task, a slight smile playing at her lips. She seemed to be thinking of something sweet, maybe her daughters, maybe her husband. She *was* married, wasn't she? Yes, he'd met her husband in this kitchen, and he hadn't seemed as warm as she. Of course, Henry couldn't blame the man. In the same situation, he wouldn't have been warm either. For a minute, the two men had stood alone, and what had the man told him? He'd picked up his pair of gloves from the table and then had walked straight over to Henry. For a moment, Henry wondered if the man was going to slap him with one of the gloves and challenge him to a duel. He hadn't. Instead he'd said, "I don't know what Lois sees in you. I don't care. But I better not catch you walking around like that in front of my girls."

Henry didn't understand, but he knew enough to keep his mouth shut. If he'd said, I don't understand, he would have ended up on his back, staring at the overhead light.

Henry backed down the hall a ways and then clomped forward again, loud enough, he hoped, for the woman to hear his approach over the radio noise and her own thoughts. The woman turned, holding the mixing spoon, which dripped icing. She wore a number of silver bracelets and silver-and-turquoise necklaces and a pair of earrings that dangled nearly to her shoulders. A day ago, Henry would have noticed only her spoon. He might have waited for her to put it down, and then gone over and started licking it like some untrained dog.

Not today. He forced himself to look at the person in front of him. "I'm sorry to bother you," he said.

"No bother," she said. "It's cold in the garage, isn't it?"

"Better than outside," he said. "I appreciate you letting me stay there these last . . ." He trailed off. What was it? Days? Weeks? Years? He hoped he hadn't stayed more than a day or two. If he had, then he'd wasted his time. He should have tried to know these people better.

She pulled a seat out from the dinette table and pointed with her spoon for him to sit down, but a thin strand of icing dripped onto the chair. "Oh well," she said. "There are three more chairs where that one came from," and she pulled another one from the table. "I'll clean this mess up later."

Henry sat down and traced a finger over the glittery finish of the tabletop.

"Have you figured out where you're going to go?" she said. She didn't seem to say it to hurry him out of her house, but rather out of concern. She sat down beside him, on the chair where she'd dripped the chocolate icing. She sounded like wind chimes when she moved.

"Sure," he said, smiling. "I have it all figured out."

"Oh, okay then," she said. She looked away and glided her finger around the rim of the bowl, collecting a big glob of chocolate icing on her finger. She put it to her lips and licked it off. Then she put a hand to her chest and her eyes bugged out. For a moment, he thought she was choking and he leaned to pat her on the back.

"No, I'm fine," she said. "I just realized how rude that was."

Henry quickly looked around, wondering what he'd done this time.

The woman laughed and brushed her hair back. Again, the wind chimes sounded. "I mean me," she said. "Sticking my finger in there like that."

Henry settled down again and placed his hands, palms up, beneath his legs. He thought if she wanted to catalogue rude behavior, she could start with him walking unannounced into her house, and traipsing around in a dirty track outfit. But he wasn't going to bring it up if she didn't.

"I guess I'm used to being criticized," the woman said. "Willy and Gail do it to me all the time. Meg's the only one who spares me anymore."

Henry nodded as though he understood and had heard it all before from her, which he might have. She might have told him all of this, and he had simply tuned her out, the way he'd been accustomed to doing for so long. He didn't remember anything, not even the names of her family, though he concentrated now, and tried hard to commit them to memory.

He didn't understand how anyone could criticize this woman, who seemed like a saint to him, but he accepted it. After all, he understood criticism, or at least he understood how to criticize. He'd been a master of it with Carla. Still, he wished he could go to Willy and Gail, whoever they were, and somehow convince them to stop criticizing this good woman. Maybe he could show them by example, convince them to be more accepting, tell them what had happened to him. But of course, it wasn't his place to intrude.

For a moment, Henry was taken away by the sound of the radio. A man with a British accent was saying: "He said the problems in Eastern Europe were caused not by too much socialism, but by the failure of certain countries to put the principles of socialism to work properly."

Henry closed his eyes and tried to remember where he was, to hang on.

"I'll be out of your way soon," he said, his eyes still shut tight. "Maybe you could tell me where I could buy some new clothes around here. And you know, you sat down in chocolate icing. It's not a criticism. I just wasn't sure if you were aware of it."

Henry opened his eyes again and looked at the woman. There. He'd said everything he'd been thinking. Maybe he could have said it better, but at least he'd said something.

"And could you tell me your name once more?" he said. "I've forgotten."

And still, she didn't get angry with him. She just told him. Yes, this woman seemed imperturbable.

TEN

L ois would have felt cruel letting Henry walk five miles in the freezing cold, dressed like he played on some junior varsity basketball team. She couldn't afford to buy clothes for him, but she could at least give him a lift to the store, even though Henry said he didn't mind walking, that he liked to walk. Lois ignored him, and asked if he had any money to *buy* these clothes. He said he did. He didn't look like he had any money, so she asked again. Again, he nodded.

Out in the car, Lois sat in the front seat with the passenger door open, but Henry just stared suspiciously at the seat.

"Maybe I can walk," he told her. "I really think I should."

"I know it looks like a junk heap," she said, "but looks can be deceiving, you know. Though not in this case."

Henry climbed in slowly, edging into the seat. He just sat there for a minute, breathing deeply, his eyes closed, and his feet still on the ground outside. Finally, he swung them in and closed the door.

Henry sat shivering, hands together as if praying, and stuck between his knees. By the time the heater in Lois's Volare kicked in, they were already halfway to Scottsdale Mall.

Even though Henry's teeth clacked, he smiled at Lois and started asking questions, which seemed like a complete turnabout to her. The day before he'd been little more than a gerbil, complacently munching food, staring vacantly, then munching again. Even so, the questions he was asking weren't too personal. Just chitchat. He asked them strangely, like he had to force them out.

"Do your children enjoy school?"

"Meg does. She likes getting good grades. Any kind of attention or praise, for that matter. Gail wants to be a heavy-metal star. She thinks it's just going to somehow happen, without her working."

Henry nodded vigorously, but Lois could see he didn't know what she meant. Still, he seemed a lot less dazed that before. He seemed, at least, to be trying.

Lois thought about what she'd just said. "I guess she gets that from me. That tendency. Wanting something without working at it."

This seemed true. That's why she'd said it. But she wasn't really sure she believed her own words. Not really. Still, this seemed like a noble admission. High-minded as she felt, she saw her spiel had been lost on Henry, who stared right past her with that silly smile.

"How long have you and your husband been married?" Henry asked her. He had his shoulders hunched forward, pushing his thin shoulder blades, like closed wings, toward his face.

She turned toward him and said, "Aren't you feeling any heat yet?"

"Yes," he said, shaking like he was about to fall apart. "Have you lived in South Bend your whole life?"

"I have it all the way up," she said.

Henry nodded and said, "F-f-f-feels good. "Are you a football fan? Do you ever go to Notre Dame games?"

Lois nudged the heat control a little farther to the right, to make sure it couldn't go any farther. It couldn't.

"Hey," Henry said.

She looked up. Henry clutched the dash with one hand, and stared out the windshield with a terrified look. She looked around, but nothing was wrong. Maybe she was following the car in front a little closely, but she had plenty of room to stop if she needed.

"Are you all right?" she said.

Henry eased his hand from the dash and settled back. Henry nodded and said, "I'm starting to feel it now. Nice and toasty. This heater works pretty well, doesn't it?"

Lois didn't say anything, though she had a million questions. She wanted to ask him something about his past, but she didn't know how to phrase it without upsetting him. Instead, she said, "Actually, Willy and I aren't married anymore. He just came over yesterday to help me move something."

Lois looked at Henry, unsure whether he understood a word she said. "How long . . ." she began at the same time Henry said, "Do you . . ."

They stopped.

"How long?" Lois said again and Henry said "Do you?"

"Go ahead," Lois said.

"No, that's all right," Henry said.

"It's not important," Lois said. "Really."

"Okay," Henry said. "Do you like driving?"

"Do I like driving?" That was certainly one question she hadn't expected.

"I used to love to drive." Henry pointed to a sports car in front of them that had just changed lanes without signaling. "That's the kind of car I always wanted to drive. This is the first I've been in a car for a long time."

Lois didn't know what to say to that. Was this a hint that he wanted to drive her car? That didn't seem like a good idea to her, not with how distracted he was.

A t the mall, Henry wandered around like a caveman who'd awakened after a million years. He walked quickly, slightly ahead of her, pausing here and there, taking in everything. First, he stopped in front of a vitamin store and said, "These aren't as good as the ones Sid Junkins sells." He said it as though Lois should know what he meant.

Then he stopped next to the game room and gazed into its dark interior lit with sharp glows and punctuated by the sounds of bombs exploding and race cars making perilous turns, brakes screeching.

While Henry looked inside, Lois regarded Henry, wondering what people must think of him as they walked by. If they even noticed or cared. Maybe they thought Henry had just come from his health club. Lois didn't mind standing next to him though, no matter what people thought. She'd grown accustomed to people thinking she was a little odd, and anyway, being a little odd was no crime in her book.

Henry walked up to a pet shop and tapped on the window and talked with a little wiener dog, who followed his finger with a drugged look while it stood on trembling legs. Casually, almost as an afterthought, the wiener dog licked the window where Henry had his hand. Then it turned away and curled up in the corner of the window. Something about this saddened her, and she'd been sad enough lately, so she said, "I think there's a men's clothing store right up here."

There was, and it was having a twofer sale.

Signs around the store announced "Twofer Madness," and a "Twofer blow-out!" On principle, Lois wanted to leave and find a store where they could spell the word "for," but Henry didn't seem to mind. He wandered among the racks, hardly seeming to notice what he chose. Lois followed Henry around and held his choices for him. Henry's limp right hand made it impossible for him to sort and gather at the same time.

The store had a kind of industrial motif, with a ceiling covered with a labyrinth of metalwork and large round ducts. Silk-screened posters hung on the walls, the posters picturing stern men from the nineteenth century who all had thick, sculpted beards that angled out from their faces. The men looked like they came off a cough drop box. Old photographs lined the walls, too, but Lois was too busy following Henry around the store to make out what the photos depicted. Assorted antiques were scattered among the clothes, a wagon wheel, a sign that read Wells Funeral Home, and a brass cash register. The drawer of the cash register was open, and each compartment held a paisley silk handkerchief. As she passed the register, she saw that it had a price tag. $1,200. She couldn't believe it. She'd seen one exactly like this go at an auction a couple of months before for $250. Maybe the same one.

The decor of the place didn't at all match the kind of clothes the store sold, most of which looked like they'd come off the set of "Dance America." And the salesmen didn't look half as dignified as the men in the posters, though they seemed to give it their all. They stood stiffly at various points in the store, bland-faced men with dull eyes like the wiener dog in the pet shop. Instead of licking their various customers, the men smiled and looked helpful, and then returned to their corners when they'd done their duty.

Lois didn't make any suggestions to Henry. She let him pick out what he wanted, except once, when she put back a pair of pants that looked like they were made out of carpet remnants.

"You don't want these Henry," she said. "Trust me."

Henry smiled like he *did* trust her and went on draping clothes over her arms.

At one point, a chubby man in a blue suit approached Lois and said, "You folks finding what you need?"

"Ask *him*," Lois said, pointing a finger through the pile at Henry.

The man gave Henry the once over and grimaced. Instead of asking him anything, the man just backed away and said, "Well, I just don't want anyone standing around not being helped."

After a while, Lois started staggering under the weight of the clothes, and then one of Henry's shirts caught on her earring, so she suggested that Henry should start trying on some of his choices. Lois draped the whole bundle over Henry's good arm, and he walked into the curtained room. Too late, she noticed a sign that read Only Three Items Allowed In The Dressing Area At Once.

She looked back and saw the chubby man in the blue suit watching her intently. For a moment, she felt insulted, but then she thought about it. What if Henry *did* steal something. He definitely wasn't the most stable person she'd ever met, and he didn't seem to understand the concept of private property either. She could easily imagine him just walking out of the store without paying. Of course, she'd be his accomplice. What would Gail think of her then? Or Willy?

He seemed to be taking forever, in fact. Lois edged away from the dressing room and headed for the silk screens and photographs.

The first photograph she came across showed five bearded men in black suits, their beards completely covering their collars. Three of the men sat in sturdy chairs, and some kind of animal pelt lay in front of them. Two other men stood in back of the three. They hardly seemed to know they were all in the same photograph. One of the standing men looked out with open hostility. The other four all looked like they had better things to do.

The caption read:

THE STUDEBAKER BROTHERS

Clem Studebaker   Henry Studebaker   J. M. Studebaker

Peter E. Studebaker   J. F. Studebaker

She should have known. From the start, there'd been something about this store that she hadn't liked, something that had set her on edge. She skimmed over the other photos on the wall near where she stood, and sure enough, they showed various scenes from the Studebaker glory days. One showed a scene in front of some bleachers: five football players on all fours pushing against the grille of a car from the Model-T era. An older man stood by the car on the driver's side. He wore boots, knickers, and a sweatshirt. The man was staring at the football players like maybe they'd been working out too hard, and had snapped under the pressure. The men had their butts sticking up in the air like horny cats. The caption read: Knute Rockne and Notre Dame football players pose with a Studebaker "Dictator Victoria" at Notre Dame Stadium. A lithograph hung beside this photo. It showed the Studebaker factory back when it made wagons: a huge Victorian complex with railroad yards, and giant gabled buildings. The caption on this one read: The Great Studebaker Wagon Works. The Largest in the World.

She turned back and saw the chubby man in the blue suit staring openly at her. She didn't care. Let him think what he wanted. She just wanted to get out of here. She hated the fact that South Bend kept lionizing the Studebakers, like nothing had really happened in 1963, like the company hadn't just ditched the town. They should have done with Studebaker what they did at the sites of horrendous airplane crashes. The authorities, Lois had heard, would sow a ton of nails into the crash site to discourage scavengers. Still, she took some satisfaction that the lofty old Studebakers had been reduced to this, silently hawking cheap clothes from the walls of a store in a mall.

Lois marched over to the dressing room and stopped. What had happened to Henry? He'd been in there for an hour, it seemed. "Henry?" Lois said into the curtained room. No one answered. Oh great, she thought. While she was having it out with the Studies on the wall, Henry had probably walked off somewhere. Well, she wasn't going to go looking for him. She had a family to take care of. How could she expect herself to help someone she didn't even know when she hardly had her own life in order?

She tried again, and this time a small voice answered. "Could you come here a second?"

Lois parted the curtain and walked in. There were six cubicles with curtains in front of them. All the cubicles were occupied. She heard a man cough. She saw a pair of hairy legs, the man's feet covered by black socks. Somewhere keys jangled. The clank of a belt buckle. Some pocket change.

Too late she realized what she'd done, invaded a domain that wasn't hers. Blame it on J. M. Studebaker, she thought. She wondered if the chubby man in the blue suit had seen her walk in. She was about to walk back out but Henry called her again. "I need your opinion on something," he said from the farthest booth. If she didn't go see what he wanted, she was afraid he'd stay there until closing.

She pulled back the curtain and whispered, "What is it?"

She thought she had walked in the wrong dressing room. She saw a short man in his late twenties or early thirties dressed in a gray wool suit, his back to her, facing a full-length mirror. He wriggled slightly in his jacket, then turned to her and said, "Does this fit?"

"I don't know," she said. "Does it?"

Except for his mussed-up hair, scraggly beard, and his untied tie, he looked like a young businessman on the rise.

"I don't know," he said. "Nothing feels right. Nothing but what I was wearing. Maybe I should join a nudist colony."

He said this with a deadpan look, and Lois wasn't sure if he was serious. "Was that a joke?" she said.

Henry looked amazed. Then he smiled, laughed, and ran a hand through his beard as though applying after-shave.

"Your pants seem a little bunched in the waist," she said. "Maybe you need the next size up."

Henry shook his head. "No, I've already got on size thirty. My pants would fall down – "

"Thirty!" Lois said. "Don't ever speak to me again, Henry."

She saw he was taking her seriously, that he thought he'd really offended her. He stared at her with a bewildered look.

"That was a joke," she said.

"Oh right," he said, smiling and nodding.

What surprised Lois when she and Henry emerged from the dressing room was that the chubby clerk in the blue suit acted as though nothing unusual had happened. He acted as though Henry and Lois were typical customers, as though Henry was dressed normally, as though he'd only taken three items with him, as though Lois belonged back there, too.

Of course, it was easier for the clerk to ignore the facts than to make a fuss. The same was true with everyone around there. That's why no one had stared at Henry as he walked through the mall. That's why South Bend still adored the Studebakers. Why Willy accumulated one junk heap after another without ever fixing one up. No one wanted to admit their mistakes.

The other night on the news, she'd seen film of a devastating downpour in Colombia. Mudslides. Buried villages. Hundreds dead. Caked arms and legs sticking out from the mud. Then the newscaster came back on, put on a concerned look, and said, "Nothing so serious around here. We could use some rain though, right Jim?"

"That's right, Sara," the weatherman had replied, smiling.

Lois was the only person she knew who sought out confusion, who was still terrified and haunted by things that happened a thousand miles away, or a thousand years before. She still didn't know how to make a smooth segue from a devastating mudslide to the local overnight forecast.

Henry decided to buy the wool suit, and he wanted to wear it out of the store, too. He also picked up a dozen pairs of socks, underwear, T-shirts, and five Arrow shirts. The number of shirts confused the clerk.

"You can get another shirt," he told Henry. "We're having Twofer Madness Days."

"That's all right," Henry said. "I don't need another one."

"But it's free," the man said. "Twofer one."

Lois and the clerk stared at Henry, who thought a second, then shook his head, and said, "No thanks."

"I'm only supposed to ring up even numbers," the man said.

"Why?" Henry said, with genuine interest.

"Twofer one," Lois and the clerk said at the same time. Lois flushed. She didn't much like the idea of sympathizing with the clerk.

Maybe this is the difference between people and the lower orders of life, Lois thought. It's not that we're aware of our own eventual deaths, as some have suggested. And it's not the fact that we can laugh, or the presence of our souls. No, the difference is that sane people and all animals live happily by routines, and people are the only animals capable of willfully, and sometimes cheerfully, breaking out of their routines, thereby destroying their lives irrevocably. Sane people choose not to exercise this difference, maybe storing it in the back of their minds as an option. Cats and wiener dogs, even chubby clerks in blue suits know enough to let their lives happen without resistance (Twofer one and onefer all!). For some, it's instinct. For others, habit.

Finally, the clerk gave up, his goodwill spent. "Cash or charge?" he demanded.

Henry slipped off his tennis shoes. In the right shoe, he had a checkbook, and a driver's license lay in his left shoe. He bent down, gathered them up, then wriggled into his shoes again. "Do you take checks?" he said.

"Local only, with proper ID," the man rattled off. He took Henry's license and compared it with the check. Lois sneaked a look at the license, too. It showed a man who looked several years younger, with fuller features, thicker hair, and no beard. But unmistakably Henry. He was dressed in a blue suit like the one the clerk was wearing now. The background was bright red and the man's pupils were little red dots.

"Everything current?" the man said.

Lois looked at the address on the check. It was hers, which shouldn't have shocked her, but it did.

"That's where *I* live," she said before she could stop herself.

Henry stopped writing. "Me too," he said with wonderment. Then he handed the clerk the pen and the check.

The clerk furrowed his brow and looked at both of them. He probably thought this was some pet game of theirs. Still, Lois wanted to set him straight. She wanted to tell him they weren't together. The man's my landlord. I'm just helping him out. That certainly sounded strange. And anyway, she didn't need to justify her actions to the man.

"You know, this expires in another month, the clerk told Henry when he handed back the license. But he didn't sound like he was trying to be helpful.

On the way home, they stopped for lunch at the Hungry Fisherman, a restaurant in downtown South Bend that looked out on the St. Joseph River. Henry ordered the all-you-can-eat Fish Bar and Lois ordered fish and chips. She was supposed to get two side orders with her meal, so she asked for corn on the cob and squash. When her meal arrived, she had everything but french fries, so she cornered the waitress, who explained that she hadn't ordered french fries.

"I ordered fish and chips," Lois said, dumbfounded.

"Yes, that's right," the waitress said, "but you got corn on the cob and squash. You ordered them *instead* of french fries."

"No I didn't," Lois said. "I ordered them *besides* french fries. I assumed I was getting french fries because it's called fish *and* chips."

"Yes," said the waitress, "but you see, you ordered corn on the cob."

"I know that, but that's ridiculous. Why is it called fish and chips if it doesn't come with chips?" Lois brought her arm up and swept her hair back.

"If you'd like to order some french fries, I can get some," the waitress said. The waitress looked calm and glassy-eyed. Her voice was smooth and automatic, the voice that tells people at airports to pick up the courtesy phone. Of course, that made Lois furious.

"No, never mind," Lois said.

"Would you like some more Coke?"

"No."

The waitress went away and a little while later another woman showed up.

"I understand you're upset about your fish and chips."

"Yes," said Lois. "I don't see why this is called fish and chips if you don't get chips."

"Yes, but no one else has problems with it," the woman said and glanced at Henry, who complacently munched on deviled crabs.

The calm manager who stood in front of her could have been a

newscaster, making segues from one disaster to another. She could
have been Willy telling her he wanted her out of his house in a week.
In the face of Lois's temper, the manager simply smiled more gro-
tesquely. Henry had stopped munching and looked at her in surprise,
as though he hadn't noticed anyone there until now.

"I ordered fish and chips," Lois said. "I didn't say fish and chips,
hold the chips." Lois felt her voice rising. "If you're not going to serve
chips, you shouldn't call it fish and chips." The manager moved her
lips while Lois talked. For some reason, people had a habit of doing
this. She couldn't figure out why; they moved their lips as though they
wanted to speak for her. Whenever this happened, it distracted and
drove her crazy. Maybe it was the way she talked. Maybe she didn't
speak fast enough or people wanted her to stop talking. Regardless,
they never realized they were mimicking her, and if she called their lip
movements to their attention, they acted like they didn't know what
she was talking about.

"You don't understand," the woman said. "We call it fish and
chips, but we mean fish *cut into* chips."

Lois couldn't believe the woman had said that. "Then you should
call it fish cut into chips," she said while the woman unconsciously
mimicked her, making little fish movements with her mouth.

Lois looked away.

"Chips mean different things," the woman explained as though she
were teaching a class of fourth-graders. "At Shoney's, if your order a
sandwich, you get potato chips."

Lois tried once more to speak rationally.

"Traditionally, fish and chips means fish and french fries. Everyone knows that."

"I'm sorry, but that's the way we do it," the woman said.

"That's the way we do it," Lois repeated. The people around her
were staring, but she didn't care. Only Henry didn't seem to mind. He
sat at the table, eating, mildly interested in what happened around
him. "I'm never coming back here, but I guess you don't care. So what
if one customer's unhappy."

"That's the way we do it here," the woman said, and kept on rattling
her inane explanations. Lois felt herself going out of control. She
didn't care about the fish and chips anymore. She'd forgotten them.

What upset her was that this woman with her ridiculous explanations thought *she* was being reasonable, and that Lois was insane for not understanding. Lois wanted to follow the woman into the kitchen and take some french fries hostage, or stand on the table and scream the Hungry Fisherman's definition of fish and chips. But she didn't. Instead, she widened her eyes and made her mouth into an O like a widemouthed bass, and moved her mouth up and down.

The woman stopped explaining. She stared at Lois, her hands locked together in front of her, while Lois made fish movements. The woman's smile froze on her face. Then, as if in some hypnotic trance, she, too, started moving her lips like a fish.

Finally, she snapped out of it. "I'll see what I can do," she said, brushing her fingers lightly across her lips. A few minutes later she brought Lois her basket of fries.

ELEVEN

The phrase just popped into Gail's head while she lay on Nathan's living-room floor.

"To our surprise, the lemon reconstituted itself."

It cracked her up.

"What's the matter?" Nathan said, looking her full in the face. He'd been staring past her shoulder, like he always did. He only looked her in the eye when he thought something was wrong.

"Nothing," she said, but she was thinking of a broken-up lemon with cartoon arms and legs, gathering up pieces of itself, and sticking them back on like Humpty-Dumpty. Only her mom made cracks as silly as that.

She remembered that day in June, driving to look at their new house, and how embarrassed she'd been when her mother had said that, though Gail wouldn't have minded so much now. Her mother never made quips anymore. Gail could hardly even remember the last time her mom had smiled. And now she'd taken in this nutcase, Henry, who'd been living in their garage for a week and a half. Gail could hardly stand going home. The house didn't feel like hers anymore, not that it ever had, but still, normal people didn't live this way. All she'd ever wanted was a normal family, but there wasn't *anything* normal about her mother.

Gail wished she could have a heart-to-heart talk with her mom to find out exactly what was wrong. Things didn't work that way. That was the opposite of how it was supposed to happen. Daughters didn't counsel their mothers. Not that Gail had ever understood what was *supposed* to happen between people, wasn't even sure anyone did. Except Nathan, who thought people shouldn't laugh during sex. That made him turn away, made him stare even closer at some minuscule spot on the rug beneath her.

"Let's make love for a change," she told him. "Don't just fuck me."

With her look Gail challenged him to be a smart-ass.

He slowly rose away from her, like some kind of street vapor from a manhole cover.

Nathan stood above her in his briefs and a T-shirt with a reproduction of the front page of a newspaper. The newspaper was one she'd never heard of, the *Sun*. The headline read: Sid Vicious Dead. That wasn't the kind of music that Nathan listened to. But he approved of it. He like iconoclastic music. Gail didn't know what that meant, but he always used the word, and she was starting to get a feel for what was iconoclastic and what wasn't. She could have looked it up, but that's what Nathan had told her to do the first time he'd used the word. She'd refused. According to Nathan, the music she listened to, heavy metal, was fake iconoclastic. Nathan called it heavy bubble. Mostly *he* played the Doors. About twenty-four hours a day. Right now, he had on "Riders on the Storm."

He clasped his hands behind his neck, sit-up style, and looked down at her, but Gail couldn't tell what he was thinking. Nathan played with his ponytail for a second, then stretched.

"You're so distant, Nathan. Where are you?"

He moved his neck around like he was doing stretching exercises or waking up from a long nap. "I don't know." He sounded baffled, his voice soft. "Somewhere. Not here. Maybe the Yucatán."

Already, she wanted him back, didn't want him to run away like that. "Come here," she said, immobile, refusing to move.

He shook his head, almost imperceptibly. "Maybe New York. Or San Francisco. Not this little shit hole on the St. Joseph."

He headed for the bathroom. On his way through the cramped apartment, strewn with stacks of music magazines and pizza boxes, he kept up the litany: "Morocco, Switzerland, Nova Scotia." Then he slammed the bathroom door, and all she could hear was him hacking his lungs out.

O n the way home, she tried to get him back. She wanted to be interesting to him again, but what could she say that would possibly keep his interest? Everything new to her was old hat to him. For a while, she just stared at the ashtray, which brimmed with butts. Nathan had the window open an inch, but the car had filled with smoke. He didn't say a word, just kept puffing away, his mind occupied with something much more important than her. He stubbed the cigarette in with the others in the ashtray, but it didn't go out. The ember smoldered against an old filter, and a wisp threaded out the ashtray. The smell of the burning filter sickened her even more than the stale tobacco smell.

"I passed my driver's ed. test last week. I've got my learner's permit now."

Nathan didn't take his eyes off the road. "Yeah, you said."

She scooted closer to him, traced a finger from his shoulder, down his arm to his elbow, then circled there and backtracked.

"Let me drive. I can do it."

"What? Right now?"

"Sure," she said. "I'm good."

Nathan thought a second, then shook his head. He smiled and gave her a look that approached affection. He seemed to be in a better mood now, and that relieved her. She nestled a little closer.

"You know, there's a lot of trust involved in that. I don't know if I trust you that much." He used his joking voice, which is what he used about three fourths of the time. Nathan had a hard time being serious about anything. It seemed like a real strain for him. Gail had learned to take this in stride, along with the rest of his character defects.

Nathan seemed pleased with what he'd said, so he said it again. "You know, you drive a man's car, there's a lot of trust involved."

"My dad's giving me a car soon. That means I won't have to get my mom to drive me to work anymore, and you won't have to drive me home. We can see each other anytime we want."

Nathan winced, then pointed to his pack of cigarettes on the dash. "Light one for me, okay?"

She punched in the cigarette lighter, took one of the cigarettes and let it droop from her lips.

"What kind of car?"

"A Studebaker."

He laughed. "A what?"

Gail lit his cigarette and handed it to him. Nathan examined the filter with a look of distaste. "You been nigger-lipping this one."

She didn't say anything, but just stared out the side window. All Nathan ever did was put down other people. Maybe that's what iconoclastic meant. She thought about the gun on her insole, the one thing permanent between her and Nathan. Until the week before, she'd suspected more. She'd kept that home pregnancy test kit at the bottom of her closet, and she'd just read the directions over and over, frantic about how late she was.

She'd wasted her money. She'd found out without the kit. A week late, but she wasn't pregnant. At first, she just cried on her bed, trembling because she wasn't sure why she was crying, had no idea what she felt.

She turned back to Nathan. That phantom baby and Nathan seemed almost inseparable to her. They were one and the same.

Nathan swung onto the bridge of Twyckenham over the St. Joseph River. Sometimes, Gail thought her town was gorgeous. The bridge was lined with evenly-spaced stone pillars, like mini–Washington Monuments, and between them and below, the St. Joe glittered, and the leafless trees arched over the river, a brocade of ice visible in their branches. Gail didn't think South Bend was a shit hole at all.

"Sometimes you disgust me," she told him. "Sometimes you make me ill."

Nathan gripped the steering wheel. "Maybe I'll take you out for a drive sometime," he said as though they'd been talking about cars all along, and nothing else. "I'm a good teacher. I've got a lot of patience. We could go out in the country and tool around, maybe have a picnic like normal people."

He looked over like he had made some incredible offer. For the first time, she noticed some uncertainty.

"What would you do if I was pregnant?" she said.

Nathan recoiled.

"I'm not," she added, "but I thought I was. I just thought you should know that."

Gail knew that Nathan wasn't much of a liar, and so he didn't bother answering difficult questions. He just glanced at her from the shadows, and a streak from a street lamp flashed across his eyes as the car made its way over the bridge.

To our surprise, the lemon reconstituted itself, she thought again.

A lemon was the name of a worthless car. She imagined a car that repaired itself as it drove, that never needed gas, that used the air itself as fuel as it glided along.

TWELVE

L ois was having more trouble than usual finding a worthwhile sale. She couldn't explain it, but *actively* searching for a good garage sale had no effect on the garage-sale gods. One had to search sideways, to empty oneself of thoughts of bargains and treasures. One had to become a bodhisattva of the secondhand, a Zen master, a decoder of koans tacked up on telephone poles.

Still, enlightenment eluded Lois. She blamed it on the dreary weather and the season. The clouds hung low and murky. The grass had turned brown and sharp-looking, and the fields around South Bend surprised Lois with their nakedness. On the outskirts of town, farm houses stood on the flat land, protected only by small stands of trees for windbreaks. Driving past a farm was a mournful experience.

She was about to call it a day when she spotted a house, a little bungalow with a concrete stoop and bright green shutters. Around it lay strewn an assortment of furniture. Most of it looked worth ignoring: cheap wicker chairs, a couple of glossy coffee tables with glass tops, a ratty couch with tears in the cushions. Still, something seemed alluring about this sale, perhaps the dozen or so thriving houseplants scattered about the lawn, which was itself an immaculately trimmed carpet of brown grass. Lois walked among these plants, marveling at how healthy they were. One rubber plant sat in a giant orange planter and reached higher than Lois could with her arms stretched. The people who were giving this garage sale obviously had a talent for making living things thrive, even though they had no eye at all for home furnishings.

She toyed with the idea of buying a fern or two, though that seemed like a dastardly fate for a houseplant. Lois hadn't kept a houseplant for almost twenty years. No matter how much she cared for them, they always withered and died. She looked for a price tag, but couldn't spot one. In fact, she hadn't even seen the people who were giving the garage sale.

"May I help you?" someone said from behind her.

A young woman wearing a Notre Dame windbreaker over a yellow jumpsuit stood on the stoop. She held a toddler in one arm, balanced on her hip.

"No, I'm just looking," Lois said, and smiled.

The woman didn't smile back. She put the child down and told him to go inside.

"You're a plant lover," Lois said to the woman, whose face didn't soften at all. "They're gorgeous. You must put a lot of care into them."

"Yes," the woman said slowly. "I guess so." Then she turned toward the house and called, "Charlie."

Lois kept browsing, but she felt uncomfortable. She was sure the woman watched every move she made. Was the woman afraid she'd steal something? Lois picked up some ivy in a hanging basket and held the plant at arm's length, admiring it in full view so the woman wouldn't suspect her of anything.

"Hey," she heard someone say.

She turned around and saw a man in a workshirt and jeans beside the woman. "May I help you?" he said, just like his wife. The way he said it, it sounded like, What the *hell* are you doing?

Lois looked at the couple like they were crazy and they looked back at her the same way.

"I'm just looking around," she said. "Are you not ready for customers?" Sometimes people didn't like you showing up early at a garage sale, and even included in their ads, "No early bird sales." But it wasn't early. It was the middle of the afternoon.

"We're not selling anything," the man said.

"We're laying down carpet," the woman said.

Lois put the ivy back on the end table she'd found it on, and started backing up. "How embarrassing," she said, and laughed. "Well, do you want to sell anything?"

She'd meant it as a joke, but they didn't seem to see anything funny. The couple just scrutinized her until she returned to her car. After she started the engine, their little boy appeared between their legs, and the three of them regarded her like hardened pioneers who'd barely beaten back a savage attack on the open plain.

L ois felt in need of a garage sale, but it was getting late. So she headed for a sure thing: the Thieves' Market, a flea market inside a building the size and shape of an airplane hangar. The building had stalls and tables crammed with antiques and manned by dealers who sat alertly, sizing you up like army recruiters.

The place didn't seem as crowded as usual today. The dealers, arms folded, chatted with one another at the boundaries of their stalls. The few customers seemed entranced, under some zombie spell, picking up decanters and old magazines, and holding them blankly before receiving the hypnotic command to replace them again. The market had the sound quality of a huge gymnasium. A low murmur of chatter bounced off the walls, and the sound of women's heels clicking on the concrete floor punctured the quiet. The place smelled like buttered popcorn.

She came to a stall where an elderly woman sat at a card table with unsteady legs, a kerosene heater aimed toward her. The woman ate peanuts from a brown bag and tossed the shells on the floor. She looked like a peanut herself, her face long and thin, and sort of caved in around the cheeks. What made Lois take notice was the assortment of junk on the table. Real junk. Absolutely worthless. A rusty doorknob, a box of metal slugs, an assortment of chipped and dirty chopsticks. And a liquor box filled with clumps of red dirt sat beside the table.

"What's that?" Lois said to the woman.

The woman glanced at the box beside her like she'd never seen it before. "I believe that's red dirt," she said. "Must be from down south. Dirt don't grow that color round these parts. But you'll have to ask George yourself, if you're interested. I believe he just stepped aside for a cup of coffee. He'll be back any second now. He never stays away long from here. George watches this place like a hawk. You know, that's what they call the wind off of Lake Michigan. You know that, don't you?"

"George?" Lois said.

The woman laughed and said, "Gracious no, the Hawk!" She said it like she had great respect for this wind.

Lois started ferreting through a box of junk on the floor. The box brimmed with trinkets and magazines. She stood up after a moment with five matchbooks in her hand.

"Look what I found," she said, holding the matchbooks in her palm as if they were diamonds.

"They're a quarter each," the woman told her.

The matchbooks looked like they were from the thirties and forties, and each one advertised a restaurant. One matchbook showed two clinking champagne glasses surrounded by cacti. It read: Eddie's Lodge Dine-Dance, Rosemead, California. On the flipside, a gunslinger had his six-shooters blazing above the caption Eddie's Lodge, More Western Than the West.

Another matchbook was from Johnny Paul's Magic Lounge in Cicero, Illinois. Magic with Laffs! Then there was Arthur's Moulin Rouge, La Vie Parisienne. And the Log Tavern in Stone Mountain, Georgia. The other was from Ettorre's Cafe in Philadelphia. Lois opened the cover. The matches were all there and some writing, too:

WHY WORRY!

There are only two things to worry about. Either you are well or you are sick. If you are well then there is nothing to worry about. But if you are sick, there are two things to worry about. Either you will get well or you will die. If you get well there is nothing to worry about. If you die there are only two things to worry about. Either you will go to heaven or hell. If you go to heaven there is nothing to worry about, but if you go to hell you'll be so damn busy shaking hands with friends, you won't have time to worry.

Lois took a match from Ettore's Cafe matchbook. The head of the matches had faded to a pale salmon color. She struck it, and it flared and caught fire, and filled the space around her with the smell of sulfur. "It works!" she told the old woman, as though she'd performed a miracle.

The woman smiled back like she thought a miracle *had* been performed. "Those are pretty long-lasting matches there," she said. "Longer than average. Here, let me try."

Lois handed her the matches from Eddie's Lodge, and the woman pried open the front cover. "George would kill me for this," she said, and she struck a match. It fired up like it had been made yesterday.

"You want to try another?" the woman said to Lois. She handed her the matchbook from Johnny Paul's Magic Lounge. The inside showed a laughing face and the words It's Fun To Be Fooled. The match heads were not red, but blue. She struck a match across the front. The head fell off. She took another and held it closer to the tip. This time, it flared and caught fire.

"Those are old matches," said the woman. "Almost old as me. I like seeing old things that still work, don't you?" and she laughed.

"Me too," Lois said, and returned the matches to the box.

"Here, have yourself a peanut," the woman said, holding out the bag to Lois. Lois grabbed a handful and thanked the woman. "Unshelled and unsalted," the woman said. "In their natural state. The best kind."

Lois knelt on the floor by some huge machine that looked like a cross between an iron lung and a vacuum cleaner. "What's this?" she said, looking up from the machine.

"I believe that's George's dictator," said the woman. "He planned to tell his life on it." The woman paused and got a thoughtful look. "You know, that machine locked up on him. He almost had it all down, too." She pointed and said, "His story's still in there somewhere, waiting to be listened. That's the problem with objects. You take this kerosene heater. About the only thing it's good for now is being a fire hazard. But I can't do without it. A body can't live without heat, even if it's only half heat. Don't want to wind up like old Evangeline Studebaker. She lived so long nobody knew she was alive, longer than me even. In one of those big old houses on Washington, you know the ones. It's all boarded up now. Such a rich old lady. You know, right around the corner from that church, St. Paul's Methodist, the Studebaker Church."

The woman pointed as though the church stood right around the corner from the Thieves' Market. "Clem Studebaker had that church built, and there's a stained glass picture of him in one of the windows. My husband and I used to go there back when we first married. Evangeline used to ride right around the corner of the church in her electric motorcar with a rod that you steered with. Oh, she was a good woman. And you know what killed her? She didn't pay her gas bill. The entire mansion was covered floor to ceiling with antiques and heirlooms. They had to cut a hole through them just to reach her body."

The woman gave Lois a big nod and said, "She was the very last of the South Bend Studebakers. My husband worked at Studebaker for seventeen years. And you know, one day he just quit. He never told me why. That popped into my head a couple of days ago, and I thought to myself, I wonder why he quit."

"My dad worked for Studebaker," Lois said. She was going to add more, but what could she say?

"Just about everybody worked for Studie's," the woman said, shaking her head.

"You don't know why he quit?" Lois said

"I don't know why. He just kept getting more and more peculiar until finally I left. That was twenty years ago. I was sixty-three. I just told him, 'I'm going to die soon and I want some time to myself.' He said, 'What do you want to leave me for? How you going to get by?' I didn't give it a thought. I knew I'd manage. But I don't know why he quit Studebaker. He hated to see a man drinking. He come home one night from a company dinner and he was disgusted. He saw a man get so drunk he just crawled on top of a table and then down under it. I never liked to see a man drink neither, but that's no reason to quit a good job.

"We never talked. I was married in 1938 and those first few years he was always telling me to be quiet and go to sleep. I said, 'When you're lying down is the only time I can catch you.'"

Then the woman's expression brightened. "They're holding a big auction of Evangeline's worldly goods come spring. You like auctions?"

The woman picked up a brick that lay on top of a stack of fliers, and handed Lois one of the sheets of green paper. The woman pointed to the paper and said, "They're advertising way in advance, because of how special this auction is going to be. It's going to be a one of a kind, once in a lifetime." As Lois read the piece of paper, the woman looked on, and started picking at something caught between two of her front teeth.

The flier read:

A Once in a Lifetime AUCTION by Richardson
Saturday, April 3, 1992, 10:00 a.m.
Rain or Shine
Personal Property from the Estate of

EVANGELINE STUDEBAKER OLIVER
Jurck Polanski, Executor
819 Washington, South Bend, Indiana

Unique Collection of Quality Merchandise — some old, some very old, some that needs to be seen to be believed — something for everyone!

1931 Studebaker President Roadster
Queen Anne Dining Room — 6 Chairs
Hand-carved mahogany sideboard
Buffet with Mirror Back Splash
Victorian Loveseat
Glass Basket
Wood frame, loose cushion sofa
Long Mahogany Coffee Table
Wooden Chair, Very old, Unique
Edison Victrola
Baby Grand Piano
Beaded Dresses from 1920's.
Asst. Occasional Chairs and Rockers
Old Wicker Furniture
Ermine Cape, Stone Marten Stole
Asst. Furs
Old Coins
Diamond Watch
Diamond Diadem

Asst. Jewelry
Old Ladies Hats
Peacock Feathers
Old Magazines
Small Oak basket — Settee
2 Oak Rolltop Desks
Asst. Steamer Trunks
Stemware
Asst. Persian Rugs
Asst. Nice China —
Hotpoint 40″ Range
Whirlpool H/D Washer
Oriental Figurines
Asst. old pictures
old frames
old bedroom suite
poster bed
maple Boston rocker
old upright radio

Numerous other items
Merchandise may be seen one hour before sale.
Sale Conducted by
RICHARDSON AUCTION COMPANY
Elkhart, Indiana
Auctioneer: T. Richardson,
Indiana License No. 47

"Maybe I'll see you there, God willing," the woman told Lois.
"Maybe," Lois said and started flipping through some 45 records.

The thought of stepping onto Studebaker property, enemy territory, didn't thrill her. Still, he figured she'd go, just like most of South Bend, purely out of curiosity.

The woman pointed to the 45s and said, "I used to have an instrument. A guitar. I used to sit on my front porch and sing. Oh, I had a lovely voice," and then she started croaking out, "Oh she wore a tulip, a big yellow tulip, and I wore a red red rose."

Lois clapped.

"I love that song," the woman said. "I love any song that's got to do with flowers."

Lois brushed her hair out of her eyes and flipped through the records. Here was one on the Decca label by Frankie Lee and The Leepers, called, "Hey, Whatchou Lookin' At? (The Albino Song)." She flipped through ten more records of bands she'd never heard of: The Restless Folk, Tod Kubek and his Merry Shriners, the Purple Pentagon, Sister Lucy Bell and Fisher (singing their smash hit: "Do Me Like a Tootsie Roll Pop"). Finally, she spotted one that she'd heard of before: The Royal Guardsmen singing "Snoopy and the Red Baron."

Lois looked up to take a breather. Sorting through these records sickened her. The past leaked off them like some rusty contagion, and she felt like washing her hands just to get rid of the feeling.

"There are some old ones in there, I suspect," the woman said. "My husband never liked old things. He just saw remembering as a waste of time. To me, it's the spice of life."

"Me, too," Lois said.

Lois cracked a peanut shell with her teeth and the woman reached out like she was trying to stop her from hurting herself. "Here now," she said. "You can't crack a peanut like that. This is how you do it." She took a peanut shell between thumb and forefinger and squeezed. The shell burst open and a puff of peanut shell smoke came out. "Empty," the woman said, and laughed. "Well, nothing's perfect in this world. Specially not the world itself. But you get the idea."

Lois nodded and returned to the records.

As Lois sorted through them, the woman started telling her about a dream she'd had the night before. Lois didn't mind hearing about this woman's life, even her dreams. The woman was just lonely.

"In my dream I was walking down the middle of the street in my nightgown. A policeman came up to me and he started acting real sassy." Then she laughed and said, "It was the strangest dream."

Lois had stopped paying attention. For a second, she just stared at the record in her hands. Then she took it from the box and flipped it over. She felt kind of queasy seeing a record with her father's name on it. One of the songs was called "True Blue Lou." The other side was "Bye Bye Blackbird," and the singer was named Rudy Walters.

Just then, George returned. He wasn't at all what she'd expected, and he definitely wasn't the Peanut Lady's son – maybe her grandson. He couldn't have been older than seventeen. His mouth looked small and defenseless against his fat cheeks, high forehead, and slightly infected-looking chin. The redness of his chin made him look like someone who'd recently shaven after going bearded for many years. He had a cup of coffee in his hand, and blew steam from the top of his cup and watched Lois. The Peanut Lady folded her hands on the card table and moved her legs closer to the kerosene heater.

"You wanting to buy?" George said. "Or you just going to look?"

Lois held up the record. "I think I'll take this," she said.

"George," said the Peanut Lady. "This woman's daddy worked for Studebaker."

George didn't seem to think much of that. He blew on his cup of coffee, and took a sip, watching Lois over the rim of the cup as though she might snatch something and run away.

"That record's two dollars," said George.

Lois wasn't fazed, even if it was an outrageous price. She took out two quarters and said, "I can give you fifty cents."

"And I can give you back your lousy fifty cents," the boy said with an ugly look. "The record's two dollars."

"You think someone's going to pay you two dollars for that record?" Lois said.

"I don't care," he said, his back turned. "I don't let no one take advantage of me."

A junkman who was loathe to bargain. Obviously, the boy had chosen the wrong line of work. The purpose of going garage sale-ing and junk-dealing was getting a bargain. And what value could George the Junkseller have seen in an old 45 with her father's name on it? None.

The boy was jacking up the price out of pure meanness.

"I don't really want it," she said and started to put the record back.

The Peanut Lady looked from her to George. "Sometimes I don't know what gets into you," she said. "Didn't I tell you her daddy worked for Studebaker? Why, she's family! As they say, you don't get to choose your family, just your friends. That's not all bad. Here, darling, you take that record. You can say it's a present from Dottie Baldwin."

George turned to the old woman, outraged. Then he glared at Lois.

Lois accepted the gift from the woman and thanked her, but she wanted to buy something, too. To make up for getting George angry.

Lois asked how much the Dictaphone was, careful to speak only to the Peanut Lady, not including George in the bargain. Not that she wanted a Dictaphone machine, but she wanted it more than a box of red clay, some dirty old chopsticks, and packs of matches.

The Peanut Lady glanced up at George and said, "Name a price, George, but say it soft and kind."

George said it soft. He mumbled into his coffee.

"George says twenty dollars," the woman said to Lois.

Lois wanted more than anything to bargain. Twenty dollars for a locked-up Dictaphone machine? It wasn't worth the price of scrap.

Lois restrained herself, but the woman saw what she was thinking. She said, "George says twenty dollars, but I say ten."

"Hey!" George said.

"No, that's all right," Lois said. "Twenty's fine."

The old woman leaned toward Lois confidentially and whispered, "My old partner, Sam McKay, had a heart pacer. He was training George to take over for him, but Sam died before the boy could learn much. Everyone I know does a lot of things to get by. I suspect George has got something else going, too. I give him food when I see him. Yesterday, I cooked up a chicken breast, and I split it, and made a sandwich for him. He was working outside, so I handed it to him through the window, and he said, 'I really do appreciate that.'" She laughed and shook her head like that was the funniest thing she'd ever said. "I really do appreciate that," she repeated, and for some reason, that struck Lois as pretty funny, and she started laughing, too.

Lois placed the gruesome-looking machine on the seat beside her in the car. On the drive home, she held the microphone, which looked like a CB attachment, and pressed the record button. The machine made a small whirring noise, clicked once, and went dead.

Lois put the mike next to her mouth and said, "Folks, you're about to hear the near-historic and semi-authorized account of Lois Kulwicki, her trials and travails, her Dickensian childhood, spent in fetters in a sweatshop where she sewed bumpers onto recreational vehicles, and how, through perseverance and industry, she was able to break out of her bonds to become the helmswoman of the largest garage sale corporation in America."

She never really seemed to find anything of much value, just broken Dictaphones, plastic dinnerware, and nude dolls. And a record with her father's name on it. Was that crazy or what?

A couple of weeks earlier, she'd bought a mug from a man at a garage sale. The mug had the name Nancy stenciled across it. Lois didn't know anyone named Nancy, but she'd felt compelled to buy this Nancy mug. Not because of its beauty. The cup, drab and stark, didn't make you want to know anyone named Nancy. It didn't even seem meant for other people to see. This mug made no apologies for its lack of looks. This mug existed only for Nancy. The name was a warning: No one else better touch this mug. The liquid inside will budge for no one else. If your name isn't Nancy or Nan, your lips will freeze on the rim, your trespassing insides will boil.

Still, she paid the man a quarter for the cup. Of course, the man asked if her name was Nancy, and she nodded.

"I've got a married daughter named Nancy," the man went on. "Lives in Kokomo with her husband, Jack. You're not married to a Jack, too, are you?"

Lois shook her head.

"That's good," said the man, "because everything they buy has got to be new. They don't want any of this old junk lying around the house, so I'm selling it lock, stock, and coffee cup."

The two of them had chatted for half an hour, Lois pretending to be a different Nancy, but a Nancy all the same, close enough to be this man's stepdaughter.

Maybe Lois wasn't after bargains. Maybe that was the least of it. If she wasn't after deals, what then? Well, some people watch soap operas. Others collect old matchbooks. Willy accumulated old Studebakers. They were his friends. They were his children. They were his family. They were all the same, none of them worked, but maybe someday, and that's what made them special. And that's why Lois went garage sale-ing, that feeling of maybe someday, of finding something worth collecting, something that didn't work now and might never work until doomsday, but something she could care about and fret over and make valuable simply by giving it her undivided devotion. Salt shakers. Avon bottles. Comic books. Cookbooks. Sheet music. Porcelain dolls. Something that needed her.

For the fifteenth time, Lois listened to both sides of the record. She sat on the living-room couch, the room darkened except for a standing lamp by the stereo. She had her feet up on the couch, her shoes off. A stranger might have thought she was relaxing there in the half dark, after a long day at work, celebrating with a drink in hand and her favorite music. But she wasn't relaxing and this wasn't her favorite music. She concentrated, trying to decipher it, to see if it had anything to do with her life.

The man on the record had a deep voice like Burl Ives or Mitch Miller, though it often cracked and skipped and popped in harmony with the countless scratches on the record. She remembered that voice. Or thought she did. Maybe her mind was playing tricks. She'd been under a lot of strain lately. Still, there was no disputing that voice, or that name: Rudy Walters.

She wished someone, at least, were here with her, someone who could tell her it didn't mean a thing. Not Henry. Henry didn't seem like much of a confidant. Anyway, he'd already gone to sleep, though it was only six-thirty. And definitely not Meg. Meg, so studious at eleven, was in her room doing a book report for extra credit. She would have tried to understand, but she couldn't have. Maybe Gail, who'd be home from work any minute now. But with Gail, asking for any kind of understanding was risky.

Lois drank and stared at the spinning label until she felt dizzy. The man kept singing, sounding sadder and sadder with every turn.

Maybe someday in Heaven above
There's a reward for that kind of love
No one could blame her
Everyone named her
True . . . Blue . . . Lou

That was her daddy's kind of song, sentimental and meant to be
crooned. She wished she'd heard him sing it once. She didn't remember either "Bye Bye Blackbird" or "True Blue Lou" (a song she'd
never even heard before) in her daddy's repertoire, but that didn't
mean anything.

"Be dead," she told the record as it spun. This time, as soon as the
song ended, she was going to take it into the kitchen and throw it in the
trash.

The song ended. She took the record off the turntable between her
hands, her thumbs pressing the label. She'd never heard of the record
company before, Parkersburg Records. It wasn't one of the big ones.

She wanted to bend the record until it broke in two, but she didn't.
She turned it over, cued the needle, and listened to the fatherlike
voice break into "Bye Bye Blackbird" for the sixteenth time.

She couldn't throw it away. She knew she'd play it over and over until the voice called her by name, soothed her, begged her forgiveness,
said, Lois, find me. I've missed you all these years.

The front door opened. She abruptly lifted the needle from the record, as though she was doing something wrong.

Gail stood there in a down jacket, with white wool mittens, a wool
cap and scarf. She didn't seem to notice Lois sitting there, and for a
second, Lois was able to watch unobserved as Gail removed her
wraps. To Lois, Gail looked like a lanky teenage boy.

Gail slowly pulled off her mittens and put them in her pockets. She
stopped and looked at the door as though waiting for someone to come
in, or deciding to go back out again. Then she started to unwrap her
scarf. Again, as slow as someone could possibly unwrap a scarf, by
centimeters, as though removing a bandage. She seemed deep in
thought, weighted down by it, *too* much so, Lois thought, for such a
young girl.

Slowly, Gail started to turn. She seemed to sense now that she was being watched. Then she saw Lois. She swung the scarf around, grabbed her knit hat, and shook her short hair loose.

"Mom, what are you doing?"

"Just sitting here." Lois patted a spot beside her. "Come sit with me."

"Why?"

"Do I need a reason?"

Gail removed her jacket, opened the hall closet, and threw it inside. Then she closed the door. Lois looked up at the ceiling, pretended not to notice.

Gail strode over to the couch and sat down, though she didn't lean back. She sat on her hands and moved her eyes from side to side, like she thought she was being observed by hundreds, thousands, a multitude of people judging her every move. She wore a knowing little smile. Her eyes narrowed.

"Okay, I'm sitting," she said.

Lois wanted to ignore that tone, to get past it. "How was work?"

The question seemed to take her by surprise, though Lois couldn't imagine why. It was innocent enough. Gail didn't answer right away. Instead, she leaned back in the couch, almost involuntarily, and touched her lip with her forefinger.

"I think I just quit."

"You think?"

"Yeah. I don't want to talk about it," but Lois could see she did.

"Are you sure?"

"Positive."

"If you change your mind . . ."

"I won't. You wouldn't understand anyway."

"Don't be so sure. I'd like to try." Lois took her daughter's hand, but Gail pulled away and held it stiffly by her side. Gail stared at her own hand as though disgusted. Obviously, there was something really wrong.

Gail sat there, looking down at her lap, saying nothing. Lois could see she was being given a chance. She knew that Gail wanted to talk to her, wanted Lois to understand, or she wouldn't still be sitting there. Lois knew that she had to say something, had to find the exact password into her daughter's world. If she said the wrong thing, used the wrong tone of voice, she'd miss her chance, and it might not come again for years.

"I've been thinking about starting a new tradition," Lois said.

Gail gave her a look.

"Ever since we left the old house, I've been carrying around a locket with me. The day the divorce became final I hung it around my neck, and every once in a while I take it out and look at it. I don't really know why. It doesn't have any incredible importance, but now it's kind of a tradition with me to carry it around, to never go anywhere without it."

She slipped the locket off her neck and unclasped it. Gail took it and studied the photographs of the little boy and girl inside.

"Who are they?" she asked, handing it back.

"Beats me," Lois said. "I prefer not knowing. Sometimes I fall asleep imagining who they might have been."

Lois looked at Gail. "That's silly, right?"

Gail looked at her. "I don't know."

"Me neither," Lois said. "We should have something that we do together each week." She thought a second. "Maybe listen to music. Like every Tuesday."

Gail ducked her head and touched her earlobe. She had a knowing little smile. "Mother," she said.

"Wait," Lois said, putting out her hand and patting her daughter's leg. "I know what you're going to say. You don't have to say it. I'm psychic, you know. You're going to say, Mother, we don't have the same taste in music at all. It won't last a minute. I'll want to listen to Megadeth, and you'll be putting on Tony Bennett. Which isn't true, by the way. I don't like Tony Bennett. I just think he's got a good voice, and I like his Christmas album. I know that's what you're thinking, isn't it?"

Gail smiled. "Almost," she said. "But not Tony Bennett. I would have said Sonny and Cher."

"That's cruel, Gail," Lois said. She sat back and thought. "Okay, maybe it won't work. It was just an idea. It doesn't have to be music."

Gail nodded solemnly, and Lois could see that her daughter wanted to start that new tradition, too. It didn't have to be music. It could be anything.

Lois took the record she'd been listening to and put it back on the turntable. She didn't know why exactly, but she wanted her daughter to hear it, though she didn't have the strength to explain right now. And maybe she never would. Gail didn't say anything, and didn't make a move. She still stared at her hand. For a while, they sat together and listened to Rudy Walters sing his rendition of "Bye Bye Blackbird."

Lois lost herself in it. She didn't know what she thought about it. She hardly knew what to think anymore. She heard Gail laughing in quick breaths through her nose, like she was trying to hide it. Lois closed her eyes, feeling like a failure. She took a deep breath and made a move to lift the tone arm. Then she felt Gail's head on her shoulder. She looked over. It wasn't laughter. Gail was crying.

"What's wrong, honey?" Lois stroked her daughter's hair.

"Don't look at me," Gail mumbled into Lois's shoulder. "Please."

Lois put her arm around Gail. She didn't understand why Gail was so sad. God knows, there were a million good reasons, but maybe she didn't need to understand. Maybe it was just enough to be allowed into that sadness, to have found the password. Whatever Gail wanted. It had been a long time since Lois had felt her daughter's tears. Maybe understanding and acceptance had nothing to do with each other.

She looked away from her daughter but kept her arm in place.

Part III

The Last
Studebaker

In our sleep, pain that cannot forget falls drop by drop upon the heart and in our own despair, against our will, comes wisdom through the awful grace of the gods.

—AESCHYLUS

THIRTEEN

Recently, a money-making idea had occurred to Lois. Antiques and collectibles, she knew, were cheaper in Indiana than just about anywhere else in the country. Partly, this had to do with economics. Indiana couldn't claim to be one of the nation's financial flashpoints and wasn't the trendsetting capital of the world either.

While Michiana wasn't the oldest settled part of the country, it still had some years on much of the nation. In 1820, Pierre Navarre had settled along the St. Joseph River, and was followed soon after by other fur traders. Massachusetts was older, but you couldn't find antiques there at a good price. That's because people *knew* about Massachusetts. They didn't know about Michiana. You could still find treasures around South Bend for next to nothing. Not so in New England, where Lois imagined everyone knew the value and history of every stray trinket and button.

Lois planned to buy antiques in Indiana and take them to one of the coasts for a profit. But not to New England. She figured they'd probably frown on antiques that weren't their own. No, she'd load up a U-Haul and take her possessions, wagon-train style, out through the plains, the desert, and over the mountains, to California. California seemed like the right place to sell antiques. There had to be people out there who wanted something old and rusted in their lives, something that didn't work anymore, or something that wasn't efficient, that didn't make sense in this day and age. For these people, she'd bring butter churns, wheelbarrows, potbellied stoves, and hand-crank Victrolas.

She'd had this plan for a month, and had thought she'd have her first load of antiques by now, but she didn't. All the great garage sales in South Bend had vanished. It almost seemed like a concerted effort, a conspiracy, to keep Lois away from personal satisfaction.

The situation reminded her of when she was little and her Uncle

Chick and her father had gone deer hunting. All summer and into the fall, they'd spot dozens of deer everywhere, but then, the day before deer season opened, the deer would suddenly go into hiding as though they knew. Neither of them had ever succeeded in bagging a deer. The closest they ever got was when Chick shot a tree branch that resembled a pair of antlers.

Of course, the lack of garage sales and good auctions and flea markets could be explained better than the collective ESP of deer. Like deer, garage sales have their season, too. Spring and summer were best, but in the fall, the garage sale column in the *Tribune* grew shorter and shorter every weekend. As much as Lois wanted to get her scheme under way, she knew she might have to wait until spring to strike it rich.

Her money from the divorce settlement was running out. Her plan to buy and sell antiques had started slow, and she hadn't even figured out how to implement the plan. Second, Henry was still living in her garage, though that wasn't much of a problem to her. She'd started getting used to his presence, even relying on him in some ways. For one thing, rent was something she no longer worried about. Henry waived it, all except for the Real Estate Guy's fifty dollars per month commission, which he offered to pay as well. Lois refused, not wanting to be indebted.

In most ways, he was the perfect housemate: unobtrusive, even invisible most of the time. But when something needed to be done, he'd burrow out of his little nest in the garage and set to work. He shoveled the driveway and the walks. He made small repairs on the house. Of course, he worked slowly, and sometimes ineffectively, since his right hand was utterly useless. Sometimes he'd stop in the middle of shoveling snow and stare off, or drop his wrench as he tightened a lug nut, as though something had jolted him. Then he'd retreat to the garage, and maybe not emerge for hours or a day, after which he'd return to his task as though nothing had happened.

He helped with the shopping too. He said he wanted to lend a hand, so he paid for half of the grocery bill. When Henry had shown up on their doorstep in December, he'd been more than a little reluctant to get in Lois's car. But by January, he seemed eager to join her on her expeditions. They never talked in the car. She drove and Henry looked out the window. "I do my best thinking when I'm looking out the window," he told her once, but didn't go into further detail. Mostly, they just went to Martin's, but sometimes they sidetracked for something special. Once, they went to Macri's for pastry. Something about Macri's seemed to make him uncomfortable, so from then on Lois went to Dainty Maid downtown when she wanted pastry. Dainty Maid often carried poppy *kolach*, a Hungarian pastry that had been a favorite of her father's, or nut *kolach*, which her mother preferred. Her mother had hated getting poppy seeds between her teeth. Lois also always picked up a dozen *kiefles* for the girls.

Henry sometimes cooked, though Lois tried to discourage him. He tended to burn things, had a hard time following recipes, and generally drove her crazy asking permission to use certain ingredients. Especially eggs. He seemed to have a phobia about eggs. No matter how many eggs she had, he'd say, "Can I use these? Do you have enough?"

At first Henry ate his meals in the garage. But Lois was sick of eating her meals alone. So, she made a new rule: Everyone had to eat their meals together. She no longer allowed Gail to eat in her room or let Meg dine in front of the TV. Gail, who didn't appreciate Henry's presence, suffered through this arrangement. Still, she didn't make a fuss. She'd been on her best behavior recently. She seemed to be trying extra hard to get along with Lois, who tried extra hard right back. They were all trying hard, except for Meg. Meg didn't have a problem with their makeshift family. She'd accepted Henry from the moment he'd come through the door. After all, she was the one who let him in.

Only two things about Henry troubled Lois. She wished he was more talkative. He was a great listener, but he never seemed to have anything to say, no real opinions or convictions. If someone had asked him what the most meaningful event of the previous year had been, Henry would have said, Why are you asking *me?*

Also, sometimes he was a little too helpful. If she refused his help, he'd get a look like he'd offended her horribly. This obsessive helpfulness disconcerted her. She was more comfortable with the opposite of helpfulness, namely Willy. Sometimes she longed to hear Willy say, Can't you see I'm busy? or When I get around to it.

In any event, Lois's new life, while not quite what she might have dreamed of as a girl, was tolerable. What might have been an intolerable situation to some (an unexpected housemate, money running out, no future) wasn't intolerable to Lois. Lois had a high tolerance threshold. She was the kind of person whom you could throw almost anything at, and she'd catch it, fashion it to fit, and make it a part of herself.

With one exception. The record. She couldn't throw it away, but she didn't ever want to hear it again. That voice just presented too many problems. It bothered her how much she still cared if her father was alive. Not that she wouldn't care, but for so long she'd assumed he was dead, which he might well be. This record didn't prove anything. It was old, though how old Lois couldn't say for sure.

One day, Lois took up pen and paper and wrote a letter to the address on the record label. Her first version began:

> Dear Sir or Madam,
>
> I'm looking for my father. Possibly, you can help me.

She tore it up and started over.

> I found a record of yours and noticed with surprise that the name on the label was identical to that of my father.

Finally, she settled on:

> I'd appreciate any information you could give me on a recording artist of yours, Rudy Walters. His whereabouts, etc. There's a possibility we're related, and I'd like to know for sure.
>
> Sincerely,
> Lois Walters Kulwicki

After sending the letter Lois was able to put it out of her mind. As the weeks went by without a reply, she figured Parkersburg Records must have gone out of business years ago, that her letter now languished in some dead-letter bin. One night she awoke thinking that maybe she'd forgotten to put a return address on the envelope. She put on her bathrobe, went to the kitchen, and wrote the letter over again, exactly the way she'd written it the first time. In the morning, she mailed it. *Then* she was able to forget about it.

Over the winter months, Lois started selling antiques at the farmer's market, which was open year-round and housed in two red barracks-like structures. The market, floored with concrete, had ceilings about twenty feet high withy fluorescent lamps and ceiling fans. Vegetable and fruit stalls lined the place, people sold handmade leather and silver goods, meat, baked goods, fresh eggs; there was even a diner with a long curving counter where people packed in for breakfast on market mornings. Often, Lois did more buying than selling. She purchased all her meat there and apples and more poppy *kolach*. A Hungarian man sold *palacsintas* a kind of crepe filled with preserves or whatever else tasted good and was handy. She also bought jewelry: silver bangles and cuffs and necklaces with turquoise.

She didn't have much to sell, mostly knickknacks: John F. Kennedy plates, a cast-iron piggy bank from the turn of the century, a glass from the 1964 world's fair. She hadn't picked up the glass at the fair, but twenty-five years later at a garage sale. The glass had a red and blue picture of the Unisphere on front, and a description on back:

> The Unisphere is a huge global representation of the world in stainless steel. This symbol was presented to the fair and New York City by the United States Steel Corp. It will stand as a permanent fixture in Flushing Meadow Park for generations to come.

When she bought the glass, she thought she could handle it, but the Unisphere depressed her, and now she only wanted to get rid of it.

The most valuable items she had for sale were pieces of her grandmother's golf-leaf china. She refused to sell the china as a set. She sold each piece separately, partly because she could make more money that way, and partly because she hated having to sell the china. She felt like she'd betrayed her grandmother, since this set of china was the only thing she owned of hers. Lois had wanted to pass it along as an heirloom to her kids.

Unfortunately, the only things of hers that people wanted to buy were her personal belongings. After a month, not one item she'd purchased at a garage sale had sold. No one, it seemed, had any use for

JFK plates, a Unisphere glass, and a Dictaphone with a stranger's life story locked up in it.

When she sold an item, she wrote a receipt. For some reason, this was her favorite part of making a sale. Her receipts were elaborate: detailed accounts in duplicate describing each item and its history. She always kept one of the receipts for herself and handed the copy to the customer, except for one man who bought a piece of her grandmother's china every week. This man was a receipt-a-phobe. Maybe he was afraid to know how much he'd spent, because when Lois tried to give him his receipt, he'd let go with a little yelp, put out his hands protectively, and take a step backwards. Every week, Lois thought of this as a contest. She wanted to give the man his receipt. It was part of her job. So she took to throwing the slip of paper at him before he could react. The man stopped showing up, and too late, Lois realized that she'd made too much of a fuss about her receipts, that she'd started turning into someone as rigid as the man selling two-for-one shirts or the fish and chippy waitress.

One day a skinny middle-aged couple stopped at her table. The man had a sharp face, but a pleasant smile, and his wife had a round face and very light skin. Both of them had lively, intelligent eyes, and they scanned Lois's table like practiced bargain hunters.

"I have a table at the Thieves' Market," the woman said by way of introduction, and then introduced her husband and herself as Roger and Annie Black.

"Pleased to meet you," the man said with a smile and slight bow. He had a voice as thin as his build and slightly nasal. He also had a Scottish accent. His wife's voice was fuller, but also slightly high-pitched though definitely midwestern.

Meeting people was the best part of having a table. Of course, some people wanted to be left alone to browse, thought if you talked to them you were just coming-on to make them buy. To other people, Lois was public property. They wanted to talk and share their lives and wanted some of Lois's life in return. Sometimes she told them the truth about herself, other times she spiced it up, figuring no harm would be done. Other dealers acted especially friendly, like they were part of one giant extended family selling bits and pieces of other people's families.

Roger and Annie Black were no exception.

"Look, honey," Annie said, tugging at Roger's sleeve. "A bank."

They both wore permanent looks of surprise, like they couldn't believe their eyes or ears or senses of touch.

"I saw it," he said, smiling. "I already have that one."

"Oh you do," she said, then turned to Lois and said, "Roger collects old mechanical banks."

"Yes," he said, "you know the kind that throw pennies into the mouths of hungry beasts," and he twisted his long fingers into a pantomime of a penny being tossed into a pair of snapping jaws.

Lois nodded and said she'd look for those. "You can take twenty percent off anything you see," Lois said, giving them the standard dealers' discount.

"What nice jewelry," the woman said, grabbing Lois's wrist and turning it to look at the silver cuff with turquoise inlay.

"Did you make it yourself?" Annie asked.

Lois thought about this and shook her head, "No, but I live in Santa Fe. I'm just up here for a while."

"Oh really?" Roger said. "All that way?" He arched his eyebrows and smiled.

"How nice," Annie said. "Do you have ties to South Bend?"

"I sure do," Lois said. She opened her silver locket and pointed to the pictures of the little boy and girl. The couple bent close. "See them?" Lois said.

"Wait a second," Roger said. He reached in his pocket and withdrew a pair of glasses.

"They were my grandparents," she said. "Have you ever heard of the Studebakers?"

Both Roger and Annie stood up and said, "Why sure!"

Lois liked this couple, the way they stood so close together, the way they spoke in unison. Their affection for each other was obvious. They seemed like the kind of people Lois wanted to know. Lois didn't want to trick them. She knew she should just shut her mouth, but they seemed so interested in what she had to say. She hadn't planned on connecting herself with the Studebakers, but she'd been thinking about Evangeline Studebaker's auction before Roger and Annie showed up.

"They were my grandparents," she repeated. "This one's Evangeline and this one's . . . Willy."

"Really? That's fascinating," Roger said, and Annie nodded agreement. Lois hardly needed to continue. Merely mentioning the Studebakers had piqued their interest.

The couple conferred for a moment in the way that couples often do: a small huddle as though the rest of the world has stopped existing.

"Evangeline and Willy," Roger said. "That's an unusual pair of names."

"Willy Studebaker," Annie said. "I don't think I've ever heard of him."

"No, you wouldn't have," Lois said, suddenly feeling a warning tinge as though something might be wrong here.

Roger peered at Lois's locket, and said, "What do the initials SG stand for?"

"Studebaker – God."

"Studebaker dash God," Roger repeated, scratching a sideburn.

"The family motto," Lois said.

"You don't say?" Roger said. "Funny I've never heard it before."

"My branch," Lois said quickly.

"The Santa Fe branch?" Annie said.

Lois nodded.

"Roger here fancies himself a bit of an expert on Studebaker lore."

"A little bit," Roger said modestly, pinching his fingers together.

"Wait a second," Roger said, tilting his head in a thoughtful way. "Didn't Evangeline Studebaker pass away recently?"

Lois nodded and swept her hair back with her arm.

"I'm so sorry," Roger said.

"Yes," Annie said.

Lois tried to look bereaved.

"Is that why you're here?" Annie said.

"To settle the estate perhaps?" Roger offered.

Lois suddenly felt like she might break into tears. She put her hand on her forehead and said hurriedly, "No . . . she didn't leave me anything."

"Oh, now!" Roger said.

"What a shame," Annie said.

Again, the couple huddled.

"Maybe she's not in a position to return to Santa Fe," Annie said in a whisper and indicated Lois's table of knickknacks with a surreptitious flick of the hand. "Let's invite her to dinner."

"Okay, let's," said Roger with a broad smile and an equal share of enthusiasm in his voice.

Lois looked up to politely decline their invitation, but instead saw a horrifying sight: Willy and Alice standing arm-in-arm beside Roger and Annie. Willy's beard was trimmed, his hair neatly combed, and he wore a sheepskin coat Lois didn't recognize, probably a gift from Alice.

"I didn't know you were down here," he said, smiling.

Alice smiled at Lois, too, a fake kind of smile that meant *fish cut into chips*.

"Hi, Willy," Lois said.

As soon as she said his name, Roger and Annie turned as one on him.

Willy picked up one of Lois's plates and said, "Say, isn't this one of your grandmother's plates? What are you doing selling these?"

"Oh my," Roger said, his eyes wide. He and Annie exchanged looks and both covetously eyed the plate Willy held.

The tears arrived. Lois wanted to do anything at that moment other than cry. Both couples looked at her in surprise.

"There, there," Annie said, taking her hand and patting it.

Roger turned to Willy. "I think she feels bad about being disowned. You can hardly blame her."

Willy didn't reply. She hated crying in front of him and Alice. He probably thought she was crying over him. She wasn't. She was crying because Roger and Annie had taken pity on her and invited her to dinner. She was crying because she was wearing a lot of southwestern jewelry she couldn't afford.

"Be seeing you," Willy said awkwardly.

"Nice meeting you," Alice said in a cheery voice as though they *had* met, as though Lois wasn't in tears.

"There, there," Annie said after Willy and Alice had left.

FOURTEEN

Gail lay on her bed staring at the poster of Axl Rose plastered on the ceiling. She didn't even like Guns n' Roses anymore. She'd grown out of them. But she figured she'd keep Axl on the ceiling a little longer, looking down on her like her guardian angel. At least until she figured out who to replace him with.

Lately, Gail and her mom had been getting along better, but sometimes all Gail wanted to do was leave, run away, hitchhike to Mars, which probably had a more normal atmosphere than her own house. Really, what she wanted was to drive off on her own, in her own car, which her dad had promised her, but kept stalling on. Over a month had already gone by since she'd passed her driver's ed. test.

She dialed her father's number, not completely conscious of what she did, and when he answered, it shocked her, like this wasn't at all what she'd expected.

"Dad?" she said.

"Hi, I was just thinking about you."

"You were?" she said hopefully.

He paused. "Yeah," he said. "I'm always thinking about you. I bet you don't think about me at all. I bet your head's too full of all your boyfriends."

"I wish," said Gail. "I don't have any boyfriends."

"Now I *know* that's not true."

She laughed. "It's true. I'm too unpoopular. I pop out at parties." That was from dad's favorite "Lucy" episode. She'd never seen it herself, but she remembered her mom and dad saying it to each other.

"Who is that?" Gail heard a screechy voice in the background.

"It's Gail," her father yelled off.

"Well, it better be. Gail, is that you?"

"Yes, it's me," Gail said.

"Jesus, don't yell," her father said. "You're going to puncture an eardrum."

"She says it's her," he told Alice.

"That's good," said Alice. "'Cause I'd bust him if it weren't. I can't trust the man farther than I can throw him. You never warned me about your dad's straying eyes."

"Seems like you could have figured that out from the beginning," Gail said.

"She says you're being unfair," her dad reported.

"Now I know *that's* a lie."

Alice swiped the phone from Gail's father. "Why are you such a stranger?" Alice said to Gail. "Why don't you and Meg come over for supper more often?"

"We will," Gail said. Something about this woman made her meeker than normal, though she had no intention of spending more time with her than was absolutely necessary.

"Good," Alice said. "Now here's your dad, but don't talk long because I'll be getting jealous."

Gail took the receiver from her ear and looked at it. She considered vomiting on the mouthpiece.

"What's up, honeybunch?" her dad said.

"Total mayhem, Dad. That's all I can say."

"Is that fellow still living with you."

"What – the missing link?"

"I need to talk to her."

"Talk to her, but it won't do any good."

He paused. "Do you know if . . . what exactly's goin' on . . . I guess you wouldn't know about that."

"Try me. I know more than you think."

"You better not. I'll come over and bust you."

Gail laughed. Then she settled her thoughts and gripped the receiver with both hands and pressed it close to her ear and mouth. "Dad," she said. "Can I come live with you?" She hadn't expected to say this, but now that she'd said it, she saw she wanted nothing more.

He didn't answer directly. That was his way. He was a slow, thoughtful man. He didn't make rash decisions like her mother, and that's what she appreciated so much about him. You could trust his choices.

Then she wasn't sure he was still on the line. She heard him clear his throat. She imagined the spot where he stood, thinking clearly, trying to make the right decision. He was using the kitchen phone that hung on the wall a few feet from an old potbellied stove they used in the winter. It was a warm spot, and to Gail it seemed warmer still on days like this. Small windows ringed the kitchen and in the winter when the snow swirled outside, you could hear the house creak slightly in the wind. Her dad had tacked plastic over the windows, and the wind bubbled them inward. The house wasn't perfect. It was old, at least a hundred years. It had stood before telephones and cars, when people had to gather round the potbellied stove for warmth. Now that wasn't necessary. Just talking to her dad, knowing he stood in that familiar spot, made her feel some of that warmth. It seemed to spill out of the telephone line itself, and she held the receiver as tightly as she could.

"Why do you want to be *here?*" he said finally. His voice sounded strained, and she wondered what was going on there. Then she heard a little cooing sound, and she realized that Alice must be standing right beside him. "Hey," he said away from the phone, like he was annoyed. Alice probably had her arms around him. She was probably doing something disgusting at that very moment. Funny, in Gail's picture of the kitchen, she'd forgotten all about Alice. She'd only imagined her dad standing there, even though Alice had spoken to her.

"Is this a bad time?" Gail said. That sounded strange saying that to her dad, but if he could sound weird, so could she. "I can call back later."

"No, now's fine," he said. He sounded forceful, and he must have given Alice a look or a push because she said, "Okay, okay!"

"Aren't things going well between you and your mom?" he said.

"Tell Gail that if she wants to come for supper, we'd be delighted to have her," Alice shouted.

"I don't know," Gail said. "Things are fine. I mean, they're crazy, but they're fine."

"What do you mean?" he said. "What's going on over there? Maybe I should come over and pick my teeth with that little fellow."

"No, it's just that Mom's crazy. You know that. It's why you divorced her, isn't it?"

"That's not why," he said. "And I didn't divorce her. We divorced each other. And your mom's not crazy. She's just a little . . ."

"Erratic," Alice shouted.

"That's right," he said.

Gail raised her eyes to Axl Rose. She figured she'd probably get that speech now that started off with: When two people live together for a long time, it's easy for them to take each other for granted. After that, Gail always stopped listening, but she knew the gist of it. The speech, or variations, had been delivered to her by her mother, her father, her driver's ed. instructor, her American history teacher. In history, it was known as the Declaration of Independence. In driver's ed. it was called "Keeping a Margin of Safety."

But he didn't start in on that one. Instead, he said, "Anytime you want, you come on over. You stay as long as you want." Then he laughed and said, "Cut that out. You better come over, Gail, so you can protect me from this woman."

"Tell her we're having leftovers tonight," Alice said. "But I could fry up some smelts for her. And we got a big old industrial-strength bottle of cherry pop."

"She doesn't like cherry pop," he said. "I don't know where you got this cherry pop notion anyway."

"I like cherry pop all right," Gail said.

"The way she sees it," he said, "the world can't get along without it. Cherry pop flows through our veins, and we worship at the altar of cherry pop."

"You're terrible," Alice said.

"I like cherry pop all right," Gail said. She wondered if it was always like this around their house now. They certainly seemed cheerful. She'd never heard her dad so giddy. Maybe it was all that cherry pop.

"Tell her we could all go to Bonnie Doon for ice cream after that," Alice said.

"That's right," her dad said. "You'd like that, wouldn't you, Gail?"

"And after that we could all fly down to the Epcot Center," Gail said.

"What do you mean?" he said. Now he had an edge to his voice. He didn't like people making fun of him. He didn't like her smarting off, but she had to do something to make him understand.

"I just want to come over, Dad. I don't want you to treat me like someone special. I want to move back home."

That stopped him. "She wants to move back home," he said.

Alice's voice came from a distance, and sounded weak. "Home?"

"Here," he said.

"Oh, well that's fine, too," Alice said.

"Whatever you think's right, honey," her dad said.

"She's certainly entitled," Alice said. "I'd never stand in her way."

"You hear that?" her dad said.

"Ask her what she likes to eat," Alice said. "A growing girl eats different from what we do. I'll probably need to go through the fridge and clear out half the garbage in it."

"Dad, tell her not to go to any trouble," Gail said. She felt her voice rising. "I don't want to be any trouble."

"Don't worry, hon. You're no trouble at all."

"I'll probably have to go to the store," Alice was saying, "and pick up some of that whole-grain bread. Ask her if that's what she eats."

"Dad, tell her to stop," Gail said.

"Hold on a sec," he said. "Will you settle down? She doesn't want us to make a fuss."

Maybe she could change the subject, Gail thought. "You know that car you promised me when I passed driver's ed?"

"Sure I do," he said. "I'm gonna fix up one of my Studies for you, just like new." Pride entered his voice and for a moment she believed him. She could almost see herself driving on a fine summer's day, along some country road, with nothing ahead or behind her for miles. She and her dad seemed to be having the same daydream. He said, "You'll look gorgeous. Your friends are gonna be green. I just need time to set to work. I've got the perfect one picked out. It's a Gran Turismo Hawk. How does that sound?"

"Ask her if American cheese will do," Alice said. "I've also got some with caraway seeds."

"Picked out?" Gail said. "The last time you said you'd picked it out. You mean you haven't started?"

"I'll get around to it," he said. "I just don't have the money for parts right now. I'm saving up for a car of my own, something special that won't come around again. A Studebaker President. It belonged to Evangeline Studebaker. They'll be auctioning it off at her estate sale. But don't worry. Your Hawk's right here. It's not going anywhere."

"Neither am I," said Gail. Blood might be thicker than water, Gail knew, but to her dad, motor oil was thicker than them both.

"Oh my God . . . Lunchmeats!" Alice screamed in the background.

Gail slammed down the receiver. She held both her hands on the phone as though it might explode otherwise. She was hyperventilating. She counted to twenty. Then she lifted the receiver and dialed her dad's number again.

Busy. Just as well. She put the receiver down again, then lifted it from its cradle and laid it on the bed. She could be busy, too. If they asked her what happened, she'd say the phone had gone dead. Knowing her dad, he wouldn't ask. He'd pretend they never had the conversation unless she brought it up. She'd go on living with her mom. That was his way. He didn't like to talk about things that made trouble in his life. If there was a problem or if someone behaved differently from the way he expected, he just ignored them and went on as if nothing unusual had happened. She imagined him staring at the wall phone, stunned for a moment, then turning around and sitting beside the potbellied stove.

Well? Alice might say.

That's a deep subject, he'd say, and leave it at that. Oh, he'd probably add something like, What are we having for lunch? He'd have to say *something* like that, something that would let them get on with their lives.

Gail left her room and wandered into the kitchen. She found Henry at the stove burning French toast, Meg on the linoleum floor with the newspaper spread in front of her, and her mother stabbing the freezer with a screwdriver. Scenes like this just depressed the hell out of her. A perfectly retarded picture, as far as she was concerned.

At the kitchen threshold, Gail announced to anyone who might listen: "Just like I thought. Dad's never going to get me that car he promised."

She didn't exactly get the reaction she'd hoped for. Henry looked at her blankly. Meg didn't look at her at all. Neither did her mom, though at least she said something.

"I didn't know he promised you a car," she said.

"Yes you did. You just forgot. You never listen to what I say."

Her mom, who seemed to have eyes only for her ice, mumbled distractedly, "That's true. I'm a horrible human being."

Gail stood above her sister and observed her. She wanted Meg to stew a bit, to sense that Gail might strike at any moment. She stood with her foot in the air, ready to stomp. Meg, who'd been pretending to read the articles on the front page (Gail knew she couldn't understand a word, that she just wanted people to think she was brainy) didn't move a muscle. She held the bottom corner of the paper, ready to turn the page. She seemed to sense imminent danger, her life in peril.

"Meg dearest," Gail said, lowering her foot so that it grazed Meg's hair.

"Mom," Meg started lowing in that dairy cow way of hers.

"Meg's reading the paper on the floor, Mom," Gail said.

She didn't seem to hear. She just kept stabbing away at the freezer. Then, almost as an afterthought, she said, "Girls, don't start anything."

Gail smiled. Sometimes there were benefits to having a distracted parent. "Do people normally read the paper on the floor?" Gail said, stepping on Meg's head and forcing her face onto the paper.

"Let me up, Gail," Meg said.

Gail released her. "I guess I didn't see you. I guess you must have fallen out of your seat at the table and gone paralyzed."

Meg stood up slowly and sat down at the table with her paper.

Gail advanced on Henry, who was whistling some tuneless tune, dreamily watching the smoke rising from the skillet.

She stood beside him and pointed. "I think your toast needs turning, Henry."

"Oh you're right," said Henry, who flipped it and said, "You want a piece?"

"No way," Gail said.

"You sure?" Henry said. "It wouldn't be any trouble."

She just looked at him and shook her head.

He didn't seem quite as retarded these days, but he was still pretty goony. She couldn't understand why her mom allowed him to stay. Luckily, there wasn't anything between them, though even if there was, the world didn't have to worry. Her mom was past her prime childbearing years. Gail shoved the thought out of her mind. The idea of certain people having sex, like her mother and father, seemed bizarre. The thought of Henry and her mother having sex was grotesque. In any event, she didn't think there was cause for alarm. Henry and her mom often sat at the kitchen table, though they didn't seem to do much talking. And they didn't moon-eye each other either. They sat together, but they didn't seem to *be* together. They seemed like they were in two different dimensions.

In science Gail had been taught about matter and antimatter. She hadn't been paying attention that day, but if she understood correctly, some things are negative and other things positive. She thought she must be positive and the rest of her family, except for her dad, was negative. That's why they clashed all the time. In another dimension, a negative Gail existed, and she didn't get along with her family either, because they were all positive. She wished she could just make the switch to her positive family, because matter and antimatter couldn't exist together. If they met, they destroyed each other. That seemed like a good description of her family.

"So Henry," she said in the friendliest tone she could muster. "Don't you think it's about time you left the nest?" Henry was now burning the other side of his toast. He looked at her but didn't move. "I mean, are you planning on staying here forever?"

Henry didn't seem to take her question as hostile, which amazed her. He just raised his eyes and considered it, as though staying forever was a rational possibility.

The smoke started rising from the skillet again, but this time, Gail wasn't going to say anything.

"Mom, how long is Henry staying?" she yelled.

Her mom paused from her chipping and drew a hand across her forehead. "I never should have let it get this bad," she said. "I think our freezer produces a new variety of indestructible ice. It's like a glacier in here."

"I asked you a question," Gail said. "I think I have a right to know how long I have to share this house with a total stranger."

Henry edged the spatula underneath the toast, loosened the bread from the skillet, but didn't turn it.

"It's not your house to share," her mom said, resuming her chipping. "Actually, it's Henry's."

"We have a lease," Gail said.

"That's funny. I don't remember you signing the lease."

Henry looked up at the ceiling as though trying to remember something. "Do you know that during the last ice age the glacier stopped at Indianapolis, and that's why most of the state's so flat? You don't get into the hills until you get past Indy."

"Really?" said Gail's mother. "Where did you ever find that out?"

"I don't know," he said. "I used to drive around Indiana a lot. I guess it's just something I picked up along the way."

Gail couldn't figure what glaciers had to do with their present situation. The two of them seemed to be conspiring against her, to drive her as crazy as they were.

"I don't have to live here, you know," she shouted. Henry backed away from her. She pointed to the skillet and said, "Flip your toast. Can't you see you're ruining it?"

Henry looked at the skillet in horror, like he'd never seen such a hideous thing before. Still, he didn't flip his toast, so she grabbed the spatula and flipped it for him.

Was it so much to ask for a normal family, not to have an airhead for a mother and a retarded stranger living with them?

Once, she'd found him alone in the kitchen, mopping the floor. For some reason, seeing this stranger mopping terrified her. She'd gone into the living room and waited for her mother to return home from her bargain hunting. As soon as her mom stepped in the front door, Gail had run up to her and yelled, "He's in the kitchen, mopping up!" Of course, it had sounded ridiculous, but family life wasn't supposed to be like this.

Gail stalked across the kitchen and stood beside the refrigerator door, which her mom blocked.

"Would you care for some fresh-squeezed orange juice, Gail?" Gail asked herself. "Why, yes, thank you so much, Mother."

"We don't have fresh," her mom said calmly. "Just frozen."

"Well, may I *have* some?" Gail said.

"In a bit. As soon as I chip it loose." She stabbed the side of the freezer and a hissing sound escaped.

"Oh no!" Her mom turned around, clutching the screwdriver, and yelled, "Now look what you made me do, Gail. Sit down at the table and don't move until I say so. I mean it."

Normally, Gail would have resisted, but she saw that her mother was serious. Anyway, the woman was crazy and pointing a screwdriver at her.

Gail retreated to the table and sat down. Meg gave her a superior look over the top of her paper.

Henry approached the table with his plate of French toast and a bottle of syrup. He looked hesitantly at Gail.

"May I sit down?"

"Hey, it's not my house," Gail said, turning her back on him.

"Don't pay attention to her," said Meg.

Henry sat down beside Gail, who turned around in her chair and stared. She put her chin on her fist and pretended she was a famous scientist, one of those people who studies apes in the wild. She felt completely nonjudgmental as she watched Henry pour his syrup on the toast. What a sight, she thought. I'm the first civilized person in the world to observe such bizarre behavior. She noted how he circled his French toast with the syrup bottle, how evenly he spread it around the piece of egg-dipped bread. He obviously knew he was being watched, but neither scientist nor specimen showed any awareness of the other.

Henry cut his toast with the side of his fork, then moved a piece, dripping syrup, into his mouth. Fascinating. Gail took a mental note. The world would be amazed when they learned of this. The thing ate like a normal human being. But wait! Here was something startling. The thing seemed to derive no special pleasure from its food. It ate with a blank expression. Its jaw was tense, and if she hadn't been observing closely, Gail might have missed its feeding altogether.

Gail pushed forward in her seat, pressing in on the thing. Now the thing shifted in its seat and held its fork in midair.

Aware of being watched, it looked at Gail. The thing's companion — the little thing pretending to read a newspaper — looked now at Gail, too.

Gail smiled at them both, to show she meant no harm. If they could have understood her, if they could have made more than meaningless noises, she would have tried to communicate. But it wasn't really necessary. A smile is universal. She hoped the big thing would continue to eat, and later, groom itself.

She wished she was still seeing Nathan. She just wanted to get away from Henry. The difference between the two men was that Nathan always acted like he knew what he was doing, even when he did something stupid. Henry, on the other hand, never acted like he knew what he was doing, even when he did something right. Gail figured that it wasn't what you did, but how you did it, the degree of certainty with which you led your life, that made you normal or abnormal. After all, Nathan had done some bizarre things in his life. He'd smuggled spider monkeys out of the Yucatán and slept on a bench in Central Park for nine months. Those had been the right things for him to do at those moments in his life. There were a lot of things wrong with Nathan, but he always knew what he wanted.

Suddenly, Henry pushed his plate toward her. He had a perplexed look. He spoke hesitantly. "Will you take a bite of this and tell me if there isn't something terribly wrong?"

"It's burnt," Gail said.

"Besides that."

"Ask Meg."

Henry handed the plate to Meg, who took a bite. As soon as she put the piece in her mouth, her expression changed.

She let her mouth drop open, the piece of French toast sitting on her tongue. She kicked back her chair and darted across the room. She spit the toast in the trash, then changed directions and headed for the sink. She turned on the tap and gathered water.

Meg had everyone's attention now, and Gail wondered if this wasn't just a show for that reason. Whatever it was, it couldn't taste *that* awful. After all, Henry had eaten half of the toast without saying a word.

Meg gulped and rinsed her mouth, then turned around. "Oh, that's gross," she said. "it's sweet and salty and gushy. You try it, Gail."

Gail waved her hand in front of her face. "It's probably poison."

"Try it, Mom" Meg said.

Gail couldn't believe it. Meg had almost died from eating tainted French toast, but her mom didn't look apprehensive at all. She set down her screwdriver and headed for the table. Henry sat placidly in his seat, arms folded, awaiting judgment like a patient awaiting a doctor's prognosis. She took his fork, cut off a hunk of toast, and swirled it in the syrup.

She took a bite.

She chewed the French toast slowly, like she was mulling it over. Then she swallowed and licked her lips.

"Oh you're right, Meg," she said. "That's truly awful." She said it as though even truly awful things weren't *that* bad. Still, she took the plate and scraped the toast into the trash. "It tasted salty," she declared with a puzzled look, still licking her lips.

"I thought something tasted off," Henry said.

"He probably would have finished it if you'd said it tasted fine," said Gail.

The hissing from the refrigerator had grown louder. Her mom stood by the freezer door looking inside. She stepped back and chewed a fingernail. Then she stepped forward and put her head inside the freezer, removed it, stepped back, then forward again, like some little dance step or ritual. Knowing her, she probably *did* know some voodoo chant to stop the Freon from leaking. Finally, she gently placed her screwdriver inside the wounded freezer and shut the door.

She looked around like she didn't know where she was, and didn't know what to do next. As far as Gail was concerned, she was acting even more schizoid than usual. Gail watched as her mom started for the breakfast table, then changed her mind and headed for the trash. She went down on her knees and sorted through it. Finally, she extracted a piece of paper dripping with egg yolk. A fine layer of coffee grounds covered the back of her hand. She glanced at the piece of paper, mumbling to herself, then put the paper back. She didn't place it on top of the trash. She burrowed her hand deep into the basket.

Then she smiled sadly, and stood up. Slowly, she walked to the sink, turned on the faucet, and ran the water over her wrists. She didn't do much washing. She just let the water splash off her skin for a minute. She seemed unaware that Gail watched her, that they were all watching her.

She drifted toward the stove and looked around. Presently, she lifted the saltshaker. "Is this what you used for your French toast?" she said.

"Is that salt?" Henry said.

"Is that salt?" Gail said.

Henry turned to her as though she'd asked the question seriously, as though she was just as perplexed as he. "I thought it was the sugar," he said.

"No harm done," her mom said. "Actually, the saltshaker looks a lot like the sugar bowl."

Gail stood up. "Why do you always protect him?"

Her mother looked at her as though she didn't know what Gail was talking about.

There was something wrong with the way her mother looked at her, but she couldn't help herself. Some things she just couldn't help. Like other people. She couldn't help them and she couldn't help herself or her family. She couldn't stop from thinking the most brutal thoughts, and she couldn't stop herself from going beyond that and giving them voice. She thought maybe that was true of others, too. That no one could help themselves. That things came out of people no matter what, even against their will. Maybe that was true of Henry, too. He couldn't stop from putting salt on his French toast. And her mother. She couldn't stop herself from poking holes in the freezer and digging through the trash. The reason people couldn't stop themselves from doing the wrong things was really so simple—because they wanted to do the wrong things. No one she knew wanted to do what was right. Matter yearned to meet antimatter, to cancel itself out, to start fresh and make things right by getting what was wrong out of the way.

In that moment of understanding Gail felt calm and forgiving. She didn't want to say what was next, but she knew she'd say it anyway. She felt it rumble to the surface.

"You know, I wouldn't protect anyone the way you protect him. I never heard you speak up for Dad the way you do for him. You don't even speak up for me or Meg that way, and we're your own children. What is he doing for you anyway?"

Her mother didn't say anything. She just pursed her lips like she had another piece of salty French toast in her mouth, like she was mulling it over.

"I'm sorry," Henry said.

"Don't apologize to her, Henry," Lois said.

"Yeah, don't apologize," Gail said. "Is he your sweetie? If he is, I feel sorry for *you*. I bet his hand isn't the only thing that doesn't work."

"I *am* sorry your father didn't give you the car he promised," he said. Gail sat back as though he'd just made some slur against her. She wanted to hit him. She didn't know what he wanted from her. He had no right being sorry for that. It was family business. He had no right criticizing her dad.

"Will you stop apologizing?" she shouted. "You're always doing that. Not everything's your fault, and even if it is, you don't have to admit it."

Henry looked as though she'd just punched him. Then he reached with his left hand and pulled Gail's face close to his. Before she knew what he was doing, he kissed her; not a gentle kiss, but desperate, like a father kissing a child good night before going off to war. Then he released her.

She touched her forehead, and felt where his lips had touched her. She didn't know what to make of this. For once, she didn't know what to say, and neither did anyone else. She wondered if she should call her father back and tell him what Henry had just done. Maybe then he'd come over and pick his teeth with Henry. But she knew that wouldn't be right, that this wasn't the right response to what Henry had just done, that maybe there *was* no response to what Henry had just done.

"Maybe I should lie down," Henry said finally.

"That's probably a good idea," her mother said.

Henry tried to stand, but sank back in his seat. Like some incredibly old man. But he wasn't old. At least not ancient. No older than Nathan.

Henry tried standing again and this time made it. Soon after he'd left, her mother turned from the freezer and said to Meg, "To hell with this. I'm going garage sale-ing. You want to go with?"

Meg jumped up, and the two of them left the kitchen. Her mother didn't say good-bye, but Meg did with a bright wave. "Be good," she said. "Maybe we'll bring something back for you." She didn't say this sarcastically either. She meant it. That was the thing about Meg. She didn't hold grudges long.

As soon as they had left, Gail remembered the piece of paper her mother had crumpled and thrown in the wastebasket. Normally, Gail was big on privacy. She didn't appreciate people snooping through the things that belonged to her, and in return, she didn't poke around in their business. Even Meg's.

She had one exception to this privacy rule. She'd break it only for someone else's own good. This phrase broke through any door. It was powerful, and not to be invoked lightly. In the past, her parents had used it on her, but not often, and usually when they punished her. *For your own good* seemed like something people said when they felt guilty about doing something awful.

Gail approached the wastebasket, knelt, and reached inside. Then, as an afterthought, she turned to see if anyone could see what she was doing. Satisfied that no one could, she stuck her hand in farther, brushing off egg yolk, coffee grounds, and discarded droopy French toast. She shook her head, hardly believing she'd stooped to this. Her mother had forced it on her.

Gail extracted a soggy piece of newspaper, a stained grocery list, and finally, a piece of white letterhead with the name of the radio station WPKB, and a few lines of scrawled script. The letters were crammed together, and each line sloped downward. It read:

> Dear Honeycomb,
>
> I'm right here where you left me. I hope you like that record. It's something we whipped up here at the station years ago as a promotion. I've still got about ten boxes sitting in the closet. I hope you and your mother and Jackie and Tim will visit me sometime soon.
>
> > Love,
> > Your Pop

Gail stared at the letter, demanding that it make sense, but it was no use, so she put the letter back where she'd found it.

She grabbed a mop and bucket from the broom closet, then went to the sink. The entire house was a pigsty, falling apart, and no one seemed to notice or care but her. The freezer had a screwdriver inside. Meg had tossed the newspaper back on the floor. Dishes were stacked up in the sink.

She opened the tap and listened to the water drum into the mop bucket. In a while, water would start dripping out of the freezer and collecting on the floor.

FIFTEEN

Some people feel oppressed by society; others don't feel oppressed enough. Every time a gruesome murder's committed, one that goes unsolved for months, at least three or four people will step forward and confess to the crime. Some people want to take the blame for everything, but taking *all* the blame is as bad as taking none. Maybe Christ died for everyone's sins, though if he did, he was the only one who could get away with it, and perhaps Mark or Matthew should have put a warning label on the Bible, reading, "Don't try this one at home." It's hard enough for people to live with their own sins, let alone die for everyone else's.

Henry didn't know that until the day Gail yelled at him for apologizing all the time. "Everything isn't your fault," she'd raged, "and even if it is, you don't have to admit it." Until then, he'd believed that everything *was* his fault, and if it wasn't, he didn't mind apologizing anyway. On that day, he realized that all his apologies did him no good. They made up for nothing, no matter how sincerely he offered them. He'd said almost the same thing to Carla back when they'd lived together in this house. Nothing had made him resent her more than those constant apologies. They were insurance to her, against the time when she'd really have something to apologize for. They were excuses, her way of saying, If I do something wrong, here's payment in advance — but it just doesn't work that way. All she'd ever proved was that she didn't know the meaning of her apologies, that she wanted to avoid blame rather than claim it.

Henry saw this when confronted by Gail. He'd recognized himself saying the same thing to Carla, and so, had reached up and kissed Gail. There was nothing else to do. Henry had never seen himself so clearly, had never realized what he'd become. Henry knew from that moment on that he needed to change his life, not that he was ready to leave this house yet. He didn't exactly feel comfortable here, but he needed to take some action, to show Gail she was wrong about him, that there *were* things about him that worked.

So he called Sid Junkins, his old landlord, and he said, "Sid, I need your help."

"If it's money, then no can do," said Sid. "Anything else spiritual or physical, I'm ready and willing. As they say, 'Buy a man a fish, he eats for a day. Teach a man to fish and he eats for a lifetime.' I've always thought you were in need of a fishing pole more than anyone I know. Maybe I'm being too blunt, but that's the way I speak."

"That's what I appreciate about you," said Henry.

The next week, Sid drove Henry to his brother, Max Junkins, who was an acupuncturist. Max lived with his wife, Joan, and their twins, Jerry and Tony, in the Campus View Apartments off Irish Way.

In the past, Henry never would have allowed himself to be dragged to an acupuncturist. He'd grown up in a family that believed people should not have problems, and if they *did* have problems, then they were limited to three sanctioned recourses. Either they could talk to their pastor, they could suffer in silence, or they could blow their brains out. Any other remedies, including therapy and off-brand religions (other than Lutheran) were strictly forbidden. Even talking with one's pastor was considered a last resort, bringing your problems outside yourself, and worse yet, outside the family, something for weak-willed sissies who couldn't "take it." Taking it was an important element in Henry's family life as a child. His parents hardly even spoke to each other for eight years, arranging their schedules so that one would be going to sleep just as the other's day began. They took it in silence, the preferred method, and his mother stopped going to church, presumably so she could take even a greater portion of It. An aunt of Henry's had taken It with sleeping pills and his own grandfather had taken It with a gun. Of course, Henry's grandfather and aunt were not talked about after that, never mentioned, because they became part of the Greater It for the next generation to take.

Now Henry's parents lived in Pasadena, the Promised Land, where they'd moved after Henry graduated from high school. As far as Henry knew, they still awoke at different times and lived separate lives, apparently waiting for the day when God called them to His Dwelling Place, offered them beer and pretzels, patted them on the back, and said, I'm proud of both you guys. You took it on the chin all this time like a couple of pros. Henry had seen his parents only once in ten years. After the accident, they'd visited him in the hospital, and when he awoke from his coma, his mother begged him to live with them in Pasadena. That solution, he knew, would have been worse than the affliction. Henry's father had hired a lawyer, who'd negotiated with the insurance company. The man in the antique car had been drunk, and the insurance company had paid for Henry's car, his hospital stay, and for long-term suffering. Henry's father thought the deal was pretty good; he'd set up his son for life, and when he went home to Pasadena he figured he'd solved just about every last one of Henry's problems.

Max Junkins, a hefty man, clean-shaven and balding, with a dark complexion and large hands, looked more suited to lifting furniture than sticking thin needles in people. He wasn't big on ceremony. When Sid knocked on the front door he yelled for them to come in, and he didn't get up from the kitchen table, where he was reading the sports section of the newspaper. "Wait a second," he said. "I'm just about done. You're early." Henry was about to turn around, but Sid said, "We're not early. We're right on time."

"Okay, okay," he said, pushing up from the table, and taking one last glance at the paper.

Max's wife appeared in the hallway, barefoot and dressed in a warm-up suit. In one arm, she carried a book; in the other, one of the twins. "Does Jerry want an apple?" she said, walking past Henry and Sid into the kitchen, where she placed the book, opened, on the counter. Jerry didn't reply, but stared dully at Henry and Sid.

The boy's mother turned and smiled warmly, and then said, "Hello," in a lilting, slightly surprised way, as though to say, What new and delightful creature are you?

"Please excuse Joan," Max said. "You'll have to attribute her rudeness to the fact that she's a graduate student, and midterms are approaching."

Joan stuck her nose in the air, and said, haughtily, "I beg your pardon. I said hello."

Max and Joan's other toddler came running down the hall at full tilt, his arms outstretched. He stopped at the end of the hall and also stared at Sid and Henry.

"Say hello, Tony," Max said. Henry smiled at the boy, who ducked his head and walked over with the determined gait to a piano that stood against a wall in the living room. He climbed up onto the piano stool, turned himself around, and started pounding on the keys.

Max asked Henry what the problem was, but Henry didn't know how to answer. He just wanted to get back on track, to start making decisions about his life again, but he doubted whether needles could help him with something so nebulous, so he said, "My right hand. I haven't felt anything in it since my accident."

"That's the least of his problems," Sid said. Sid was dressed that day in jungle fatigues and boots. He flanked Henry in the middle of Max's living room, which was cluttered with toys. Sid looked like a general doling out battle strategy. "Give him the works," Sid told Max. "Look at him. He's all nerves. He's skinny. He's a mental and physical wreck."

Sid continued down a checklist of Henry's disorders, while Max nodded and stroked his dark beard, which was flecked with gray, and made noises of agreement. Every once in a while, he'd tilt his head and look up, as if to say, "I don't know if I can help with *that*."

Then Max reached out and took Henry's right hand. Henry drew the whole arm back. Max raised his eyes to Henry and gave him a questioning look, then took Henry's arm again and quietly examined him. First, Max placed two fingers on Henry's wrist, feeling his pulse. Then he inspected Henry's fingers, probing the joints and skin, a finger at a time. He looked as though this were his first encounter with hands and fingers. He seemed to see something very important in every inch of skin.

Abruptly, Max held up a hand and said, "Okay, I think I can take it from here," and he led Henry, without a word to Max or Joan, into a small room off the living room.

The room was bare except for a bureau and a high metal table, like the kind in doctor's offices, with a white sheet draped over it, and a space heater in the corner. He instructed Henry to strip down to his underwear, and meanwhile, turned on the space heater. "Can you feel this?" he said, aiming the heater at the table. The coils hadn't heated yet, but Henry nodded and unbuttoned his shirt, though he wasn't nodding so much to affirm his warmth. It was a general kind of nod, a big assent to new experience and trust.

Max told Henry his problem was in his shoulders. That's where, according to Max, Henry collected all his tension. Henry felt some of this tension collecting at that very moment as he sat in his underwear on the table, and watched Max at the bureau tear off the top of a sterile packet, and remove a needle about three inches long, with a plastic grip at its top.

"How long have you and your wife been married?" Henry asked. He figured that if he acted friendly to Max, then the man might hurt him less. In Henry's mind, the pain caused by doctors was inversely proportional to their personal attachment to you.

Max turned around. He didn't look the right sort of person to be poking needles in people. His eyes looked bright and amused and a little crazed.

Max seemed to sense this. He faced Henry and said, "You ever have a tattoo? Now that hurts. These needles don't hurt at all. Unless you look, you don't even know what's going on, though if it bothers you, then you can put on your clothes and walk right now. Not everyone's problems have to have the same cure."

Henry thought about this. He didn't want to walk. He remembered the Alamo, the film, that is, in which the captain had drawn a line in the sand with his saber and told anyone who didn't want to stay and fight to cross the line. No one would think worse of them, he told his men, but of course, everyone *would* think worse of them, regardless of what the captain said. Henry knew if he left now, he'd never try again, he'd never find the strength.

"No, I'll stay," Henry said.

Max didn't say anything, but looked pleased and nodded. "These needles," Max said as he took Henry's right hand and positioned it flat on Henry's knee, "are a kind of outlet, a conduit for the things that are locked up inside you. The Chinese believe that your life energy flows through a series of pathways, or meridians, and when you have a disease, it's caused by an imbalance in your energy flow." As he said this, he gestured with the needle like a conductor with a baton. "I'm a practical man," he told Henry. "Before this, I studied law. I didn't like it. The more I understood about the law, the more I realized it helped almost no one. Now acupuncture's completely the opposite. I don't claim to understand it completely. As far as I'm concerned, it's a mystery. But I can live with that. My motto is, 'Whatever works.' For

Sid, it's vitamins. Religion for other people. Now, hold still, Henry."
He pinched the skin in the middle of the back of Henry's hand and
flicked the needle into it. He gave the needle a spin, and the skin
twisted in response. He let go and the needle stayed there, wobbling
back and forth, seeming almost to hover above the hand.

Max grabbed another needle from the packet and said, "You know,
in every society, from so-called primitive cultures to our own so-called
advanced society, people hate not knowing what's wrong with them.
They automatically feel better if they have a name for their disease.
Then they feel cured. In primitive cultures, in the absence of conven-
tional medicine, people believe that their diseases are caused by
curses. When you're sick, the first thing you try to find out is who
cursed you, who gave you the evil eye. Then, when you find out, you're
able to learn the magic to counter their magic." Max paused and said,
"Anyone curse you, Henry?"

Henry thought back. He remembered Carla clutching his leg, saying "Are you crazy?" That was as close to a curse as he'd come. He was
about to tell Max this, but Max laughed and said, "I'm just kidding,
Henry. The first thing we're going to have to do is unblock your sense
of humor."

Max inserted one needle after another into Henry's hand, and continued to explain the procedure. He said that you could either use the
needles to increase energy flow or you could use them to drain away
excessive energy and break down blocks in the flow. You took a person's pulse on each wrist to find out what needed to be done. In
Henry's case, according to Max, there were a lot of dams that needed
to be unblocked. The aim, he said, was to reach equilibrium in the
body.

By the end of this explanation, Henry had eight needles wobbling
in his hand. Strangely, he did not mind this, though his hand looked
like a biology experiment, like something you'd do to a frog. Partly,
what made him calm and relaxed was Max's self-assured voice, his
talk of culture and belief, his conviction that what he was doing to
Henry would have some good effect.

He returned the next week, and this time Max worked on his shoulder. Henry lay on his stomach, naked except for a towel covering his
buttocks, the heater again pointed at the table. Max left Henry alone
this way for twenty minutes while the needles supposedly did their

work, then when he returned he removed them and tried something else called "cupping." This procedure seemed even stranger to Henry than being stuck with needles. Max took six jars with candles in them and lit each one. Then he placed the mouths of the jars on Henry's back. The fire didn't burn Henry's back; it almost immediately used up the oxygen in the jar and created a vacuum. Again, Henry was left alone for twenty minutes, with six jars affixed with suction to his back. Whether it worked or not, Henry felt there was something cosmically silly about this procedure. The jars left red blotches on Henry's skin for nearly a week.

Henry didn't think he was getting much out of the treatment, but he liked Max and his family, so he kept going. Max would talk gently to him as he worked. Sometimes, Henry felt like crying for no reason, or grew silently enraged, which Max said was natural. "All your emotions are pent up in you. We're letting them out little by little."

Outside the room, life was happening. A child pounded a piano. Another one cried. Sid's brash voice boomed and was answered by Joan's laughter. To Henry, all this was a call, a summons. He answered with the thin breath through his nostrils, and a tightness in his jaws, a trembling around his face, all the tunings and misgivings of his body.

Henry thought he was getting used to the treatment, but during his next visit, as he sat on the table staring at the needles in his hands, he suddenly felt flushed and anxious, then nauseated. The room seemed like an inferno. He stood and felt dizzy, then weaved to the heater, and turned it off. That didn't do any good, so he opened the door and stumbled into the living room.

"For God's sake, Henry," Sid said, leaping up from the couch. "Put on some clothes. There are children here." Henry glanced over at the toddlers, but they were standing in diapers in their playpen and didn't seem to mind. Neither did Joan, who was reading a thick blue book at the table. She glanced up, then went back to her book. Henry couldn't help himself anyway. He needed to find his way outside. He could barely focus his thoughts, though one rational perception passed through his mind: he realized that Sid always saw him at his worst.

"Max!" Sid yelled down the hall. "Get in here. Henry's freaking out."

Henry heard a toilet flush. He didn't think he was freaking out, just hot, so incredibly hot. He opened the living-room door and started down the steps, which wound around the wall. He held on to the banister with his good hand to keep his balance. Finally, he made it downstairs. He opened the door and burst out into the cold, fresh-smelling air. He was in the parking lot of the apartment complex. He looked up and saw the curtain pulled back from an apartment window.

Henry walked over the salt-whitened parking lot to the edge, where the accumulated snow of an entire winter had been plowed. The snow, piled up three feet, looked hard and gray, but Henry still felt too warm, much too warm, and plunged into the drift and covered his burning skin with snow.

Presently, he looked up and saw Max standing in front of him, with his hand extended. Max looked a little concerned, but otherwise calm and forgiving, and Henry didn't mind accepting the offer of assistance.

"I guess we let out too many emotions at once," Max said.

Henry glanced down at his right hand and saw that the needles had fallen out, but they hadn't broken and there wasn't any blood. Slowly, he got to his feet and gave Max his good hand, and followed him back across the lot. He could have apologized to Max, and maybe should have, but Max didn't seem to need an apology.

SIXTEEN

When Willy called, she knew what he was going to say before he said it. "You're getting married, right?"

"That's right," he said.

"Go ahead," she said. "I don't care."

"I don't need your permission," he said.

"Okay, good-bye."

"Wait, that's not why I called."

"Okay," she said. She stood in her kitchen, listening to his faint voice, eager to hang up so she could start out on her first garage sale-ing expedition of the spring.

"I'm wondering," said Willy, "when you're going to throw that weirdo living with you out on his ear. Any normal person would have done it long ago."

"Henry?" she said. "Are you talking about Henry?"

"I'm not going to call him by name," Willy said. "'That weirdo' fits him just fine.'"

"Okay," said Lois in a singsong. "Thanks for calling."

"Lois," he said. "Don't hang up. I'm taking you to lunch."

"How gallant," Lois said. "But I'm going out garage sale-ing, and I don't want to go to lunch with you. We have nothing to talk about." Then she reconsidered. There were a couple of things she wanted to discuss with him, after all. "If you're treating and I get to choose where, then maybe I'll go," she said.

"Sure. I'll treat." Willy sounded surprised.

"Okay, I'll meet you at Tippecanoe Place at one o'clock. Don't forget to call for a reservation, Willy."

"Tippecanoe Place?" Willy said. He sounded even more surprised.

Lois hung up on him. She stood there without moving for a minute, staring at the receiver. Then she unscrewed it, extracted the cotton ball, and threw it in the trash.

Normally, she wouldn't have set foot in Tippecanoe Place, but she wanted to go just this once. The meals, she'd heard, were expensive. After all, if he could take Alice to brunch there, he could do the same for his ex-wife. When they were married, Willy rarely took her out to eat, and never anywhere fancy. Usually, when they ate out, they went to Godfather's Pizza or the Ponderosa Steak House. Willy had always acted worse than the girls when it came to varieties of food. At least you could take them to the Olive Garden or the Hacienda. Lois, though, was the only one in her family who liked places like the Cornucopia downtown. The girls' reaction to the Cornucopia was, "Bean sprouts. Yuck."

All of a sudden, Willy had acquired expensive tastes — in clothing, cars, and food — but not for his family. Now, she wanted him to buy *her* an expensive lunch for once. She wanted to eat and enjoy her meal and she wanted to tell him what a tightwad he was. And she was going to give him hell for breaking his promise to Gail to fix up a car for her.

Lois was ten minutes late. Of course, Willy had arrived on time, and had been waiting in the middle of Tippecanoe Place's Great Hall. Dressed in a blue blazer with a fat red tie, he sat on one of the couches with his legs thrust out and crossed at the ankles, and his arms folded. With his full beard, and an implacable expression, he looked like he'd been waiting a century.

"About time," he said, getting to his feet slowly and giving Lois the once-over. "Glad to see you dressed up for the occasion. I would have bet money on you showing up in jeans and one of your yard-sale vests."

"Since when are you the fashion critic?" she said. "Did you save that tie from the last time you ate lobster?"

Actually, Lois had considered wearing her usual attire, but had settled on a summery dress with a multicolored scarf draped over her shoulders. She hated having to fit in at Tippecanoe Place, but she didn't want to be kicked out either.

A young woman dressed in a ruffled skirt and ruffled blouse with a sweetheart neckline led them to their seats. She looked like an MGM version of a peasant, a stylish peasant, and seemed completely at ease in these surroundings. Lois wondered if maybe her father or grandfather had worked for Studebaker.

Despite herself, she couldn't help being a little impressed by the opulence of the mansion. The high ceilings were paneled with oak, and so were the walls. As they walked past the Grand Staircase, Lois noticed its intricately-detailed carvings.

They ate on the mansion's veranda. She and Willy sat in huge white wicker chairs that swallowed them up despite how tall both of them were. The walls were granite, and fringed lamps from the twenties hung above each table.

During their appetizer, terrine of duck, they didn't talk at all. And they didn't talk through their main course. They both ate like they had nothing else on their minds but eating. Willy had the filet mignon and Lois had the salmon.

Willy probably had some kind of speech prepared for her, but he didn't use it. Lois had one prepared for him, but she didn't use hers either. When Willy finally set down his fork and wiped his mouth with his cloth napkin, she started talking, but she hardly knew what she was going to say next. Words just formed and seemed to say themselves without any effort on her part.

"When I was growing up," she started, "I used to watch this TV show called 'Coronet Blue.' Do you remember that show, Willy?"

Willy shook his head, halfway opened his mouth, and stuck his tongue back in one of his molars to dislodge some meat.

"It was about this man who was being threatened, but he had amnesia, and he didn't know what was going on. All he could remember were the words 'Coronet Blue.' There was no last episode of the show, and for years, I wondered why. I was so disappointed. I figured there had to be some good reason, and I'd never find out. You know, it's silly, but I must have thought about that show a hundred times in twenty years, wondering what I had missed."

Willy, she noticed, moved his lips while she talked. He was distracting her, but she knew he wasn't aware of what he was doing. She leaned forward, across the table, and brushed her hair back. She wore all her bangles, all her southwestern jewelry, and the sun coming through the veranda windows glinted off the silver.

"You know, last week," she continued, "I found out what had happened. I was reading the magazine section of the Sunday paper, and I found out that there *was* no last episode of the show because the writers couldn't decide why the man was being chased or what 'Coronet Blue' meant."

Willy chortled and finally closed his mouth. "Figures," he said.

"No, it's not funny," she said, pointing at him. "Don't laugh. It's not funny at all. The point is that I had something of myself invested in that show."

He gave her a bewildered look. She didn't expect him to understand. "Look, Willy," she said. "What I want to know is this. Do you lead a charmed life or something? That has to be it. No matter how you treat Gail, no matter how you neglect her and break promises, she still makes allowances that she'd never make for me. Or anyone else."

"Is that all?" Willy said, setting his napkin on the table.

"No, that's not all," Lois said. "I just think it's strange how some people can get away with so much and others can't make one mistake without their lives being ruined. You, for instance are obnoxious, rude, crude, selfish, and generally undependable except that you always show up on time. But no one takes you to task for your behavior. Why? Is it because you never make any apologies for the way you act? The people who love you, and I still include myself among this group though I'd be hard-pressed to say why, speak fondly of your flaws as though they're eccentricities, somehow offset by all your good deeds.

"I, on the other hand, can't make a move without being criticized by Gail. That's how it is, and how it will always be, so I might as well get used to it. Lately, Gail's been on a rampage because I'm not rich enough. She's decided recently that she deserves to be rich, that only an accident of birth has deprived her of this right. Of course, she blames her mother for this accident, not her father."

As usual, Willy didn't seem at all upset. He scratched his beard and said, "Maybe if you kicked out that weirdo, for starters, got your life – "

Lois didn't let him finish. She picked up her dessert fork and jabbed him in the forearm.

"Hey, Lois!" he said. "That hurts."

"Good," she said. "Don't instruct me," and she jabbed him again. Lois looked across at Willy, who was rubbing his hurt arm.

She stood up and threw her napkin down. Her wicker chair fell behind her and she screamed, "What the hell does 'Coronet Blue' mean? That's what I want to know."

"Lois," Willy said. You're the only person I know who can get all upset over some TV show that ended twenty years ago."

She ran from the veranda through the rooms leading back to the Great Hall. Instead of leaving, she turned and ran up the Grand Staircase. She knew Willy. He'd get up slowly and follow her if she went outside. He'd try to talk calmly to her, reasonably, and she didn't want any part of it.

She ran up to the third floor, which had a hall with pictures of the Studebaker brothers and the original wagon works and an engraving of President Lincoln's Studebaker carriage. She ended up in the children's playroom. There were no dining facilities up there. The playroom was being used now for storage, and contained mostly empty coatracks. Lois pushed past them and made her way to the window, where she could see all of downtown South Bend. For a while, she just stood there, collecting herself, then getting angry again. She wanted to stay angry. What she saw in front of her wasn't just the St. Joseph Bank building or the Indiana Bell building. And not Willy either. What she saw, or what she tried to see, was her father, twenty-five years older than he was when she'd last seen him. She still couldn't believe the tone of the letter he'd sent her ("I'm right here where you left me"). She just didn't see how it was possible for him to have gone on living after they'd left his life. If he *had* lived, she'd always thought, if he was *somehow* still alive, then he didn't love her, maybe never had. Or else he would have been in touch.

Well, she had some news for him. If she went, she'd be making that trip on her own. Jackie was dead, hit by a train in high school, while playing with some friends on the tracks. Tim was somewhere on the high seas, in the merchant marine. She hadn't spoken to him in ten years. Her mother had died long ago, when Lois and Willy had been married only a few years. Lois's mother had died embittered and silent, never mentioning her husband and always walking out of a room if someone brought him up.

Lois opened her locket with the pictures of the two children and stared at them. That locket was the last thing she needed — two children she didn't even know. Let them be orphans, she decided. Join the club. She placed it on the windowsill and left the room.

SEVENTEEN

Evangeline, the daughter of George W. Studebaker, had been the last Studebaker to grow up in Tippecanoe Place. Her father had sold the mansion during the depression for a fraction of its worth, because he'd invested all *he* was worth in two local companies that had collapsed: the South Bend Watch Company and the Kennedy Radio Corporation. Even if he'd invested in the company that bore his surname, he wouldn't have fared much better. Studebaker barely survived the depression. The chairman of the board, Albert Erskine, shot himself. There were massive layoffs. The plant operated only two days a week. Studebaker survived only because of new management and the loyalty of the workers, who helped save the company by investing their money in it and taking huge cuts in their wages. Not that they had much choice about pay-cuts, but Erskine had once said of his factory workers: "Every man eats and thinks and dreams Studebaker."

Maybe that was true of the workers, though not of the Studebakers themselves, who might have felt uncomfortable with the implied narcissism. The Studebakers hadn't had much to do with the company since 1915, when John Mohler Studebaker retired at eighty-one as company director.

Over the years the Studebaker family receded from the public consciousness. When someone mentioned Studebaker, they mostly meant the car or company, not the people, not the way the world *Israel* in the Old Testament means both the land and the people. As the public's memory of the Studebakers faded, so too did the family, until only Evangeline Studebaker remained in South Bend, quietly leading a life to which no one paid particular attention. There almost seemed a correlation here, the way the gods of a culture vanish when the people stop burning incense for them. Maybe the citizens of South Bend would have done well to remember the Studebakers as people, not only cars, because, as the city's awareness of them slipped, so did the fortunes of the company.

Through all those years, Evangeline lived alone in a turreted lime-stone house on Washington Avenue, a street downtown where the wealthy had once built their homes. The street had suffered decades of neglect and decay, but at the time of Evangeline's death it was being renovated and refurbished house by house. Tippecanoe Place, with its giant limestone blocks and round arches, stood foremost among the houses. You could tell that almost all the houses were important on this street because they all had names: the DeRhodes House, de-signed by Frank Lloyd Wright; Copshaholm, a combination Roman-esque and Queen Anne—style mansion with Italian sunken gardens; the Cushing House built in 1872 in second empire style.

The only large house on Washington that didn't have a name was Evangeline's, a smaller version of Tippecanoe Place, but with none of Tippecanoe's generous grounds. Evangeline's house seemed cramped on its busy street corner, with only a run-down garage in back.

At first, the *Tribune* reported her death quietly with a simple obitu-ary. Half of the obituary explained that Evangeline had absolutely no connection to the company. Other than that, there didn't seem to be many facts about her. She was born in 1905, went east to school at Bryn Mawr. She'd never married. The paper seemed almost embar-rassed by her death, maybe saddened that it had missed a great inter-view, a tremendous human-interest story.

Perhaps a shake-up occurred at the *Tribune*, because three days af-ter the obituary ran, the paper made her death seem *extremely* impor-tant, as though Queen Victoria had died all over again, or at least South Bend's favorite aunt. The *Tribune* ran a banner headline and carried a special souvenir supplement devoted to Studebaker family lore. There were photographs as well: The family scions. A magnifi-cent frontal view of the plant. An interior shot taken from a great height showing dozens of men in rubber aprons standing along a con-veyor belt. The men looked up at the camera in bewilderment as though the photographer had just shouted, You're all docked a week's pay!

Still, no one had much to say about Evangeline. The only tidbit was the circumstance of her death. Apparently, as wealthy as she un-doubtedly was, she hadn't paid her heating bill, and so had died of ex-posure. Not only that, but piles of antiques and heirlooms filled her entire house. The people who found her had had to wade through her possessions to reach her body.

A week passed before anything else appeared in the paper about Evangeline. Maybe another shake-up occurred. This time, the *Tribune* ran an editorial questioning all the hoopla surrounding Evangeline's passing. "Here was no kingmaker, no industrial giant," the paper eulogized, "but a quiet woman who shied away from publicity and lived a simple, honest life. Let's not falsely glorify her memory. Instead, let's dignify it by respecting her as an ordinary but true citizen of South Bend."

L ois stood by a window that looked out onto a scraggly fir tree and the street beyond. Over fifty people packed into the room, and others jammed the doorway right outside. A young man with a ponytail and his Mediterranean-looking girlfriend held hands in front of her, occasionally whispering to each other. She figured they had their eyes on the phonograph, but then they abruptly turned around and made their way out of the room. The hardwood floor creaked underneath their weight, but other than normal shifting around and whispering, people in the crowd were quiet, almost respectful.

The people in the corridor were noisier, less intent on the proceedings. Three children raced one another on the carpeted hallway, past Lois's line of vision. In their wake, someone yelled, "Keith, watch out! Don't get runned over!" Then they must have sprinted up the stairs, because a minute later she heard squeals and thumping sounds above the heads of the auctiongoers. Lois, like the rest, looked up at the ceiling as though she might see through it. A middle-aged man with a massive gut got an impatient look and waded through the crowd into the hall. Their father, Lois assumed.

It seemed to Lois that half of Michiana had shown up by 10:00 A.M. to see Evangeline Studebaker's estate auctioned off, the other half appearing by noon: gawkers, browsers, and bidders alike jamming Evangeline's house. Among the treasures to be sold were two oak rolltop desks, a baby grand piano, a player piano, a score of oil paintings by nineteenth-century American artists, steamer trunks full of beaded dresses from the twenties, a set of gold-leaf china, and a 1931 Studebaker President that hadn't been driven in ages. Other oddities included a barrel of peacock feathers, a pantry stocked with jars of capers and boxes of Chef Boyardee pizza mix, and a nearly complete set of *Better Homes and Gardens*.

The auctioneer, a lanky man with stooped shoulders and hawkish features, seemed more long-winded than most people in that line of work. He didn't simply sell off objects, but always told the crowd a little story surrounding each item, as though each of Evangeline's belongings had personal significance to him as well. Up on his makeshift stage, he sometimes seemed more like a eulogizer than an auctioneer. He wore a lime green sports jacket about twenty years out of fashion, with wide lapels, and a tie the size of a dinner napkin. The man had a habit that Lois found annoying. As he spoke, he kept touching his nose, rubbing it along the bridge, as though his nose were something he'd just awakened with that morning and he was trying to worry away with his finger.

The man's wife, two grown sons, and a teenage daughter all assisted him with the auction. The wife charged folks a dollar at the door, signed them up, and gave them a numbered paddle. The daughter and one of the sons zeroed in on bidders in the crowd, she with a sharp yelp and a fixed stare, he with a pointed finger and a guttural "Ho!"—both of them seemed twice as animated as their father. The other son moved boxes and furniture up to his father's place, and never spoke a word. Together the three of them orbited their father, took their cues from him, and seemed in step with his every gesture. From time to time, one of them would speak in a low voice or whisper in his ear, and he'd smile and nod or shake his head. Then his attention would turn to the crowd again, and he'd look at them with something approaching concern, a sense of responsibility for their welfare. Lois noticed this look, or rather, absorbed it, and the deliberate way he worked the crowd. She started to feel reassured, despite that annoying habit of rubbing the bridge of his nose, and she began to trust him. She believed that bargains could be had here, and believed him when he said something was one of a kind or worth twice the highest bid.

Lois examined the wallpaper by the window. The paper was peeling off, and without realizing, she grabbed a corner and started tearing it away. The paper was salmon-colored and showed chrysanthemums surrounded by twin branches with evenly spaced gold leaves. Beneath the wallpaper was only plaster, not more wallpaper.

Near the window a trove of knickknacks were spread out on tables along the wall: framed family photographs of Studebaker men, women, and children, hats in their original boxes, and two glass cases with Evangeline's jewelry inside. Lois sifted through them like an archaeologist. She catalogued every object as testimony of another woman's life. Where was the proof that *her* life had not always been this fractured? She tried on a curved velvet hat with a veil, then returned it to its box. She felt like a widow.

Other people's lives weren't good enough for her anymore.

Outside, it was a crisp blue day, the clouds blown away by the wind. A light sweater kind of day. A large bird circled around in the distance.

While the auctioneer chattered away in a singsong voice, Lois tried to ignore him. Lois could never figure out why that singsong voice, so difficult to understand, was such an important aspect of an auctioneer's job, but all auctioneers had it, and seemed to consider it a badge of honor rather than a speech defect.

The rolltop desks went first, then the nineteenth-century American paintings, removed from their hooks and leaning against the wall, and also the stuffed chair in which Evangeline had died. After the auctioneer finished with the chair (it sold for $225), he moved on to a dozen Victorian porcelain dolls and from there to an Edison phonograph from the turn of the century.

Lois, of course, wanted it all, but could afford none of it, which just depressed her. She had only $115 in her bank account, which had to last her the better part of the next two weeks. By March she'd nearly gone through the settlement money, her scheme to get rich with antiques in California had faltered, and the child support hardly even kept the girls in clothes.

Now would have been a good time to go searching for Gail and Meg and Henry, who had disappeared half an hour earlier, Henry and Meg in one direction and Gail in the other. The amazing thing was that Gail had come of her own volition. Usually, she wouldn't be seen dead at an auction or garage sale, and had only deigned to show her face at this one because she knew her father was going to be there. Lois had already spotted him outside, arm-in-arm with Alice, the two of them ogling the canary-yellow Studebaker. Or maybe Gail just wanted to see how a lady as rich as Evangeline had lived her life.

The auctioneer touched his nose and said, "I want to tell you a little history on this item. Now I wouldn't be at all surprised if John M. Studebaker himself used this Edison phonograph." He pronounced the word "Stoodiebaker" and the name Edison became "Ederson." "Mr. Stoodiebaker, I hear, was a personal friend of Thomas Ederson." The auctioneer leaned forward and said, "Thomas Ederson used to maintain that he never slept more than one hour a night. Maybe that's true because the man couldn't have had eight hours' beauty rest and accomplish all he did in one lifetime. But my personal opinion is that Mr. Ederson took a lot of catnaps during the day. You know why I think that? You just look at a photograph of Ederson, and in every one of them, he's got his eyes closed." The man straightened up and gave the crowd a wide-eyed look. They stared at him, entranced for a second, then broke into laughter.

While the man told his little story, Lois tried to ignore him. She noticed one young man who was looking hungrily toward the record player. She recognized him from somewhere, a skinny boy with a bad complexion and thin red hair, but she couldn't quite place him. The boy sipped a diet pop while the bidding went on, eyeing the crowd warily over the lip of the can.

The auctioneer raised his hand and ticked off Edison's accomplishments: "The incandescent light bulb, celluloid film, the movie projector, the alkaline battery . . . and this . . . " he patted the oak cabinet of the phonograph and said, "This was the invention he was proudest of.

"All in all, the man conjured up over a thousand strange and useful products, some you've heard of, some you use everyday and don't think twice about, some you'd think I was pulling your leg if I told you about." He put his hand back down and rubbed the bridge of his nose with it, and he leaned forward even closer to the crowd. "At the end of his life, you know what he was working on?" Here, the auctioneer raised his hand and put on an "honest truth" look, his lips clamped, his eyes looking off sideways at his raised hand. "A machine to communicate with them that had gone off into the great hereafter."

A few people laughed nervously and shook their heads and the auctioneer nodded his and said, "That's exactly correct. It's unbelievable that a genius like Thomas Ederson could have such a jughead idea. I was surprised as you when I first heard that. But I guess when you've invented just about everything you can invent on this earth, you just naturally start aiming for the heavens."

That didn't sound so bizarre to Lois. After all, she knew how to communicate with the dead, and she didn't even need a machine. All you had to do was listen to them sing and write them letters. They'd write back and say, I'm right where you left me. And they made more sense than the living who'd try to sell you fish *cut into* chips every chance they got. Who knows? Maybe Evangeline Studebaker herself stood right beside Lois at this moment, waiting to be communicated with. Lois turned and stared at a rotund woman beside her. The woman wore a large Notre Dame T-shirt with stains on it, shorts, and flip-flops. The woman had her neck stuck out like a turtle, her attention directed up front, her head bobbing for a better view.

The woman turned and regarded Lois with mild disapproval, obviously misunderstanding why Lois was staring at her. Lois put a hand through her hair, then touched the place where her locket had been. Her breath caught, and for a moment, she thought she'd lost it. Then she remembered.

The auctioneer handed a record each to his son and daughter, and they waved them in front of the eyes of the bidders as though they were holy relics. He stroked the glory horn of the phonograph and cranked its arm. A song from World War I filled the room. A chorus of earnest men shouted.

> The Kaiser called the devil up
> on the telephone one day;
> The girl at central listened to
> all they had to say.
>
> The devil said 'Hello, Bill,'
> and Bill said 'How are you?
> I'm running here a hell on earth,
> so tell me what to do.

My army went through Belgium —
Shooting women and children down.
We tore up all her country
and blew up every town.

My Zeps dropped bombs on cities
killing both old and young;
and those the Zeppelins didn't get
were taken out and hung.'

The auctioneer lifted the heavy tone arm from the record and the men stopped marching. "You know, Ederson also invented the electric chair," he said, holding up a hand. "But he invented it to discourage folks from using George Westinghouse's alternating current instead of his own direct current. For the electric chair he used AC just to convince folks of the hazards of it. When someone died in the chair, he said they'd been Westinghoused." He looked around the room to see the reaction. "It's true," he said. "Look it up." Then he started into the bidding. The words all ran together, and Lois could hardly make sense of them.

"Nuhnuhnuhnuhnuhnuhnuhnuhnuh," he said, an outboard motor starting up. "Neeeneeneeneeneeneeeeneeenee ALL RIGHT NOW! Somebody give me two hundred bid two hundred bid two hundred Okay one-ninety okay one-fifty who'll start me out at one-fifty one-fifty nee nee nee nee nee My goodness! No interest in it? Now now now now now nee nee nee UNusual REAL HANDY Give me a bid, folks Look, you snooze, you gonna lose — Wake up and bid."

"Yowp!" his daughter shouted like she'd just been pinched, and she pointed to the culprit, the boy with the pop can and the suspicious expression. He peered at the phonograph over the rim of his can, and his eyes glinted with excitement.

"Okay I've got forty and I want fifty," the auctioneer shouted. "Neeneeeeneeeneeneenee."

"Yowp!"

"Now fifty now five!"

"Yowp!"

"Now sixty now five nuhnuhnuhnuhnuhnuhnuhnuh!"

"Yep!"

Lois turned her head back and forth, trying to keep track of the bidding, but the only person she saw bidding on it for sure was the skinny boy with the diet pop.

The boy sliced his hand through the air, which meant that he wanted to bid half what the auctioneer was suggesting.

"Okay sixty-two-and-a-half I got sixty-two-and-a-half and I want sixty-five nuhnuhnuhnuhnuhnuhnuh!"

"Yo!"

"Sixty-five now seventy sixty-five now seventy let's go OKAY."

The auctioneer's son raised seven fingers above his head.

"I've got sixty-five and I want seventy," the auctioneer said. "Neeneeeneeneeneeeeneeeneeeeeeee . . ." He seemed stalled. "My goodness, someone's getting a steal."

Lois started peeling the wallpaper again. She'd succeeded in tearing an apple-core-sized hole in it before she realized what she was doing and stopped. The man was right. She hated to see such a bargain go by the wayside. The man with the diet pop looked straight ahead at the Edison phonograph.

Lois couldn't stand it any longer and raised her paddle.

No one noticed her.

The auctioneer's son and daughter were both looking off in other directions and the auctioneer had his eyes on the phonograph. He was still stroking the glory horn saying, "Nuhnuhnuhnuhnuhnuh."

"Hey, I want to bid," Lois shouted, perhaps a little louder than absolutely necessary.

The people in the front of the room shuffled and some of them turned to look at her.

"OKAY," the auctioneer shouted ecstatically, pointing to Lois himself. "I've got seventy and I want eighty now eighty now eighty now eighty now eighty now eighty now eighty."

"HOW!"

"Now ninety now ninety now ninety."

Lois raised her paddle.

"NOW!"

The man with the diet pop glanced her way and gave her an angry look, like she'd done it to personally foil him. Maybe he was on a budget, too.

"Now a hundred now a hundred now a hundred UNUSUAL!"

No one raised a hand and the man pointed to Lois and said, "You stole it! For ninety dollars. Your number?"

Lois raised her paddle and her stomach sank. All of a sudden, she knew what she'd done. She'd reduced her family to poverty for the sake of an old record player.

The auctioneer's wife took down the number on Lois's paddle.

Lois approached the man with the diet pop, her main competition. He glowered at her as she neared, holding his diet pop at his side like a gun he was going to draw if she made a false move.

"Listen, mister," she said. "I'll sell you that phonograph if you want."

The man turned away, took a sip of pop, and said. "You paid too much for it."

She studied the boy, his red hair, his glum expression, the tight way he held his infected chin, and then she recognized him, George the junkseller from the Thieves' Market.

"Where's Dottie?" she said.

The question seemed to take the man by surprise. He turned his head abruptly and gave her a strange look. Now that she'd asked the question, she supposed it sounded like she was scolding him, like he'd been bad and she was going to tell on him.

"You were a friend of hers?" the boy asked. "She was looking forward to this auction," he went on. "She'd been wanting a phonograph like the one you got. Had her eye on it some time. The auctioneer was right. You stole it."

"I'm sorry," Lois said.

"Why? You didn't do nothing." He crossed his arms. He looked like he didn't want her to be sorry, like that was the last thing he expected or wanted. "It was her own damn fault," the man said. "That heater of hers. I kept telling her to get rid of it."

The man looked around the room. "Stop by the stall sometime. I got some things you might be interested in, some of her jewelry and things like that."

"Do you want the phonograph?" she said. "I'll give it to you for what I paid."

George just shook his head. "No, you keep it," he said, setting his diet pop down on the windowsill. "It won't do me no good. None at all."

Faintly, she heard another voice – Evangeline's, Dottie's? – she couldn't make out what was being said exactly, but the tone was one of great disappointment, as though something badly needed had slipped forever, just out of reach.

EIGHTEEN

The car, canary-yellow, newly waxed and shined, sat underneath a huge red tent between the house and the garage. Twenty rows of folding chairs had been arranged to face the car, and now every seat was full or reserved with someone's sweater or jacket, or bidding paddle. Meg, with Henry in tow, waded through the crush of people. Normally, Henry would have hung back, but Meg had, from the outset, taken control, leading him to every nook of the auction, darting through the crowd and pulling him along. While she cruised past people's knees and elbows, Henry bumped into one person after another, whisked along before he could apologize. He looked in his wake at the bruised and jostled people, most of whom smiled or put up a friendly hand as if to say, We have children, too. We know what it's like to be a family man.

Henry didn't do anything to correct their impressions. In some ways, he *was* a family man, though with someone else's family. Meg could have been his daughter. They *thought* she was his daughter, and proportionally, they seemed to go together. She was short and so was he, and they dressed alike, she in her blue-jean overalls and white T-shirt, he in jeans and loafers (no socks), and a loose Cubs sweatshirt. Only recently had he been able to dress without feeling confined.

This Studebaker didn't seem like any other Studebaker Henry had ever seen. For one thing, this car looked too elegant to be a Studebaker. Its top was down, as well as its rumble seat. It also had a large brown storage box that looked like an old steamer trunk, attached to the back. The car had whitewalls and gently curving running boards painted dark brown. The body and the spokes of the wheels were yellow, and two extra wheels, canvas-covered, were strapped to either side of the car.

Henry had always thought of Studebakers as monstrous things, too large for the road. Travel had been so conspicuous back then. When you went somewhere, you wanted people to take notice: Get out of the way, it's a Studebaker! might have been the company slogan.

Partly, this impression had to do with Henry's dad, who hadn't grown up in South Bend. "If you didn't come from South Bend," his dad had told him once, "Studebaker was a laughingstock. The Studebaker dealer was next to the Rescue Mission across from the Nash dealer."

Fair or not, that's how Henry had always thought of Studebakers, until now. If they'd made more cars like this, he thought, maybe they wouldn't have folded.

As Meg craned her head inside, Henry ran his good hand along the giant wheel well, and thought of how long it had been since he'd driven a car. Even now, he found it difficult to rely on others for transportation. Unless he hopped on his bike, he was always at Lois's mercy. Sometimes he wanted to go farther than a bike could go, and in less time. Sometimes he missed the person he used to be, not that he wanted to *become* that selfish again. He just missed himself, or the part of him that was the flip side of selfishness, the self-reliant side.

"I think we should find a place to stand, don't you?" Henry said, and Meg jumped down from the running board. She grabbed his hand unself-consciously and started leading him toward the seats. The auctioneer was setting up his microphone near them.

Suddenly, Gail sprung into their path. "Where's Mom?" she said, looking at them both as though keeping track of Lois was their responsibility.

"What's that you're wearing?" Meg said, letting Henry's hand go. Gail didn't wear her jeans frayed and torn these days, nor as many bandanas and heavy-metal T-shirts as she had when Henry had first shown up. Now she went for stone-washed blue jeans and high-top sneakers with thick tongues and the laces untied. She'd also traded in her black T-shirt for a black lace bustier. But now she was also wearing a hat with a plume.

"Do you like it?" Gail said, placing a hand behind the hat and another on her hip. "It's the latest in Paris fashion."

"Where'd you get it?" Meg said.

Gail looked up in the air and said, "Oh, some guy gave it to me, one of my many admirers. Where's Mom?"

"She stole it," Meg confided to Henry and took his hand again as if to show an alliance with him against her sister. "She always looks up in the air when she's lying."

"So I swiped it off a table," Gail said. A couple of people looked over their shoulders at her. "Nobody cares."

"Put it back, Gail," Meg said, taking an ineffectual swipe at Gail's head. Meg seemed genuinely shocked and offended by her sister's transgression. She looked up at Henry and said, "Tell her to put it back."

"Yeah, Henry," said Gail, mimicking Meg's intensity.

"It looks good on you," Henry said, smiling at her. "How about if I buy it for you?"

"Oh, shut up," she said. "That wouldn't be any fun. Where's your sense of adventure? Don't you have any guts?"

Henry looked around at the crowd. A few people still milled by the Studebaker, but most had gathered along the invisible walls of the tent, or in the seats. A general murmur rose among the people, and the auctioneer stood patiently in front of them like a choir director.

A man sitting in one of the folding chairs caught his eye. The man looked familiar but Henry couldn't place him. He stood up and handed the woman in the next seat a bidding paddle, and then started toward Henry. He had a beard and shaggy hair, a creased, leathery face, and his eyes looked like he constantly squinted in the sun. A big silver belt buckle with a turquoise inset studded his midsection.

Meg glanced where Henry was looking and darted toward the man. She met him halfway and put her arms around his middle.

"Dad, Gail stole a hat from one of the tables," Meg said as they approached.

"That so?"

Gail didn't answer but looked up in the air.

"Where's your mother?" Willy said to Meg. "She doesn't know better than to leave you running around alone?"

"We're not alone," Meg said, indicating Henry. "Gail just does whatever she wants."

Willy rubbed his finger under his nose as though he'd just been seized by a violent itch. Then he looked at Henry as though he'd just noticed him. Henry shifted his weight under Willy's scrutiny. Henry had the feeling Willy had disliked him from the moment they'd met, not for anything Henry had done or said, but simply for existing. Whether or not Henry had taken up residence with Willy's ex-wife was immaterial to the man. He would have been disgusted by Henry if he'd passed him on the street or if he'd spied him through an intergalactic telescope.

"What did *you* steal?" Willy said to Henry.

"Some eggs," Henry answered. "But I wouldn't really call it stealing, because I thought they were mine. I wouldn't have taken them otherwise."

Willy scratched a sideburn and said, "You stole eggs?"

"Eggs and other assorted groceries. I don't remember it all too clearly."

Willy looked Henry up and down, then turned to Gail. "Well, put it back before somebody notices," he said to Gail. "I don't want to pay for some junk hat. It makes you look retarded. It makes you look like you just stepped off some banana boat."

Willy said all this from the side of his mouth. Gail stared fixedly past her father's shoulder, seemingly unmoved, and Meg acted like the one who'd been ridiculed. She looked down at the ground, kicked some dirt, sneaked a look at her sister, and bent her head again.

Willy jerked his head, and Henry imagined Willy's marble-sized brain knocking against his skull. Henry didn't like Willy much. In fact, he didn't like him at all, and hadn't liked him from the moment they'd met. This was a big admission for Henry. For a couple of years now the only person he'd allowed himself to dislike was himself. Willy was just the kind of person Henry had once been before the accident. Maybe that's what Willy needed. An accident.

"I'm not asking you to pay for it," Gail said. "I don't want you to pay for it."

Henry tapped Willy on the arm and Willy turned around. Henry backed off and said, "I was just going to say I stole a few other things. I went on a shoplifting spree when I was nine. I went into a Walgreen's with a heavy coat in the middle of summer and started putting everything in sight into my pockets: a French-English pocket dictionary, a Russian-English dictionary, some plastic nose-and-glasses, and a whole cardboard display of those razors that cut your hair while you comb it. I did it in full view of everyone. I suppose I wanted to get caught but no one stopped me."

Henry wasn't sure why he'd told Willy all of that, except that when people made him nervous he talked. It almost didn't matter what he was saying, because sooner or later he'd run across something they wanted to hear. Not with Willy, however. Willy cleaned an ear with an index finger while Henry talked. When Henry finished he turned to Gail as though Henry wasn't there. "It's *your* ass," he said. He jerked his thumb over his shoulder. "I'm going to sit down. They're about ready to start the bidding on my car. Watch me. I'm going to try to pick it up for twenty thousand, but I don't know. I wish I had fifty grand. The place is packed with collectors."

Henry tapped Willy again, and Willy turned around slowly. "Yeah," he said.

"Are you buying that car with money from the girls' college fund? For five hundred dollars you could buy a car for Gail. You can't spare five hundred dollars?"

Gail looked at Henry, horrified. He felt horrified, too. Every muscle in his body told him to turn around and run.

"What are you doing?" Gail yelled. "What exactly are you trying to do?" Gail pushed her way between two people and hurried away.

Willy didn't look angry, but amused. "Where did Lois meet you anyway? Some animal husbandry class? On a chinchilla farm?"

Then Willy turned around and left. Henry sat down on the grass, then lay back on his elbows and looked up at the clouds. Presently, Meg sat down beside him and handed him his paddle. She didn't say anything, and looked where he was looking. People stepped around them, and Henry felt comfortable there. Henry absently picked a dandelion and set it down on its side, then glided his hand over the tops of the grass, letting the blades tickle his palms.

Henry didn't stay there. A couple of months before he might have. But having rejoined the human race, he had a responsibility to stand upright and act the way people around him acted.

Henry didn't know how these auctions worked, really. He'd just picked up a paddle because it seemed like the thing to do. It made him feel like he fitted in. Up until now, he hadn't been paying attention, and for all he knew the bidding had already begun.

The auctioneer stood up front, a hand on the great grinning grille of the automobile. He was talking so low Henry could barely hear him, and he seemed to be talking directly to the car itself, not the people. The man rubbed the bridge of his nose and said, "You know, Studebaker had a knack for making the right decisions at the wrong time. First, they decided to go into the luxury car business, so they bought the Pierce-Arrow Motor Company. That was 1928, the year before the depression. When the depression hit, no one seemed to want luxury cars no more. Back in the thirties they *had* an impressive lineup: the President, the Commander, the Rockne, the Erskine, the Pierce-Arrow, and their lower-priced car, the Dictator." Here, the auctioneer paused and rubbed his nose as though he was excessively weary. "They also made some *wrong* decisions at the wrong time. Now I'm not saying anything against Studebaker, but let me ask you something. Does it make sense to name a car the Dictator in the thirties? Who'd want to ride around in a Mussolini car?" the auctioneer asked, pronouncing the name muscle-lini. "Does it make sense building luxury cars during the depression?" he continued. "Not much. That's why the company went into receivership in 1933. That's why the man running the company, Albert Erskine, shot himself. After that, Studebaker started making cars that made more sense, even though they still made some jughead decisions, like merging with Packard in the fifties. Not a smart move. You ever see one of them Packards? That's one damn ugly automobile."

Here, the auctioneer patted the hood of the car, and said, "But this car is a throwback. This is one damn pretty car, even if it don't make no sense. Whoever buys this car, and I use the word *car* advisedly because that's just too tame a classification for a thing of such beauty, ought to head to the Hoosier Auto Show and Swap Meet down in Indy in September, just to show off some. Everything's in working order, too, and that's unconditionally guaranteed. The wigwag stoplights in back. The horn." He reached in and tooted it. "The fold-down windshield. The rumble seat. My son, Myron, took it out for a spin this morning, just to make sure it worked, didn't you, Myron?"

Myron, who stood on the other side of the car from his father, made the A-OK sign with his fingers.

"Myron knows just about everything about cars," the auctioneer said proudly and then took a long look at the Studebaker again.

The auctioneer looked at the crowd. "Okay, now for the big one, boys." He stopped and stared at the crowd, smiling that big smile of his and rubbing his nose. There was a low whispering among them. Then the auctioneer took a breath and said, "The book value on this car in this condition is about fifty-five thousand, but I can tell that you're looking for a bargain, so who'll start us off at twenty."

Henry glanced in Willy's direction and saw him raise both hands.

"Yo!" Myron shouted and the auctioneer started up his motor.

"All right then, I've got ten and I want fifteen. I've got ten and I want fifteen."

"Fifty!" Henry offered.

A stray syllable tumbled out of the auctioneer's mouth like a broken tooth. His mouth remained open, his jaw slack. People turned to look at Henry, but no one said a word, the only sound being the breeze in the uppermost branches of the surrounding oaks and firs.

"I was asking fifteen," the auctioneer said. "Did you say fifty, five-oh?"

Henry nodded and said, "If that's all right." Henry had never felt a stronger desire to buy anything. It was almost as though a voice in his ear had guided him, telling him that this car was something he couldn't live without. He had the money. He had plenty of money left from the insurance. Willy didn't deserve this car. The car was something Henry could be proud of. He was tired of standing still.

He looked around him. Gail shaded her forehead with a hand, and she squinted at him. Meg stared at him like he'd suddenly shot up into the clouds. Willy chewed on a blade of grass, his mouth working furiously, drawing the grass in until it disappeared.

"Fifty." Henry finally said. "Fifty grand."

"Well, there's a man who don't mess around," said the auctioneer. "Do I hear sixty thousand?"

Even the breeze died down, and people looked at their feet and froze in place. The auctioneer roved the crowd once with his eyes, as though trying to etch the scene in his memory, then pointed to Henry and said, "You bought yourself a piece of history, mister. You can't put a price on that. Hold up your paddle so I can see your number."

Henry held his paddle high. He felt slightly nauseated and on edge. Something felt wrong, and his whole arm tingled. He looked at his hand holding the paddle. It wasn't his good one.

"Number three-twelve," the auctioneer's son reported, and it was good he got it, because Henry couldn't have held his hand up a second more. It dropped now and the paddle fell out of his hand, and he lost all feeling in it again. He stood still and stared at the fallen paddle.

A bald man approached Henry, picked up his paddle and handed it to Henry, who tried to take it with his right hand, but couldn't now. So he took the paddle with his left.

"That's all right, son" the man said to him. "Post auction shock. It happens to the best of us. You paid a pretty penny, that's for sure, but it's still a damn fine car."

"That it is," said another man beside the first, and the two of them disappeared into the milling crowd, shaking their heads and talking history and automobiles.

Then Meg and Gail appeared in front of him, but didn't say a thing. They just stood and stared as though he was someone they thought they'd known but hadn't really, like some movie or rock star who'd been living with them incognito all this time.

"I'm flabbergasted," Meg said.

"Can we take it for a ride, Henry?" Gail said, her voice quivering slightly. She didn't give him time to answer. Her eyes brightened, and she said, "Oh God, you should see Dad." There was more approval in Gail's voice than he'd ever heard.

"Where's Mom?" Meg said. "We can all go for a ride together."

"Maybe she's waiting in the car," Gail suggested.

And so, while Henry made his way up front to settle his account, Meg and Gail headed off to check Lois's car. He tried to write his check with his right hand, but couldn't. Whatever had allowed him to raise it before had vanished, and with it, most of the sensation, except for the faintest tingling.

NINETEEN

irth trauma. To Lois, her treatment at birth explained a lot about her life. She'd read an article on obstetrics that claimed that people who had come painfully into the world often replayed their trauma later, either by killing themselves or running amok. Her mother had told her that she'd been the most difficult of her three children to deliver. Thirty-seven hours Lois had played hide-and-seek, sticking her head out for a glimpse, then rushing back inside before she could get caught. Finally, the doctor pulled her out with forceps.

Lois had always done things in her own time. When people told her to hurry up, she slowed down. She hadn't spoken until she was nearly four, and in grade school she often refused to go on to the next subject if she didn't feel ready. On the other hand, when people told her to wait, she rushed forward, skipping two grades in high school and graduating at sixteen. That was also the year she married Willy, who thought they should wait a few years before getting married. But Lois needed him right away, sure that life's transitions would come easy with such a monolith of patience and self-assurance by her side.

At least, that's how she felt until she and Willy married. Then her outlook changed. From day one, she convinced herself Willy wouldn't live to be eighteen. He seemed too guileless, too unselfish, too good for her. Certainly, one day soon he'd fall down a shaft at the construction site where he worked, or suddenly go to sleep in her arms, the victim of something even medical science couldn't have predicted: an undeserving wife.

Her dreams and premonitions intensified over the first year, but still nothing happened to Willy. He just grew stronger and healthier and shone with confidence. She almost wished something *would* happen so she'd be proven right. She didn't want him dead, did she? Sometimes she wondered. That was ridiculous, and to prove it she told Willy she wanted to start a family.

Now, twenty years later, she was running away from that family, running amok. It had to be birth trauma. Lois hadn't exactly planned to run away. Leaving had been an impulse decision – she'd been at wits' end for weeks now, months, years, her whole life even. Or maybe birth trauma didn't explain her behavior at all. Maybe it was all her father's fault, like being at wits' end ran in the family, some kind of genetic disorder. She'd held herself together until the auction. When she bought the phonograph, nearly spent her last dime, that finished her off. She knew she couldn't face them with what she'd done.

She headed south on Highway 31, arguing with herself for fifty miles, checking in her rearview every ten seconds as though someone might be following her. The phonograph lay across her backseat, her only luggage.

After a while she lost focus on the road and then awoke to realize she'd already driven a hundred miles. She couldn't remember a thing she'd passed. To keep her mind alert, she started singing. She sang whatever came to mind.

In this way, she was able to survive. As long as words that rhymed and didn't mean anything formed in her mouth, she didn't think about what she was doing or why. As soon as she closed her mouth and the last note faded, her voice turned into a sob and she almost choked.

She had to keep telling herself that she'd run them into the ground, that, in a situation like this, she couldn't say good-bye or tell them where she was headed, they'd all have to adjust somehow.

Then she pulled off onto the shoulder of the highway, opened her door, and retched, but nothing came up.

Gail and Willy had been right about her all along. She wasn't fit to take care of herself, let alone anyone else. Willy would take care of them. Willy and his new wife. They wouldn't want for anything from now on because Willy was so levelheaded.

At Naptown she took I-465 around the city, which flung her off into a different orbit onto Interstate 70 East, heading toward Ohio and West Virginia, and she left the state at Richmond, singing a song about Cuba, where she'd never been and likely would never see. There were so many places in the world she knew about, had known about her whole life, had taken on faith existed. Cuba, Afghanistan, Liberia. Except for that trip to the world's fair in 1964, she'd barely stepped outside of Indiana. She'd never seen Europe, the industrialized nations, the Third World, the Free World, Asia. Georgia, for Christ's sake. She'd never been to Georgia. She would have sung "Georgia on My Mind," but she didn't know how it went, except for the refrain.

After she ran out of songs, she repeated her repertoire, made up new ones, and then in the middle of the night, as she started to approach her destination, she fell silent and didn't utter another word. All she heard was the hum of her tires on the road.

The rest of the way she listened to the radio, at first anything that she could receive, but then, she kept it on AM, and tuned to the dial number of the radio station where her dad worked. The number was just a hole on the dial, and nothing but fuzz filled the car. Some people liked that, Lois knew. Nothing but white noise surrounding them. Some people paid big money for that. She could get used to it, too, she figured.

Toward morning, the station started coming in, and then it went again. The voices were indistinct, and she couldn't make out what they were saying. Behind the voices was something that sounded like the steady blast of a foghorn, and Lois imagined the people at sea, trying to be heard between the foghorn above them and the white foam below.

She felt like the radio pulled her along, like she could take her hands off the wheel and her father would reel her in from his station. At one point, she lifted her hands off the steering wheel as an experiment, and the car pulled toward the center line. Maybe he didn't want her to reach him, after all. She knew how easy it would be to allow him to pull her off the road into a tree, how easy to surrender, a giving in to her natural relationship with her father.

She arrived on the outskirts of Parkersburg by noon and didn't need directions. The station, a low concrete building no bigger than a bunker, stood off the highway in clear view. A gigantic tower — it must have been three hundred feet high — rose behind the station. There weren't any windows in the building. The only ornaments were the four plastic call letters on the side facing the highway, and a marquee with a fortune cookie message: To See The View, You Have To Climb The Mountain. Lois knew about that mountain. One minute you think you're on top of it, and the next day you're under two thousand pounds of sand.

The parking lot was immense, much larger than such a tiny building needed, but then Lois saw that on the far end of the lot was another building. She'd been so intent on finding the station, she'd hardly taken in the rest of her surroundings. Now she stopped in the middle of the nearly empty parking lot, her car straddling the line between two spaces. And she stared out the window, not at the radio station, but at the other building across the lot.

The light of the sun shone on the Stuckey's as though it was some holy place. She turned away from it, and for a while, she just sat with her hands folded over the steering wheel, contemplating where she was. She looked back again and the Stuckey's was still there. She looked at the sign on the building, and marveled at how little Stuckey's had changed. Most businesses, she knew, tended to make some basic changes over the years, but not Stuckey's. It looked as it had when she was a child – the sign written in a kind of 1950s slanting script, the building white with a bright blue roof and STUCKEY'S emblazoned across it.

So he hadn't budged in thirty years. She imagined he'd simply walked across the parking lot after they'd abandoned him, and found himself a job at the station. Perhaps that was the easiest thing for him to do, though she hoped he'd done it to keep vigil close by, waiting for them to turn around and retrieve him. It must have been difficult to keep vigil in a building without windows.

Lois got out of her car, but was struck by an attack of indecision. She wanted to use the rest room at Stuckey's before she found her father, who wasn't even expecting her. She didn't have a good feeling about that Stuckey's. She didn't want to go inside. She thought something bad might happen if she did. Maybe her dad would have a heart attack when he saw her, or someone would steal her car and leave her without any escape.

She decided she'd parked too far away, and got back inside her car, and crept toward the radio station. Actually, she inched there. She barely moved. She approached the building with caution, as though it *were* an enemy bunker.

She parked again and got out, only to realize that this time she'd parked in a handicap space, of which there were ten or so along the wall. Did that many handicapped people work there? she wondered. Again, she stood outside the car, pondering whether she should move or not.

Now she noticed something different – steam rising from her hood, and when she turned on the ignition the needle on her temperature gauge slowly rose toward the red, quivered, and kept on rising.

She walked around the side of the building to the entrance – green indoor/outdoor carpeting that led up two concrete steps and through a glass door to an empty lobby the size of a doctor's waiting room. There was a receptionist's window, but no receptionist.

"Hello," she called. "Is anybody home?" she said. The word *home* sounded so strange to her now. This was her home. She was home to stay. Home, home on the range.

Slowly, she took off her earrings. One by one, she removed the rest of her bracelets and necklaces and left them on one of the chairs. She wanted to look right for him. She wanted him to recognize her.

She set her purse down and started fumbling for the letter that her father had sent her, as though it might give her some clue as to how to act with him. She looked in and saw a pack of sugarless gum. On another day Meg had been looking for some, and Lois had forgotten it was in there.

"I saw you put it in there, Mom," she had said.

"I don't remember having any gum, honey," Lois said.

"Well, when you find it, remember that I told you it was there. In the meantime, I guess I'll have to go without," and Meg had sighed dramatically.

Lois closed her eyes and let go of the gum, and wanted to die. She stopped ferreting around. She just kept her hand in her purse.

There didn't seem to be anyone around. She made her way down a short hallway with the same indoor/outdoor carpeting that covered the outside steps, past two closed doors on one side and two sound booths on the other side. The sound booths had long windows that faced the hallway. In one of them she saw a man, and she heard music. Afraid to knock, she waited outside.

Finally, she opened the door and he turned around.

Lois recognized him at once: his flat features, his nose, which had been broken in a fight in the merchant marine. She recognized his single sharp feature, his eyes; blue dots in an otherwise wide face. She recognized the way he wore his hair, close to the scalp, though his hair had changed from black to white. However, he seemed shorter and the muscles he'd developed in the factory had gone soft.

He looked like he'd hardly seen the light of day in the thirty years since Lois saw him last. His complexion was pasty and mottled in different shades of white and yellow, ranging from a margarine tint to patches the color of ocean foam. He wore bright red slacks, slightly short, and a pullover green sports shirt, too tight, which emphasized the rolling hill and dale of his upper body. His arms were covered with fine white hair that Lois remembered as black.

Even though she recognized him, she didn't say anything. She wanted *him* to say something, to recognize her as well, but he regarded her like she was some stranger off the street. Then, slowly, his expression changed. His face clouded momentarily, and she couldn't make out right away what he was feeling: uncertainty, fear, suspicion?

"I left my family," she confessed. "I drove all night to get here. I haven't slept or anything."

Standing there, waiting, she felt ashamed of her body, her age, the fact that she wasn't a girl anymore peering out the car window as her father waltzed into Stuckey's, humming a tune, and disappeared, supposedly forever. She was taller than him now. She wasn't dressed right.

He waved her into the sound booth, and then turned to his microphone. "We have a visitor, folks. Somebody's stopped by to chat. A pretty woman to keep me company."

He still didn't recognize her. Lois wanted to turn around and run. She felt foolish, and wasn't sure she wanted him to recognize her. Maybe he wasn't her father at all, or maybe he knew who she was but refused to admit it. Still, she obeyed him and sat down. His chair was a big leather easy chair, like the one he sat in at home when she was little. Her chair was a gray metal folding one, the auditorium kind. Stencilled across its front were the words Property of Wood County.

His desk was covered with paper bags from Stuckey's and candy wrappers with half-eaten candy inside: pecan logs, a box of maple pralines, a bag of peanut brittle, and another of saltwater taffy. He cleared the desk of some of the wrappers, then offered her a pecan log.

"These are my favorite," he said.

She took the log and unwrapped it, but the thought of putting the log into her mouth disgusted her so she just held it. Her dad had one, too, but he ate his, and smiled at her. Lois wanted to talk to him, to sit facing him and hold his hand, and learn to be with him again. But her hands were sticky with the pecan log and so were his, so she kept them to herself.

"Where you from?" he said cheerily.

"South Bend, Indiana," she said, staring at the microphone, wondering how many people were listening.

Her dad's expression clouded and he stopped chewing. Then he recovered and said, slowly, "I used to live there."

"I know," Lois said. "You used to work for Studebaker. You had a family and you took them to the world's fair." She looked down at her lap and said, "The fair world. The world's fair." Then she looked at him again.

He moved closer to her and didn't take his eyes from her. He zoomed in on her like some giant lens. "We'll talk later," he said. "I'm doing my show."

He pushed a button and said, "Howdy." His voice trembled, his hands shook, and he wouldn't look at Lois.

A woman's voice said, "Howdy, Rudy!"

"Howdy, ma'am," he answered in his deep voice. "And to whom do I have the pleasure of talking?"

"My name's Laura."

"That's a fine name," he said slowly. "My daughter's name is Lois. She's come down all the way from South Bend, Indiana, to visit me. She's sitting right here with me now." To Lois, he didn't sound too enthusiastic. He sounded like a prisoner of war rattling off the articles of the Geneva Convention.

"How nice," the woman said. "Howdy, Lois," the woman said.

For a second, Lois couldn't find her voice. "Hi," she said, which sounded more like something had caught in her throat than a greeting. "Hi," she repeated.

Her father looked at her and smiled. He patted her hand and his shoulders dropped a bit. She was afraid he might start telling his listeners more about her. She abandoned me once, she imagined him saying, and now she's abandoned her family.

He didn't say that. Instead, he asked the woman why she'd called and she said, "Rudy, I want to give your listeners a recipe for eggs and asparagus."

"Sounds like a tasty morsel," he said when she was finished. "Thanks, Laura."

"Is this what you do around here?" Lois said, which sounded like a criticism, but she hadn't meant it that way. What she meant was, Did he need any help? How could she lend a hand? She wanted to start right away. She wanted to stay busy.

"Well," he said and paused. "Night watchman," he ticked off on his finger. "Record librarian. Janitor... and receptionist. While Faye's gone. Station manager. Owner. Disc jockey. We do one show here. It's mine. People call in from all over, travelers passing through, people who can't sleep, and they say, howdy. We talk. Sometimes I sing for them. You'll see. How long you planning on staying?"

Lois thought about this. "You live here?" she said. "You don't go anywhere?"

"Well," he said and paused. "Stuckey's. Maybe we can talk about this later."

He pushed a button in front of him and another voice entered the room, this time a man who said, "Howdy, Rudy."

"Howdy, sir, and what do you want to talk about?"

"On a fishing expedition last summer," the man said, "I discovered something very useful that can be done with discarded fish heads and entrails."

Lois ignored the caller and said, "Why didn't you ever get in touch with me? If I hadn't found that record that you made, I'd never have known you still existed."

"How do you think I feel?" he told her, putting a hand to his chest. "I've still got three boxes of them records." He turned to the microphone again and said, "Sir, would you like one of my records? I'll send it for free."

There was silence on the other end. "Must have hung up," he said. He looked down at his lap. "I didn't get in touch with you because I thought you'd be better off. I figured I'd just gum up the works. So'd your mother, I guess. Anyway, I figured you'd be happy. You were a happy little girl."

"Daddy," she said. "It didn't work."

"I suppose not," he said and turned away.

Lois's dad looked thoughtful and flicked a switch.

The next caller was the mother of a thirteen-year-old boy who wet his bed every night. The woman said, "I've tried grounding him. I've tried whuppin' him. Nothing works. What should I do next?"

The woman sounded more concerned about the stains on her sheets than about her son.

Lois felt flushed and nauseated. She had no right to be horrified by anything people did to their children. At least this woman had called in. At least she was trying to work things out.

"Tell you what, ma'am," he said. "I don't know much about this problem, but I bet you're not doing much good by whuppin' your son. I don't know if punishment is the route. What do the rest of you think? Anyone out there can help with this problem of bed-wetting? This is WPKB, 1290 on your AM dial. Some talk, some music, some of the time. You're listening to the 'Howdy Rudy Show.' You're on the air."

"Howdy, Rudy," a woman said.

"Howdy, ma'am. What do you know about bed-wetting?

"Not a blessed thing," the woman said, "but I want to know your opinion on the issue of forced busing. I don't see why my children got to suffer, going to some low-rent school in the worst neighborhood. Do you think that's fair, making little children suffer?"

Lois suddenly felt shy, and didn't want to sit down next to her father, so she wandered slowly around his sound booth. There was a plant on top of a filing cabinet, and she started absently fiddling with its leaves. It had pink blooms and long green arms like a cactus, but without stickers.

"I like plants," Lois said, "but I always wind up killing them."

Her father turned in his chair. The leather of his chair made a scrunching noise when he turned. "Plants don't take that much."

"Too much for me," Lois said.

He turned back to the microphone and said, "Caller, what'd you say your name was?"

"Shirma."

"Shirma," he repeated. "Is that like Sherpa, you know those little people who climb mountains and whatnot?"

"It's a family name," the woman said, sounding offended. "Is that your daughter with you?"

He didn't answer her, but scratched an ear and turned to Lois again. "That's a Star Bright plant," he said. "I've had it for twenty years. Folks generally hand them down from one generation to the next. Your mother and I had one of these plants when we were first married. It belonged to Grandmother Redemacher, and that's what we called it, our grandma plant. Then her dog got into it, tore it out by the roots."

"Was that Buster?" Lois asked. "I remember Buster."

"No – Daisy. This was before you were born."

"Oh."

"Anyway, your mother never forgave me for that."

"Never forgave you?"

Her dad shrugged and picked at his pecan log. "That's how she was." He turned again and said, "You have any hobbies, Shirma?"

"I go clogging most every night of the week."

"Good for you," said Lois's dad. "Keep out of trouble," and he disconnected her.

There was something Lois didn't understand, but she was hesitant. She didn't want to upset him too much. "What about when Mom left you here?" she said. "She seemed pretty angry at you. I mean, whose fault was that?"

Her dad looked at the ceiling.

Next, a man called who said he was a guidance counselor at Wofford Middle School in Frankfort, Kentucky. "About the bed-wetting?" he said. "You're right. Punishment's way out of line. A problem like this stems from psychological insecurity. When children feel out of control of their lives they sometimes manifest this by losing control of their body. The way to help kids is to bolster their self-confidence. Bed-wetting is infantile behavior, a subconscious need to regress to a time when people took care of you, when they gave you their unconditional love. If you feel like no one's taking care of you, it's like calling out for help."

"That sounds sensible to me, sir," Lois's dad said. I hope you're listening, ma'am. Unconditional love, not punishment. Is that about the gist of it?"

"That's it," the man said.

"Wait a second," Lois said. "You bought a new car. You took us out east when we were broke."

"You left me on the side of the road, not the other way around," he said, pinching his shirt at a place below his collar, and plucking at it a couple of times like he wanted to remove some lint.

Lois suddenly felt the need to pee, even though she'd been just half an hour ago.

"You were broke," Lois pressed, her voice rising. "You weren't even headed home. You were headed south. Mama said you would have driven us into the ocean, except you would have run out of gas long before then."

"I was crazy with worry," he said, not looking at her, but addressing the microphone like someone at a congressional hearing. "About the money, about her. I knew it was coming. I knew she was waiting to punish me."

Lois wasn't sure whether he was talking about her mother or God. Lois remembered her mother as quiet and dour, not the vengeful creature Lois's dad made her out to be. She never spoke against him. She just didn't want to speak or hear about him at all. She just wanted to pretend he never existed.

"So when the boy wets his bed," Lois's dad said into the microphone, "that boy's mother should maybe give him an ice cream cone?"

The guidance counselor didn't reply immediately. Then Lois heard his voice, more nervous than before. "Maybe I could call back some other time," he suggested. "If now's not convenient."

Lois's father gripped the sides of his leather easy chair and said, "This is my show. There *is* no more convenient time."

"I wouldn't necessarily reward the boy," the man said, "but I wouldn't punish him. I'd ignore the bed-wetting. And I'd spend more time with him . . . "

Lois wanted to listen some more, but she couldn't hold it any longer. She flew out of the room and made it to the rest room barely in time.

When she returned, her father stood by the filing cabinet, eating a pecan log.

"We're taking a break," he said curtly, ripping off a hunk and depositing it in his mouth.

"I'm not going home," she forced herself to say.

"Where you heading then?"

"Nowhere," she said. "You're not going to kick me out, are you?"

He just looked at her sadly and she felt sick and desperate. She thought maybe if she gave him a present, he'd let her stay, and then she remembered the phonograph on her backseat. Yes, that was her dad's kind of music.

He opened one of the drawers and started flipping through some papers.

"Here, I found it," he said, pulling out a square of green cardboard. He handed her a game of auto bingo. In the right-hand corner there was a stylized drawing of a mom and dad zipping along in a car while their two kids played auto bingo in the back.

The card had little windows with objects to look for while traveling. Each window had a red plastic shade to pull across when the object was sighted. There was a picture of a policeman, a mailbox, a dog, a fruit stand, a train, an airplane, a train gate, a billboard, a stoplight, a fountain, a cow, a fireplug, a boy, a bird . . .

Lois held the game and closed one of the red windows over a truck. She looked at her father, wondering what it meant.

"I just wanted you to know," he said. "I bought that for you. I thought this was something you'd like."

"Lois didn't know what he meant. He hadn't known she was coming, and this was something for a child, not a grown woman.

"Don't you remember?" he said. "I told you I'd buy you something and I did. You weren't happy with me that day. You wouldn't even look at me. Never mind trying to get you to smile. I thought this would get me back in your good graces."

"You've kept this game for thirty years?" she said, waving the card at him.

"I thought maybe you'd come back," he said, "and I could give it to you. Then I just forgot about it, until now."

"You knew where it was," she said. "You knew exactly where it was. It didn't take you long at all to find it." That was important to her and she wanted to know if that was important to him. She peered into his eyes. She looked harder at him than she'd ever looked at anyone before. He looked down at his shoes, and toed the floor with one of them. Then he scratched the back of his neck.

"I don't have much," he said. "When you don't have much, you don't do a lot of searching around."

Lois nodded slowly. She could agree with that. Slowly, she sat down on the floor, like someone on a picnic who's just thrown a blanket over the perfect spot. She sat in the middle of the room. She knew she'd never budge again, that she couldn't take a step farther. Columbus was wrong. She'd fallen off the edge. All these years she'd seen her father one way. All these years she'd seen her mother another way. She moved the auto bingo window over the policeman back and forth. She kept staring at the policeman in the window. She was afraid to take her eyes off him. She thought he might sneak up and arrest her if she did. She kept sliding the window, picking up speed, faster, until he was just a red blur. And then she couldn't make it go any faster, and she grabbed the opposite corners of the auto bingo card and ripped the game from one end to the other.

TWENTY

From the window of her dad's bedroom on the second floor, Gail pondered why a piece of underwear and a man's shoe were stuck on the eaves below her. The underwear, crumpled and gray, lay plastered to the shingles. The shoe was in the gutter below the underwear.

Meg stood beside her, her hand on her chin, wrestling with the same riddle.

"Maybe a bird stole them for its nest," Meg conjectured.

"A bird?" Gail said. "What would a bird want with a shoe?"

"It could be the whole nest," Meg said. "It wouldn't need anything else."

"Like a bird trailer?" Gail said. A month ago, she would have told Meg to stop being stupid, but now she went with it. She placed her hand on the back of Meg's neck, and Meg looked up at her.

"What do you think Dad will do when he finds out?" Meg said.

"I don't know," Gail said. "Don't worry about it."

"He'll probably think we've run away," Meg said.

"Maybe someone broke into the house," Gail said, pointing to the shoe and underwear. "Some juvenile delinquents, like the McKee brothers. They're a couple of j.d.'s. They were probably getting their kicks."

Meg shook her head. "I doubt it." A moment later she added, "Maybe he'll think we've been kidnapped."

"Look, do you want me to leave a note?" Gail said. "Would that make you feel better?"

Meg nodded.

Gail thought about it and realized that Meg was right. She wasn't lazy; she just didn't know what to tell her father, even in a note. But it was only fair. Her mother hadn't even left that much.

Meg searched for something to write on and with, and found a yellow-ruled pad and a nubby pencil without an eraser. She returned to the window, where Meg still stood, biting her nails and gazing out at the road.

"Do you think he's been in an accident?" she said.

"No," Gail said. "He'll be here. Now hold still." She placed a piece of paper on Meg's back and said, "What do you want to say?"

"'Dear Dad,'" Meg started.

"I know that much," Gail said. "I mean, after that."

"'We know you'll worry, but don't,'" Meg dictated.

Gail started to write it on Meg's back. The paper wasn't level. Part of it covered the straps of Meg's overalls and part lay over her thin T-shirt. A couple of times the pencil poked through the paper. Gail got as far as "We'll know you'll worry," then stopped.

"If he's going to worry anyway," she said, "what good is telling him not to?"

Meg considered this. "At least he'll know we care."

"Okay, what next?" Gail said, convinced, pencil poised.

"How about 'Sincerely, Meg and Gail.'"

Carefully, Gail wrote, "Sincerely, Gail and Meg," and then walked over to the brass bed in the middle of the room and placed it on one of the pillows. She wasn't sure which side her dad slept on, but she thought he probably claimed the one closest to the door. Still, she didn't want to put it on Alice's side of the bed by mistake. So she picked up the note again and put it in the exact center.

She returned to the window and resumed her lookout. Maybe he *had* been in an accident. He said he'd be here forty-five minutes ago. Maybe he'd lost his way. Alice had gone to pick Gail's dad up from work at the ethanol plant, and if he returned home before they left, then everything would be ruined. He'd kill Henry as soon as look at him, especially if he found him on his property.

For a week now, ever since the auction, her father had been sneezing and his eyes had been watering. He blamed it on Gail's mom and Henry, said every time he thought about what they'd done to him, he had to blow his nose. Gail couldn't tell what rankled him more, getting beat out on the bidding for the Studebaker or having his ex-wife run off and saddle him with a couple of kids. Gail knew that's how he thought of them. Even Meg knew it. Gail wouldn't have bothered to write a note if Meg hadn't insisted.

Her father still hadn't even started fixing up any of the rusted heaps he had over by the barn. From where she stood, she could see them all clearly – a Hawk, a Lark Daytona, a Wagonaire, a Regal – Gail knew all their names. They'd been a part of her alphabet, learned on her daddy's knee. They were older than her, in far worse shape, entangled with weeds. They weren't going anywhere. Gail knew that for sure. Even if he devoted the rest of his life to the project, he wouldn't be able to get any of them going. He couldn't make one decent car from the lot of them.

The real reason her dad sneezed so much was because of the ethanol plant. Even Alice knew that much. The city didn't smell like ethanol anymore – not that it ever had this far out in the country. They'd finally solved the problem, but now the plant shot out a fine mist of corn dust over the city. Her dad would never have admitted it. He wasn't about to blame the place where he worked for his problems. Instead, he blamed the newspaper for spreading rumors.

Gail heard Henry before she saw him, a steady grinding noise and then he poked around the curve about a mile away from the house, going no more than ten miles per hour, gravel and dust spurting around him.

"Why is he going so slow?" Meg asked.

Gail didn't answer, but watched the car as it made its slow progress toward them. She knew the car was an antique, but she hoped it went more than ten miles an hour. She didn't want to spend two months traveling to Parkersburg. Before too much longer, she wanted life to return to . . . well, normal wasn't quite the right word. At least, she wanted things to be abnormal in the ordinary way. This limbo with her dad and Alice had to end.

Everyone had been jumpy for the last week, expecting some news of Gail's mom or waiting for her to call. Whenever the phone rang, Willy clumped over to it and jerked it off its hook. "Yeah?" he'd say, daring it to be her, but it never turned out that way. Gail had wondered, too, how she'd react if she heard her mother's voice on the other end. At first, she thought she didn't want to talk to her ever again. Then she figured she wanted to talk to her only long enough to tell her she never wanted to talk to her again. She wanted to punish her. She wanted her to suffer. She had it all rehearsed. That was a pretty dumb stunt you pulled, Mom. Don't think we're just going to let you come waltzing back into our lives, because we're not. Meg felt more forgiving. More confident, too. Whenever the phone rang, Meg ran to it and said, "If that's Mom tell her to come back. Now!" Meg had been braver than Gail would have guessed. She'd cried only once or twice. She'd been on a think-positive kick all week, refusing to allow for the possibility that her mother might not return. She also started doing strange things, all kinds of rituals that didn't make sense. Whenever she went down the stairs, she stepped back up the last three stairs and went down them again. When she closed a door, she'd open it again, and leave it slightly ajar. When she left the house, she'd wave, even if the house stood empty.

Every day, Meg tacked on a new ritual, and although Gail thought they were stupid and embarrassing, she didn't say anything about them.

The night before, her dad had been out in the barn working on one of his secret projects, and Alice had been sitting on the front porch reading a book called *Before You Conceive*. Gail noted the book, lifted her eyes to heaven, and thought, Oh God, save us from this unholy union. What kind of stunt was this anyway, getting pregnant in this day and age? Gail couldn't see any point at all in raising a family. Why would her dad want another one anyway? The first one hadn't brought him any luck. She guessed it must be merely instinct, that humans, no matter how disappointed they were in the people around them, couldn't help themselves from creating more, from thinking they could beat the odds. In any case, she felt relieved she wasn't *with little monster*, as she once thought she'd been. She looked with disgust at Alice. Inside, the phone started ringing. Alice put down her book and smiled and said, "Oh, hi, Gail. I didn't notice you there."

"Get a life," Gail said and went inside to answer. She picked it up, and a man started talking. He had a deep voice and spoke like one of those people who make sales pitches over the phone.

"Who *are* you?" she said. She expected maybe some pervert who was going to ask her, What color is your underwear? Mr. Sims, her driver's ed. instructor, had been caught doing that, and fired. He'd always had his head up his duffel bag. Still, everyone at school had been jolted. Somewhere, she had a paper on which he'd written some notes in the margin complimenting her writing. She couldn't locate the paper, but if she found it, she'd toss it. The comments didn't mean much now, coming from a creep.

"If you're Gail or Meg, then I'm your grandfather," the man on the other end said. This was a sales pitch different from any other she'd ever heard.

He told her a long involved story about his life, how he'd always been an honest man, and had trusted people to do right by him, the same way he acted to those around him. He told her his world had always been simple, that you worked for an honest wage, and raised a decent family. He said he'd grown up in South Bend, and thought about it often, but never wanted to return. He talked a lot about betrayal, said he still loved the place he'd worked, and the people he'd worked for. He talked about the satisfaction that can come only from loving a job, from knowing that the people you work for are looking out for you, and he talked about the satisfaction that can come only from giving what you earn to your family, from looking out for them. He said it's a great cycle, and that's the way God meant things to work.

She didn't have the foggiest idea what he meant. She wanted him to stop, to get to the point. "Look, can I put you on hold?" she said, breaking him off in mid-sentence.

She put the phone down on the kitchen counter and looked out the window at the fields. Then she picked it up again and said, "Okay, I'm back. Now does this have anything to do with my mother, because if it doesn't, I'm hanging up and having this call traced."

The man sounded disappointed, hurt, but what could he expect? She didn't know him, after all, and he didn't make sense. Grandfather or not, he meant nothing to her.

He got to the point. He said Gail's mom had come for a visit, but her car had broken down, and someone needed to pick her up.

"Why doesn't she take a bus?" Gail said, outraged at the thought of doing her mother any favors.

"Believe me," said the man, "If I could get her on a bus, I'd send her directly."

"I thought you said she was visiting," Gail said.

"Sort of," he said. "That's what I *thought* she wanted to do. She's got some crazy idea of staying here with me. Or bringing me back with her. She says she's not going home without me. She says she's not budging. Please, will you take her off my hands? I can't have her tagging after me every step I take."

"If she wants to stay with you, let her," Gail said. "We don't want her back."

He didn't say anything for a moment. "Honeycomb, I don't know what she looks like normally, but she don't look good at all."

"That's normal," said Gail.

"I'm telling you. If you don't come get her, you're going to regret it someday. There are some people who can live all right on their own and some people who need constant companionship. Me, I have all the companions I need here at the station."

"I'm putting you on hold again," Gail said and put down the receiver. She gazed at the fields again.

Gail put the receiver to her ear. "Okay, I'll come get her," she said flatly.

"I tell you, she's the type who's got to tag after someone," her grandfather went on. "The long and short of it is I love her, but there's not much I can do for her."

"I said I'll come get her," Gail said.

Her grandfather seemed like he had more to say, more of a sales pitch, but she finally broke through to him, and he told her where her mother was. "I'll call you when I get there," she said and hung up.

Immediately, she called Henry. Haltingly—after all, she'd never done *him* any favors—she asked if he'd help her. She knew she couldn't go to her father.

Henry hadn't even hesitated. He acted like they'd been best friends for years.

"It's lonely here without you guys," he'd told her.

"Hah!" Gail said, "If I were you, I'd be jumping for joy to see us hit the road."

"Not really," he said. "I was happier with the three of you than I've ever been in my life."

"Okay," she said, "don't go overboard." Why had he acted that way to her? she wondered after she'd hung up. She wouldn't have done any favors for her if she'd been him. One thing she knew for sure. As long as she lived, she'd never figure that guy out.

Now Henry was threading toward them, turning slowly into their long driveway. Meg ran out of the room and down the stairs. A moment later, Gail heard the front door slam, and Meg bounded off the porch.

Then Meg came to a halt and turned around. She walked back to the porch slowly. Gail thought maybe she'd forgotten this time to leave the door cracked.

Gail took her time. Leisurely, she made her way out of the room, taking one last look at the note she'd written, and closed the door. Then she thought better of it and left it ajar. No one would know, she thought.

As she walked across the front lawn to meet Henry's car, she almost stepped on something flesh-colored. She recoiled, thinking it alive, then realized it was only some kind of doll. A nude doll with a pot belly. Old Ken. She'd loathed that fat old doll when her mother brought it home that time. White gloves. No balls. Arched gray eyebrows and gray hair. Its stupid smile. And worst of all, its flexible limbs. That's what made her hate that doll the most, how you could twist it around in any stupid shape you wanted, and it would still be smiling. That was the biggest difference between her and her mother. She did not find stupid things funny. "Campy" is what her mom called it.

Still, she rescued the doll from the lawn. It looked about the same, but with chew marks on its torso. She'd seen one of her dad's dogs, Dale Earnhardt, with the doll in its mouth a few times. The dogs were gone now. Dale Earnhardt, Rusty Wallace, Bill Elliot. Alice had developed a sudden allergy to dogs, and so her dad had found new homes for them. At least that's the version he told Meg to keep her from bawling. Gail knew better. "Found homes" was his way of saying he'd taken them to the pound or else shot them himself.

Gail dangled the doll from one of its white-gloved hands and brought it to Henry's car.

"Old Ken!" Meg shouted.

Henry wore a flat cap, shorts, and a short-sleeved shirt. Gail had never seen him look so breezy, so casual. The hat made him look like a dope—she couldn't expect him to be perfect—but she couldn't find any fault with his car. She'd never seen a richer-looking car, with its white tires and yellow spokes, and the brown running boards that curved over the wheels and along the side. Even the spare tires, canvas-wrapped on each of the running boards, added to the elegance of the car. Suddenly, she wished her father *had* bought the car at the auction. At least then it would be in the family. Maybe she would have inherited it eventually.

She stopped that line of thought. She didn't want her dad to die, even if he did act like a jerk. Anyway, it would have been his car, no one else's. He wouldn't have allowed anyone to inherit the car. He would have been buried in it, or better yet, floated down the St. Joseph River in the car, lit on fire like one of those Viking funeral ships she'd read about in Western Civ. class.

Henry had the top down, and sat smiling at her. Meg stood on the running board and clambered into the seat without opening the door. Gail wondered how the four of them would fit into the car on the way back. Her mom, she decided on the spot, would have to sit in the rumble seat. That would be a fitting punishment.

Henry tipped his cap and tooted the car's horn.

"What took you so long?" she said, opening the door and handing Old Ken to Meg, who took the doll and started maniacally twisting its limbs.

He pointed with his left hand to his right. "I can't shift without taking my hand off the wheel. I had to drive in first all the way here. I keep expecting my hand to wake up. I raised it for a few seconds at the auction, but that was it."

"Wake up?" Meg said. "I didn't know it fell asleep. What do you think it's dreaming about?"

Henry thought about this, looking ahead at the barn.

"We can't drive to West Virginia in first gear," Gail said. "Let me drive, Henry. I'm good at it."

Henry didn't seem wild about the idea. "I suppose it would be safer," he said, reluctance edging his voice. "On the other hand, more accidents are caused by your age group than any other. I don't want to have an accident. We're not having an accident, no matter what." He said this like a promise.

"I'm not going to have an accident, Henry. Just give me a chance."

He shook his head. "This car's my responsibility. So are you, at least until we get down to West Virginia. I'm sorry, Gail."

She saw she couldn't budge him, and that in itself seemed remarkable.

"I guess we can't go then," Gail said, kicking a foot against the running board.

Henry didn't say anything.

"You guys," Meg said, alarm in her voice.

"Did you learn automatic or shift?" Henry asked.

She saw what he was thinking and said, "Yeah, right, that's going to be safe, me shifting and you driving. If you don't let me drive, Henry, you're going to kill us all. Guaranteed accident."

Henry looked down at his hand and said, "You're right. We'd better not go."

Gail scraped her foot on the running board, like she had dog dirt on her. "Get out," she told Meg.

Meg looked up at her. "But Gail," she said.

"Stop whining and get out."

Reluctantly, Meg obeyed. Then Gail slipped into the seat where Meg had been, placed Old Ken on the dash, and told Meg to get back in. She did, in an instant.

As they pulled away, Meg waved at the empty house.

Henry noticed this and said, "Who are you waving good-bye to, Meg?"

"It's not a wave good-bye," she said. "It's a wave hello. It'll be waiting for us when we get back and I won't have to do it again."

"Oh, I get you," said Henry, but to Gail, it made no sense at all. Like shifting gears for someone else. Like retrieving her runaway mother.

From the passenger side, and with her left hand, she couldn't shift easily. Everything felt wrong. Slowly, she got her bearings. She'd never seen a more unusual dashboard. Along with the usual gauges for fuel, temperature, and the speedometer, she noticed an eight-day clock, an odometer and tripmeter, which she set on zero, and something called an ammeter.

"Second," he said as they headed up the gravel road, and she did some quick mental picturing and pulled the shift back and toward Henry.

"Okay?" he said.

"Yeah," she said, perspiration collecting on her forehead.

"You can let go now," he said.

"What? Oh." She still held on to the stick, leaning in toward Henry. Slowly, she took her hand off the stick and sat back in the seat next to Meg, who seemed to be finding endless amusement with Old Ken. "Tell me when you need me again," she said to Henry.

"Sure thing," he said, and then started whistling some mindless tune. Unfortunately, the car had no radio.

At the end of the gravel road, Henry stopped, and then turned onto the highway. Henry's tongue poked out the corner of his mouth as he drove, like he had to exert all his energy to keep his concentration.

"Okay, first," he said and she pushed the stick up and left. This time, she kept her hand on the gearshift. As they picked up speed, he said, "Now second again," and she pulled it toward her and over to Henry. The needle started climbing, and now they were picking up speed, passing the familiar sights of South Bend in an unfamiliar vehicle. A cement truck went around them and the driver tapped his horn. Henry took his hand off the steering wheel and touched the brim of his hat.

"Okay, third," Henry said after the truck had passed them.

This car had only three gears. The one she'd learned on had five.

Gail pushed the stick up and jiggled it toward Henry, but it didn't want to go. Finally, she pushed and forced it into place. "Okay," she said and Henry took his foot off the clutch. The speedometer read thirty-five.

The car made a grating noise. Henry flew forward against the steering column. Gail bounced off Henry. The chrome button on the glove compartment whisked past her, and the next thing she saw were the tops of Henry's tennis shoes. In the small space, she turned her head and saw Meg on all fours beside her.

"What happened?" Meg said.

Slowly, Gail clambered back to her seat.

"I guess I got it into first somehow instead of third," Gail said.

Everyone seemed all right, though a strange sour smell pervaded the car now. Henry, who still sat shivering, had wet his pants. If Meg had wet her pants, Gail would have made fun of her, but with Henry, she pretended not to notice.

Meg screamed and pointed. Gail, still disoriented, thought someone must be dead. For a second, the image of her mother pinned under the wheels of the car flashed in front of her.

Old Ken sat at the end of the hood, his arms held straight over his head, white-gloved hands making an arch like a ballerina's.

Cars passed them, about one every twenty seconds, some slowly, the passengers gawking, trying to determine if any blood had spilled. Some cars sped by, horns blasting, as if Gail, Meg, and Henry had stalled in the middle of the highway for kicks.

"Trade places with me, Henry," she said.

Henry looked over at her like he'd never seen her before. He had his hands in between his legs, resting against the wet spot.

"Move, Henry," she said, and she pointed toward Meg. "I'm not getting out of the car to trade places with you. Not here."

She nudged him and he started sliding over. She clambered over him, knocked her knee against his stomach, used his shoulder as a brace, then twisted herself around.

Meg wanted to collect Old Ken before they headed off again, but Gail wouldn't let her. For twenty-five miles, he gamely hung on, then slowly jiggled across the hood and slid off. Luckily, Meg was asleep when it happened, or she would have had a fit. Gail felt some regret seeing the little doll meet his end, but she preferred to look at it another way, to say he'd found a new home. She reached her hand up and waved good-bye.

For a hundred miles, Henry shivered and stared at the road, ashen-faced. Slowly, he came out of it and pointed to cars as they passed, saying, "You're drifting," or, "Maybe you should pass this guy."

Finally, she said, "Henry, I don't need a backseat driver," and he stopped, but kept eyeing the road.

Then he took out a pad of Mad Libs from a bag at his feet and he and Meg occupied themselves for a while. Gail didn't want to join in. She didn't want to talk at all. She felt grim and determined, and as they drew closer to their destination, she kept herself occupied with the different ways she planned to punish her mother.

They traveled through the night, stopping only briefly at rest stops for quick cafeteria-style meals and gas. The car had definitely been built before anyone cared about fuel economy. It got only about fifteen miles per gallon. Each time they stopped, Henry handed her his wallet. He didn't have any credit cards, only cash, but lots of it. Handling all that money, she imagined that she was a strong and powerful woman who owned a fleet of antique cars. She depended on no one, was impossible to deal with, men and women alike feared her. She peeled off twenties and bought premium.

Other travelers openly admired the car, and when they said something, if she'd gone out of Henry's earshot, she'd point to him and say, "My daddy bought it for me."

"That's a nice daddy," one man said, shaking his head with envy. "I hope you appreciate him."

"I do," she said, confidentially, "but I do my best to hide it."

At six that morning, they reached the outskirts of Parkersburg, and Gail pulled over by a pay phone. Her grandfather, who didn't even sound sleepy when she reached him, told her she had less than five miles to go.

"I can't wait to meet you," he said. "Lois has told me your whole life story, you and Meg. We can all have a nice breakfast at Stuckey's, and do some catching up before you have to head out again."

"We don't want breakfast," she said. "We've already eaten. We've got to head right back. My dad's expecting us."

"Don't you want to stay for a few minutes, get to know me a bit?" he said.

"Why?" she asked.

"I'm your grandfather," he said.

"Maybe some other time. Is she ready to go?"

He didn't say anything right away. "She's ready," he said finally, and now Gail could detect some weariness in his voice.

Gail hung up and returned to the car. Meg had just awakened. She yawned. "Where are we?"

"Nearly there," Gail said.

"How's your mother?" Henry asked.

"I didn't speak to her," she said.

"Gail?" he said.

"I'm right here."

"I've been thinking. I don't need one."

"One what?"

"A car. They just cause trouble."

Gail shook her head. "I don't want it," she said. She would have died for that car, but if her own father couldn't come through, she'd feel ashamed to accept something like that from Henry.

"I'll take it," Meg said.

"No you won't," Gail said, pointing. Then she turned to Henry. "But thanks."

"Why not?" Henry said. "You need a car to get around."

Henry took off his cap, and started rolling it up on his lap, then slowly unrolling it, a look of concentration on his face like he'd never come to a more difficult decision. "I really want you to have it," he said. "I insist."

She gave him one of her mom's old killer looks. "I insist back. I don't want it."

"Why not?" He looked down at his lap and rolled his cap up again.

"Stop that, Henry," she said.

He looked at her in bewilderment and she pointed to the hat.

"Watch where you're going," Meg said.

"I really really really want you to have it, Gail" Henry said, continuing to roll and unroll his cap.

"You're annoying me, Henry. Why do you want to give it to me anyway? What have I ever done for you?"

"Please take it," he said, the cap getting tighter with each twist.

"This is creepy," she said to Meg. ·

"You'd better take it," Meg said with a look of concern.

"In Japan, it's rude not to accept a gift," he said.

"This is America, Henry. Don't you even know where you are?"

Henry looked around. "Yeah, well not exactly."

"Just because you have a little accident is no reason –"

Henry shouted and she almost swerved off the road. It was a little animal shout, like he'd just been hit with a hunter's bullet. Then he started shouting in earnest – with words attached. She'd never heard Henry shout before. His voice rose higher and his face turned instantly red through his scraggly beard. He sounded like he might start bawling at any moment. "This has nothing to do with them!" he yelled. "Why do you have to bring them into this? This has nothing to do with Carla and Matthew!"

"Are you crazy?" Gail shouted back. She didn't even know what he meant. She'd been referring to the little accident they'd had with the stick shift, and he'd gone off the deep end. When she said, "Are you crazy?" that made him even wilder. His eyes bulged and spit formed at the corners of his mouth.

"Stop it," he said. "Don't ask me that. Why is it crazy to give something for a change? Why is that?"

He bent his face close to hers and she wanted to bite his nose off. She'd never appreciated being yelled at. She grabbed his cap out of his hand and threw it over her head.

Again, Henry let out a little yelp, and craned around to look back.

"Gail," Meg said. "That was mean."

"Let me out," Henry said.

"No, Henry. I'm sick of your goddamn car and I hate your little cap. What do you think of that?"

"Let me out," he said, reaching across Meg as though he planned to hijack the steering wheel.

Gail turned the wheel and the car swerved into the other lane. A car's horn mooed at them. "You're going to kill us, Henry," she said.

"Let me out," he said, flinging open the door. It flapped out and banged shut. Henry opened it again and leaned out across the pavement.

"Get back in here," she said.

"I want my cap," he said.

"I told you. I hate your cap, and I hate your scraggly beard, and how skinny you are, and the way you dress. You look like a freak."

"I'm going to jump," he said, leaning out.

"Gail!" Meg shouted. "He means it."

Gail slowed down and stopped on the gravel shoulder. Even though he was a lunatic, a certified weirdo, she didn't want his blood on her hands.

Henry leaped out and started walking back down the road. He walked slowly. She hated his walk. He had a bowlegged gait, chimplike. She'd forgotten to tell him that and made a mental note to remind herself when he returned. In the rearview she saw him dance into traffic, run back onto the shoulder, and elaborately dust off his cap. He beat it against each leg as if he were playing a tambourine. Then he stuck it on his head. All the while, Meg chastised her the way their mother did.

"Don't you know how to be nice?" Meg said. "Didn't anyone ever teach you that?" She put a hand to her chest and said, "I could never get away with that kind of behavior. I have feelings. I know how to get along in society with other people. You know what you are, Gail? You're antisocial, and that's not a nice thing to be. If you want to function in society, you're going to have to control your temper. You know what I do when I'm angry? I play basketball in my head. I know I'm not tall like you, but I pretend I am. I pretend I'm taller than any basketball player in existence, and I'm going one on one with them, and none of them can beat me. Maybe you should try something like that."

Gail tuned out her little sister as much as possible. She kept her eyes on Henry and nodded her head like she cared.

"What's he doing now?" Gail said, breaking Meg off mid-sentence in her Learn To Be Nice speech. Instead of walking back to the car, Henry crossed the highway to the other side. Then he started walking back the way they had come.

Gail started the car, eased back into traffic after a couple of cars had passed, then headed across the median, a strip of grass about thirty feet wide that dipped into a gully. She bumped the car across the strip at about five miles an hour.

"Isn't this illegal?" Meg said, touching her arm.

"You're dead meat if you say another word about what's right and wrong," Gail told her calmly, and Meg shut up.

When they caught up with Henry, he kept walking a straight line, his jaw set. Gail could see his red face and his quiet crying, mouth open, eyes swollen. Meg looked at Gail with disapproval, her little lips pinched, and breathing hard through her pug nose, but she didn't dare say anything.

"I'm sorry I made you cry, Henry," she said. "Get in the car."

"You didn't," he said. "Go away," and he waved her away with his good hand.

Then he pulled his cap down farther and turned his face at an angle from them.

"Come on, Henry. Don't be a baby."

Meg looked at her again and said, "You're a real charmer, Gail. Don't strain yourself." Then she looked at Henry and said, "Please, Henry. Gail's a jerk, but she'll grow out of it. She really *is* sorry. I've never heard her apologize before."

Henry shook his head and tried to speak, but just kept swallowing.

Gail couldn't stand to see a man cry. She didn't know how to react, or what to say that would make him get back in the car, so she kept on saying the same lame things. "Come on, Henry, let's go." She repeated it over and over until she realized she sounded like *he* had a few minutes before when he kept telling her, "Come on, take it. Please take it."

Finally, Henry found his voice. He touched his chest, then gave his arm a little slap as though he didn't like his arm. "I can't do it," he said. "You're right. You don't have to take the car. Just do whatever you want with it. You can leave it on the side of the road for all I care."

"Fine, Henry," Gail said, "when we get home."

Henry shook his head. He'd stopped crying, but still swallowed a lot. "I don't belong with you. I have to try living on my own."

Then he started running ahead of the car. He ran at full speed, but his bad arm flopped beside him, so he looked like a retard. She overtook him easily and contemplated running him down, but stayed with him, though he wouldn't look at her. Finally, he ran off the shoulder into the weeds and disappeared.

Gail didn't know what to do. If he didn't want to go on with them, she couldn't force him. Slowly, she crept back across the median and headed away. Meg looked stonily ahead, arms crossed, and after a minute said, "I'm never going to forgive you for this, Gail."

When they pulled into the radio station parking lot Gail spotted her mom right away, standing in front of the station, holding some kind of potted plant. Just like her mom, Gail thought, always collecting things.

She didn't seem to notice them immediately. She gazed steadily at the ground. Then slowly, she looked up, and seemed startled to see them. It must be the car, Gail thought.

She dropped the plant and the pot shattered. She turned and hurried into the building.

Gail parked alongside the shattered pot, in a handicap space.

"What's wrong?" Meg asked. "Doesn't she want to go home?"

"Who knows?" said Gail. "You know Mom. Just wait here. I'll bring her back if I have to drag her."

"Don't hurt her," Meg said. She looked like she meant it. Gail had never seen her sister look so fierce or unforgiving.

"I wasn't speaking literally, Meg. I'm just saying this might take some doing."

She opened the door and found her mother sitting in one of the reception-area chairs, her feet stuck out in front of her, a hand tugging through her hair. She looked like someone had just taken a flying leap and tackled her. She looked like she might wet her pants. A man stood behind her dressed in radioactively bright colors: a yellow sports shirt and bright blue pants. He looked pale. He had the whitest skin she'd ever seen and white hair, too. In those clothes, he looked like the invisible man trying to attract attention. She hoped this geezer wasn't her grandad, but she had a bad feeling about him. He had a hand on the back of her mom's shoulder as he tried to nudge her out of her chair.

"Come on, Lois," he said gently. "It's time to go home."

"Come on, Mom," Gail said, her words harsher than she meant. "Let's get the hell out of here." She stood over her mom, then knelt down and tried to take her hand. That hand lashed out and slapped Gail hard across her cheek. Gail fell backwards and her mother leaped out of her chair.

"Jesus, what was that for?" Gail said.

Her mom glared down at her. "What's that you're driving?" she said, her voice enraged but barely reaching over a whisper.

"A car, Mom. It's a car. What do you think it is? Do you think we came . . ." She wanted to say, Do you think we came down in a wagon, but she happened to catch the old man's eye. He stood behind her mom, and spun his finger around his temple and pointed to the back of her mother's head. Then he tucked his head into his chin and pushed the air in front of him with his fingers, like he had his hands on some invisible piano. Gail knew it meant, Take it easy.

Gail didn't want to take it easy. Slowly, she got to her feet and stood face to face with her mom.

"What kind of car?" her mom said.

"It's a Studebaker, Mom," Gail said. "Henry bought it at the auction."

Her mother gave Gail a look like she'd betrayed her.

"A Studie," said the old man, rubbing his chin. "You don't say? Let's go out and take a gander. What model?" He started to head for the door, but neither Gail nor her mom followed, so he stopped.

"Why did you come down here?" Gail asked. "Why didn't you tell us at least?"

Her mother pointed to the old man. "Him," she said.

"It had nothing to do with us?" Gail said.

Her mom gave her a long sad look and reached a hand toward her, but Gail flinched, then realized her mother didn't intend to slap her. She let her mother touch her cheek.

Her mom smiled, about to say something, but the old man moved to her side and said, "I've been trying to tell her all week that everybody's got their reasons. I didn't leave them. I'm the one who got left behind. Seems like somebody might have wondered about my whereabouts before now." He looked at Gail's mom and said, "At least, somebody's come after you."

"It wouldn't have killed *you* to be in touch with *us*," she replied.

"We've been through that," he said. "It wouldn't have killed me, but listen to your own daughter, honeycomb. She says your problems had nothing to do with her. Mine had nothing to do with you. They were between me and your mother. That doesn't mean you weren't all affected. Hell, Studebaker shut down without any warning. If you ask me, that started the whole thing. Sort of set a precedent. Just think, if they hadn't folded, we'd still be a family."

The old man took Gail's mom by the shoulder and started guiding her to the door. Gail walked alongside them, trying to sort things out.

They went outside, where Meg stood now beside the car. When Meg spotted them, she rushed the few feet into her mother's arms. For a while the two of them stood this way.

Slowly, they walked toward the car. "Henry gave it to me," Gail said, "Sort of. I told him no."

"What a beauty," Gail's grandad said. He reached out and stroked the car. "A little before my time, but I worked on some others just as pretty. Lord, this brings back memories," and he gave a little sniffle.

Gail looked at her mother, but she wasn't where she'd been standing a second before. She'd retreated to the building again. Great, Gail thought. At this rate, she'd need all day to get her mother into the car.

And probably all week to make it home. Maybe they should have flown.

"Mom!" Gail said, following her mother, who didn't go back inside, but instead knelt beside the building and picked up a brick. She stood up again, holding the brick at neck level.

Gail backed off. She could take being slapped, but not being hit with a brick. Gail thought maybe her mom planned on hitting her grandad with the brick, but she didn't. She whacked the hood of the car. The metal buckled and dented, and the force of the blow boomed around them. Everyone backed off and the old man put a hand to his heart.

"What are you doing?" he shouted.

She turned around and looked him directly in the eye and slammed the brick down even harder on the hood.

Flakes, Gail thought. I'm surrounded by them. I'm the only sane soul for a thousand miles. For a moment, Gail thought that her mom wanted to get back at her by doing this. After all, Gail sort of owned the car now, but she had no real connection to it. What her mother was doing didn't hurt her feelings. And anyway, she didn't have her eyes on Gail.

Methodically, her mom walked around the car, bludgeoning it. She cuffed the Studebaker with the edge of the brick, a backhand blow. She dimpled the running boards and dented the fenders. She clubbed the hood and pounded the rumble seat. The brick made a clanging like a dull gong. She raked the paint off the side of the car with a screeching noise that made Gail's neck tingle and her shoulders tense.

"Stop it," the old man said. "You don't know what you're doing."

Actually, Gail's mom looked like she knew exactly what she was doing. She seemed completely calm. She had the same serene expression she'd had that day when she'd defrosted the refrigerator with a screwdriver. That time, Gail had looked on her mother with disdain, but now, mixed with shock, she also felt a crazy kind of admiration, as if maybe her mom had absolutely flipped out, but she had guts at least. Like getting a tattoo on your insole. Doing something wild to prove you could do it.

The old man was having a shit fit. He didn't try to stop her, but with every blow, his knees buckled, and finally, he sank down. "What have you done?" he said feebly.

She stood by the rumble seat. She looked tired now, completely exhausted, but she kept on beating the metal until Gail walked up to her
and put out her hand. She felt like someone on a police show who's had
a gun trained on her, but bravely walks up and says, Give me the gun.

But she didn't say anything. After she had given her the brick Gail
tossed it aside, put her arm across her mom's shoulder, and said, "Are
you all right?"

Her mom smiled, swiped at her hair, and said, "Much better,
thanks."

Then her mother turned and said in a cheery voice, "Okay, let's get
going." She sounded like some happy mom rounding up her wander-
ing children at a roadside oasis. Meg obeyed right away. Gail stood
still for a moment. She didn't know what to think anymore. She'd
hardly had any sleep. That had to be the reason why she didn't move,
her heart crashing in her ears. She didn't know what made sense anymore, or how to sort through her feelings. Right now, she didn't care
about the car. She felt almost relieved that her mother had beaten it to
a pulp. Something seemed to have been released, and already her
mother looked less tense and worn. The only person who seemed upset
was the old man, who looked devastated. She stood right next to him.
She could hear his small sobs. Finally, she tore herself off the spot and
ran around to the driver's side of the car. Gail got behind the wheel and
her mother sat beside her.

There must have been at least fifty dents in the car. Pockmarks covered the body from the roof to the hood to the rumble seat. It didn't look
like it had been in a wreck. The car looked like it had traveled through
an asteroid belt. Gail didn't know much about cars, but she knew that
her mother had sent the book value of this one plummeting. She imagined people gawking at them on the road back, not out of envy or admiration, but out of shock and bewilderment. At least it still worked. It
started up without a problem. Gail adjusted the rearview and saw her
grandad still on his knees behind them, his hands over his eyes, as
though afraid to look up.

"Where we headed anyway?" Gail asked a mile down the road.

"I don't know. Where do you want to go?" said her mom.

Gail didn't know. She reached for the radio, but remembered the
car didn't have one.

As they drove along, Gail expected to see Henry around every turn, with his cap perched on his head, or beating it like a tambourine against his leg. She kept an eye out for him, and Meg did the same, scanning the roadside, leaning forward, hands on knees.

Gail and Meg didn't exchange a word. She knew Meg blamed her for leaving Henry, but she had no choice. She couldn't drive alongside him all day. She'd assumed he'd be walking along the shoulder when they returned, that he'd be hot and out of breath, grateful for a ride.

But with every passing mile, she started to realize she'd left him behind. Maybe he was resting in some weeds along the road, or had turned back the other way, or accepted a ride from another driver.

"Aren't you going to turn around?" Meg finally asked her.

Gail's mom looked at them both. "We're not turning around," she said. "Why would you want to turn around?"

"Henry's back there, Mom," Meg said, her voice turning up to whining volume.

Gail wanted to turn around and search for him, but even if she found him, she doubted she'd be able to coax him into the car again.

"He came down here with us," she explained. "We had a fight and he got out of the car and wouldn't get back in. He wants to live on his own now."

"There's more to it than that," Meg said. "Henry's gone and it's her fault." Meg pointed the accusatory finger. "She threw his cap away," was all she managed before her voice broke and her face reddened and she couldn't say any more.

Her mother gave Gail a dumbfounded look, and brushed Meg's hair with her hand. "There, there," she said. "I'm sure he'll be all right."

"No he won't," Meg said bitterly. "Not just because you say so."

Something flashed across her mother's face, and she sat back straight in the seat, but kept her hand on Meg's hair. "There, there," she said in a weakened voice.

"He'll get in touch with us," Gail said. "He didn't give me the title to the car, so he's got to come back for it sooner or later, right Mom?"

Her mother looked at her uncertainly and Meg didn't buy it either. With Henry, you could never tell. She'd never met anyone like him before. He'd get rid of a car in a second, but he stuck with people no matter how hard they wanted to be rid of him.

Then, she spotted something up ahead on the side of the road, a piece of clothing. It looked like shorts, but she passed it before she could tell. She slowed down and saw a short-sleeved shirt a little farther along. There wasn't any reason to think it was Henry's shirt. It looked like his shirt, light blue with a white collar, but a lot of guys wore shirts like that, and why would Henry get rid of his shirt and trousers anyway? It didn't make sense, not that Henry ever did, and she'd seen plenty of strange things on the road up to now: a couch, a TV, a blender. Just about any object that people filled up their lives with could be found on the side of the road, discarded.

Then she saw something that had to be Henry's, and she stopped the car. She didn't have to say why, because as soon as Meg saw the cap, her eyes widened, and she rushed over to it. Gail followed and then her mother, and the three of them stood on the gravel around the cap, looking down on it, like Henry had shrunk or melted underneath it.

"He must have found a ride," Gail said as though that explained everything.

"Maybe someone kidnapped him," Meg said, looking up at them.

Gail's mom cupped her hands around her mouth. "Henry," she yelled, louder than Gail had ever heard her mother. If he was anywhere around, he couldn't have missed *that*. Gail looked over at her mom in admiration. She could have won some 4-H contest with a yell like that.

But he didn't answer. The three of them walked back toward the other clothes to see if he'd left any clues.

Gail glanced over at the field that bordered the road. Henry was standing in the middle of it like some scrawny scarecrow. He hardly had any clothes on — just his underwear, which she could barely make out through the weeds.

"He's in there," Gail shouted, but as she spoke, Henry ducked in the weeds.

"Henry," Meg yelled in a desperate voice. "Come here right now."

He didn't answer and didn't appear. They waited five minutes, ten, calling after him, but he wouldn't show himself. This time, Gail wasn't going to leave him, and even if she'd wanted to, Meg would never have allowed it. Even their mother seemed resolved to find him.

The three of them fanned out and walked slowly into the weeds, which were half as tall as Meg. As Gail called out for Henry, she pushed back her fears, mostly of mice and ticks and snakes. She wanted another chance to find him and convince him to come home with them again. And why not? She stopped and looked around her. The hills of West Virginia surrounded them. She seemed to be walking through some flat basin, like the inside of an extinct volcano. In the middle of the field stood a single tree with silver bark sparkling in the sun. She headed for that one, sure that she'd find him behind it. As she approached, nervous, trying to think of something that would make him come back, she wondered how the boundaries of her family could have possibly grown as large and mysterious as this field she was plunging through in the middle of nowhere.